CW00517336

Edge of Empire

Hunt

By Alistair Tosh

For Andrea

Copyright © Alistair Tosh 2022.

The right of Alistair Tosh to be identified as the author of this work has been asserted by him in accordance with the Copyright, Designs and Patents Act, 1988.

First published in 2022 by Sharpe Books.

Table of Contents

24

25

26

27

28

29

30

31

32

33

34

35

36

37

38

39

40

41

42

43

44

45

46

47

48

HUNT

1

Her son was dead. She would die soon too, but would be made to suffer greatly before the end.

As the bow of the boat crashed again into the rising swell, soaking all onboard, Alyn allowed her grief to fill her once more.

She sat with her back against the mast, arms wrapped tightly around her knees. Salt water dripped from her dark hair that hung in long, tangled strips. The island they had been approaching from the north all morning filled her vision. A single, huge mountain stood proud, its sharp peak kissing the low, grey cloud.

So consumed was Alyn in her misery she no longer noticed the grunts of the ten men at their rowing benches, as they pulled hard against the current. Nor did she take note of the sails of the other boats ahead of them.

At least during the two days of the voyage he had left her alone. He and his band had been absorbed in a continual struggle to keep the boat afloat in the rough, grey waters of the Hibernian sea.

On the first two occasions he had taken her, during their flight across the Novantae lands, she had fought him with all her strength. The agony he inflicted to her face and body with his fists had left her with a closed eye and a pain in her ribs that, days later, ached with every breath. Now she no longer resisted him. The final time had been on the night before they reached the boats. He had simply pushed her from his horse and dragged her into dense

1

brush. She remembered little of the physical act, only the intense smell of damp moss and rotting leaves as her face was pushed into the soft earth.

Alyn had yet to hear his true name. His men addressed him only as lord. However, on the night before they sailed, he had left their camp on horseback, leaving her bound to a tall beech sapling. His warband sat around their campfires. She was ignored, a mere slave, so in the darkness, she listened to their talk. Even though their accents were thick, she understood most of the words and as the night wore on, she heard his byname. All had turned in fear to stare, wide-eyed, into the darkness as if expecting to see their lord reappear. This was not a name to be said in his presence and it was clear the beast's men feared him.

As the morning wore on, the weather calmed and the boat slipped past the western shore of the island. As the sun was reaching its zenith the small flotilla entered a broad bay overshadowed by a huge promontory with sheer granite cliffs, from which screeching seabirds launched themselves.

What caught Alyn's attention was not this great edifice; rather what appeared to be their destination at the bay's far side. There, behind a rock strewn shoreline was a huge palisade. Unlike most settlements, she saw no peaked, thatched roofs of the population's homes appearing above the stout wooden barrier. Instead, there were the dark maws of three caves set into the overhang of a cliff, partly shrouded with bracken and underbrush.

With a start, Alyn felt the rough tangle of a beard pressed against her cheek.

'Do you like your new home, slave?' He breathed the words into her ear. Alyn flinched from him. Her owner laughed, she pressed her head against the mast in a vain attempt to escape the stench of his breath. He gripped her hair, yanking it hard, forcing her to stare into his eyes and seeing the madness there once more. 'You will be my thing here. You will see to my needs and warm my cot. And…if you displease me,' he said, nestling his nose into the tangle of her hair, taking a long lingering sniff. 'I will give you to my warband.' He released her.

Alyn turned to the men before her who sweated at the oars. Each had the so familiar shaven and darkly tattooed heads. All stared at her with a renewed hunger. Alyn lowered her head and began to shake uncontrollably as her ears filled with the sound of his laughter.

2

AD 149 Northern Britannia

Cai Martis, Prefectus of cavalry, knew the only hope he had of finding the woman he loved was to seek the aid of his enemy.

Despite his initial anger at Lucius for preventing him from pursuing Alyn's captors, he came to accept his friend had been right to do so. Riding into the confused ranks of a fleeing and defeated enemy in the aftermath of a battle, would have been futile and most certainly led to his death.

Now, after days of planning, he was desperate to begin the hunt. Each passing day took her further away from him and beyond help. If she still lived.

Before sunrise, he and the boy had passed through the open gates of an abandoned turret on the Wall of Aelius and into the lands of the Carvetii. They had left the military road some time since and, with the Sula's silver waters on their right shoulder, rode along a wide track cut through lush green pastureland and the fallow fields of long-since harvested corn. They had been riding in silence for a time, Cai deep in thought, so he did not immediately register that the boy had spoken.

'But why can't I come with you?' Beren said, his voice impatient. 'She's my mother.' Cai sighed. The lad's anguish was understandable; however, this refrain was wearing on his nerves.

Cai turned in his saddle, taking in the fair-haired boy at his back who was the very image of his father. He held back his words of anger as he saw the tears pooling in

4

Beren's eyes. Man and boy held the other's gaze for a moment longer. Cai took a deep calming breath.

'You are your father's son, Beren. He would be proud that you would rush into danger to seek to free your mother. But, I know too, neither he nor your mam would forgive me if I allowed it.'

'But—' Beren began. Cai cut across him.

'No, Beren. The search will be impossible if I have to constantly worry for your safety. Nor will I put the others at even greater risk. That's my final word.' Cai turned back and nudged his pony into movement once more, the patches of brown on the animal's hide glistening with sweat from the long ride and the effort of pulling the other two horses along with her.

Mascellus had agreed to take care of Adela and Epona on his farm, which he'd returned to the day after the battle. Lucius had not been happy to leave his beloved warhorse behind but they could not take Roman-branded mounts where they were headed.

As the track passed through a small copse of tall oak, their destination came into view. Three low, single-storey buildings nestled in a bend of a fast flowing stream whose waters foamed over grey rock enroute to the Sula. All three structures had been built in the Roman style. Two were square in design with roofs of thatch; however, it was the central building that drew Cai's attention. It was long, with a covered walkway running along its length, finished off with a roof made of tan coloured tiles. Cai smiled despite his mood.

'Just like one of the ala's barrack blocks.'

The sound of a woman singing floated to him from somewhere within the farm. The movement of the strengthening morning breeze made it difficult to discern from where it emanated. To Cai's left were penned-in

5

fields, empty of cattle, and to his right was a small enclosure holding four horses, all chestnut in colour. Three were tethered to the corral's fence whilst the fourth trotted in a circle at the end of a long rope held by a man standing at its centre. A man instantly recognisable to Cai. Mascellus.

Cai directed his mount towards his old comrade, who was dressed in leggings and a worn tunic which his stout belly pressed against. His long fair hair with yet only a few streaks of grey hung loose, forcing him to flick his head continually as the breeze blew it across his eyes. At the sound of the approaching horses Cai saw Mascellus turn, a momentary look of confusion passing across the old veteran's face. When he saw Beren's head pop out from behind Cai's back a broad smile instantly lit his grey bearded face.

'By the gods, sir. I took you for a damned Greek wine trader,' Mascellus said, as he tied the horse he had been training to a post.

Cai moved his hand self-consciously across his shaven jaw. It had been Lucius's idea to crop his hair short and pass a blade over his chin. If they were to survive more than a day amongst the tribes, they must conceal who they were. Even after several days, the touch of air against his skin still felt strange.

'It will take some getting used to, brother. But a necessary deceit.'

'Husband.' The sound of the woman's voice startled the old veteran. 'This is no way to treat guests, you must bring them inside'

'Now, now, Enid I was just about to.'

'Well, is that you Cai?' The woman continued, as if Mascellus hadn't spoken. She was of middle years with the dark hair of the Carvetii, touched with speckles of grey. Thin lines creased the corners of her eyes and lips, the result of regular laughter, Cai knew. Her green dress barely contained her broad and rounded hips that swayed as she walked towards them.

'Greetings, Enid. It's good to see you again,' Cai said, with genuine warmth.

'Thank you for letting me have my man back,' she said. 'Although he will need some feeding before he will be useful around this place again.' Cai saw the quick smiles exchanged between Mascellus and his wife and was filled with an unexpected feeling of loneliness.

'And this must be young Beren. You're right, husband. He is the image of Adal.' Enid smiled up at Beren, who still sat unhappily behind Cai. 'Well,' she said, placing her hands on her hips. 'A growing warrior like you must like honey cakes?' Cai saw the flicker of a smile pass across the boy's face. 'Let's get you inside and washed. Then you can help yourself.'

Mascellus refilled Cai's cup with more of the dark ale. They sat side by side on a bench placed at the far end of the veranda of the farmhouse.

'Your fields are empty,' Cai said.

'My man should arrive with the kine in the next day or so. They've been sheltered by Enid's folk whilst I was away.'

Both men were silent for a moment, lost in their own thoughts.

'Thank you, my friend,' Cai said, keeping his voice low. 'It's no small thing you do for me. I won't return until I find her, living or dead. You know what that may mean.'

'It is my honour, brother, to care for the son of Adal. I know he is as kin to you too. But are you sure about this?

7

You must know the odds of finding Alyn in the barbarian wilds are not good.'

'If it were Enid, what would you do?'

Mascellus turned on the bench to study Cai, before nodding slowly. 'The same.'

The friends looked up at the sound of slow approaching footsteps. Beren sat between the two men. Cai was saddened to see the boy, who was usually so full of questions, reduced to silence. Placing his hand on Beren's shoulder, he attempted to put some levity into his voice.

'Whilst I am gone, Mascellus has agreed to teach you swordcraft with the spatha and how to ride like a Nervii.'

'That's right lad. You can help me and Enid around the place and in return we'll spend our evenings turning you into a trooper of the ala. Fit to join the Nervana when you reach manhood.'

Beren stared at his hands, picking at the skin around his nails. A habit Cai had noticed in Alyn. 'I want to find my Ma,' Beren said, his voice almost a whisper.

'I know, Beren,' Cai replied, his hand still on the boy's shoulder. 'But it will give me great comfort whilst I am gone to know you are safe.'

After a moment Beren gave a barely perceptible nod. Cai squeezed his shoulder gently. 'Well, I must be away. Lucius is waiting for me near the coast road. I must reach him before the last light is gone.'

Moments later, Cai contemplated Beren from his new mount. 'I will find your Mam. You have my word.' The boy, who Cai had come to love as a son, stood on the veranda. His eyes were dry and to Cai his face seemed filled with determination. Beren nodded once but said nothing.

After clasping arms with Mascellus, Cai trotted his mount back along the track. Upon reaching the small copse of oak he turned back to look once more upon the farm. Beren had remained on the veranda, unmoving. Cai raised his hand in farewell, but after holding it there for a moment he was disappointed to see the lad didn't return it.

Clicking his tongue, he nudged his mount and moved into the trees, the farm disappearing from view.

3

Lucius Faenius Felix, Tribunus of the First Nervana, awoke with a start. His heart pounded, the sound of men's agonised screams still echoing in his ears.

It took a moment for him to remember where he was. Steadying his frantic breathing, he squinted at the cloud flecked sky from where he lay in the long grass. A pair of red kites circled in the distant heights, before a current of air took the graceful birds out of his field of view.

He had slept little over the days since the Twentieth had finally reached them. Ending the desperate battle with the tribes. On each occasion that he had slipped into a fitful sleep, he was awoken by the tormented cries of his men.

He raised himself gingerly onto one elbow, taking in his surroundings from his position near the river's edge. Hrindenus was hunched by the campfire. The big Tungrian watched over two freshly caught trout as they cooked slowly, their sightless eyes staring into the flames.

Further along the bank was Castellanos. The Greek medicus was lazily skimming stones across the dark, languid surface of the Anam. He had been the surprise addition to their small party. Lucius let his mind drift into memory. Two days passed, since they'd met in the ruins of the headquarters building.

'Where should we start the search?' Lucius had asked. 'From the reports the tribes have scattered throughout the great forest and beyond. Many will have gone to ground. No doubt some will continue their flight. Perhaps even by sea.'

'I don't know, Lucius,' Cai replied, failing to hide his exasperation. His almost perpetual frown appeared once more, darkening his eyes. 'I have only one thought. And it is a desperate one.' Lucius waited for his friend to go on. When he said no more, he guessed at Cai's intention.

'You want to seek out their warchief.' After a moment Cai nodded, almost reluctantly.

'Barra might be prepared to help us. It was Alyn, after all, who treated his nephew Herne.' Even as he had said it, Lucius heard the doubt in his friend's voice.

'We defeated the Novantae,' Lucius said, 'We killed many of his men, perhaps even kin. He may feel humiliated that you spared his life.'

'I know,' Cai said, his voice resigned.

Both sat in silence for a time harbouring their own thoughts, when suddenly an idea had come to Lucius.

'I know where we can at least start our search,' he said. 'Do you remember what Nepos told us when we visited his command?' Before Cai could ask what he meant, a sharp double rap at the door interrupted them.

'Come.'

The door swung open and in walked Castellanos. Even after conversing with the Greek many times over recent days the medicus's appearance never failed to shock Lucius. His face was pale and drawn, and his dark eyes were underscored by even darker rings, giving them a sunken demeanour. His shoulders stooped, bestowing him with an aura of defeat. It was understandable, Lucius had supposed; the horror filled days of the recent past had weighed heavily. Even so, the man of middle years who stood before him had aged greatly.

'Can I speak with you, sir?' His words firm, belying his appearance.

'I'll wait outside,' Cai said.

11

'No, Praefectus. This concerns you too.'

'Very well, Castellanos, what is it?' Lucius said, more brusquely than intended, but the interruption was irksome.

The physician took a deep, controlling breath. 'I want to come with you.' Lucius and Cai glanced at one another before examining Castellanos. 'Hrindenus is not quite as discreet as you have been.'

'That big ox, wait till I—'

Castellanos cut across Cai.

'He came to me, asking for medical supplies. I eventually wheedled it out of him. He wouldn't tell me your purpose, though there could only be one reason that would take a small band into the wild lands. You seek Alyn.'

'It's too great a risk, I could not ask it of you,' Cai said.

'Please understand, I do this for my own reasons. Yes, I grew to like Alyn very much as a friend. But…'

'What?'

Lucius smiled to himself, remembering his impatience with the medicus, and his reply.

'I cannot bear this place of death and suffering any longer. My orderlies can now look to the care of the men that remain in need. I find I am no longer able to face their suffering.' He lowered his head, shamed by his words. After a few moments, as he and Cai had watched on in silence, the medicus raised it once more, a ghost of a smile flickered on his lips. 'And besides, I have a plan that may help, if we find ourselves in the lands beyond the Novantae's.'

And it had been a good plan. So, they had become a party of four.

Looking now at Castellanos as he tossed another pebble into the slow moving waters, Lucius sensed a renewed energy about him. The medicus still appeared careworn, but he stood taller, his movements lithe and purposeful. Lucius well understood the weight that had been lifted from them all to finally have left that place of death.

It was one of those autumn days that gave lie to the summer's ending. The sun warmed the air, making a cloak unnecessary. The long reeds by the riverbank were still lush. Though the nearby oak trees were almost naked of their foliage, there was barely a breath of wind to stir the fallen accumulation of nut-brown leaves.

'They're ready,' Hrindenus shouted over his shoulder, before stalking to the Anam's edge to fill the canteens. Lucius arose on stiff legs and felt a wrench of pain in his shield arm. A constant reminder of the price of victory.

The two trout had been laid on a flat river-stone and Lucius peeled away the dappled skin of one and picked off some large flakes of the succulent, blush coloured flesh from its carcass. A line of oily liquid ran down the back of his hand as he dropped the hot meat into his upraised mouth.

'Not bad,' he said, as Hrindenus returned, handing a canteen to Lucius. The Tungrian gave him a lopsided smile.

'The cooking is the easy part,' he said. 'It's the catching takes the real skill. You're indeed fortunate to have such as me on this journey. Else I fear you all would starve for lack of a mess slave to provide for you.'

Lucius laughed, well used to the Vexillarius's familiarity. Their ruse, if it was to work, would require that they all adopt a greater informality. With the exception of the medicus. Of course Hrindenus had taken to it with alacrity.

'How much longer do you think he will be?' Castellanos asked, taking a place at the fireside. 'Shouldn't he have been here by now?'

'Keen to be on our way, are you, medicus?' Hrindenus said, with some amusement. 'Well, I suppose someone has to prick all of those putrid barbarian arse boils.'

'I merely wondered if we should be concerned,' Castellanos said, not hiding his irritation. Lucius smiled to himself, amused at the Greek's discomfiture.

'It's a long day's riding to Mascellus's farm,' Lucius responded. 'He would have spent some time getting the boy settled in. Not to mention the visit to the town of the Carvetii to acquire the other supplies we need. 'There's still a good time yet before we should be concerned.' Castellanos harrumphed, but said no more, instead reaching for a share of the fish.

Lucius turned at a whicker from one of the mounts. All four horses had been hobbled a few paces away amongst a swathe of long grass. A moment later he heard an answering whicker from further down the river. One or more horsemen was approaching their camp. All three jumped up from the fireside. Lucius clasped his dagger's hilt at his belt.

Moments later, a rider came into view, mounted on a native pony. Its coat was white with brown patches, much like their horses. He pulled a packhorse along with him, loaded down with goods hidden under leather covers. The rider wore a thick leather vest atop a dull brown tunic. His short-cropped hair was fair, turning to grey, his face clean shaven. Cai raised a weary arm in salutation.

'Greetings, brother,' Lucius said, as Cai halted and dismounted stiffly before the fire. 'How was your visit to our friend's farm? Did you get the lad situated?'

Cai grimaced. 'Mascellus has enthusiastically reembraced the life of a farmer. Almost as if he never left, and is well pleased to be back with his wife. And who can blame him, she is a fine woman. As to Beren...' he

14

shrugged. 'It may be some time before the boy forgives me for leaving him behind.' A rueful smile crossed Cai's face. 'One day he will be a fierce warrior, like his father.'

'Were you able to trade for all we need?' Lucius asked.

'More or less,' Cai said, as he arched his back, stretching his aching body. He moved to the packhorse, unlashing the leather cover. Accompanied by a clattering sound he rolled it out on the soft grassy bank of the Anam. Three long spears and three scabbarded swords were revealed, pommels shining dully in the afternoon light.

Hrindenus was first to step forward and pick up one of the swords, swiftly drawing it. 'It's ancient,' he said, his voice full of disgust as he took in the rust-mottled blade.

'They're all serviceable,' Cai replied. 'They just need some attention with a whetstone. Besides, we're mercenaries, remember. Our kit doesn't need to be of parade ground standard. The spears are made of new, solid ash, so we'll look the part.' Hrindenus grumbled something unintelligible.

'Well then,' Lucius said, 'let's spend what's left of the day's light making our final preparations.'

As night fell, Lucius peered across the campfire at the other three men as they took their ease. They picked at some of the fresh bread and cheese. 'So our plan is unchanged,' Castellanos said, around a mouthful of cheese.

'We take the coast road to its terminus at the fort on the estuary,' Cai said. 'From there on into the great forest making our way to where the Sula meets the Sea of Hibernia. That's where our old colleague Nepos said he thought the capital of the Novantae would be found.'

'But,' Hrindenus said, pausing to swallow the lump of bread he'd been working at, 'but isn't there a good chance

15

Barra has gone to ground near their settlement by the lake? Shouldn't we make for there first?'

'We've discussed this,' Lucius cut in. 'The boys of the Twentieth will have swept through there. Most of the stragglers of the tribes will either be headed further north or will take refuge in the heart of the Novantae lands in the far western reaches.'

'What if we're stopped and questioned by our own troops?' Hrindenus tried again.

'I have something to see us through any such difficulty, though that's as much as you need to know.' Lucius gave the big Tungrian a hard stare to make it clear this line of questioning was at an end. Hrindenus stared back, but eventually shrugged and smiled.

'Did you really have to make me take a blade to my chin? It took me a year to grow my whiskers out to their full lustrous length. How will I get a woman, now that I look like one of you Roman pretty boys?'

'I've heard the women of the Caledonae tribes are not particular,' Lucius said. 'So even a wool-clipped Tungrian might have a chance. Besides, it's I who should feel sorry for himself. Having to grow this itchy devil of a beard.'

'It's better than being recognised by our enemies,' Cai said, a smile flashing across his lips in the flickering light of the fire. 'We spilled so much of their blood defending the Sack's ramparts, our images must be emblazoned on their souls. If we're captured, at least we might receive a quick death, rather than a slow, agonised one as we're cooked over a fire.'

'You Nervii are a bundle of laughs,' Hrindenus said. Lucius thought the big man had sensed, as he had, some of the old humour was creeping back into their brother. Humour that had been sadly missing in recent days.

Lucius turned to Castellanos. 'Well, my friend, let's hope your idea works, because from this moment on we are the guards of Castellanos the Greek, who has a curative for every ailment.'

4

They pushed the horses hard, covering ground in a day that had taken them three when last they came this way with the full ala. After only brief stops to water the horses, and talking little, they neared the fort as the light began to fade, Cai signalled a change of pace to a walk.

He had been riding beside Lucius for much of the journey, but eased back to let Hrindenus come alongside him. 'How does it feel to be returning to your old post?' he asked, reaching down to pat the neck of his mount.

'Strange,' Hrindenus said. 'Almost like that life belonged to someone else.' He paused for a moment. 'So much has passed in the few short weeks since I last patrolled this ground.' Again, the big man was quiet for a short time before continuing. 'I'm glad to have the opportunity to look over Hediste's burial place. Hopefully it hasn't been disturbed by any beast. Perhaps the river stones I covered it with have been sufficient to protect it. The work was done in a hurry, with no time for care.'

'It's good to honour the dead. Especially those closest to us,' Cai said. The pair rode on for a while longer. 'I wanted to thank you, brother.'

'For what? I hope you're not going to get all womanly on me, sir?'

Cai laughed. He'd grown so used to the standard bearer's brusque mockery he didn't think he could be surprised any more. But he became serious. 'I had no right to ask you to ride with me on this....' Cai paused, seeking the right words. 'This hunt has so little chance of success, and yet carries a high risk for us all. As much as I hate to say it Tungrian, I've come to rely on your presence and courage in battle.' Cai fell silent, unsure what else to say. He expected Hrindenus to make the usual offhand comment, instead he too fell to silence.

Hrindenus made a hooming sound from deep within his broad chest. 'You are my commander, that is the truth of it,' he said. 'But I know you would have allowed me to refuse you, had I wished it. We are of different tribes, you and I, and different ranks. And divided by a generation of battle experience. Still, I also know we have shed blood together, and have stepped in the way of an enemy blade to defend the other. To me, at least, we are brothers, and brothers do not abandon kin in time of need. I did not come to know your woman well. But, she is important to you, so she is important to me.' Hrindenus hoomed once more.

Cai gazed at the big man. His face, in that moment, seemed so unfamiliar without its beard and long fair hair framing it. Hrindenus continued to stare at the road ahead.

'Brothers. Yes.' Cai nodded, knowing any words from him would be inadequate thanks for the gift the Tungrian had given him. He hoped they would serve.

As the small party approached a low rise in the military coast road, Cai became aware of a rhythmic, tramping sound. It could only be made by a large formation of infantry on the march, progressing at an unhurried, steady pace.

Lucius led the four and their two baggage mounts from the surfaced road, crossing the shallow drainage ditch to wait for the formation to pass. Moments later the bobbing plume of a centurion's helmet appeared above the lip of the rise. Behind it, the fluttering standard of a charging boar, held aloft by a mean looking Vexillarius. Cai smiled at an old memory as the officer and the first line of legionaries came fully into view.

19

The centurion knocked the knob of his vine stick against the rim of his helmet in greeting as he reached them. 'A glorious evening, gentlemen, is it not?' he said, in a gruff tone, before moving passed. Followed by the ordered ranks of his command.

'Why are they on the road as dusk approaches?' Lucius asked.

'It would seem the Twentieth have little fear of our blue-painted friends,' Cai responded.

'They still have time to stop and prepare a marching camp before nightfall.'

'A full cohort,' Castellanos said, moving his mount in between the pair, as century after century passed them by. When the last of the infantry was cresting the rise, a new rumbling sound caught their attention: the cohort's baggage train, filled with all the supplies the unit would need on campaign. The first of the ox-drawn wagons held a number of wounded men, though no more than a score, Cai thought.

'It seems the tribes are too busy running to put up much of a fight,' he said.

'Or have already been caught,' Lucius replied, his voice grim as he nodded further down the road. Beyond the last wagon came two long lines of shuffling captives. As they neared the four riders, Cai was able to distinguish both Novantae and Damnonii. Each former warrior was tethered to the next by a rope and iron ring looped around their necks. The leading slaves were hitched to the last wagon, wrists trussed behind backs by thin, leather straps. One or two stared defiantly ahead. However, most had heads bowed, immersed in their own misery.

'No wonder that Centurion was so damned chirpy,' Hrindenus said. 'They have near fifty quality slaves for the market.'

Behind the tribesmen came the rearguard. A full turma of cavalry moving at a slow walk to match the pace of the oxen. 'Tungrians,' Cai said. 'Hrindenus, go and have a chat with the Decurion, see if you can get the lay of the land in the direction we're headed. Remember our cover story. We're lowly guards for the good medicus here.' He watched as the big man trotted his mount towards the cavalry officer, who peered at his fellow tribesman with disdain. Well at least our dishevelled appearance seems to be working, Cai thought.

Hrindenus greeted the Decurion in his own language and his face visibly relaxed. He even laughed at some quip from his countryman, who now pointed back towards the other three, causing the officer to laugh once more. The turma didn't halt, as Hrindenus rode alongside the cavalry officer at the head of the formation, both talking animatedly as they passed by. The officer roared another deep belly laugh.

'What's so damned funny?' Lucius asked, confused.

'I expect our oversized Vexillarius is expounding on the folly of our plan to bring healing to the great unwashed,' Cai responded. 'Look at them,' he nodded at the passing cavalrymen. 'Shields hanging from saddle horns, men bantering with their mates as if escorting a routine grain delivery and not in enemy territory. These men have become complacent.'

'Perhaps the Novantae have given them little cause to be on their guard,' Castellanos said, in a low voice. 'Surely the fight will have gone out of them after seeing so much death and having victory snatched from them at the moment of triumph over us.'

'Well, they've seen some action,' Cai said. 'Look at their saddles.'

Lucius curled his lip in distaste. Severed heads hung from the saddle horns of many of the riders. The grotesque trophies bounced with the movement of the horses. Each was tethered by their long plaited hair, except for the Damnonii victims who lacked any. Instead, those were held by iron nails driven into the top of their skulls. In turn the nails had been forced through strips of leather, which were strapped to the cavalrymen's saddles.

'This will certainly help to endear us to the Novantae,' Castellanos said, not able to hide his own disgust at the sight.

'Cocky bastard,' Hrindenus said ruefully as he pulled his mount to a halt. 'They've spent too long attached to the Twentieth in comfortable barracks in Castra Deva. He thinks it's easy to kill barbarians.' The big Tungrian spat. 'It's easy to chase down a fleeing enemy when someone else has done the hard fighting for you.'

'Did you discover anything of use?' Lucius said.

'Aye,' he said. 'Turns out he's from a neighbouring village to mine, so we became quite pally. He reckons the tribes are done. There's been a few minor skirmishes, mostly they've been driving them deeper into the great forest. Their Legatus kept up the pursuit for a few miles beyond the terminus fort, but has called a halt for fear of losing too many of his infantry unnecessarily. It appears he's claimed it as a great victory. Our part in it is already forgotten.'

'Our standard will have a new battle honour, that's what matters,' Lucius said. 'But it may be that the heroic Legatus of the Twentieth has left the job half done. If he has truly halted his foray into the west, it would appear we will soon be moving into enemy-held territory.'

'It might also mean Barra is still at large in Novantae lands,' Cai said, his voice sounding grim. 'And we may yet find him in their capital.'

'If we get that far,' Hrindenus chipped in.

5

'Halt. State your business,' the Optio of the gate section snarled.

Lucius had been reflecting on his last visit to the fort, the memory of Nepos, its last commander, coming to him with some fondness. The old Decurion, blind in one eye and with his distinctive teardrop scar, had given his life in the defence of the fort. The image of Barra holding a raised spear with Nepos's severed head impaled upon it flashed to mind, filling Lucius with the familiar sense of rage. How would he feel if they eventually found the Novantae warchief?

Castellanos nudged his mount forward a step. 'I am Castellanos the Greek, healer of the poor wretches of the world. I and my companions seek shelter for the night and to commune with your commander.'

'Did you hear that, lads? Castellanos the Greek here wants to commune with the Tribunus.' Lucius noted only two of the eight man section laughed, the others simply looking on sullenly. This particular junior officer was not well liked by his men. 'Well Greek, you can go fuck—'

'What's going on here, Gratius?' The men of the guard section came to attention as a Centurion strode through the main gate and onto the causeway. Lucius had to hide a smirk at the sight. For the officer was tall, nearly as big as Hrindenus. However, where the Tungrian was built like an ox the Centurion was twig-thin. His long skinny legs gave his stride the appearance of a new-born foal.

'Sir. I was just telling these gentlemen we have no room to house them or their mounts for the night,' the Optio began.

'We're happy to make our camp outside of your walls if need be,' Castellanos interrupted. 'We journey into the lands of the tribes and simply seek some intelligence from your commander.' The Centurion scrutinised Castellanos followed by the others of the party, appraising them for a few moments in silence. He continually pursed his lips as he did so.

'Very well,' he said. 'Dismount. Leave your horses and weapons here and follow me. Gratius, see to the stabling of their horses.'

'Yes sir,' the Optio responded smartly, whilst simultaneously giving the group a filthy stare.

'Thank you,' said Castellanos, as he handed the reins of his horse ostentatiously to the Optio, whose face immediately turned a bright shade of pink. ''I am in your debt.' The Centurion nodded curtly before turning on his heels. Lucius and the others attempted to keep pace with his long stride.

Lucius took in the familiar sight of the cavalry barrack blocks. Only a small number of horses stood in the front stabling areas. The smell of cooking reached him from the numerous three-man rooms at the rear. As they approached the doorway to the small principia, the Centurion suddenly turned to face them.

'Wait here, whilst I speak with the Tribunus. And if he agrees to an audience, you'd better damn well tell the fucking truth. I know soldiers when I see them. You're as much paid-for guards as I'm the Emperor's mother.' The Centurion removed his helmet, ducked his tall frame under the doorway, and was gone.

'What do you think?' Cai said.

'Let's wait and see who we're dealing with first,' Lucius said. 'It appears the Centurion, at least, is not fooled by our ruse. If pressed we'll have to try our alternate fabrication about making contact with Urbicus's agent. We don't want to be mistaken for deserters after all.'

'Do I look like I have the fucking time to see every stray turning up at our gates, Malor?' Lucius and the others heard the raised and exasperated voice of, presumably, the fort's commanding officer. Followed by the muffled response of the Centurion.

'Well, well, it's a small world,' Cai said. 'I'd know that lisp anywhere.'

'Very well, show them in,' came the booming voice once more. And before Lucius could ask Cai what he meant the tall Centurion returned.

'Right, in you come. And remember what I said, any fucking lies and I'll have your guts for a spatha belt.'

'How very descriptive,' Castellanos said, still in character. The Centurion gave him a withering look, before striding off along the internal walkway. As he reached the open doorway to what had been Nepos's quarters, the Centurion rapped his knuckles against the wooden frame.

'The four *gentlemen*, sir,' he said.

The man behind the old wooden desk was of middle years, perhaps the same age as Lucius. His hair was thinning, turning to grey, and there was a chunk of flesh missing from the top of his right ear, leaving wine-red and puckered scarring. His chainmail shirt lay on the small bunk behind him and he wore only his red military tunic. His cloak was wrapped around his shoulders to stave off the evening chill.

'Right, who the fuck are you and what are you doing heading into enemy territory? You look like fucking spies to me, no matter what Malor here says.'

Lucius felt Cai brush by his shoulder to stand to attention in front of the Tribunus's desk. 'It's Tribunus Marcellus isn't it, sir?' he said.

'Yes. How—'

Cai gave the military salute. 'Praefectus Martis of the First Nervana, sir. You may remember we met once on the eve of the battle at the Novantae's hill? You were Legatus Verus's adjutant at the time.' Marcellus stared back at Cai, his brow furrowed, his eyes showing no sign he recognised his colleague. 'I had longer hair and an unshaven chin until a few days ago,' Cai said, seeing his confusion.

The Tribunus's eyes widened in surprise. 'Martis, yes of course,' he said, though his bewilderment returned. 'What the hell are you doing here, clearly attempting to conceal your identities, only days after seeing off a siege of barbarians? Have you abandoned your post?'

Lucius stepped forward. 'Tribunus Felix of the Nervana. Can we speak in private? I will explain all.'

'Jupiter! Felix, what the—?' Marcellus faltered. He scrutinised Lucius's unkempt appearance for a short time. 'Well,' he said, recovering his composure. 'This should indeed be an interesting tale.' His tone was dubious. He flashed a wry smile at Lucius. 'But Malor stays. I suspect I may, one day, need a witness to our meeting.'

'Very well,' Lucius said, and reached into a fold of his cloak, retrieving a tightly rolled scroll. 'These are my orders, I cannot reveal all to you but, you will recognise the seal?'

The fort's commander stared at the wax daub, indented with the image of a big cat. Lucius had once been told by Verus it was called a cheetah, an animal native to Numidia. 'Urbicus?'

Lucius nodded.

27

'Malor, get some chairs brought in. This may take some telling.'

In moments all were seated. The small room felt cramped as the six men squeezed around the commander's table.

'My apologies, I have no decent wine, but there's plenty of posca to go around,' Marcellus said, handing a leather canteen to Lucius, who took a mouthful before passing it on. 'Well, let's have it, Felix, what's so important our former Governor orders you into barbarian lands in the middle of a war?'

Lucius, scratched at his new and increasingly scruffy beard. 'Urbicus has an agent planted within the Novantae.' He paused, gathering his thoughts. 'The revolt of the tribes may be far from over. Indeed, the intended incursion across the Wall my men halted may have been a prelude to a wider conflict. One involving those tribes beyond the Emperor's new wall. Urbicus believes they plan to move against our northern garrisons.'

Marcellus seemed unconvinced. 'The Novantae and their allies are beaten. My command barely had a scratch.'

'You may have found it a different story if your Legatus had the balls to push on deeper towards the Novantae capital,' Hrindenus said, his voice dripping with scorn.

'Shut your mouth, Hrindenus, you forget yourself,' Lucius interjected, seeing Marcellus's features darken. His eyes locked on the Tungrian, his knuckles whitening as they gripped the arms of his chair. Lucius pushed on. 'The decision to halt further advances may aid our mission.'

'How so?' Marcellus asked, still not removing his glare from Hrindenus, who returned it with a hint of a smile.

'The agent is a member of the Novantae's ruling elite. He may not have fled their lands yet. If we can make contact he may be able to reveal the wider plan of these damned barbarians.'

'So let me understand this,' Marcellus said, incredulous. 'Your plan is to sneak into a tribe's lands that are in turmoil, making your way through near impenetrable forest. Somehow make contact with this agent. Get him to reveal all and then hightail it back out again. Do I have the right of it?

'No, colleague,' Lucius said, a wide smile spreading across his bearded face. 'We're going to ride in. In full view of the Novantae and they will lead us to their capital. Whereupon the agent will contact us.' Lucius laughed at the other's incredulous look, before continuing. 'Castellanos the Greek here,' he continued, indicating the medicus, who nodded in mock solemnity. 'Is indeed Greek and a healer. In fact, he's our cohort's very own medicus. Our subterfuge is a wandering healer and his escort, come to bring succour in the Novantae's greatest time of need. For a small fee.'

'Are you mad?' Marcellus interjected, his lisp becoming more pronounced. 'The blue-faces will see right through you. They'll, rightly, assume you are spies and have the skin flayed from your bodies. Before burning you slowly as a sacrifice to their heathen gods.'

'Perhaps,' Lucius conceded. 'Though once the medicus here starts working on their sick and wounded, of which there must now be many, we'll be able to persuade them of our good intentions.'

Marcellus stared at Lucius and his companions, before turning to his Centurion, who had kept his own counsel throughout. 'What do you think, Malor?'

The tall officer looked like he had been folded into his campaign chair, his knees almost touching his chest. He glanced at each of the four men, who were strangers to him. Lucius felt the intelligence in his scrutinising eyes, before Malor returned his attention to his commander.

'Something doesn't smell right with any of this, sir, in my opinion. If they speak the truth they're either the bravest men I have met or the most stupid. Or both. I think it unlikely they'll return. If they are lucky, they may get the chance to spend the rest of their miserable lives as slaves to the Novantae. With the delight of having their arseholes pummelled each night by some big hairy bastard,' Marcellus snorted at the image. 'But,' Malor shrugged his shoulders. 'If by some miracle, resulting from the great many sacrifices these men must have already made to divine Fortuna, they make it back with intelligence on what the blue-faces are up to. Well then, they might just save a great many lives.' All in the room were quiet for a moment, before the Centurion spoke once more, a leer of a smile spreading across his face.

'My money is on a lingering and painful death.'

6

'That was a hell of defence you and your lads put up against the blue-faces.'

Cai was saddling his mount inside one of the cavalry barrack blocks. A flickering oil lamp gave some additional light on the dull autumnal morning as Centurion Malor entered its wide doorway. Cai finished tightening the straps under the horse's broad belly and stood, arching his back as he did so.

'Aye, though we suffered grievous losses,' Cai said, turning to Malor. 'At least enough survived that we can rebuild the cohort, thanks to the timely arrival of the Twentieth.'

'It was a bastard of a march from Deva,' Malor said. 'The Legatus had us at double pace before first light each day and well into the night. Still, my long legs make keeping up with the pace the least of my worries.'

Cai laughed. 'How in Hades does someone with your frame survive so long in the shield wall? You must stand head and shoulders above everyone else?'

It was the Centurion's turn to laugh, or at least that is what Cai assumed the blast of a snort from the tall man's nose was. 'I always have the longest reach. Makes it hard for any blue-faced bastard with a spear to get close.' Cai smiled at the image.

'It makes a kind of sense I suppose.'

Malor became serious. 'Look Martis,' he said. 'I'm not sure I believe much of your Tribunus's tale. But men who have defended their standard for days of bloody battle can only have honourable intentions. So I wish you luck.' The Centurion held out his arm, which Cai gripped.

'Thank you. We'll need it.'

'I don't suppose you'll have much to warm you at night around the campfire, so I brought you this,' Malor held out a water skin. 'A supply of posca to keep you going for a while.'

'Thank you, brother,' Cai said. 'That's most welcome, although I think I'll keep it away from the big Tungrian oaf, otherwise it won't last a single watch.'

A short while later all four were mounted once more and waited outside of the fort's main gate along with the packhorses. Marcellus approached them on foot, stopping at the side of Lucius's horse.

'This will see you safely through any of our mounted patrols, should you encounter them,' Marcellus said, in his familiar lisp, handing Lucius a wooden tablet. He nodded his thanks, stuffing the pass into his saddle bag. 'The route west through the forest is obvious for two or three miles. Soon after it splits into a number of narrow game trails and the travel will be tougher. But if you stay close enough to the Sula to smell its salty waters, you shouldn't stray too far from the right path,'

Lucius held out his hand. 'My thanks for your help. Perhaps we'll meet again one day and I'll regale you with the story of our triumphant mission.'

Marcellus smiled solemnly at Lucius. 'I pray it is so, Felix.'

'I remember him when he was a nervous adjutant,' Cai said, shortly after they left the causeway. 'Jumping like a frightened rabbit every time Verus spoke. It's hard to reconcile with the hard bitten commander we've just left. I would have expected him to be in the Senate by now. Isn't that what your lot all eventually do?'

'I had a good long chat with my colleague last night over his skin of posca. For Marcellus, achieving election to the senate was certainly what was expected of him. He is the youngest of four boys, it appears his father no longer had sufficient personal wealth to fund Marcellus's election, as he had done for his other sons. As it turns out, however, the youth you encountered all those years ago took to military life better than Verus or even he had expected. He distinguished himself during Urbicus's campaign and afterwards decided to make a life in the Eagles his career.'

'By the way, what was in that letter you plucked from the folds of your tunic last night?'

Lucius rumbled a low laugh. 'It was an old instruction from Urbicus to find a land agent for his newly acquired estates in Britannia. But it still held his seal intact. I didn't want to risk bringing along his last set of orders. That will be required to secure passage for my journey to Baetica.'

The small party turned towards the river's ford. Cai glanced at the earth-strewn outline of the ala's old overnight camp. The faces of some of his men came to mind. So many had been lost.

'They did well, the lads,' Lucius said, sensing his friend's mood.

'Aye,' Cai said, before nudging his mount into the shallow, fast moving waters.

By the time the sun broke above the eastern hills behind them the four had reached the point where the broad track became confused. The trees, which had been fairly sparse until then, darkened into a dense cover of oak and red pine. The forest floor was strewn with fern, green fronds covered with brown spots like the rust on untended chainmail.

'What do you think?' Lucius asked Cai, as he took in what seemed to be at least three pathways.

'Hrindenus,' Cai called over his shoulder. 'Are you familiar with this ground?'

'Aye, some,' he said.

'I presume the southernmost path will keep us nearest the Sula?'

The Tungrian scratched at the fair whiskers of the returning growth. 'That trail, as I remember, finishes by a sandy beach a mile or so further on. The central one goes directly west for some way before turning to follow closer to the coastline, still heading westward. The other I don't know.'

'The middle path it is. I'll take point,' Lucius said, kicking his horse into a canter to be quickly swallowed by the dense cover of the forest.

'You bring up the rear, Hrindenus,' Cai said. 'We must keep our eyes skinned from here on. Just because the damned Twentieth have decided the tribes are beaten, we won't be so complacent. Castellanos, stay close to me.'

After an hour the narrow path they had been following changed course as Hrindenus had described, and the silver waters of the Sula could be glimpsed through gaps in the trees.

'A beautiful land, is it not?' Castellanos said. Cai jumped in surprise, not realising the Greek had moved up onto his shoulder. Castellanos had kept his own counsel in recent days, rarely talking unless directly addressed by one of the others. It was jarring to hear him speak now in the quiet of the forest. 'It seems after so many years living in this land I am seeing it for the first time.'

'Aye well,' Cai said. 'It does have a kind of beauty all its own. As long as you can avoid being skewered by one of the locals.' The medicus smiled.

A short while later, Lucius trotted back down the path towards the others. 'There's a stream ahead where we can water the horses and stretch our legs. I suggest we take the opportunity while we can.'

'I'll take over from you,' Cai said.

'Keep a sharp watch, brother,' Lucius returned. 'I'm surprised we haven't come across any of the legion's mounted patrols yet. Something doesn't feel right.'

The three walked their horses to the stream and dismounted as Cai took up watch further along the pathway. The waters gurgled over smooth, dark pebbles just below its surface. Hrindenus pulled several large dock leaves from the bank.

'I'm off to get rid of this morning's grains,' he said, disappearing amongst a stand of dense bush.

'Charming man,' Castellanos said, before kneeling down at the stream's edge and drinking directly from its crystalline water.

Lucius turned at the sound of heavy rustling in the undergrowth. Hrindenus reappeared, pulling his troos back up over his hips as he moved.

'A rider,' he said in an urgent whisper, moving swiftly towards the horses. He drew his sword from its scabbard, slung over his saddle.

Lucius crouched, listening. It was a moment before he heard the muffled rumble of fast moving hoof beats. They came from the east. Were they being followed? By hand signal to Hrindenus, Lucius indicated he should find cover, whilst he would take the other side of the pathway. The big man nodded his understanding.

'Hide,' he hissed at Castellanos, before turning sharply at the sound of splashing footsteps in the stream. Cai had heard the approaching horseman too. His friend knelt beside the Tungrian, sword gripped in hand, panting heavily.

The rumbling sound grew louder, accompanied by the snapping of twigs and the alarmed calls of birds disturbed by his passing. This rider is careless of the noise he's making, Lucius thought.

An instant later a chestnut horse burst into the small clearing. Its rider pulled up hard, a wild state of alarm in his eyes, at the sight of the horses by the stream, blocking his route. His mount brayed its annoyance at the sudden halt.

Lucius and the others leapt from their hiding places. Cai took hold of the horse's reins as Lucius and Hrindenus raised their sword points towards the horseman.

'Mascellus,' Cai exclaimed. The fair hair of the rider and long grey beard were dishevelled, but Lucius saw immediately it was indeed the old Decurion. Still wild-eyed and breathing heavily, he fought to bring his horse under control. Recognition dawned in the veteran's eyes.

'Thank the gods. I feared I wouldn't catch you.'

'What is it Mascellus?' Cai said. 'What are you doing here?' Lucius heard his own concern echoed in his friend's voice.

'It's Beren. He's gone.'

7

Beren was lost.

He'd left the road as daylight began to fade, in order to lose Mascellus. He'd caught sight of him in the distance. He couldn't discern the rider's features, but who else would be riding an identical chestnut-coloured mount at such a hard pace? Now with the gloom of the forest enclosed around him he had no sense of where he was.

He had slept little during the night, jolted awake by every rustle of the undergrowth. He had not dared to make a fire so awoke stiff and cold on the soft ground, damp with dew. He mounted the horse he had borrowed, no, stolen, from Mascellus's corral and nibbled distractedly at the bread made by Enid he had taken from the hearth. He felt a greater guilt at that small theft than he did the taking of the chestnut mare. Enid had been nothing but kind to him. Beren knew his mam would have scolded him for betraying her hospitality. He brushed at his eyes with the back of his hand before the tears could tumble from them.

The day before, with the brooding presence of the mountain of Criffel on his right shoulder, he had been able to keep his bearings, even in the depths of the forest. Now its familiar company was gone and he was left alone amongst the ancient oak and red pine. The forest was silent, the morning birdsong gone, the only sound coming from the rustle of leaf fall as his mount pushed through the thick golden carpet.

The sky above was overcast, thick grey cloud cover hiding the sun. Which direction should he take? He knew Cai was headed west, deep into Novantae lands, but which way was it? A feeling of hopelessness began to fill him as he gazed at the dense woodland.

'Divine Epona, help me,' Beren whispered the prayer into the still morning air. He cast around hoping for some sign, perhaps a hint of a trail he could follow. Nothing. He didn't know how to go on and couldn't even return the way he had come, the blanket of leaves hiding his passing. He had been foolish, thinking he could follow Cai and aid him in the search. 'Stupid, stupid, stupid,' he spat.

Beren stared despondently at a broad red pine that had emerged like a great sentinel barring his path. Its bark was obscured by a thick cloak of moss. A memory sprang into his mind's-eye of the day Cai took him on his first hunt. His friend had spent most of the morning talking to him about the different kinds of trees or the signs to watch for to identify the passing of game. He had eventually become frustrated, wondering when they would actually get the chance to make a kill.

One particular memory came to him. Moss thrives best on the north facing side of a tree's trunk. Beren almost shouted with joy. If he was looking directly at the moss covered side of this great tree, it meant he was facing southwards. If he turned to the right he would be headed west once more.

'Come,' he said, nudging his mount into a trot, the chestnut happily obliging, keen to be moving once more.

As the morning wore on the land began to rise gradually. The landscape became difficult as broad, grey, lichen-covered rock protruded from the forest floor, forcing Beren to take a winding route. Red pine became the dominant cover, the soft undergrowth of wind-fallen leaves replaced by dense bramble bushes, whose unpicked berries hung thick and withering on their barbed and tangled branches. His mount snorted great gusts of air with the effort of the climb, her nostrils flaring, head swaying from side to side. Beren was forced to let her walk. Moving any faster risked a stumble.

The ground became abruptly steep. He sensed the summit was close. The light ahead, seen through the filter of the trees, was brighter. Moments later horse and rider entered a clearing.

'Come on girl,' Beren spoke quietly to his mount. 'Let's see what we can see, shall we?' He halted at the centre of the glade, which was little more than a hundred paces across. He breathed a sigh of relief as there, to the south, across the treetops, was the distant slash of the Sula, its waters shining dully. He was headed in the right direction.

The cloud cover was low this high up. Moments later the view of the estuary was snatched away by a descending mist. In an instant all around him was obscured. He could see no more than ten paces in any direction. The light wind dropped. The only sound was his own breathing. It felt like he had been drawn into a ghostly realm, the slow movement of the cloud seeming to give glimpses of wraith-like creatures darting within in the mist.

Fear began to creep into his very bones. His breathing became rapid and ragged, his heart beating hard against his chest. Beren fought down the panic threatening to overwhelm him. 'Let's go,' Beren whispered to his mount, clicking his tongue and turning the chestnut westward once more. He wanted away from this place.

A snapping sound resounded sharply in the still air. Beren whipped his head in its direction. A horse whinnied from behind him, close by the forest's edge.

Beren kicked hard. The mare protested as it leapt forward, towards the opposite side of the clearing. A dark spear thumped into the ground immediately in his path.

39

Beren yanked hard on the reins, horse and rider swerved around the shaft, which stood at a drunken angle. The sound of shrill warcries burst all around him.

The chestnut shrieked as a second spear impaled her neck. Her front legs buckled under her. Beren was thrown clear, crashing to the soft ground. Breath was driven from his body, agonising and sharp. White light filled his mind. He tried to rise but couldn't, the pain in his lungs vying for supremacy over the agony assailing his head.

He felt, though did not see, rough hands grab the neck of his tunic. 'So what do we have here? A Roman whelp, is it?'

Beren's mother was of the Carvetii tribe, who spoke the language of the People, and although this one's accent was thick he understood the words and heard their malevolence. Beren's vision slowly began to clear. He stared into a hate-twisted, thickly bearded, face.

'Let's see what colour you bleed, shall we Roman?' Beren felt the cold edge of a blade against his throat and a sharp prick as the metal broke skin.

'Hold your hand, Tegan! I know him.'

This new voice tugged at the edge of a memory. The thought faded as darkness took him.

8

'He slipped away before first light yesterday,' Mascellus said. 'He took one of my horses and a small loaf of bread. The dogs didn't raise the alarm because they knew him.' The old veteran accepted the water canteen handed to him by Hrindenus with a nod of gratitude.

His next words held a tone of admiration. 'The little shit made away without a sound. It wasn't until my Enid went to his cot to wake him that we realised he was gone.'

Cai felt his chest tighten. He had lost Alyn and now Beren. Hopelessness threatened to overwhelm him. What could he do?

'And you haven't seen any sign of the boy in all the time you have been in pursuit?' Lucius asked.

'I came across a half turma patrol around midday yesterday. Their Duplicarius said they'd seen a rider, from a distance, haring along the coast road an hour earlier. They had been coming out of the hills and were some way off. He thought the horse might have been chestnut coloured.'

Mascellus took another pull from the canteen. 'As dusk began to fall, I thought I caught a glimpse of a rider in the distance along the military road as he disappeared over a rise. When I reached it there was no sign of him. He may have left the road and entered the forest, or it might have been my old eyes playing tricks on me.'

'Are we really so sure Beren has come after us?' Castellanos spoke quietly from behind them.

'Aye, he's followed us, that's for sure,' Cai said, resigned. 'He'd been determined to come, but I thought

41

he had accepted his fate, if grudgingly, when we reached the farm. I should have known better.'

'You couldn't have known, brother,' Lucius said. 'A few days ago, he barely knew how to ride a horse.'

'He's too much like his damned father,' Cai said with some vehemence. 'Stubborn.'

'And never wanting to let his brothers face danger alone,' Mascellus said, with a sad smile. Cai snorted in response.

'If it was the lad the Decurion saw,' Hrindenus said, 'and he has taken to the forest, well…' the Tungrian's words trailed off for a moment. 'I've known experienced troopers lose their way in this place. I know these lands better than any of you. If we are to hunt for him, I should be the one to go.'

'Not on your own you won't,' Cai said.

'We'll all go,' Castellanos said.

'No,' Lucius said, his tone commanding. Cai turned to his friend in surprise. 'There's little point in the five of us blundering around this damned forest.' He gathered his thoughts for a moment. 'Mascellus, return the way you have come. Follow the forest's edge once you reach the military way. Search for any sign of the boy's passage into the trees. Report back to me here if you cross his trail. If not, go back to your farm.'

'But—' Mascellus made to protest. Lucius held up his hand to curtail it.

'It may be Beren comes to regret his rashness and finds his way home to you and Enid with his tail between his legs. You must be there so you can get word to us.' The old Nervii nodded. 'The good medicus and I will make camp here, whilst Cai and Hrindenus try to track him down.'

'Aye, there's sense in that,' Cai said, before turning to Hrindenus. 'Let's get going.'

A short time later Mascellus had disappeared back down the trail and Cai sat astride his mount. 'I'll see you soon, brother.'

'If you're not back in two days, we'll return to the fort and await you there,' Lucius said. 'We're too exposed here and we've been lucky so far not to run into any bands of vengeful Novantae.' Cai nodded, staring directly at his friend.

'If we don't find him in two days, the boy is likely dead.'

'Let's make for the north,' Cai said. 'If Beren is headed westward we might cut across his trail.'

'The sheep-humpers are running scared from the boys of the Twentieth,' Hrindenus said. 'They'll have left so many damned trails criss-crossing the forest floor the land will look like a gyrus after a day breaking in new mounts.'

'Mascellus's horses are shod,' Cai said, 'We might be able to pick out Beren's trail from the rest.'

Hrindenus grumbled noncommittally. Not having a better idea, he kicked his mount northwards. For the remainder of the day the pair headed inland. As Hrindenus had predicted they came across signs of men both on foot and mounted. Most headed westward.

As dusk fell, they came to a halt on the brow of a small, wooded rise overlooking a narrow, sheer-sided stream whose waters crashed over slick grey rocks protruding from its surface. The water foamed and sprayed as if the stream was fighting its way out of the clutches of the forest.

'These hoof prints are days old,' Hrindenus said. 'This is as good a place as any to make camp for the night.'

43

'We have light yet,' Cai said, not hiding his annoyance.

'No. At most we have half an hour before the ground is masked by the dark. The horses must be rested and watered.' Without waiting for a response Hrindenus spurred his mount down to a clearing near the stream's edge. Cai stared at his retreating back, anger surging through him. Unthinking he kicked his horse hard, causing the animal to leap after the other. Not slowing, as he came alongside the Tungrian, Cai kicked out. With a yelp of surprise the big man was flung from his saddle, landing with an expelled groan onto the forest floor.

'You forget yourself, *Tungrian*,' Cai's words were spat, his face flushing deep red. 'If I say we ride on. We. Ride. On.'

Hrindenus rose slowly to his feet, taking quick breaths as he struggled to get air back into his lungs. Lines of pain and anger creased his brow as he stared up at Cai.

'You do what you damned well like, *Nervii*. Go stumbling about in the dark like a lost child, and risk your horse breaking a leg. I'm staying here.' Without another word, Hrindenus took the bridle of his mount and led it towards a patch of tall, tangled grass where he hobbled it, before taking his water canteen and stalking towards the stream's edge.

Cai observed this, sitting rigid in his saddle. A burning sensation filled him; this time it wasn't anger, but shame. 'Shit,' he whispered into the evening air. Dismounting he hobbled his mount near to the other, leaving plenty of slack for it to graze freely. He too retrieved his canteen, before following the trail Hrindenus had taken.

He found him sitting on a smooth grey rock, staring into the surging waters of the burn. His waterskin lay abandoned on the ground nearby. Cai lowered himself to the ground across from Hrindenus, emitting an

44

involuntary groan, stiff from the effort of a long day in the saddle. He retrieved a small rock, so he could sit more comfortably, tossing it casually into the maelstrom.

'Forgive me, brother,' Cai said. 'You're right, and it seems I am not in my right mind.'

'I know,' Hrindenus said, not taking his eyes from the crashing water. 'It's why I let you live.'

For the first time that day, Cai laughed, deep and full throated. Hrindenus turned to him a wry smile creasing his young face. 'My thanks,' Cai said in mock solemnity. After a moment he became quiet, staring into the middle distance to the stout stands of red pine beyond the stream. 'This is a hopeless search,' he said. 'The boy is lost. Alyn is lost. And I have failed in my promise to a friend.'

'Gods you're a cheerful bastard,' Hrindenus said, turning to face Cai directly. 'Give the lad some credit. He's a tough little nut, that one. I saw him during the days at the Sack, when all was going to shit around him. Most his age would cower in the corner, holding onto their mother's skirts. Not him. He helped his mam tend to the wounded. Beren must have seen some terrible sights. He's a survivor and we mustn't give up on him.'

Cai nodded, hearing the sense in the words of his friend. 'Aye, you're right. He has a little woodcraft too from our hunting trip. Perhaps it'll help him.' Both were silent for a time, deep in their own thoughts. 'I'll take first watch,' Cai said. 'We'd best take up a position on the rise. Those waters are so loud down here a Novantae warband could creep up on us and take us up the arse before we had the chance to decline their amorous intentions.'

Next day they set off at the first hint of light, long before the rays of the low autumn sun broke above the tree canopy. As the morning progressed the trees began to thin, allowing more light onto the forest floor. Which was as well, as the ground had become covered with a dense and tangled undergrowth. The land began to rise too, making the going increasingly arduous.

The pair continued to see signs of the passing of many feet and hooves. Much as with the previous day, they were not fresh. Towards noon a mist descended, accompanied by a drizzling rain hiding much of the way ahead in its gloom. Hrindenus continued to lead the way. Cai halted from time to time, doubling back on the trail, to ensure they themselves were not being hunted.

The afternoon wore on and the rain ceased. For a time, their passage was accompanied by a continuous drip, dripping sound. As they progressed along the bank of a narrow stream, Hrindenus suddenly pulled up and dismounted.

'What do you see?' Cai asked.

'There are signs of shod horses passing this way. I nearly missed it amongst all of the others.'

'Could it be Beren?'

'There are many. A patrol, I think. The sign is fresh. Perhaps they came across the boy. Shall we follow?'

Cai thought for a moment. 'Well, we've nothing else to go on. Perhaps the gods are pointing the way?'

'I don't think the gods give a fuck about us. That doesn't mean it isn't a good idea to track them. They may at least give us some intelligence.'

'Lead the way,' Cai said.

Even in the leaf-strewn forest floor the sign of the patrol's passing was easy to pursue. It had left the edge of the stream and moved deeper into dense woodland of oak, alder and hawthorn. The birdsong that had been the perpetual background noise to their journey had faded to near silence.

'There can't be more than a section,' Hrindenus said. 'I don't understand. Only eight men so deep into hostile territory?'

'It's as we have seen already, brother,' Cai said. 'Complacency has set in amongst the command of the Twentieth.'

They pushed on. Though to Cai, the crunching and shushing of the passing of their mount's hooves through the golden leaf-fall trumpeted their presence. The gentle rise of the ground had continued. As the pair ascended through a tangle of underbrush, Hrindenus raised his hand sharply.

'What—' Cai began.

'Listen.'

At first all he could hear was the sound of the gentle breeze in the treetops and the gusted snorts of the horses. Then he caught it.

'Crows.'

'They could just be feasting on an animal carcass?'

Cai didn't respond, he kicked his mount towards the distant clamour. In a matter of moments, the raucous caws and clicks of the carrion birds was not all that drew them onwards. The smell. A reek that had become so familiar to the two men.

As they closed in on the cacophony, Cai dismounted. He slowly drew his sword from its scabbard slung across his saddle. Hrindenus followed suit. Cai crept through the undergrowth, each footstep carefully placed. He pulled back a final branch of a rowan tree, heavy with its small red berries. His heart sank at the sight before him.

A small glade, perhaps fifty paces wide, was filled with shafts of bright sunlight. Though, instead of shimmering from the tall, dry winter grasses at its heart, it reflected from the sleek, black backs of a carpet of hooded crows, rooks and ravens. The birds hopped gleefully from place to place as if at their own festival.

As Cai stepped fully into the clearing the dark cloak erupted into the air, accompanied by piercing cries and croaks of alarm. Immediately the source of the feast was revealed. Eight bodies lay discarded on the ground around the blackened remains of a campfire. Though they no longer wore their chainmail shirts it was clear they had found the patrol.

All still wore chequered troos and leather cavalry boots. Their weapons and horses had been looted along with armour and helmets. Although, given that clouds of flies now buzzed frantically around the bloody stumps of the auxiliary's necks, the latter would not be missed.

'The bastards beheaded them,' Hrindenus said, cold anger lacing his words.

'A habit enthusiastically embraced by that turma of Tungrians we met not so long ago.'

Cai ignored his friend's glare. Some of the carrion birds began to settle back onto the ground, tentatively making hopping steps towards the corpses. Moving around the edge of the glade, Cai searched the undergrowth.

'No sign of Beren,' he said, but he felt no relief.

'The ashes of the fire still have some warmth, perhaps we could still catch up to the bastards.'

'Perhaps,' Cai said. He looked down at one of the bodies. 'What were these fools thinking? Making a hot camp, and in a place so easy to ambush.' He shook the questions from his mind, what good did it do now? 'Mount up, let's follow. But have a care. I don't want to end up like these poor bastards.'

'This way,' Hrindenus said, after leaving the glade. 'There must be at least twenty of them.'

They entered dense woodland that closed tightly in on the pair. They followed the trail for a time. Signs of the warband's passing were often obscured as it crossed a series of others, both old and fresh.

'I've lost them,' Hrindenus said. 'I—' The ground had begun to rise sharply. Cai had been so focussed on ensuring his mount didn't stumble he almost walked her into the rear of Hrindenus's horse, which had come to a halt.

'What the—' The Tungrian was staring at the brush-covered ground. He dismounted, going onto one knee.

'This sign is fresh,' he said. 'No more than a day old.' The big man moved rapidly over the ground searching the undergrowth. 'Perhaps thirty mounted warriors. Headed that way.' He indicated the rising ground before them, through which an open area of the hill's summit could be seen.

Cai dismounted. The pair stalked carefully through the undergrowth to the clearing's edge.

'Look,' Hrindenus said. Pointing to the far side of the open ground. It took a moment for Cai to pick it out. A spear, its shaft protruding from the long grass at an angle. A moment later, the tainted smell of death hit them.

9

In the near darkness, Lucius sat with his back against the trunk of a stout red pine, its rough bark chafing even through his cloak. Castellanos's gentle snoring had become the background noise to his thoughts, which had returned first to his postponed journey to Baetica, the land of his birth, and from there to the meeting with Urbicus's mysterious agent among the Novantae. How was he meant to make contact?

'Damn the Numidian and his secrets,' Lucius hissed through gritted teeth, hurling the twig he had been idly turning between his fingers, into the darkness. He told Castellanos he would take the first watch, but had not woken the Greek for his turn, knowing, from long experience, sleep would not find him this night.

The journey home would be a long one. Over land would be safer, which would take many months. Or he could take the sea route, cutting the journey time in half. It would mean risking the waters around the great peninsula in winter. They had become the last resting place of many a stout merchantman. Perhaps—

Lucius's senses pricked, alerted by the sound of rustling in the undergrowth to his right. It stopped as suddenly as it had started. He had grown used to the night-sounds of the small creatures in the forest. This had seemed somehow different, not the scurrying of a ground dweller. He felt blindly along the damp earth until he located his scabbard and his sword sheathed within. Slowly, he freed the long blade. The sound came again; this time it was further away. Lucius relaxed. A small soul of the woodlands after all.

'Hello, Roman,' said a voice from behind in perfect, though accented, Latin. 'What brings you to my lands?'

Lucius dared not move, feeling the pressure of the cold steel of this stranger's long blade against his neck. He heard more movement out in the darkness as outlines of more figures emerged from the gloom. All the while Castellanos snored on.

'Let's talk, you and I, shall we?' His captor spoke again. 'Then I can decide if you're worth killing or not.'

10

'It's one of Mascellus's horses,' Cai said quietly.

'You can't be sure,' Hrindenus said. 'Chestnuts are used by our cavalry. The undergrowth is so disturbed here. Perhaps another of our patrols?'

Cai searched the ground around the carcass of the horse, avoiding the spear protruding from its neck. A metallic glint flashed from the long grass near his feet. He knelt, searching amongst the scrub grass.

'What is it?'

'The boy's in trouble,' Cai said, the words flat and toneless. He showed the big man what he had seen.

'A pugio?' Hrindenus said. 'Then it *was* another of our patrols. Surely?'

Cai turned the dagger over. 'Do you see the hilt?' Hrindenus peered at the metal bar closely, picking out the letter M scratched into the metal. The Tungrian shrugged a puzzled expression wrinkling his brow.

'The M is for Martis. I gifted this to Beren on the eve of the battle at the Sack.' Cai hung his head. 'The bastards have him.'

'If the boy was dead,' Hrindenus said, his voice filled with an assurance he did not feel, 'we would have found his body with the horse. Which means they've taken him captive. And look.' He pointed to the forest edge. 'The blue-faces have left a wide trail for us to follow. We'll find him.'

Cai saw the Tungrian was right. A wide swathe of trampled ground led directly to the western end of the small hilltop glade. He snapped into movement, striding through the tall grass towards his horse, mounting in one swift movement. Hrindenus close on his heels.

'We've no time to lose,' he said, driving his heels into the rump of his mount.

The trail was easy to follow. By noon the sign had become fresher. Their quarry was not in a hurry, it seemed.

'They're close,' Hrindenus said from behind Cai. They had stopped in a thick stand of oak where the soft ground had been churned by the passing of many hooves.

They set off again at a walk, both men straining to hear any sound of the enemy. As the watery autumnal sun reached its highest point, the great forest came to an abrupt end. From the edge of the last line of trees the view ahead revealed a landscape of low, rolling hills, wide pastureland, and beyond, the Sula. The estuary was much wider at this point where it emptied into the sea of Hibernia. Visibility had improved, and as Cai observed the distant horizon he was able to discern the dark, distant mountains of that mysterious land.

'There!' the big man said excitedly. It took a moment for Cai to pick them out. A warband of around twenty horses cresting a distant rise and moving at a walking pace.

'Can you see him? Can you see if they carry Beren?' Cai asked.

'I can't be sure. But I think at least one horse is doubled up. Who else could it be? They aren't pulling any empty horses either. This might not be the party who ambushed those lads back there.' Hrindenus nudged his mount.

'Wait.' Cai said, 'If one of them turns to look back down the trail, we'll be seen. Let them descend out of sight first.' Moments later, when the last of the horsemen disappeared from view the pair set off at a trot.

'They seem to be heading in the direction of the coastline,' Hrindenus said, raising his voice to be heard over the rumble of hooves. 'Perhaps their destination is nearby?' A short while later, ascending the rise they had seen the Novantae pass over from the forest's edge, Cai saw that Hrindenus's guess was right.

The warband had halted, its warriors dismounting outside a small fortress gateway. No, Cai realised, not so much a fort as a defended farmstead. It was perched on a sheer cliff top, overlooking the sea's green waters. A stout, circular palisade stood tall and imposing behind a single, deep ditch. Within, four peaked roofs of round houses rose above the wooden wall. However, the farmstead did not sit in isolation. Nestling outside the ditch were a large number of smaller structures which, to Cai, even at some distance, had a makeshift appearance.

'Nowhere else to run,' Hrindenus said, echoing Cai's own thoughts. As they watched, Cai noticed three individuals detach from the warband and walk towards the open gates in the palisade. One was a tall warrior, the other two were clearly boys. One of the youths had bright red hair. There was no mistaking the quick stride of the other fair haired lad next to him. Beren.

'They'll have us strung up by our balls before a word passes our lips.'

'Then stay, brother,' Cai said coolly. 'There'll be no shame in it. But I see no other option. It's too well defended to sneak in after dark. And two swords are not enough to fight our way to the boy.'

'No shame?' Hrindenus spluttered. 'I'd never be able to face my comrades if they were to learn that a Tungrian dared not follow where a damned Nervii went. Even if it was to his own foolish death.'

'Come, my friend,' Cai said, unable to hide his amusement. 'Have a little faith. The Novantae would not disrespect their own laws and harm travellers come to them under a sign of truce. We just need to find an oak tree.'

As the light of the setting sun silhouetted the distant Hibernian mountains, Cai and Hrindenus walked their small horses towards the edge of the settlement. For a time, they went unnoticed, until a stout, dark haired woman, straining under the weight of a full pail of water collected from the nearby stream, saw their approach. At first, she gazed at them with a calm curiosity. Until an almost comical look crossed her features and her jaw opened and shut multiple times, like a fish stranded on the beach. Her shrill scream pierced the air.

'That should do it,' Hrindenus said.

Tribespeople emerged from many of the low buildings outside of the ditch. Some gripped spears, others whatever tool had readily come to hand.

'Unstrap your sword and make a show of tossing it to the ground,' Cai said. Both men lifted the sheathed blades hanging from their saddle horns. In unison they raised the weapons above their heads. Holding them for a time to ensure they were seen, they threw them into the dirt.

'Devine Epona, protect these two fools from their own idiocy,' Hrindenus said. Cai unstrapped the oak branch still thick with golden, autumnal leaves, holding it high for all to see.

'Let's walk the horses a little closer, so they get a better view of us,' Cai said.

'I think they can see us just fine from here. Any closer and they'll see the damp patch of piss on my troos.'

The pair nudged their mounts to within a spear's throw distance of the nearest hovels and, for the first time, Cai saw movement around the gateway to the enclosure.

'Here they come,' Cai said. 'We're in the hands of the gods now.' Six mounted warriors emerged through the gates, their horses' hooves rattling across the wooden planking of the small bridge spanning the ditch. The crowd of villagers gathered at the edge of the ramshackle settlement rushed to get out of the way of the horsemen. They drove their mounts hard towards where Cai and Hrindenus waited, unmoving.

At first, it appeared that the warriors were going to charge straight at them. But, at a shouted command, they pulled up, quickly taking up positions around the pair.

'Well, what do we have here,' said a big red-headed warrior, in perfect Latin. A wolf-like grin spread across his lips. 'Our land is thick with Roman spies this day, it seems.'

'Greetings, Barra,' Cai said.

HUNT

11

The sound of waves crashing against the base of the cliff was their constant companion. Faint evening light filtered through the wooden slats of the hatch to the cool, stone lined storage pit. Lucius was still able to see the outline of Castellanos's dark features.

'What do you think?' the medicus asked. 'An attack?'

'It's gone quiet, so not an attack, I think.'

Lucius shifted uncomfortably. The rough floor of the cramped space made it impossible to sit in one position for any length of time.

'I wish they would get on with whatever they plan to do with us,' Castellanos said. 'If I don't take a piss soon I'll have to humiliate myself.'

'We've both been through worse, brother—wait, they're coming back,' The sound of approaching horses grew louder as they entered the settlement. 'They're not in a hurry this time, it seems.' Lucius fell silent. A hurried conversation was taking place nearby. Even with his good understanding of the language of the People, he could not pick out anything meaningful in the muffled words.

Time dragged. The last of the light disappeared, leaving the pair in complete darkness, until a flame burst into life close by. A torch, presumably lit by the sentries who guarded them.

'It's no good, I have to go,' Castellanos said, with an air of resignation. The Greek shuffled onto his knees, his neck bent against the trapdoor. Lucius heard the rustling as Castellanos undid the ties of his troos, followed shortly after by the splash of liquid on the stone floor accompanied by a sigh of relief. The small space filled with the smell of ammonia, and after what seemed an age, Castellanos re-tied himself and shuffled back into a seated position.

'Bollocks. It's everywhere,' Castellanos said. Lucius squeezed himself tighter against the side of the wall.

An instant later the hatch was flung open and the face of a large, red-headed warrior stared down at them. His freckled features instantly turned to disgust at the smell of piss.

'Romans out,' he commanded in halting Latin, raising the point of his spear for emphasis.

Neither needed a second invitation to get out of the dark, and now damp, hole. Hours of confinement had left them stiff and their movements laboured.

'Out!' The warrior pointed the tip of his spear threateningly at the pair.

Lucius scrambled over the lip of the pit first, before pulling Castellanos up alongside him. He looked around, the familiar smells of horse and cattle mixed with the salt air of the light breeze. Two other guards waited nearby. Both were as threatening as the first, with spears levelled. A faint orange glow still pervaded the western skyline, throwing the settlement's palisade into a dark silhouette. Lucius picked out the movement of sentries on its walkway. The sound of the waves from the Hibernian sea were louder above ground and mingled with the shrieking clamour of the gulls as they settled for the night.

A spearbutt struck painfully against Lucius's shoulder.

'Move, Roman,' the fierce warrior barked, simultaneously nodding his head towards the nearest of the four roundhouses. The inhabitants moved about their business; few, other than a group of curious children, paid them any heed. Lucius approached the entrance-place which appeared to sprout from the low lying eaves of the thatched, conical roof. He halted in expectation that someone would pull back the wooden doors before he could enter. A heavy thump of the spearbutt on his back disabused him of this.

'Inside,' came the truculent voice once more.

Lucius pushed open both narrow doors and ducked inside, hearing Castellanos shuffling behind, close on his heels. He sensed though could not yet fully see a large open space ahead of him, hidden as it was in a fug of smoke emanating from the dulled yellow flames of the fire. He choked as he moved deeper into the interior, taking slow careful steps in the gloom. Vague shapes flitted briefly into view to his right and left as he progressed towards the flickering flames at the building's heart. Castellanos coughed. As Lucius neared the round stone hearth, the shapes of two sitting silhouettes coalesced before him. Both stared silently into the flames. The nearest turned at the approach of these new visitors, a bright smile instantly lighting his face.

'Hello, brother,' Cai said.

'Cai? How—' Lucius began.

Cai smiled, relieved to see his friend alive and seemingly none the worse for his captivity. "Let's keep our own counsel, for now, until we know how the land lies. But I've found my old friend and one time rescuer.'

'Barra? I know we—'

'Sit, Roman,' the warrior growled. 'And keep mouths closed, until my lord comes.'

'His Latin is hurting my ears,' Hrindenus grumbled under his breath.

Cai shuffled over to allow Lucius to sit next to him, his friend easing himself stiffly to the earthen floor. He acknowledged the Tungrian with a nod.

'Gods I hurt,' Castellanos said, as he lowered himself gingerly next to Hrindenus, who smiled amiably in greeting.

The three warriors who had escorted Lucius and Castellanos withdrew into the smoky haze, taking up stations near the doorway.

'Here, brother. You look like you need it,' Cai said, handing a water skin to Lucius who took it gratefully, slaking his thirst with deep gulps before passing it to the medicus, wiping stray droplets from his chin as he did so.

'How were you captured?' Cai asked, his voice low.

'I'm almost too embarrassed to say,' Lucius said, and did indeed seem sheepish as he responded to Cai. 'The Novantae bastard got right up to me, as I kept watch. He had his sword at my throat before I saw or heard him.'

'You mean Barra?' Cai said.

'Tut, tut, falling asleep on watch, sir?' Hrindenus said, from the other side of the fire. 'That's a capital offence.' The big man grinned as Lucius bridled.

'I did no such thing you Tungrian oaf, you—'

The doors to the roundhouse burst open. A surprised warrior cursed as one bashed against his knee.

'Cai?' The excited shout, so familiar.

'Over here, lad,' Cai returned, standing so the boy could see. Filled with relief, he laughed as Beren ran the short distance from the doorway, leaping into his friend's arms. Cai raised him from the floor into a tight embrace, the boy's legs dangling freely.

'I found you,' Beren said excitedly, his arms wrapped tightly around Cai's neck.

'Indeed, you did, lad,' Cai couldn't hide the smile from his voice. 'Even though I told you to stay put, with our good friend Mascellus.'

'I had to, Cai. I had to find her.'

60

'I know, lad. Let's talk later, I…' Cai turned as a larger shadow stepped close to them.

'It seems our families are destined to come to each other's aid, Nervii,' Barra said, his voice appearing strangely sombre.

'You found him?' Cai asked. 'Thank you for—'

'My nephew found him,' Barra said. 'And not a moment too soon.' Cai turned, releasing Beren as he did so. He took in the figure standing behind Barra, face flickering brightly in the light cast by the flames of the hearth fire.

'Greetings, Herne,' Cai said. 'I'm glad to see you well, and my thanks for Beren's life.'

The Novantae boy gave Cai a solemn look, nodding in acknowledgement.

'We have sought you out—' Cai began, speaking in the tongue of the People. Barra raised his hand to forestall him.

'Let us sit first. You are guests in my home,' Barra turned to the fierce warrior, who had continued to stare at the group, appearing caught between curiosity and distrust. 'Join us, Keefe. Send the others away.'

'Lord,' the big red-headed warrior said brusquely.

Appearing out of the shadows, four women bustled between the men carrying low, age-worn benches. In moments all were seated around the fire. Barra was joined on his bench by the warrior, Keefe and Herne. Cai sat with Lucius and Beren, Hrindenus and Castellanos taking the final seat. Cups of frothy, dark ale were served.

For a time, there was silence between them. Beren and Herne stared into their cups with almost identical expressions of distaste. Cai might have laughed if not for the tension he felt. Hrindenus took deep swallows, mirrored a moment later by Keefe. Barra's eyes roved between Cai and Lucius. It was the first time Cai had been

61

able to scrutinise the Novantae since their arrival. Away from the battlefield he seemed different somehow. Not just that he no longer wore his armour, or his hair was unbound. He seemed in his natural environment. At home. Finally, Barra spoke, once more in Latin.

'Your Tribunus's disguise is not a very good one. Even with the scruffy fresh growth on his chin, I knew him. After seeing this Roman everyday astride the walls of your fort, how could I not? If he wishes to be seen as a hired sword for your healer,' Barra indicated Castellanos with the hand holding his cup, the action sloshing some of the ale onto the nearest hearthstone, causing it to hiss, 'he should lose some of his aristocratic bearing.' Cai snorted, as Lucius opened and closed his mouth in surprise.

'Your pretence is a desperate one. Had you stumbled into any other warband...well you assuredly would have met a painful ending. It will be many years before foreigners are welcomed into our lands once more.' Cai, knowing this was the only man who could help him, held back the words he had rehearsed over and over in his head these last few days. He sensed the warchief had more to say.

'Your boy is a brave one.' Barra turned to Beren and for the first time smiled, making the boy blush. 'Foolish. But brave. He has told me the tale of his mother's abduction. I am sorry. I liked her.'

'Will you help us in our search for her?' Cai said, fighting to keep the emotions from his voice. Barra gazed long at Cai, his eyes piercing, expression unmoving. The silence grew, the two enemy's eyes locked upon one another.

'I know that must have cost you to ask, Nervii,' Barra said, after taking a deep breath. 'I will help. Not only because I owe her a debt, but because Herne here, it appears, has already promised it.' Barra looked ruefully at his nephew, who flushed. 'Keefe will ride to Rerigon in the morning to seek word of her. But I must tell you. I hold out little hope. There were few captives taken. And none by my people. Our only thought was escape.'

'Rerigon? Is your tribe's capital?' Lucius asked.

'Rerigon, Roman, is the last untouched stronghold of our people. The place of power. The seat of my now dead king. It is closer to Hibernia than to our nearest land neighbours.' Barra turned to Beren, looking kindly at the boy and speaking softly. 'If there is no sign of her there, my young friend, I fear she has gone to meet her ancestors.'

12

Shortly after, Barra, Herne and Keefe left them. A meal of bread and strong tasting flounders was served, the flat fish a welcome repast after the recent days. The group talked little whilst they ate. The women hovered around them, not hiding their glances of disdain, if not outright loathing. They were provided with soft deer or cattle hide as bedding, then left alone.

As the doors closed behind the last of the women, Lucius broke the silence.

'Do you trust him?'

'Believe it or not, I do. He has always acted with honour. Or at least his own version of it.'

Hrindenus snorted. 'Have you already forgotten young Lenius? He seemed happy enough to kill the boy to get at our standard.'

'No, I haven't forgotten,' Cai said, discomforted by the Tungrian's vehemence.

'Well, there's nothing to be done,' Lucius said. 'Let's get some rest and see what tomorrow throws at us.'

For a time, Lucius lay on his back staring up at the roundhouse's roof, watching the flickering light of the flames play on its blackened thatch. It was clear to him Alyn was lost. He grieved for his friend. However, it also meant that he could finally make the journey to his homeland. Perhaps he could convince Cai and the boy to come with him? The thought cheered him. It would be a great comfort to have the companionship and counsel of the fierce Nervii in the dangerous months ahead.

***

HUNT

Cai was awakened in darkness by the shrieking cries of seabirds. Turning his head at a rustling sound, he saw the outline of Beren, sitting up, his knees drawn to his chest.

'Can't sleep lad?'

'No,' Beren said after a short delay. Cai heard the thickness in the boy's throat. 'Do you think my mam is dead?' The words followed by a sniff of snot.

'I pray to the gods she is not,' he said. 'And, if there is a chance she is alive, I'll not give up searching for her.'

'Do you promise?' Childish hope filled his words.

'I swear it.'

There was a slight creaking sound as a lone woman entered through the doorway, briefly letting faint early morning light into the gloom, before it was extinguished as the door closed behind her. To Cai, she appeared only a few short years into womanhood. Not one of the older women who had attended them the evening before. She moved on swift, silent steps to the hearth. With practised hands she cleared away the charred remains. In silence, Cai and Beren watched as she built a stack of kindling at its centre. In a matter of moments, a new flame was burning brightly, blooming further as she added the logs. Gradually the rest of the party stirred, awoken by her bustling.

'Do we have anything to eat?' Hrindenus addressed the woman haltingly in the language of the People.

'You'll have to wait, you big ox.' Her harsh words did not match the smile that brushed her lips, quickly hidden by her long dark, unbound, hair as it fell across her cheek as she bent to add more fuel to the flames. The woman next moved to a small alcove, returning with a metal pot filled with water and hanging it from the frame over the fire. She continued to cast surreptitious glances in the direction of the Tungrian as she hastened about her work.

'What's your name?' Hrindenus asked, rising from his furs to sit facing the growing flames.

'Who's asking?' she responded, a challenge in her strangely lilting words.

'I am Hrindenus, Wolf of the Tungrii.' Cai hid his smile at the earnestness of the big man. Since they had met all those weeks ago, he had known him only as the fierce and fearless warrior. For the first time, he saw him for the young man he was.

The dark haired woman stood tall, brushing soot from her hands on the green chequered weave of her skirt. She looked at Hrindenus, matching his own proud gaze. 'Well, Hrindenus Wolf, I am Niamh, once of the Robogdii.' With the slightest of flushes she turned and walked briskly towards the doorway. 'The oats will be ready soon,' Niamh said over her shoulder. And with that she was gone.

'Who are the Robogdii?' Castellanos asked, his voice croaked with fatigue. His question was met with shrugs.

'She's the sister of the warrior, Keefe,' Beren chirped up enthusiastically. 'She's nice.'

Cai flashed a broad grin at Hrindenus. 'Well, Vexillarius, I think you might want to reconsider any thoughts you may have about the lovely Niamh. Especially if you treasure those big Tungrian balls.' Hrindenus harrumphed, still staring at the closed doors.

'As we appear to be guests rather than prisoners,' Lucius said, as he and Cai sat by the fire, empty bowls of oats set aside by the hearth stones, 'shall we take a stroll? It's stuffy in here.'

'I'm going to find Herne,' Beren said, dashing towards the door before Cai could say a word.

'Let's tread carefully, brother,' Cai said. 'If Barra recognised you, he may not be the only one. This tribe's wounds are raw and may welcome the opportunity of easy vengeance.'

'Well, I'm going to catch up on some sleep,' Castellanos said, returning to his furs.

'All you do is sleep, medicus,' Hrindenus said affably. The Greek's response was unintelligible, his words muffled from under the deer skin.

'I'll go and see to the horses,' Hrindenus said.

As Lucius left the hut, Cai close behind, he shielded his eyes against the sharp brightness of the low autumn sun as it broke above the settlement's gateway. People moved purposefully about their daily chores. The pair drew some attention, and a few hostile looks, as they passed by. But they went unmolested.

'I think our host's word is law here,' Lucius said. 'Though I wouldn't like to put it to the test. We should find a quieter spot.' He nodded towards the gateway, whose stout oak doors were open to the makeshift village beyond.

Once outside of the palisade the pair took a path which passed along the outer edge of the deep ditch. Cai walked by Lucius's side, seeming deep in thought.

'You're worried the word Barra's man returns with will be grievous?' Cai stared across the grey waters of the sea that had come into view.

'No, Lucius. I worry he will return with no news at all.'

Rounding the last bend in the ditch they came upon the cliff edge and to their surprise saw the broad back of the Novantae warchief. Barra was standing by the cliff's edge watching the activity below. A line of four fishing boats were being hauled by groups of men towards the waiting waters that lapped gently upon a pebbled beach. The horizon was obscured by a light mist descended in the middle distance.

Barra turned, hearing them approach. He acknowledged them with a nod, before returning to watch the fishermen.

'You are well rested?' He asked.

'Our thanks for your hospitality,' Lucius said.

'You did not expect it from a barbarian?' Barra said, showing the slightest of smiles.

'After recent events, lesser men may not have been so welcoming,' Lucius returned.

'Anyone who comes to my home in peace will be welcomed at my hearth. Besides, I have more pressing matters to attend to than vengeance. We don't have sufficient stores to feed the growing numbers of people seeking shelter under the ramparts of my farmstead. What was already going to be a bad winter could be ruinous. The catch of those few boats may just stave off starvation. We must hope the winter storms do not come early. Although your legion may decide to venture further into our lands and destroy what little we do have.'

'From what we've seen and heard,' Lucius said. 'The decision has been taken not to push further west.'

'They believe we are beaten,' Barra said, his tone flat. 'And they are right. For now.' The three were silent for a time, watching as the men pulled on their oars, driving them through the silver-flecked water, bobbing lightly on the gently rolling waves.

'Has your man left yet?' Cai asked, his voice outwardly calm to Lucius's ear, but there was a tightness to his words.

'He left during the night. There are people he would speak to first. Men he knows who have their ears and eyes on the comings and goings in the harbour.'

'You think Alyn was taken by boat?' Cai asked.

As he spoke, Barra continued to watch the horizon. 'As I said last night, I doubt she will be amongst my people. If she is, and yet lives, Keefe will find her. But it may be that she was taken in the boats of the Damnonii.'

'And if she was?' Cai asked, his voice losing its earlier calm. Barra turned to his erstwhile enemy and simply grimaced.

13

'Still no word?' Castellanos asked, as Cai and Lucius returned to sit by the hearth. Cai's slightest of headshakes was his only response.

'Where are Beren and Hrindenus?' Cai asked, as he took his seat on the low bench.

'Neither have returned since you left.'

'I hope the big lump isn't up to something we will all regret,' Cai said, his tone morose.

'There's warm, fresh bread.' The medicus indicated the large, rounded loaf sitting upon a broad dish by the hearth. Lucius reached forward, breaking off a chunk and poured himself a cup of milk from a jug set nearby. For a time, they sat in silence, caught up in their own thoughts.

'I'll see if I can make myself useful,' Castellanos said. 'There will be many ailments amongst these people.'

'A good thought,' Lucius said. 'Speak to Barra first, get his permission. We left him by the cliffs outside of the palisade.' Castellanos nodded, gathering up his dark wooden box that held his precious potions and instruments.

Cai could feel Lucius's eyes upon him from across the fire. He seemed on the point of speaking; instead, he simply reached again for the bread, ripping another chunk from its thick crust.

'I'm going to search for Beren,' Cai said, unable to do nothing. Sitting there in the silence of the roundhouse was like waiting for his own execution. He rose to leave. The doors to the hut burst open.

'He's back,' Beren shouted, his face a confusion of excitement and fear. The boy looked at Cai in expectation. He turned to leave.

'Wait, Beren,' Cai said. 'Let's go together. We will not show our fear, even though it may tear at us.' He went to the boy's side, placing a hand on his shoulder. They walked together into the open air.

Cai immediately saw the warrior Keefe by the entrance to another of the roundhouses. He had dismounted and held the harness of a grey, dappled horse. Steam arose from its flanks into the afternoon air. It must have been ridden hard. The big red-headed warrior wore a chainmail shirt, Roman to Cai's eye. His left hand rested on the pommel of his long sword, which hung from a broad leather belt. He was speaking in quiet tones to Barra.

Barra broke off the conversation at seeing Cai and Beren approach. He beckoned them to join him. Lucius followed at a distance.

'Did you find my mam?' The words burst from Beren, unable to contain himself. Cai clasped the boy's shoulder a little more firmly, in part for his own comfort.

Barra studied Beren, a sad smile on his lips. 'No. Keefe was not able to find your mother. There is some news.' The Novantae glanced meaningfully at Cai. 'Come. Let us go into my hall and I can tell you what Keefe has discovered.'

Barra's hall was larger than the roundhouse they had slept in the previous night. By a good ten paces. A group of four women, the ones who had served them on the previous night. appeared from a low table at the rear of the dwelling.

In moments, Barra, Cai, Lucius and Beren were seated on benches by the hearth. Herne appeared in the doorway, curiosity lighting his freckled face.

'Herne,' Barra said. 'Come join us.' The warrior's nephew approached, sitting by his uncle.

Barra's eyes moved from Beren to Cai, before resting his sight firmly on the boy. For a moment the Novantae warchief seemed lost for what to say. To Cai, he appeared to be considering his next words carefully.

'Keefe was unable to find your mam. She is not amongst the Novantae.' Barra briefly glanced at Cai. 'But...' Barra paused again. 'There was a sighting of a woman. Just one. She was carried away in one of the Damnonii boats.'

'Was it my mam?' Beren's eyes filled with hope.

'It's impossible to know. From the description Keefe received from one of the local boatmen, it could be.' Barra addressed Cai. 'We know this Damnonii who sailed from Rerigon. And we know where he has taken his boats.'

'Who is he?' Cai demanded. 'Where has this Damnonii gone? How do we find him?' Barra held up his hands.

'Peace, Nervii,' he said. 'There is something I must speak to you of first.' Barra turned to Herne. 'Nephew, take Beren and practise your skills with the hunting bow on the beach.'

'But—' Herne began.

'Go!' Barra ordered, brooking no further discussion. Beren too seemed about to object.

'We are guests here, Beren,' Cai said. 'Do as you're asked.' Beren gave Cai a look that he had seen before on the journey to Mascellus's farm. Both boys got to their feet and stalked shoulder to shoulder to the doorway, heads together in whispered conversation.

Barra shook his head as he watched them leave.

'Those two are going to be trouble,' he said with a smirk. 'Already they share a strong bond.'

'You wish to keep something from the boy.' Lucius said, it wasn't a question. Barra pinched the hairs of his long red moustache between finger and thumb, drawing them downwards in repeated strokes. A habit Cai had noticed on his first meeting with the Novantae outside the gates of the Sack's village.

'This Damnonii is well known to me. There is no mistaking who it was. His tattoos are distinctive. One in particular. He stands alone from his own tribe. Commanding a band of wretches no honourable chieftain would have as his hearth warriors. His true name is Blue Wolf or at least it is what he calls himself. Although he is better known amongst the People as Blue Dog. And he is mad.'

14

'Mad! What does that—' Cai began.

The door to the hall was flung open. The big warrior Keefe filled its frame. 'Lord. Riders approach. Moving fast.'

'Stay here,' Barra said, rising. The Novantae strode from his hall. The doors slammed behind him.

'Trouble?' Lucius asked.

'Let's find out,' Cai said. He strode to the entrance. Lucius followed. There was no way to see what was happening outside, though both could hear the muffled tones of Barra and Keefe. Moments later the rapid rumbling of hoofbeats could be discerned. The sound came to a crescendo, suddenly halting, replaced by the heavy snorting of the beasts.

'Two horses?' Lucius mouthed. Cai nodded.

'Why do you ride with such abandon into my land, Frang son of Goraidh?' Barra's voice was clear and unruffled.

'You shelter our enemies here.' A new voice, filled with disdain.

'Who are you to speak to your lord in this way, runt?' Keefe growled, his voice filled with hot menace.

'You're not of this tribe, *Hibernian*. You have no say here.'

'Keefe leads my war-band, as well you know,' Barra said. 'Keep a civil tongue in your head. Unless you want to lose it.' There was silence for a few heartbeats.

'You shelter Romans in your hall,' Frang said sullenly, his voice kept low, no less blunt. 'Where are they? I will deal with them, if you don't have the stomach.'

HUNT

'Why you—' Frang's words were cut off. There was a yelp, followed by the sounds of a scuffle.

'Stay your hand, Keefe,' Barra said, his voice urgent. 'We'll not spill blood this day. Unless we're driven to it.'

'Get to your feet. *Runt,*' Keefe snarled. 'Be on your way, unless you want my blade in your belly.'

'I won't forget this, *Hibernian*,' Frang said, his voice holding a strangled tone. 'And you will never be king, cousin. You'll not replace Cynbel. I will make sure of that.' There was the rumble of hooves once more, gradually fading as the riders left the farmstead.

'You're going to have to kill him, Lord,' Keefe said.

An instant later the doors were flung open and Lucius and Cai came face to face with Barra and the truculent warrior. The warchief's eyes widened.

'I take it you heard all?' His tone was brusque.

'You are to be king?' Lucius asked. Barra's eyes narrowed. Would he enlighten his former enemies?

'If only it was that simple, Roman. Cynbel, our king, was my uncle. He had no sons. Thus, the succession passes onto the king's nephews. Of which there are only two living. Frang and I.'

'Frang is a snake,' Keefe said, his voice adopting its previous moroseness.

'Perhaps. But he has his supporters and he holds Rerigon. We are weak. Most of my people are scattered throughout the great forest and beyond.'

'As I said, Lord. You will have to kill him.'

Barra turned to Cai. 'Well Nervii, it seems our paths may have aligned.'

'I don't understand,' Cai said.

'I will aid you in the hunt for your woman.'

Barra left them, saying only he would tell them more that evening. 'Can we trust him, brother?' Lucius asked,

75

as the pair lingered outside the hall, preferring to be in the open air than the stifling, smoky interior. Across from them two women gutted and hung fish on wooden poles, ready for the smoking hut. The slick skins glistened silver and grey. Gulls screeched overhead, eyeing the fish-gut in the hope of an easy meal.

'I trust he means what he says,' Cai said. 'If he wanted to do us harm, he could have. At any time. He has shown us only courtesy. I do sense he is withholding something. If he has designs on becoming the high king of the Novantae, he will have to deal with his rival. How can he risk leaving his lands to help us before securing them?'

Both continued watching the women for a time before Lucius spoke again. He coughed to clear his throat. Cai was familiar with this unintended signal of a change to a difficult matter.

'I'm sorry to ask this, brother. Do you truly believe Alyn yet lives?' Cai turned to his friend, taking in his now full-bearded face, seeing the concern in his eyes. He looked at the women once more as he responded.

'The odds are heavily against it. I know this. But I have to try. I will hunt down this Blue Dog. If Alyn lives, I will take her back. If she is dead, and the Damnonii did take her, I will gut him from balls to neck.' Cai turned back to his friend. 'I cannot ask you and the others follow where I go. The risk is much too great. You must go get your lands back, Lucius. Go, before the winter seas make the journey perilous.'

Lucius gave a quiet, throaty chuckle. 'Would you abandon me, if our fortunes were reversed? I think not. You'll not get rid of me that easily my friend. Baetica can wait a while longer.'

'Lucius I—'

A great shout, almost a warcry, burst from beyond the fish-smoking hut. Hrindenus appeared, thrown backwards from behind the stout pinewood structure. He landed in the dirt. An instant later Keefe appeared, followed by the woman Niamh on his heels.

'You dare to lay a hand on my sister,' the Hibernian bawled once more. The big warrior's face was contorted by rage.

'Keefe, we were only talking,' Niamh said, her words frantic. She took hold of her brother's arm. It gave Hrindenus an instant to get to his feet. The Hibernian shook her off roughly. Lucius saw the Tungrian brace in readiness. Both men were of equal height and build.

Keefe crashed into Hrindenus, driving him towards the ground once more. This time however, he was able to grasp the Hibernian's arms, twisting his body so they fell together, landing in a tangle of limbs. They grappled with one another, each trying to gain the upper hand. Keefe attempted a punch. The force of it, had it connected, would have felled any other man. Hrindenus blocked it with his upper arm.

'Stop it, the pair of you,' Niamh shouted in her strangely lilting accent.

'We'd best intervene,' Lucius said. 'We don't want to draw more attention to ourselves.'

'Get in between those two giants?' Cai said. 'I don't think so. But it seems we won't have to.' Cai indicated Niamh with a nod of his head.

Her long, dark hair flying loose, the Hibernian woman carried the bucket that had been used by the fisher women, both of whom looked on, laughter creasing their already lined faces.

'Get up, I'm warning the pair of you,' Niamh tried again. The two continued to tussle oblivious to her words.

'That's not water,' Lucius said, as Niamh upended the bucket's contents over the faces of the two prone men.

'What the fuck,' Hrindenus shouted, as fish guts slopped into his eyes. The two warriors rolled apart, wiping frantically at the stinking slime encasing their faces. Getting to their feet, the pair glowered at one another. Keefe turned to his sister, fury in his eyes.

'You will not speak to him again,' he said, returning his stare to Hrindenus to emphasise the point.

'Who do you think you are?' Niamh said, her voice filled with indignation. 'I'm not your woman.'

'You live under my roof and under my protection,' he bit back at her.

'I think your memory is short, brother,' Niamh said, with some vehemence. 'If not for I, you would not be alive to have a roof.' With that said she turned on her heel and strode off towards Barra's hall, where Lucius and Cai still waited. When she was halfway towards them, she glanced over her shoulder, gracing Hrindenus with a long lingering smile.

Keefe glowered at the Tungrian as he saw him return it. Suddenly sensing the Hibernian watching, Hrindenus straightened his features and made off in the opposite direction.

'I hope we leave soon,' Lucius said. 'This place is too small for those three to be in close proximity to one another.'

15

'We must leave before first light,' Barra said. The women had cleared away the evening meal and departed. The six men were once more seated around the hearth of Barra's hall. Keefe and Hrindenus studiously ignored one another as the company had eaten the meal of bread and thick white fish. 'We must go unseen until we depart Novantae lands. Frang will have eyes watching.'

'We make our first camp in the forest near to Rerigon,' Keefe said. 'Under cover of darkness we take the boat that has been prepared for us.'

'How long by sea?' Cai asked, as he cast the whetstone along the blade of his sword.

'If the weather stays fair,' Barra said, 'it should take two days to reach Blue Dog's isle.'

'I hate the sea,' Castellanos groaned.

'You'll be fine, medicus,' Hrindenus said, clapping the Greek on the shoulder.

Cai scrutinised the Novantae warchief. 'You haven't yet told us why you're going to make this journey with us.'

Barra smirked. 'I told you. I owe a debt to your woman.'

'If you say so,' Cai said. 'It doesn't sit well with me. You have your hands full here. You must get your people through a difficult winter.' Barra acknowledged this with a nod, saying nothing. 'You also mean to lead your people and must secure this land from rivals.'

Barra and Keefe exchanged a look. The Hibernian's face was inscrutable. Barra shrugged as if making a decision. As was his habit, the warchief pulled at his long moustaches.

'I must do more than win these lands to call myself king.' Barra gazed into the flames. 'I must be sanctified at our most holy place. Our sacred isle. As all those who rule tribes of the People must. The ceremony is carried out by the high priest himself. I travel by sea. The old land route has been closed off by your new wall.' He looked at Cai, but with none of his former rancour. 'The journey will take us past Blue Dog's isle. So, you see, I can both repay my debt and be confirmed lord of the Novantae.'

'I know you wish to come, lad,' Cai said to Beren. 'You must not defy me on this again. If you want us to have the best chance of finding your mam.' Cai had been expecting a repeat of the same arguments from when he'd taken Beren to Mascellus's farm. To his surprise, the boy appeared to accept his words with no further discussion. Perhaps his friendship with Herne had made the difference?

Man and boy waited by the farmstead's gateway. Cai held the bridle of his horse, preparing to leave. The others were close by, making final preparations.

'Bring back my mam, Cai.' Beren said, his voice kept low in the dark of the early morning.

Cai placed his hand on the boy's shoulder, bending down to speak quietly into his ear. 'I will do all that is in my power to do,'' he said earnestly, before raising his voice into greater cheer. 'Keep up your practice with that new hunting bow of yours and we'll spend a day in the forest upon our return. Let's see if we can bring down a deer or two, eh!' He ruffled Beren's hair. The boy giggled.

'Or three,' Beren responded enthusiastically.

'Well, young hunter, we must leave some game in the forest for others.' Cai placed his hand on Beren's shoulder one final time. 'I will see you soon my friend.'

HUNT

'Are we ready?' Barra asked of the men around him. All were in silhouette. The torches over the gateway had been extinguished so watchers would not see them leave.

The group of horsemen left Barra's farmstead. They walked the horses through the makeshift village. Cai thought he saw movement in the darkness, but it was gone in an instant. Perhaps nothing, he thought.

16

The arrow flew direct and true.

'Not bad for a Carvetii,' Herne said.

Beren laughed. 'Half Carvetii, half Nervii, remember?' he said over his shoulder as he went to retrieve his arrows. Two had struck either side of the knot of the ancient oak, with his final one splitting them, near to its centre.

Neither had been able to sleep once Cai, Barra, Lucius and the others had departed. Herne had suggested that as there was now no one to stop them, they take the horses into the forest and try some real hunting. They rode out in the gloom of the early morning light and were soon amongst the trees.

'I think you might be ready for the hunt,' Herne said in mock seriousness.

'Just you watch. I'll be the first to kill a deer. Maybe even one of the roebuck with the big antlers.'

'Ha. We'll see. Let's go then,' Herne said, a gleam of excitement in his eyes.

They hobbled the horses in a small secluded glade, leaving them to graze on the lush, dew-covered, scrub grass.

This part of the forest was filled with oak and silver birch. Gold and brown leaves fell from above in an almost continual cascade. Their footsteps rustled continuously as they progressed across the forest floor.

'This is useless,' Herne said, 'Every deer will hear us coming.'

'Look,' Beren said, pointing in the direction they were headed.

'What?' Herne said, puzzled.

'Red pine. We'll make less sound.' The broad, rust coloured trunks were topped with a dense canopy of deep green.

'Do deer like red pine?' Herne asked, answered by Beren's quick shrug.

They entered the gloom of the closely packed trees. For an hour or more they moved in near silence on a carpet of soft needles. However there was neither sight nor sound of any game. Not even the normally ceaseless birdsong accompanied them.

Beren was becoming bored. 'Let's go back to—'

Herne held up his hand. Beren instantly froze beside him.

'What?' Beren whispered. Herne put a finger to his lips and crept slowly forward, Beren following his lead. A horse's whinny brought them up short. It had come from close by. Both boys dropped onto one knee, listening. A faint murmuring sound could be heard.

Herne cupped his hand to Beren's ear and whispered. 'Voices. Let's get closer. Beren nodded. The pair edged forward under the canopy of low branches. The sound became clearer. Voices of men. They spoke the language of the People, not Latin. Beren was about to speak, thinking they could not be enemies. But Herne put his hand across his friend's mouth, shaking his head urgently.

The Novantae boy got onto his hands and knees and crawled slowly forward, Beren behind. The voices became louder still as they reached the trunk of a wind-fallen pine, its roots naked to the sky, like the splayed fingers of a hand.

The men were close. They dared not risk a glance beyond the trunk. A horse whinnied again, perhaps sensing their presence. The boys lay against the rough bark, its dark moss covering moist against their cheeks.

'They must be spies?' This from a man with a rasp of a voice.

'I'm not sure,' said another, his words slow and deliberate. 'One is a healer. He tended to my neighbours' feet. Swollen red they were. I—'

'They can still be spies. Fool,' said the rasper.

'Be quiet,' said a third voice. Herne turned to Beren, his eyes wide. 'Whatever my cousin's motives for sheltering these strangers, you can be sure it will be to his advantage. Perhaps he seeks Rome's aid in some way to secure his journey to the sacred citadel? Whatever it is he will not reach it. I want him dead before he ever departs our lands.'

'He doesn't know he was seen leaving, lord,' said the slow speaker.

'Are you sure *you* weren't observed?'

'Yes, lord.'

'They will wait until darkness, somewhere in the great forest, close to Rerigon. We must seek them out and butcher them all.'

'Our men are ready, lord,' said the rasper. 'Ten should be enough to ensure it is you who will be confirmed as king by the holy ones.'

'Good. Let's go. I want the severed heads of my treacherous cousin, and those Roman spies, on display above the gates of Rerigon by morning.'

Moments later, the rumbling hooves of horses dimmed as they left the glade. 'We must warn them,' Beren said, his voice frantic. 'Do you know where they have camped?'

'No, but we must try,' Herne said. Both boys set off at a run to get back to their horses, this time uncaring of the noise they made as they crashed through the undergrowth.

84

HUNT

17

'Stay away from him,' Cai said.

They had been travelling for most of the day, staying within the treeline as far as possible. They had reached a small open area, surrounded by a dense, tangled undergrowth. A place to lie low. And wait. Cai had volunteered himself and Hrindenus to collect firewood. He wanted to speak with the Tungrian alone.

'How the fuck am I meant to do that?' Hrindenus said, incredulous. 'We're going to be in each other's company for days. Not to mention being stuck in a boat in the middle of the damned sea.'

'Just try not to antagonise him. You know how spikey he is.'

'Spikey? These Hibernians are humourless.'

'Well, you were trying to get into his sister's skirt.' Hrindenus gave Cai a hurt look. Which, for once, seemed sincere.

'No, sir. I wasn't. She's a rare beauty though, is she not? A fine woman.' A smile lit the big man's face.

'I hadn't noticed. I thank the gods you won't be seeing her again, Vexillarius.'

'Oh, I'll be seeing her again all right. I gave her my promise. When we return I would come for her. She likes the idea of being wed to a fine Tungrian warrior such as myself.'

'Jupiter's balls! You were only there for two days. You haven't told Keefe, have you? I don't want to have to watch your back for weeks on end.'

'Of course not. I'm not a complete fool. And besides, you don't have to watch my back. The Hibernian is no coward. He'll come at me from the front.'

'It's not funny,' Cai said, with a sigh. 'Just try to ignore each other as best you can.

'Oh, don't you worry about it, sir. I think we'll be best of friends before long.' Hrindenus beamed a great toothy smile at Cai. 'Besides, I will need his permission to wed her.'

By the gods, the man was besotted. Cai shook his head in frustration.

'We thought you might have lost your way in the woods,' Barra said, with a sardonic smile, as Cai and Hrindenus reappeared through the screen of brush. They dropped their armfuls of windfall branches into a pile.

'Are you sure it's wise to build a fire this close to Rerigon?' Lucius asked.

'Nervous, Roman?' Barra asked, shaking his head. He quickly became serious. 'We are away from any trackways. This is not a commonly hunted area. Besides, my people are staying behind their palisades at night. And will for some time to come.'

'What of Frang?' Cai interjected. 'Won't he be searching for you?'

'My cousin's a coward. He'll be waiting for us to enter Rerigon's walls and attack us in numbers. We, however, won't be dancing to his reel. Besides, this might be our last warm meal for some time.'

As night fell, the small company relaxed around the fire picking flakes of steaming white flesh from the carcasses of six fish.

'What is this fish?' Castellanos asked, his fingers and chin glistened with grease. He spoke in the language of

86

the People. His words were still halting, but had rapidly improved over recent days. 'It's delicious.'

Barra smiled. 'We call it pollack. I would have thought this is very simple fair for a man from the great city of Athens.'

'How did you know I was—oh yes. Your nephew.'

'Perhaps you will share some tales of your home as we travel?' Barra said.

'I'm not much of a storyteller, though we Athenians need little excuse to talk about the civilised world's greatest city.'

Barra laughed, a deep, mirthful sound. Cai noted how at ease the Novantae was. More at home in the forest, away from his duties.

'We should set a watch, lord,' Keefe said, his manner dour.

'You do not wish to hear our Greek friend's tales, Keefe?' The big man's grunt was his only response. He pushed his way through the tangled brush, disappearing from sight.

A full moon had risen, casting a faint white glow on the forest floor. Cai sat against the rough, narrow trunk of a silver birch. Keefe had returned to the camp with barely a word when he had taken over the watch. He had positioned himself some twenty paces from their hide. Close enough that he could still hear the medicus's deep snores and smell the smoke of the dying fire.

He had slept little in recent weeks. In part because of the tortured images of dying men that floated through his nightmares. Worse was the same dream which awoke him each night. He would find himself walking through a deep, dark cave. He could hear the sea and the cries of gulls. The complete blackness prevented him from seeing what was before him. Then, out of the darkness, a woman's anguished scream filled his mind. He would awake in a sweat, his heart pounding. What he wouldn't give for one night of oblivion.

You gave me your word. Adal's voice would come to him unbidden. Accusing.

'I'm sorry, brother,' Cai whispered into the night. 'I *will* find her.'

He tried not to imagine what day to day existence must be like for Alyn. If she lived. He blocked out any thoughts of her as soon as they arose, but sometimes, as now, they resisted. The memory of their walk by the riverside. Their passionate kiss.

A rustle in the undergrowth. Cai was instantly alert. A man's dark silhouette, outlined by faint moonlight, emerged slowly from the woodland, spear in hand. Had he been seen in the darkness? Cai moved his hand slowly to his sword's pommel, sheathed on the ground next to him.

A scream escaped the silhouette's throat. The man dropped his spear, clutching at his thigh.

'Awake, uncle. You are attacked.' A boy's voice shouted shrilly from the darkness. Cai didn't have time to wonder at the warning, as warcries erupted from all around him.

He leapt to his feet, drawing his blade, tossing its scabbard aside. He ran at the only attacker he could see: the stricken spearman. Down on one knee, frantically pulling at what appeared to be an arrow shaft, the silhouette looked up in time to see the glint of Cai's blade before it sliced deeply into his neck.

Another dark shadow burst from a thicket to Cai's right. It took two attempts for Cai to rip his blade free, giving this new enemy time to cross the small clearing. He wielded a sword too. Its point thrust towards Cai's face. He slashed instinctively right to left, parrying the warrior's blade, but only onto his exposed shoulder. He shrieked as icy pain lanced along his arm. His enemy roared at his sight of victory.

But, Cai knew how to fight in the darkness. He dropped to his knees, the assailant's sword point freed by the movement. Ignoring the pain, Cai thrust his own blade upwards. Its steel bit deep into the soft groin of his enemy. A high pitched squeal filled the darkness, more akin to the slaughter of a boar than a man. Cai twisted his sword's pommel to make sure, before yanking it clear as the body fell at his feet.

All around was chaos.

'Tungrii!' Hrindenus's battlecry came from behind Cai. The big man ensured the enemy knew what awaited them and any friends would take care to avoid him.

'Over here, Vexillarius,' Cai yelled into the night. An instant later Hrindenus was by Cai's side, his face fierce in the moonlight, his mouth twisted in a manic grin. Eyes wide, searching for an enemy.

'Let's kill the bastards,' Hrindenus screamed.

'Stay by me, we'll meet them together,' Cai yelled back. Hrindenus growled.

More shadows burst from the undergrowth. Cai couldn't tell how many, as the next instant his blade rang with the sound of steel on steel. Sparks flashed, for an instant lighting a dark bearded face as Cai parried his assailant's stroke. For a heartbeat Cai smelled the strange sweetness of his enemy's breath as they strained for dominance over one another. He was strong. Cai was forced to take slow steps backwards. He kicked out, connecting with the warrior's shin, drawing a sharp cry.

Cai's strength was ebbing fast. His shoulder screamed with the pain of its wound. Their blades crossed, a metallic grinding sound accompanied by the heavy, straining breath of both men. He was pushed back further. Cai kicked out desperately again, but this time missed. The unknown warrior shoved hard, freeing his own sword. Cai stumbled, his heel catching on an exposed root. He took a step back in a desperate attempt to prevent his fall. There was no stopping his momentum and an instant later he was on his arse.

The warrior took his chance. He strode towards Cai, a feral grin creasing his lips. Raising his sword two-handed to make a killing stroke, his blade a blurred, lethal shadow. Cai knew he was finished.

18

The warrior grunted. His back arched. Sword falling from his grip as he tried desperately, to reach, two-handed, at something unseen behind him.

Cai seized this unexpected salvation. Still sitting, he thrust the point of his long blade at the exposed belly of his attacker. The man's scream became a wail as he clutched at his abdomen, an instant later collapsing to his knees and onto his front. His head came to rest in Cai's lap, as if in sleep.

For a moment Cai was dazed. In the moonlight he saw the cause of the warrior's scream. Two arrow shafts stood proud, buried deep in the bare, darkly tattooed back of the corpse. How?

'Tungrii!' Cai peered in the direction of Hrindenus's warcry. He could see only the dark, confused shapes of undergrowth. He sensed movement ahead of him, a faint rusting almost hidden by the sound of the raging battle. Two shadows emerged. His mind struggled to understand. The shadows were too small for men.

'Cai?' The voice was unsteady, and instantly recognisable.

'Beren?' Cai called. He tossed the limp body of the warrior aside, scrambling to his feet. He rushed to the boy's side, recognising Herne as the other. 'What are you doing here?' Anguish filled his words.

'We came to—' Cai cut Beren off.

'Get behind me,' he said, backing them away from the battle's din.

A great crashing sound came from Cai's right. He cursed, realising he no longer held his sword. He searched frantically for it, the forest floor still too dark to see. The crashing continued, followed by a wild battlecry as a huge warrior broke into the small clearing.

The warrior, seeing movement before him, let out another great bellow.

'Hold, Keefe!' Herne's high pitched shout came from Cai's side. The warrior froze instantly.

'Herne?' the big Hibernian said in confusion. 'What are you doing here?'

The Novantae boy had no time to answer as another beast-like bellow erupted from the bushes directly behind the Hibernian. The big warrior turned, his sword already swinging in a great arc, meeting the sword of the shadowed enemy. The two blades clashed, the metallic sound ringing around the small space.

'It's Hrindenus,' Beren screeched. Keefe didn't seem to hear as he drove his head into the face of the Tungrian. Stumbling backwards, blood streaming from his nose, Hrindenus swung his blade blindly in a desperate attempt to buy himself time.

Cai moved swiftly. Flinging himself into the side of Barra's man, driving him into the morass of bushes. They both landed hard and in a tangle of limbs. The warrior reacted furiously, kicking out in an attempt to free himself. Cai grabbed Keefe's arms, desperately holding on, knowing the warrior was in the battle madness. 'Stay your hand Keefe,' Cai wheezed desperately.

'Keefe, hold!' Herne's voice shouted again, from close by. The warrior looked around, his eyes wild. 'Hold, Keefe. It is I. Herne.'

'Herne?' Keefe said, his voice calming though still uncertain.

Cai felt the warrior's grappling ease. He stared, with bulging eyes, into Cai's own for an instant. Before his face relaxed and, much to Cai's relief, he ceased to struggle.

'Get off me, Roman,' Keefe said, contemptuously. Cai released his hold. Both men scrambled to their feet.

The sound of battle continued but had moved further away.

'They're running,' Hrindenus said, his voice sounding muffled.

'Hrindenus, stay with the boys,' Cai said. 'Keefe, let's find out what is going on.'

The big warrior growled, turning to Hrindenus. The pair locked eyes.

'Watch over them, Roman,' Keefe said, the threat implicit in his tone. Hrindenus, pinching his nostrils between finger and thumb, said nothing.

Cai and Keefe ran into the near darkness. The clash of swords had stilled. The only sound was their feet as they stumbled blindly through the forest's undergrowth.

'Lord? Barra?' Keefe called.

'Here,' came the response out of the darkness, a short distance ahead. Reaching the Novantae warchief's side, they found him crouched over a body. 'This is Obran, one of my cousin's band. He always was a shit fighter. His mother is a good woman though. A friend to my wife when she lay on her death-bed. I grieve for her. She did not deserve such a son.'

'Frang is not the fool you thought, Lord,' Keefe said, his tone flat.

'No.'

Cai turned to Keefe. 'How did they find us? I—'

All three tensed at the crunching sound of heavy footsteps approaching them. Barra stood, sliding his sword from its scabbard. The tangle of branches before them parted and Lucius stepped through.

Barra puffed out a breath of relief. 'You will get yourself killed one of these days, Roman.'

'Undoubtedly,' Lucius said. 'The others?'

'Hrindenus is behind us watching over the boys. Castellanos—'

'Herne! I heard Herne. He shouted a warning,' Barra said, his voice filled with sudden concern.

'He's safe,' Cai said. 'Along with Beren.'

You're injured, brother,' Lucius said, seeing Cai holding his hand to his shoulder, blood oozing slowly through his fingers.

'It's nothing,' Cai said, irritated.

'Let's have the good medicus take a look, shall we?' Lucius said. 'Where is the Greek?

'We must leave, Lord,' Keefe interrupted. 'Frang must kill you now before you leave our lands. He must know we plan to use the sea road. He will be waiting for us at Rerigon's harbour. Once he remembers to stop running.'

'I must speak with my nephew first.'

They found Hrindenus and the two boys at the camp. The three were watching on, in silence, as Castellanos attempted to staunch the flow of blood from the neck of a warrior, over whom he was bent. To Cai, in the faint light, the medicus's hand appeared black as if wearing a glove. The battle to save the unknown man's life was lost, the Greek continued to hold his hand over the wound, unable to accept what his years of experience would normally already have told him.

'Come, Castellanos,' Cai said, resting his own hand on the shoulder of the medicus. 'He's dead. And a good thing it is too. He would have killed you if you'd given him the chance.' Castellanos simply shook his head, pressing against the wound that had ceased to pump blood.

19

'It was you who loosed those arrows?' Cai asked, not able to hide his surprise.

He and Barra looked upon the two young friends. They glanced at each other, and Cai could tell his former enemy, too, was struggling with mixed emotions. He was angry at Beren's disobedience, and filled with pride at his bravery, all at once.

'I hit the first man in the leg,' Beren said. 'I was aiming for his back, but I walked into a branch in the dark and released too soon.' Beren sounded disappointed with himself, though he rallied. 'Then me and Herne both shot that warrior who was trying to kill you, Cai.'

'You have done well, my brave young warriors,' Barra said. 'I cannot find it in me to be angry at your disobedience. Your warning saved lives.' Cai smiled as he saw both boys, who still held tight to the bows, puff out their chests. 'You must now return home. Only there will you be protected. My hearth warriors will see to it.'

'Keep to the forest until you reach Barra's farm,' Cai said, a few moments later, as he held onto the halter of Beren's dappled white pony, his other hand on the boy's shoulder. The early morning light enabled them to see each other's face clearly, even though the trees still loomed darkly over them.

'We will Cai,' Beren said. 'I don't fear the forest.'

'I know you don't,' Cai said, a smile breaking across his lips. 'I will return before the heart of winter, I hope. Perhaps before the first snows.' Cai didn't offer him any false hope about his mother and Beren didn't ask for it. 'Well then, it's time for you to be on your way.' He cupped his hands and boosted the lad onto the pony's back.

Barra was nearby, speaking in low tones to Herne. Cai was surprised to see the two embrace fiercely, before Barra too hoisted his nephew onto the back of his mount.

'You must be like brothers,' Barra said, as he and Cai faced them. 'You need fear nothing if you act together.' The boys looked at one another, their excitement returning. Raising hands in farewell they kicked the mounts into motion. Cai watched their rapidly retreating backs until the forest swallowed them. He felt his throat tighten. He hoped fervently, in that moment, he could one day return to the life he had hoped for, with Alyn and the boy.

'They will be fine warriors one day,' Barra said, as he too observed the same piece of forest. 'Now it is time to be on our way. We have a boat to find.'

20

Keefe rapped firmly on the ancient, salt stained door of the roundhouse.

The small hut sat upon a gentle rise above the tideline, with the waters of the long bay lapping gently against the pebbled shore below. Nets, old and new, lay strewn to either side of the doorway, along with several piles of driftwood. Kindling for the hearth-fire. The whole place stank of fish-rot.

Most of the fishing boats had left in the early hours as the first signs of light showed in the eastern sky. Lucius gazed across the grey waters, seeing their dark pinpricks in the distance. One, however, lay, forlorn, against the bank.

'What do you want?' A voice croaked from within.

'Open up old man, you know who it is,' Keefe said, his words a hissed whisper.

The door creaked open a handspan and two eyes peered through the gap from the darkness within. Lucius saw a wisp of a man, whose thinning grey hair lay in matted strips across his shoulder. His matted beard hung in tendrils covering a stained and fading tunic.

'Take the boat and go,' croaked the old fisherman.

'What of your son, Old One? He is to guide us to the island,' Keefe said, his annoyance rising.

'He ran, like the coward he is. He fears Frang. You know how to sail as well as any man, Keefe. If you keep to the north star you'll come to the isle you seek. Its lone peak is hard to miss. There is food and water stowed aboard. Enough for three days. Now begone.' The ancient door slammed shut, followed by the distinctive thud of the locking bar falling into place.

Keefe turned to face the others, who were gathered on the slope between the roundhouse and the shore.

'We have no choice,' Barra said. 'Besides, old Ougien is right, the island is hard to miss.'

'Unless a mist comes down and we run into rocks.' Keefe's voice was even more morose than usual.

'Let's load up,' Lucius said addressing the others. Cai wore his green chequered cloak, scabbarded sword in hand. At his shoulder, Hrindenus, eyes blackened and swollen, his nose crusted red, looked around continually, expecting trouble. Castellanos, whose olive skin appeared to have turned a sickly grey, peering fretfully at the waiting boat. His dark wooden box, held against his chest like a precious child. 'The sooner we are out of here the better.'

He gazed along the coastline. The palisade of the Novantae capital was no more than a hundred paces from the fisherman's hut. The stout wooden wall protruded from steep turf ramparts. Its base rested against a ragged line of sharp grey rocks that appeared and disappeared with the rolling movement of the dark waters. A dense, smoky fug lay above the peaked and thatched roofs of many huts, mingling with the low oppressive cloud.

Two men watched from its parapet, resting their elbows on the top of the wooden barrier. To Lucius they appeared only mildly curious, rather than on the lookout for Frang's enemies.

'It seems my cousin has not made it known that we are to be stopped,' Barra remarked. 'Or perhaps he is not as respected as he believes. But let us not tempt the gods.'

All heads turned at the rumbling sound of many hooves. Massed riders, approaching rapidly.

'Perhaps the gods are already tempted,' Lucius said. 'Get to the boat.'

The six men scrambled down the bank, tossing weapons and supplies into the stern of the vessel. Without further instruction each gripped its stout oak sides and dragged it across the pebbles, their footsteps crunching and slipping as they went. A shout of alarm came from behind them. But none looked back. They reached the lapping waves, splashing into the cold waters.

'Get in,' Keefe shouted as the boat became buoyant. He manhandled Castellanos into the bow, the Greek yelping with surprise. Lucius heard a splash to his right and saw a spear shaft bob back to the surface an arms-length away. With no additional encouragement needed he threw himself over the gunwale of the craft.

'Oars,' Keefe commanded. From his position at the stern, he took hold of the tiller. Lucius and Barra sat side by side, scrambling to get the oars into their slots, Hrindenus and Cai behind them doing the same. Castellanos, seated in the bow, held tight to his box.

A spear clattered against the boat's narrow aft, before slopping into the growing swell. The four men rowed. At first in a frantic, uncoordinated fashion as they fought desperately to escape the shore. Soon they found a rhythm. In moments they were beyond the range of their enemy's spears.

'Hold here,' Barra said.

'Lord?'

'Hold I said,' Barra shipped his oar. Lucius did likewise, wondering what was to come. He scrutinised the beach. A line of horsemen, fifteen at his count, sat their mounts, calling insults Lucius did not understand. As the boat steadied, Barra stood.

'We'll meet again, cousin,' Barra called. 'When I am anointed, I will return for your head.' One of the waiting riders nudged his horse onto the shingle, coming to rest as its front hooves entered the lapping water. Lucius found it strange that these two men were related by blood. The cousin's physical differences were marked. Where Barra was tall and well built, the body of a man familiar with war, this one was shorter, almost diminutive. Wiry muscles knotted his forearms and his head was shaved in the fashion of the Damnonii. His face twisted with hatred. As he spoke, his voice became shrill.

'I will reach the citadel long before you and your mongrel crew, cousin. It is I who the Holy One will bless.' There was a moment's silence before Frang spoke again. 'I know you also seek my friend the Blue Wolf?' he smirked. 'I almost pity you. Well, at least it saves me the task of killing you myself.'

'You are a frightened weasel, Frang. I saw you at the battle for the Romans' fort. Always drinking around the campfire, boasting of your courage. Not once did I see you amongst the vanguard of our warriors. You were pissing yourself, hiding amongst the bracken, awaiting our victory.'

Frang's voice became a screech. 'It is you who are the coward. Come ashore and face me.'

'One day soon, cousin,' Barra said, his voice filled with amusement. 'Be patient. Your death is coming.' He sat back down on the bench. 'Row.'

'I think you may have touched a nerve,' Lucius said.

Barra made a grumbling sound and turned to Lucius.

'Yes. Though now it appears I have two madmen to kill.'

HUNT

21

The breeze stiffened as they rowed out into the bay. Keefe ordered the mast to be raised and he unfurled the sail. Frang and his band shadowed them for a time, following the shoreline. As the long sea lake widened, they gave up and returned in the direction of Rerigon.

The fisherman's boat was stout and swift, cutting through the swell. As Cai sat on his bench, he observed the warrior, Keefe. His face had taken on new life, and whilst he didn't exactly smile, his conversations with Barra became almost light-hearted.

'A fine craft, this one,' Keefe said.

'Better than that leaking bucket I rescued you and little Niamh from, all those years ago.' Cai realised that Keefe was more than Barra's shield-bearer, they were as brothers. Much like himself and Lucius.

As the morning reached its midpoint, the craft passed through the narrow neck of the bay and into the sea of Hibernia proper. The keel immediately began to rise and fall as they headed directly into the oncoming swell. Cai heard Castellanos groan from behind him.

'Why did I ask to come on this damned journey?' Moments later there was a retching sound. Cai was forced to concentrate on not emptying his own stomach over the side.

'More food for the fish,' Keefe said, delighting in the Greek's discomfort.

Once they were well out to sea, the waters calmed somewhat, enabling them all to rest. The low cloud cover fragmented, allowing brighter light to filter through. As noon approached, Cai spotted a distant, dark island

101

beginning to emerge on the horizon. As the afternoon wore on, the island grew in their vision, revealing granite coloured cliffs, its summit shaped like a bannock.

'What is that place?' Cai asked.

'It is Ailsa's Isle,' Barra said, his voice flat. 'A place of the gods. We will drop the anchor stone off its shore for the night.'

For a time the small band were quiet. In the end it was Lucius who broke the silence, echoing what had also been on Cai's mind.

'How could Frang know we searched for Blue Dog?'

'Because,' Barra said, his voice filled with a simmering anger, 'there is a traitor amongst my people.'

The memory of Urbicus's letter to Lucius flashed into Cai's mind. Was this the man? The Numidian's agent, who betrayed Barra and the Novantae people? The warchief said no more and Cai sensed he should not push further.

'Frang seemed confident he would overhaul you on this journey,' Cai said. 'How could that be?'

'Unless we meet disaster on the sea road,' Keefe cut in, 'he cannot.'

'I've been thinking on it,' Barra said, his voice seeming distant to Cai. 'The land route, even if it wasn't closed off to us, would take longer in any case. It makes no sense.'

'He believes this Blue Dog will kill you,' Hrindenus said from his rowing bench. The small party turned to the Tungrian in puzzlement. 'He knows we go first to seek out this Damnonii. He must have already sent a messenger ahead of us.' Hrindenus grinned at the surprised looks of Barra and Keefe. It gave his black and swollen eyes the appearance of being shut tight. Barra stared into the dark waters of the Hibernian Sea.

As the bright autumn sun disappeared below the western horizon, Keefe lowered the sail before calling to Castellanos, who was still sitting hunched in the bow of the boat.

'Greek, throw the anchor stone over the side.' The medicus cast around in confusion. 'By your feet,' the big Hibernian said, not hiding his exasperation. With some effort and a helping hand from Hrindenus the sandstone ball was dropped over the side with a splash. The coiled rope rushed after it, like a serpent chasing its quarry into the depths.

'My name is Castellanos,' the Athenian said to Keefe, with his professional smile fixed. 'You may call me by name, or medicus, if you wish to be more formal.'

Cai was surprised to see the big man smile back. A grin of genuine mirth. He nodded his head once in affirmation.

The boat turned slowly in the continual rolling swell. Barra got up from the bench, stretching his back, legs splayed to keep his balance. For a moment he peered northwards. 'There's our destination,' he said. All stared in the direction the warchief surveyed. In the dying light, Cai was able to make out the dark purple outline of a distant sharp peak.

Barra turned to Cai. 'Blue Dog's island.'

22

Lucius slept fitfully. The wind had stiffened during the night, causing the rolling waters, gentle as darkness descended, to rise and fall alarmingly at times. He and Cai had lain back to back under the aft rowing bench, more for stability in the heaving boat than warmth. From Cai's restive movements he guessed his friend didn't sleep much either.

Indeed, the only members of the party who had were Keefe, who had barely moved during the night, his arm and head resting against the tiller. The other was Hrindenus, who slept next to Castellanos in the bow. The big men appeared to compete with each other as to who could snore loudest. To Lucius's dulled mind the Tungrian's broken nose took the acclaim.

As soon as the high cliffs of Ailsa's Isle could be seen in the early grey murk, Keefe raised the sail. The makeshift crew passed around cold rations of dried fish and hard cheese. Lucius gripped his cloak tightly about his shoulders. The wind had become bitter, sea spray from the tossing bows soaked them, chilling all. Castellanos in particular struggled with the cold. The Greek shivered continually as he held tightly to his wooden box for fear it would be lost overboard.

As they left the bannock-shaped crown of Ailsa's Isle behind, Lucius looked upon the mountain on Blue Dog's island. 'How long?' he asked.

'If we keep this wind,' Keefe said, 'we'll reach the island as the sun begins its descent.'

'Blue Dog's lair is on the western shore,' Barra said. 'We can't get close without giving warning of our approach. There's a steep spur of cliffs to its south. They jut out into the sea about a half day's walk away. We can beach the boat there. We'll be able to move quickly across the moorland between. The bracken and heather will hide us.'

'You've been to this place before?' Cai asked. Barra nodded.

'Once. When we were seeking allies.' Lucius knew without asking what he had been seeking allies for. 'It's a grim place. He and his people dwell in caves cut deep into the cliff face.'

'They live like animals,' Keefe interjected.

'The caves are protected by a rocky shoreline and a large, well-made palisade,' Barra continued. 'It would take a great force of warriors to overwhelm it. Neither can it be attacked from above as the cliff overhangs. Our only chance is stealth.'

Keefe made a hooming sound. 'His men are ever watchful and diligent in their duties. They fear their master's wrath. Which is always swift and brutal. It will not be easy to get past them.'

'We must try at night—' Barra began.

'Is that a sail?' Castellanos said, searching the horizon beyond Keefe in the boats aft.

Lucius initially saw only sky. But, as the boat rose to the peak of a swell he glimpsed a flash of red. Keefe scrambled towards the mast, nimbly shinning up the oak pole, his feet gripping the damp wood. He stared southwards.

'Two sails,' he shouted. 'Broad and red.'

Lucius turned to Cai. 'One of our patrols?'

'They've already seen us,' Keefe said. 'Their oars are out. They mean to snare us.' He slid back down the mast.

'I don't think they would believe our story,' Lucius said. 'Can we reach the island before they overrun us?' Keefe turned to the north.

'Perhaps. We'll have to take to the oars. We must make for the island's southernmost point. I'm unfamiliar with it.'

'We have little choice,' Barra said, retrieving his oar and fitting it between its wooden slats. Cai, Lucius and Hrindenus made haste to do likewise. They were soon rowing hard, adding their strength to the power of the wind.

'You must find an easier rhythm,' Keefe shouted. 'Or you will soon be exhausted.' At first Lucius didn't understand what the Hibernian meant, but by matching Barra's stroke he eventually achieved a steady tempo.

'They're gaining,' Castellanos shouted from the bow. It didn't need to be said. All four rowers were transfixed by the sight of the red sails. Lucius's arms and shoulders burned. How much longer could they keep this up?

'Roman,' Keefe said. Lucius looked up, before realising the Hibernian was addressing Cai behind him. 'You steer. I row.' Lucius had forgotten about Cai's wound. He must be struggling. Cai tried to protest but the big warrior was already moving, brooking no dissent. Soon he took the tiller and Lucius could see from his friend's white pallor he was almost spent.

How near were they to the island? Lucius dared not risk a glance over his shoulder for fear of breaking the rhythm. His lungs ached, his breaths came in great, heaving gusts, matching Barra's next to him. The ships appeared to loom larger with each stroke, closing in on the fishing craft. A single bank of fifteen rowers on each side moved to the thunking sound of the timing mallet, the pulsing clatter reverberating across the water to Lucius and the others.

'They're loading scorpios,' Cai said. 'The nearest will soon be close enough to chance its luck.' Lucius could see the red cloaks of the two-man ballista section, clearly visible on the bow platform of the leading patrol boat. The ship's bows were painted with a pair of large eyes that stared, unblinking, at their quarry. Lucius's oar thumped against his chest as the fishing boat lurched hard to the left. Cai had turned the tiller arm.

'What are you doing, Roman?' Keefe gasped, unable to manage a shout.

'Rocks,' was all Cai said in reply. The four rowers were nearing exhaustion. There was a sudden sharp thud, and Lucius was showered with splinters of wood.

'Shit, they've got our range. Row.' Cai bellowed. Lucius fought the desire to look at the short scorpion bolt that must now be protruding from the mast. A smooth, slick, grey rock passed within touching distance to his left. The paddle of Lucius's oar clattered against it.

'You're mad,' Keefe wheezed. The boat lurched again, this time to the right. Another rock passed perilously close, its surface broken, jagged and obscured by barnacles.

There was a thudding sound followed instantly by a shriek from Castellanos.

'He's hit,' Hrindenus panted, with little air left in his lungs. 'Castellanos.'

'Leave him,' Keefe said, the words gasped.

Lucius glanced towards the Roman pursuers. The nearest ship was backing its oars. They had escaped capture.

'Hold on,' Cai screamed. Lucius had an instant to see the alarm in his friend's eyes before he was tossed from the boat, to be swallowed by the cold waters of the Hibernian sea.

23

Cai broke the surface. He gasped for breath, spitting out salty bile.

He had seen the rock, an instant before they struck it, and been able to brace. He could not, however, prevent himself from being flung overboard by the impact. He filled his lungs once more, choking as he breathed in more seawater.

'Help me!' It was Castellanos, his voice panicked. A wave hit Cai full in the face, stinging his eyes. It took him a moment to get his bearings.

'Help!'

Castellanos was trapped. The wooden hull of the fishing boat was shattered, a great split ripped down its right side. It listed at an alarming angle and was sinking. Water gushed into its interior. The medicus was caught beneath both the shattered mast, which hung at a drunken angle, and the rigging that was dragging like an anchor in the roiling water.

The Athenian struggled frantically to free himself from under the leather sail. If Cai could not reach him in time, he would be dragged to the bottom. Treading water, Cai quickly searched around. There was no one else to be seen. Another wave drove him away from the wreck.

Cai kicked hard for the flotsam. It took several exhausting strokes, eventually reaching the boat's near-submerged gunwale. Using a piece of the tangled rigging for purchase, he slid over its side.

'Help me.' The Athenian's shout was spluttered. Castellanos was being pulled under.

'Hold on, Castellanos,' Cai hollered, coughing up more water. There was no further response from the medicus. The whole of the right side of the boat was entirely submerged. Cai pulled himself under the sail, casting around frantically. He felt a forearm and grabbed it, his own instantly gripped by Castellanos. Cai pulled hard. The Greek's head bobbed to the surface. He gasped for breath. Cai pulled again.

'Wait,' the medicus spluttered. 'My box.'

'To Hades with your box,' Cai said. The medicus pulled back, disappearing below the surface once more, though still gripping Cai's arm. If they didn't go soon, they would both be lost. He was on the point of dragging the Greek away when he resurfaced, dark hair plastered to his forehead.

Cai pulled hard and Castellanos kicked himself free. Both slipped into the waves, the medicus's small medical trunk held under one arm as he gasped for air.

'Are you alright?' Cai asked. 'Can you swim.'

'Yes. Hold onto my box.'

The dark wooden container, from which protruded the short shaft and flights of a scorpio bolt, floated easily on the surface. Cai grasped for it. He was exhausted. His shoulder was aching horribly. As the pair bobbed together on the swell, Cai looked towards the two Roman galleys. Both stood off impotently.

He looked towards the shore. A sandy beach was perhaps two hundred paces from their position. Beyond he was able to make out a dark treeline. For an instant he saw a flash of red hair, midway between them and the land. He could not tell if it was Barra of Keefe; whoever it was made easy, languid strokes towards the shoreline. There was no sight of Lucius nor Hrindenus. He turned right and left hoping for a glimpse of his comrades, seeing only the grey spume of the sea as it battered the rocks around them. There was nothing to be done. His strength was waning fast.

'Let's make for the beach,' Cai said.

'What about the others?' Castellanos replied. Cai only shook his head and began to kick towards the shore.

Lucius held onto the oar's spar with his left hand as he floated on his back. He had kicked hard away from the wreckage, and towards land, he hoped. He held his right hand under the chin of Hrindenus. The unconscious Tungrian's forehead and eyes were streaked with blood that flowed steadily from a gash in his hairline. His features were continually washed clean with every dip in the sea's swell.

Despite being encumbered he had managed to get some distance from the wreck. By turns, kicking hard for a few seconds and resting for a time, he had made progress. The waves too seemed to assist him, driving the pair towards land. Even so, the effort was draining. At first, the big man's bulk had only seemed to hinder him a little in the buoyancy of the Hibernian sea. But their leather armour was becoming saturated. The weight was beginning to drag.

He heard a shout, the call unintelligible. The sound of splashing came from behind. 'You are safe, Roman,' Barra said from behind, a hand resting on his shoulder. 'You can stand.' Keefe appeared too, the lapping waves reaching his chest.

The big Hibernian took hold of Hrindenus under his arms and began to drag him to safety. Lucius released his grip on the spar. Letting his feet drift downwards they soon touched the firm sandy bottom.

'Come,' Barra said, pulling at his arm.

Lucius looked at the Novantae, whose long red hair clung to his cheeks in sodden strands. 'Cai?' Lucius asked, suddenly fearful for his friend.

'He's close. Look.' Barra said, pointing. Sure enough, there was Cai and Castellanos a short distance along the coastline. Both held onto the medicus's ever present box as they kicked hard for the beach. Lucius let Barra help him through the surf, until his feet felt the crunch of pebbles.

'My thanks,' he said. 'I can manage from here.' Lucius saw Cai and Castellanos wading ashore, the medicus clutching his box.

In moments the group lay exhausted in a small huddle of sand dunes, whose dry scrub grass hissed as a sea breeze passed through it. Castellanos and Cai attended Hrindenus.

'You're getting in the way, Praefectus,' the medicus said as he tried to examine the deep gash in his hairline. Cai moved aside but remained nearby.

'That box of yours really does save lives,' Lucius said, as he spotted the flights of the scorpio bolt protruding from its wooden lid. Castellanos ignored him, continuing to examine the wound.

Lucius turned his gaze out to sea. The two galleys were returning to their patrol, it seemed. For a few short strokes the banks of oars rowed in unison, manoeuvring the warships back into deeper waters. Soon after, by an unheard order, the oars were withdrawn, allowing wind power to take the strain.

'That was a close run thing,' Barra said, the Novantae coming to stand by Lucius's shoulder. 'The weight of my sword almost dragged me under.' Lucius looked at Barra's hip and was surprised to see the warrior's sword still hung at his side, the fur-lined, leather scabbard sodden and streaked white with salt.

'Mine is at the bottom,' he said. 'Along with the fisherman's boat. And the remains of our food.'

'Keefe held onto his blade,' Barra said. If he was making a point of honour, Lucius chose to ignore it. He turned instead at the sound of a groan. Hrindenus was conscious.

'How is he?' Lucius asked, as he reached the medicus.

'I'm fine,' Hrindenus interrupted. The Athenian had bound the gash with a dressing, a bright red stain already spreading like a red eagle's wings across its front. 'I've got a bit of a headache, that's all.' An instant later the Tungrian turned onto his side and retched onto the sand.

'He's had a blow to the head,' Castellanos said. 'He must rest for a few hours to see how it develops. I worry about brain swelling.'

'What brain,' Keefe said from behind the group. His tone, flat.

'We cannot stay here,' Barra said. 'We're too exposed.'

'I'll stay with him,' Castellanos said. 'You go ahead without us.'

'No,' Barra said firmly. 'We will not have time to return for you. Already we must hope there is another boat we can take from Blue Dog's lair, once we have dealt with him. I have no time for delay.'

'I can walk, Medicus,' Hrindenus said. Lucius saw the white pallor of the Tungrian's face that even the two day old growth on his chin and bruised eyes couldn't hide. His skin glistened with moisture. The last time he had seen such a sight was when he knelt by the Baetican assassin. Moments before he died.

24

'No. The shortest route is to cut inland,' Barra said. 'It will take us over the mountain and will be tough going for your man. But to go around will delay us by a day.'

Cai stared back along the trackway. Hrindenus leant against the trunk of a gnarled and wind-bent ash tree. Clusters of red berries hung heavily, framed by its yellowing leaves. They had been walking for only an hour and the big man already appeared spent. 'It will kill him,' Cai said.

'Then we must leave him,' Barra responded, his tone brusque. Cai rounded on the Novantae.

'Would you leave your man?' Cai flicked his head at Keefe, who was at his side. Barra gazed beyond Cai's shoulder for a moment before responding.

'No. I would not.'

'I'll take him,' Keefe said, brushing past Cai, his heavy footsteps crunching against loose stone as he returned along the narrow path. The Hibernian spoke quietly to Hrindenus. Cai couldn't make out what was said though it was clear the big red-headed warrior brooked no argument. A moment later the pair approached Cai and Barra. Keefe held Hrindenus tightly under the shoulder and the Tungrian had his arm around Keefe's waist. Like a pair of mismatched lovers.

'See, I told you, sir,' Hrindenus said with a weak grin. 'Didn't I say he and I would become firm friends?'

'Quiet, Roman,' Keefe grumbled. 'Keep bumping your gums and I'll drop you over that cliff yonder.'

Cai observed the route ahead. The pathway rose steeply from this point. It did indeed pass near to a drop, although not quite a cliff. Hrindenus would be more likely to roll, end over end, than fall. The trail disappeared over a rise before merging with the drying purple heather. Beyond that, there was a dark line of red pine.

Lucius and Castellanos caught up with Cai. His friend had been chivvying the medicus along. 'What I wouldn't give for a good mule,' Castellanos said.

'Let me carry your box for a time,' Cai said, holding out his hand.

'No, no,' he returned. 'It's my burden to bear.'

'Then you must keep up, brother,' Lucius said. 'Hrindenus will need your services soon enough.'

'If his brain is swelling under his thick skull,' Castellanos said, 'this ascent may finish him.'

They climbed for a while longer, following a narrow, fast moving stream whose waters tumbled over smooth rocks slick with slimy, green algae. Castellanos moved to Hrindenus's side, examining his head as they walked.

'We must rest here,' he said. 'The bleeding is getting worse. I must halt its flow.'

'S'fine,' Hrindenus mumbled, sounding drunk.

Keefe lowered the Tungrian to a grey boulder. His head lolled against his chest and only the big warrior's close attention prevented Hrindenus from slipping into the heather.

'Hold him upright,' Castellanos said, Cai moved to help Keefe, who gently raised Hrindenus's head. With alarm Cai realised the Tungrian's eyes had closed as if in sleep. The medicus had seen it too and worked quickly. He unbound the dressing, now caked in congealed blood. A splintered hole in the lid of his box where the bolt had pierced it shed thin shards of wood as he opened it. He removed a tightly wound ball of animal gut. Next he retrieved a slim needle, threading a line of the sinew through its eye.

Between finger and thumb the Greek pinched the two sides of the gash together. With an expert hand he briskly made the first pass with the needle. Hrindenus did not stir. In moments the wound was closed and bound in a fresh dressing.

'That has stopped the bleed,' Castellanos said. 'He cannot be moved further. He will die.'

'We must rest for the night,' Cai said, addressing the others. 'There's water here and undergrowth in which to conceal our presence.' Barra turned, staring at the route ahead.

'Very well,' he said. 'There's still two or three hours of light left in the day. Keefe and I will continue. We should be able to reach Blue Dog's settlement before last light. We'll watch for a time and return as soon as we can. At least that way we will know what we are up against.' The Novantae chieftain left them, running at a steady pace up the mountainside, shadowed by Keefe. Cai noted, despite their size, both warriors moved on swift, near silent, feet.

Hrindenus murmured, his words unintelligible. He had not woken since Barra's departure. Cai hoped it was a good sign. He turned to Castellanos for confirmation. The Athenian looked over his patient, though appeared unconcerned.

'He fights,' was all he said.

It was close to complete darkness. Sufficient light was left in the dying day to enable each to see the other, as they crouched, concealed, amongst the heather and bracken. The dense cover gave them some protection from the chill of the stiffening breeze. Even so, Cai's troos had begun to stiffen from the drying salt water, making the enforced inaction uncomfortable.

'Do you think they will return tonight?' Castellanos asked, his tone flat. The question, it seemed to Cai, arising more out of boredom than curiosity.

'I hope so,' Lucius said. 'These damned flies are a misery; they've taken a liking to me.'

'Perhaps it's your noble blood they like so much, brother,' Cai said, his grin standing out even in the gloom.

'It may be your Nervii blood is too nasty for their taste?' Lucius responded.

'Too tight to give any away more like,' a voice croaked. All three turned to where Hrindenus lay. His eyes were open.

'So you have returned to us,' Castellanos said. 'The bone of your skull must be even thicker than I thought.' Hrindenus gave a throaty chuckle that immediately turned into a groan. 'I'll fetch more water.' The medicus crouched low, disappearing through the undergrowth towards the gurgling sound of the stream.

'How long?' Hrindenus asked.

'Only a couple of hours,' Cai replied. 'How's the head?'

'Like divine Epona's own mount is trying to kick its way out of it,' Hrindenus said. Puzzlement creased his eyes. 'Where are the Novantae?'

'Gone to scout Blue Dog's lair,' Lucius said. 'We must be ready to move in the morning.' A rustling sound came from behind Cai, and Castellanos reappeared. They had lost their skins in the wreck so the medicus carried the water in a clay mixing bowl. He raised the Tungrian's head, lifting the bowl to his lips. Hrindenus took deep swallows.

'You must rest,' Castellanos said. 'If you are to be fit enough to move again.' Cai was surprised to see the big man drift almost immediately into a deep sleep. The medicus saw Cai's eyes widen in alarm.

'I mixed a little milk of the poppy in with the water. Enough to dull the pain and help him sleep. Rest will speed his recovery.'

'Speaking of which,' Lucius interjected. 'We should take the opportunity to get some shut-eye while we can.'

Some hours later, as Cai sat amongst the undergrowth, having relieved Lucius of the watch. He listened to Hrindenus's deep wheeze-grumble of a snore. 'Enough to wake the dead from their long sleep,' Cai murmured.

He turned sharply at the sound of a splash. Before Cai could react, a dark image appeared above him. 'We thought we might pass you in the darkness,' the shadow said with Barra's voice. 'But we could hear your man's snores some way up the pathway as if to guide us home. Perhaps the gods are smiling upon us.'

Lucius stirred beside Cai, Castellanos and Hrindenus continued the deep slumber of the exhausted. A shadow moved behind Barra. Keefe, silent at his chief's shoulder.

'Did you reach the settlement?' Cai asked, wincing internally as he heard the note of expectation in his own voice.

'Yes,' Barra said, as he slumped into the bracken next to the dark hump of the prone Hrindenus. 'How is he?' Cai ignored the Novantae's question.

'What is it?' Cai asked. 'What are you not telling me?'

Barra blew out a long slow breath, his shoulders slumping in weariness. 'Blue Dog is not there.'

25

'How can you be sure?' Lucius asked.

They had set out as soon as the pathway could be discerned in the early gloom. By mid-morning, they had crossed over the lone peak. As the sun attained its zenith the group lay amongst deep clumps of ferns, whose summer green had turned to a mottled brown of winter.

'Look at the palisade walkway,' Keefe said, losing patience. 'There is only one sentry and he stands with his back against the parapet. He does not fear Blue Dog's wrath for his laziness, because his master has gone from here.'

'There are few men, it would seem,' Lucius said. He turned to Cai. 'There are women and children, though.' His friend nodded, not taking his eyes from the sight below. He had barely done so since they had reached this concealed spot on the cliffs. All knew what he looked for 'Do we wait until nightfall to take them?' he asked Barra.

'No,' the warchief said. 'I have a better plan. We will walk through those gates in daylight and those Damnonii rats will let us.'

Thirty minutes later, the six had scrambled from the cliffs and onto the rocky shoreline. A cleft in the jagged, grey rocks hid the party still.

'Once we step out into the open,' Keefe said. 'The Damnonii will smell a deception if you don't play your part well.'

'Don't worry,' Lucius said with a grin. 'I've seen many plays at the theatres in my homeland. I know how to put on an act.' The big Hibernian gave Lucius a jaundiced look.

'Just don't get me killed, Roman,' he said, wrapping his arm around Lucius's back. Barra did likewise from the other side. Behind the trio, Cai and Castellanos held Hrindenus in a similar fashion, although in their case the casualty was real. The Tungrian, although improved from the day before, was worn out after the long slog.

'Let's go,' Barra said.

The six moved from the cover of the rocks. Still some distance from the palisade. they were not immediately spotted.

'What do you see?' Lucius asked, braced between the two warriors, his head hanging low.

'Women outside of the gateway, mending nets,' Keefe said. 'But no men. The fool on the walkway is not in sight.'

'Saa!' Barra exclaimed under his breath. 'There's a boat pulled up above the shoreline at the palisade's far end. We can take it once we are done here.' With the sea to their left and the cliffs to the right, they continued unnoticed for a few moments longer.

A slight, dark-haired boy of perhaps six summers appeared from behind a rock where he had been crouching by a sea pool. He stared at the six men in surprise, but not fear, Lucius thought. He held a long piece of animal gut in his right hand, and at its end hung the remains of a dark blue mussel shell. In the other he gripped a small wooden bucket, filled with seawater, whose surface writhed with movement. Crabs.

The boy turned suddenly and dashed towards the settlement. 'Mam!' he shouted in excitement. 'Warriors.'

'It's all right lad,' Barra started to say. It was of no use. The boy moved on nimble feet, skipping between the rock

119

pools as both water and crabs sloshed from his bucket with each step.

The women around the gateway arose, watching the slow approach of this band of strangers. They spoke rapidly between one another, before walking swiftly through the open, heavy wooden gates. Surprisingly, to Lucius, they raised no cries of alarm.

'Well, we must have their attention now,' Barra said.

A head appeared over the parapet, before disappearing again. Shortly afterwards the doors swung shut with a heavy crash.

'I saw three men before the gates closed,' Barra said.

'We only have two swords,' Lucius reminded him.

'We must hope our deception is persuasive enough to get them to open up again. When they do, Keefe and I will attack. Once we have killed the first, you must take his sword and lend a hand.' Lucius felt the familiar tug of fear. But also the familiar rush of blood, as it surged around his body, preparing him for battle.

Lucius glanced towards the settlement before letting his head flop once more, as if the effort of raising it had been too much. Three bearded faces had appeared above the parapet, confirming Barra's count. One balded with age, the other two broad and red-headed.

'The Twins,' Keefe hissed.

'Shit. This might not be as straightforward as I'd hoped.' Barra said.

'Who the fuck are The Twins?' Lucius said, his voice barely a whisper.

Barra hawked and spat. 'Let's just say if Blue Dog has truly gone from this place, he has left two of his best warriors behind.'

'That's not saying much,' Keefe said. Lucius could sense the Hibernian's unease despite his scorn.

'Stop there. Don't come any nearer. Strangers are not welcome here.' The voice sounded reedy. The older man, Lucius thought.

'The Blue Wolf's hospitality seems sadly lacking these days,' Barra returned, his voice loud and filled with irony. 'Will you not welcome brothers in need?'

The older man cackled. 'You must not know our lord well if you think him hospitable. How is it that you have come to this place?'

'Do you not recognise me, old goat?' Barra said. There was silence from the palisade for a time. 'It is I, Barra. Warchief of the Novantae people and now king.' Lucius could hear the murmur of voices as the three conferred with one another. 'Let us in for pity's sake, we have injured men.'

'You're not looking so lordly these days, Barra of the Novantae.' This voice was younger, and deep, dripping with malice. 'Your grand plan came to nought under the walls of the Romans' fort. Begone, ragged king of a conquered land. The Romans will soon have you and your people under their boot once again.'

Lucius felt his shoulder drop as Keefe stepped forward. The additional weight forced Barra to lower Lucius to the ground. In that instant he saw a face appear over the palisade at the other side of the gateway. A woman's face. She watched Barra before turning her attention to where Cai and Castellanos held Hrindenus between them. She vanished, back into the settlement.

'You dare insult a king, Damnonii cur? You are truly one of Blue Dog's cowards. Where were you when the fighting was fiercest? Hiding in the forest awaiting our victory. A victory that would have been ours but for the arrival of the Eagles. I challenge you now. Fight cowards.' The Hibernian's face and neck was flushed

121

with anger. The three on the palisade glanced at each other for an instant, before exploding with laughter.

'Why should we waste our time on a boggy bastard like you? Robogdii water-rat.' This from the other twin.

'What now?' Lucius said under his breath, as he lay on the wet rocky ground, the smell of seaweed keen in his nostrils.

'We'll have to wait till darkness and—What's that?' Barra said, confused. Lucius turned his head slightly. One of the gates was opening.'

'Someone wants to help us,' Lucius said. 'No time. Run.' Lucius leapt to his feet and began to sprint for the gateway, jumping rock pools, careless of how he landed on the uneven and slick ground. He hoped the others followed, his own breath and crashing of the sea concealed all other sound.

He glanced up at the wooden parapet. The three warriors looked puzzled. He prayed they would remain so for a while longer. Suddenly the older man turned sharply towards the gateway. He let out a high-pitched yell of fear and ran to where the palisade's walkway met the supports for the nearest of the heavy wooden doors.

'The gates,' he screamed. The Twins reacted, running towards where the elder had disappeared from view.

Lucius ran on. His lungs burned. He was no more than twenty strides from the opening. The gate began to move. It was closing, tentatively at first, but soon picking up momentum. 'No,' he gasped.

With no more than a few strides to reach the opening, the gate crashed shut. He despaired. Only for an instant, as the heavy door rebounded against the central, vertical spar. A gap of around a handspan appeared. Lucius slammed, shoulder first, into its solid, bark-rough surface. The force of his impact opened the small gap further. He

122

was thrown to the ground by the impact on the solid door. Agonising pain lanced along his arm and side.

Through the agony's red mist Lucius saw the door was shutting again, as the defenders within renewed their efforts. But he had done enough. Barra and Keefe leapt over Lucius and smashed against the wood, driving the gate inwards. A gap of an arm's length opened up. Barra and Keefe slipped through, sweeping swords from their scabbards as they moved. The door slammed shut behind them.

Instantaneously the clash of steel and screams of war-cries erupted. Lucius got back onto his feet, and despite the pain, shoved his shoulder against the heavy door once more. It wouldn't budge.

'Make way, sir,' the shout came from behind him. It was Hrindenus. Lucius rolled to the side before getting to his feet. In that instant the blood encrusted head of the Tungrian filled his vision. The big man's bulk impacted against the door, immediately followed by Cai's. The iron hinges groaned. The gate swung wide as Lucius added his own weight.

All was chaos. Women screamed, pulling children to them as they dashed towards the dark entrances to three caves like deep ragged wounds in the cliff. Two individual duals were taking place. Barra and Keefe each battled with one of the twins. Keefe was forcing his red haired foe backwards with great sweeps of his sword, towards one of the cave mouths. Barra was on the backfoot, as he parried attack after attack from the other brother.

On the ground before them was the third defender. The older warrior had been propelled backwards as the door swung inwards. His eyes were wild with fear as, still on his arse, he attempted to draw his sword from its salt-

123

stained scabbard. But Hrindenus was quicker. The Tungrian stamped hard onto the desperately flailing man's arm. Lucius heard a sharp snap, accompanied by a piercing shriek. Hrindenus followed up with a swift punch to the prone warrior's jaw. He collapsed. Whether dead or unconscious, Lucius couldn't tell.

'Help Barra,' Cai shouted. Hrindenus grabbed the hilt of the half-drawn sword from the limp fingers of the old warrior.

'Tungriii!' Hrindenus charged towards the where the embattled warchief was being driven back against the palisade. The rocky ground was uneven and with each backward step Lucius saw the Novantae stumble, making it impossible for him to attempt a counter thrust.

However, Hrindenus's battlecry had shaken the Damnonii. The red-headed warrior, who wore only a sleeveless tunic and filthy chequered troos, turned sharply, the battle-lust dying in his eyes. His long fat-matted beard was flecked with spittle as his mouth twisted with fear at the unexpected arrival of this new enemy. The instant of distraction was enough.

Barra lunged. He knocked the Damnonii's blade aside and buried the point of his own into the warrior's shoulder. Barra's thrust must have sliced through tendons as an instant later the warrior's sword dropped to the rocky ground, released by lifeless fingers. Bemused, he stared at his arm as if willing it to move. Hrindenus swung his blade. A woman at the cave mouth screamed as the warrior's head bounced across the stony ground. It came to rest, with a squelch, in a narrow cleft between two rocks.

Lucius tore his sight from the Damnonii's headless body at the sound of strangled choking. He turned, in time to see Keefe end his own battle. The other twin had been pressed back against the wall of the cliff. He had raised his hands in an attempt to grasp the Hibernian's blood-covered blade that was embedded in his neck. Keefe twisted his sword pommel and Lucius heard its steel point grind against the stone of the cliff. The light fled from the Damnonii's eyes.

26

Cai took in the open ground around him. The settlement, if it could be called that, was a disordered mess. Jumbled branches of wood, washed white by the sea, lay in heaps around the interior. Wooden ribs from the wrecks of old boats were piled against the palisade, interspersed with the tangled remains of ancient fishing nests.

The whole place stank. A combination of rotting animal flesh and discarded fish carcasses, remnants of which were scattered all around. There were no buildings to speak of, only a few low huts only large enough for storage. But Cai cared nothing for this. He sought only one thing. One person.

He turned towards the dark maw of the largest cave entrance. A small group of women had gathered there, huddled closely together, casting fearful glances at this new band of men who had brought death to their community. However, not all appeared to dread the appearance of these strangers.

To the fore of the group stood a lone woman. She was short, though not stout. Muscled forearms, no doubt from long years of hauling nets, were crossed over her chest. Her long dark hair lay across her shoulders and, unlike the other women, appeared to be well kept.

A small head peered from behind the worn green material of her calf-length dress. Cai recognised the lad they had first seen on the shoreline with his bucket of crabs. The woman stared at the men, defiance in her eyes.

'Stay here,' Cai said to the others.

'There may be other men hidden within the caves,' Barra said. 'I'll come with you.'

'No,' Cai said, firmly. 'Their men are gone.' Barra snorted, but said no more.

Cai walked slowly towards the waiting women, his arms held out wide, the palms of his hands open to show he was unarmed. As he neared the lone woman and her son, she drew herself up, showing no fear. Cai knew it was an act and admired her for it.

When he was no more than ten paced from her, she spoke for the first time. 'Come no closer, we are armed.' Cai smiled, but stopped where he was.

'We mean you no harm,' Cai said. A sudden thought came to him. 'Are you the one who opened the gate to us?'

'Was it a mistake?' she asked.

'We seek only shelter. And for a woman who might have been brought captive to this place. My name is Cai.'

He saw the woman's shoulders noticeably relax and her scowl instantly transform with the slightest of smiles. Her voice softened as she spoke. 'I am Moira, Cai of the Nervii. Alyn said you would come.'

'Where is she?' Cai cast about, his sight roving between the other cave openings.

'She has gone from this place,' she said. The despair that instantly filled Cai must have been plain for Moira to see. 'She lives.'

'Where—'

'Come inside,' Moira said. 'I will tell you all.'

A short while later the group was seated around a hearth fire as the women brought them food, mainly bread and dried fish and a few mixed berries too. Cai and Moira sat on the furs of a cot towards the rear of the cave. Water dripped from the slick moss-covered walls, pooling in hollows at their base. The air was damp, not a place he would want to bide for very long. Despite the smell of

127

mould and rot, Moira had clearly made an attempt to keep this sleeping space clean. Her son, whose dark hair and brown eyes were the echo of his mother's, perched on a boulder nearby. He pretended to play with a stick, making regular, surreptitious glances towards Cai. Moira had told him to give them some privacy; the small distance was as far as the boy was prepared to concede.

'He wishes to protect his mother,' Cai said. 'A brave lad.'

'She saved him,' Moira said, and Cai heard the wonder in her voice. 'Alyn saved him.'

'How?'

'Fynn woke one morning with a cough,' she began, her words quiet so the boy didn't overhear. 'Over the next two days it got worse and his breathing became difficult. Until, eventually, each breath was a struggle. He was fading before my eyes. I felt powerless.

'Alyn sent women into the hills to gather all manner of herbs. She mixed some into a concoction that I helped him to drink. Others she crushed into a steaming cauldron and built a small canopy over it in which she had Fynn lie down. She repeated this over and over for the next two days and nights. His breathing bit by bit became less laboured, until he was almost himself again. He's still not as strong as he was, though he has improved with each rising of the sun.' She smiled at her son.

'Where is she, Moira?' he asked softly, dreading her answer.

'Blue Dog has taken her with him to the king making. Along with most of his warband. He left only those three behind. Not to protect us. To ensure we did not flee.' Her voice became a growl. 'We women are not their slaves. We are cattle.'

'Why didn't he leave her behind with the rest of the women?' Cai asked.

Moira stared at her hands, unconsciously picking at the dirt she saw there.

'I have to know, Moira. No matter the cost to me.'

She raised her head, meeting his eyes. She spoke quietly, but resolutely. 'Blue Dog wants to be king of the Damnonii. He has gone to stake his claim. He is not a normal man, you must understand this. He has an evil inside of him and much hatred. He is also cunning. As I understand it, the old king was not able to father children, no matter how many wives he took. Blue Dog thinks if he can prove his own virility, making future conflict over succession less likely, the Damnonii elite will look upon him with greater favour.'

'I'm sorry Moira,' Cai said. 'I still don't understand.'

She took a deep breath, not breaking eye contact with him. 'She tried to fight him for so long, you must know this. Until she could no longer. Alyn is with child.'

27

'Well, it appears that if Frang did indeed send a messenger to Blue Dog about our arrival, he didn't reach this island.' Barra said.

Moments before, Cai had relayed to Lucius and the others what the woman Moira had told him of Blue Dog's ambitions. His friend crouched by the fire and had disappeared into his own silent world of pain. Lucius looked on in silence as the Novantae paced before the hearth. He had not seen him so unsettled. 'Perhaps they met the fate that we narrowly evaded.'

'But why does Blue Dog believe he can be king?' Caden of the Damnonii was well when last I saw him. I sought him out in Rerigon before he took ship with the remainder of his men. Cynbel, our king, had been killed on the final day of the battle. I went to Caden to solicit his support, if it was needed, should there be a challenge to my consecration. He promised it. It makes no sense.'

'This stretch of water can be treacherous,' Keefe said. 'His boat could have foundered, or been caught in a storm.'

'Perhaps,' Barra said. 'But how would news of his loss travel so swiftly to Blue Dog's ears?'

Lucius kept his own counsel, waiting for the Novantae to settle. Barra stared silently into the flames, deep in thought. He turned suddenly, towards where the captive lay. The old man cradled his shattered arm, whimpering occasionally. They hadn't bothered to tie him up. If he attempted to run, he wouldn't get far.

Barra stepped from the fireside, striding over to the dishevelled warrior. He grabbed a handful of his tunic, yanking him to his feet, before manhandling him over to the others. The cave echoed with his childlike sobs.

He pushed the old man onto the rocky ground in front of the fire. Keefe, Hrindenus and Castellanos stared back at him in silence. Even Cai shook himself from his internal torment, if only for a short time.

Barra knelt by the prisoner, who flinched away from his malevolent stare. The warleader gently took hold of the old man's shattered arm as if tending an injured child. The Damnonii hissed but said nothing. When Barra spoke, it was with the calmest of voices, making his words all the more chilling.

'Tell me why Blue Dog thinks he can be king of the Damnonii?' he said, all the while gently holding the other's forearm. The answer immediately tumbled from the old man. His words fell over one another in a race to escape his tongue.

'Caden is dead. Blue Dog believes the other chiefs of the Damnonii fear him and will dare not challenge him when he makes his claim. He has taken his full warband to enforce his will should they try,' the warrior finished, breathing heavily.

'How does Blue Dog know that Caden is dead?' Barra persisted. 'How could news of this import have reached this shit hole so soon?' The Damnonii shrugged, lowering his head so as not to meet Barra's eyes.

A scream echoed around the cave.

'Please. I'll tell you.'

Barra eased his grip. The prisoner's howl turned to sobs, fat tears cascading across his cheeks. The Novantae gently held the old warrior's forearm once more in his left hand. With his right he gently stroked the injury as if he was one of his favoured hounds.

'How does he know the Damnonii king is dead?' Barra repeated. This time the old man answered, his voice shrill as he fought the pain.

'Caden and a small band foundered on the rocks on the eastern side of the island. They must have become separated from his other ships. Some of our men, out hunting, spotted them from their hiding place and recognised the king. They brought the news to Blue Dog.' The old man became silent again. Barra gently raised his damaged arm, the threat implicit.

'He killed the king, didn't he?' Barra's lips curled into a snarl. The old man nodded. 'How?'

'Blue Dog's plan was to meet them at their camp, where he would make his supplication and offer shelter and hospitality. Then when we had got them good and drunk with the ale we carried with us, we would slit their throats. But by the time we reached Caden's camp, night had almost fallen. So Blue Dog changed the plan. We would wait until full darkness and attack them as they slept.

'It was easy. They had camped in the shelter of sand dunes by the shoreline. Their fire could be seen from a great distance.' The words continued to tumble from the Damnonii, as if he wished to get his tale over with as quickly as possible. 'There were only eight of them and it was all over in moments. Their sentry had fallen asleep in the long grass of the dunes. The soft sand muffled our approach. We finished them off before they realised what was happening.'

'Who killed Caden?'

The prisoner's terror-filled eyes now met Barra's. 'Blue Dog. With his own knife.' A piercing shriek resounded from the cave walls as Barra gripped the damaged arm. Lucius saw the Novantae's face was almost white. Silent fury filled his eyes. The warchief recovered his composure.

'You will come with us to the king-making and tell this tale before the Damnonii chiefs. They may give you a quick death if you tell it true.' The old man folded in on himself, his head sinking to his knees. His shoulders shook as sobs overtook him once more.

Without a word Barra strode towards the cave entrance. Lucius followed. He caught up with the warchief as he reached the rocky shoreline. The sea was calm. Almost like smooth glass, Lucius thought. He waited at the big red-headed warrior's side. After some moments of listening to the gentle lapping of the waves and the cry of the gulls, Barra spoke.

'Caden was a fine warleader. I fought with him for many years against the Eagles. We came to respect one another, though we were not friends. I think he truly loved war. It was perhaps why he so readily raised the war banner when Cynbel asked for his support to drive the Romans from our lands.

'It grieves me he was murdered in such a cowardly way. It was his greatest weakness. He led in battle, less so during peace times. He should have dealt with the menace of Blue Dog long since. He was ever a thorn in his heel. He owed Caden his allegiance but continuously raided Damnonii lands, and others, from this island. I was surprised when Blue Dog answered the call to arms. Caden welcomed him to his warband. I think he reasoned it was better to keep him close than allow him freedom to raid.'

'I'm sorry,' Lucius said. Barra shrugged. Lucius asked the obvious question. 'What now?'

Barra nodded towards the old fishing boat. 'We will take that, and sail for the king-making. I'll take that wretch in the cave with me as proof of Blue Dog's treachery. You must decide if you will accompany us. It will be perilous for you. As a king I can offer my protection. But, I am not yet consecrated, and, perhaps, in the eyes of a few, not yet a true king. Some may choose to ignore the protection my status provides. Especially if your true identities become known.'

'If Cai goes, I go. I cannot speak for the others.'

'They must understand what they risk,' Barra said. 'They may lose more than their lives.'

HUNT

28

Cai had wedged himself into the bows of the fishing boat and was huddled inside the cloak he had taken from one of the dead Damnonii twins. The band had stayed in Blue Dog's settlement for the night, but he had spoken little to the others. They had sailed from the island, whose single peak was hidden from view by low cloud cover. His last words with Moira echoed continually in his mind.

'Alyn thought only of you. She knew you would come. But she has suffered greatly at the hands of Blue Dog. You must know she couldn't fight him anymore.' Could she not? His unspoken words of accusation caused a wave of shame to wash over him.

He had not been able to speak of it. Even with Lucius. How could he tell him the woman he sought had Blue Dog's child growing in her belly?

Lucius had told him he and the others had spoken and would not abandon him. They would meet their fate together. He had tried to dissuade them. Cai knew in his heart that it had only been a cursory attempt. He needed them. But knowing this only added to his misery.

As before, Keefe was at the tiller. The sail billowed in the strengthening wind, driving them northwards. There were two oars used for pushing away from rocks. They would be of little use if the band were unlucky enough to come across a naval patrol again.

Barra and Lucius sat in the stern, near the Hibernian. They spoke to one another in quiet tones. Castellanos and Hrindenus were seated side by side to the fore of Cai, his knees almost touching their backs. The pain of the Tungrian's head wound had made him morose and he

135

barely muttered when the Greek had tried to engage him in conversation. Completing the party was the prisoner. No one had bothered to ask his name. They did not want to feel any pity for a dead man. He sat by the mast. The medicus had set his arm and strapped it, but the old man still cradled it with the other.

Keefe had told them the journey by sea would take them no more than a further two days if the weather held. Followed by another to negotiate a winding river.

'What is that land to the west?' Lucius asked Barra, nodding over the Novantae's shoulder.

'It is the kingdom of the Epidii,' Barra replied.

'It is a long arm of land thrust into the sea of Hibernia,' Keefe added. 'On a good day its southern extreme can be seen from the lands of my people. We will follow its coastline until evening and anchor off it for the night.'

Castellanos groaned. 'Another night at sea.'

'It's too great a risk to make a landing for the night,' Barra said. 'The Epidii are an insular people who seldom welcome strangers. Only our holy men are unmolested. They think nothing of the People's fight with the Eagles, who have always been wise enough to leave the Epidii lands untouched.'

'You do not see them as of the People?' Lucius asked.

'If you saw them, you would see why,' Barra said, becoming thoughtful. 'They are an ancient tribe. Perhaps descended from the original men who lived in this land in the time before time, whose tales are long forgotten.'

'They sound just delightful,' Hrindenus chirped in. 'Let's not go there.'

Cai listened to the exchange as if from another world. His mind and body were drained. Despite the discomfort of the cramped conditions, he drifted into an exhausted sleep.

136

HUNT

A woman screamed in the darkness. Cai was startled awake, his heart pounding. All was grey. The crew of the boat were as they had been before, but they inhabited a world of mist.

'We cannot go on in this,' Keefe said, his voice a whisper. 'Our course was taking us close to the shoreline before we lost sight of it. We risk losing another boat on the rocks if we push on.'

'It's not yet midday,' Barra said, letting his frustration show. 'What do you suggest?

'Drop the anchor stone, lord,' Keefe replied. 'Wait for this to pass.'

Barra made a grumbling sound. 'Very well. Let it be done.'

Cai touched Hrindenus on the shoulder. The big man nodded. With a grunt of effort, he picked up the heavy brown stone at his feet, held in a mesh of knots. He dropped it over the side. In moments the line was taut, the side of the boat listing slightly with its weight.

'It hasn't touched bottom,' Hrindenus said.

'Shit. We'll have to move closer to shore.' The Hibernian closed his eyes, listening. 'That way,' he said pointing.

'How do you know?' Hrindenus asked, sceptically.

'Because, *Roman,* I have ears,' Keefe replied, giving Hrindenus a stare that Cai had seen many a time on the face of a Centurion on the parade-ground. 'I can hear the waves rush across the pebbles as they meet the beach.' The Hibernian addressed the others in hushed tones. 'We must only speak in whispers. If there are Epidii nearby, our voices may carry to them.' He turned back to Hrindenus. 'Take an oar,' Hrindenus smiled and shrugged, moving to the bench behind the mast. Lucius did likewise. Cai hauled up the anchor stone.

'Slow strokes,' Keefe said. 'No splashes.' Hrindenus and Lucius did as instructed, their oar paddles lightly caressing the water. In moments, the shushing of waves advancing and retreating on the shoreline was clear for all to hear.

'Rocks,' Barra hissed a warning.

'The anchor,' Keefe commanded. Cai moved quickly, dropping the heavy stone over the side with a splash. The sound, loud in the still air, caused the others to wince. The stone hit bottom and Cai grabbed the rope, halting the boat's momentum. The rocks were perilously close, their peaks covered and uncovered with each rise and fall of the swell.

Keefe cast around, surveying the location. Nothing could be seen beyond three or four spear lengths. 'We can't stay here. The anchor stone will drag on the bottom and we will be pulled towards the rocks.'

'Let's try farther along the coast,' Lucius suggested.

Keefe shook his head. 'It's too great a risk in this murk.'

'There's only one option,' Cai said from behind them all. 'We must chance the shore. If we have not already been overheard, we can drag the boat above the tideline and take cover as best we can until this mist clears.' Both Keefe and Barra were unhappy with the idea. In fact, Cai saw fear in their eyes. Which worried him all the more.

'Very well then,' Barra said. Castellanos groaned and touched the dark wood of his box as if for luck.

'No,' the prisoner whined. 'We must not go there.'

'Shut your hole, wretch,' Keefe snarled. The old Damnonii recoiled.

Using the oars to fend off the rocks they advanced towards the rising sound of the surf. All strained their eyes and ears for any sign a hidden enemy awaited them. The bows of the fishing boat came to a juddering halt as it crunched against the shingle.

Cai was first to step from the boat into the shallow, chill waters of the Epidii's kingdom. He drew his sword slowly from its scabbard. Another gift from the twin. The others did the same. Only Castellanos had no weapon. All six waited, as if frozen, for a time, as the surf rose and fell around their knees. They listened, ready to push the boat back out to sea at the first sign of an attack. Nothing. Not even of sea birds. Only the gentle ebb and flow of the waves.

29

Lucius came to sit next to Cai, who leant against a rock. His head rested against the pale green lichen that obscured the true nature of the stone below. His friend stared towards the mist-shrouded beach.

They had pulled the boat onto the shingle, the crunching sound of their passing seeming to call out their presence. There was a patch of bedraggled and wind-bent trees nestled amongst low sand dunes. No place to build a camp, but good enough, they hoped, to conceal them for a brief time. Keefe and Barra kept a watch at opposite ends of their hiding place, a spears-throw apart.

Lucius slid down the rock so his shoulder touched Cai's. He spoke, his voice barely above a whisper. 'Tell me what ails you, brother? Not finding Alyn is a great disappointment, but there is still hope we will discover her at their holy place. There must be more to this than you have told me.'

Cai did not immediately respond. Lucius waited, knowing something must be greatly amiss. Cai rubbed the heels of his hands into his eyes as if trying to clear his vision.

'She's with child,' he said. 'She has that bastard's spawn growing inside her.' Lucius heard the rage in his friend's voice. 'I am going to kill him slowly for this.' Cai fell silent, and Lucius again waited. 'What am I to do, Lucius? If we find her, what am I to do? She carries another man's child. I swore to protect and watch over her. But how...'

'One step at a time, Cai,' Lucius said. 'First we must find her. Though remember this is not her doing.' Lucius gathered his thoughts. 'I know you love her still, that cannot have changed?'

Cai nodded. Lucius noted there was no hesitation from his friend.

'Well, that's the starting point. She will have been changed by her ordeals. But time can heal many wounds, even the most egregious.' A sudden thought came to Lucius. 'Has it occurred to you that the babe could be yours?'

Cai turned sharply to Lucius, his eyes wide with surprise. It was clear his friend had not thought of it. 'But—' Cai began.

Lucius cut across him.

'Surely the timing works? I saw how close you were on the eve of the battle,' Lucius smiled at Cai. He saw his friend's eyes fill with hope.

'Perhaps,' Cai said. Even though it is a small hope Lucius thought, it was still hope.

A horse whinnied. Both turned sharply towards the sound, coming from the direction over which Barra kept watch. They could see nothing in the dense sea mist. Both men reached for their sword hilts. Lucius saw Hrindenus, who sat nearby with the shivering Castellanos, had already drawn his and was in a crouching stance. The prisoner whimpered from where he lay.

An instant later Barra appeared from the murk. 'Horsemen,' he whispered. 'I couldn't tell how many.' Moments later the big shape of Keefe emerged on near-silent feet.

'We're surrounded on three sides,' he said.

'Can we get to the boat?' Lucius asked.

'Let's try,' Barra responded. He waved his hand at Hrindenus and Castellanos to gather in close. As a group, they moved back-to-back, crab-like, edging towards where the fishing boat lay. As they reached the beach they crunched onto the shingle. A shrill shout, in a language Lucius did not recognise, pierced the still air. There was a rumble of hooves, swiftly turning to a grinding, mashing sound. The dark shapes of mounted men swam in and out of the mist. A yip-yipping cry erupted around them. For the first time Lucius caught sight of one of the horsemen. He had long dark hair that stuck out in wide spikes, greased by yellowing animal fat. His chin was scraped clean. Unlike the warriors Lucius was familiar with, he had no discernible tattoos on his dark skin. He wore troos and a jerkin made of a grey-coloured animal skin.

The horse he rode was even smaller than the ones he was used to seeing the other tribes ride. It gave him an almost childlike look. If a child had a fierce face, baring wolf-like teeth and holding a vicious-looking spear. The riders circled the six so rapidly it was impossible to count their numbers. Still, Lucius saw they were greatly outnumbered. There was no escape.

30

The dark, snaking waters of the river were a welcome relief to Alyn. The discomfort of the continual toss and roll of the sea journey northwards had been difficult. She had emptied her stomach over the side more than once much to the amusement of the crew. Now, with the steady dip and rise of the oars, they were making progress towards their destination. Wherever that was.

She sat upon a coiled rope next to the mast, whose sail had been stowed as soon as they had reached the river's mouth. Low, tree covered hills could be seen to the west and east, yet at some distance. At first the river's edge had been shrouded by tall, straw-coloured reeds eventually given way to fallow fields, the harvesting time long past.

Two bands of horsemen appeared on either bank. Perhaps forty in total. They were silent. Even when Blue Dog hailed them. This was no honour-guard, she thought. Urgent discussion ensued within the crew of the boat that was cut off by a snarled command from their lord. It appeared this was not the welcome they had hoped for. She had smiled at that.

Four other boats accompanied them. The sum total of Blue Dog's warband. She feared for Moira and the others, left behind with those three animals.

The past two weeks had been a blur. Starting with his discovery she was with child. She had barely acknowledged it to herself, not wanting to accept the possibility of a child being brought into the barbaric world Blue Dog had created on his godforsaken island. When her sickness had made it obvious, to the other women at least, she had hoped they would remain silent and that she could hide it from him for a time. The brute still came to her each night, or any other time he wanted to quench his lust. Eventually, he had uncovered her secret. She shuddered at the memory.

With a final sigh, he had rolled from her and lay on his back in the furs of her cot. His chest rising and falling briskly from his exertions. He had reeked of sweat, his breath foetid with the stench of ale and dried fish.

Since she had stopped resisting him, he had ceased the beatings. As long as she welcomed him to her bed, her life, in its own way, had become almost bearable. Her skills as a healer had been welcomed by the women. Even by some of the men, who approached her with all manner of ailments. She had come to be respected to a small degree. But try as she might, she could not shut out the memories of her former life. The grief felt for the loss of Beren and for the man she loved at times overwhelmed her.

When she thought of Cai it was with a mixture of hope and despair. Because she knew he would come for her. And he would find her, she was convinced of it. When he found her, Blue Dog would kill him.

That night as she lay next to the mad Damnonii, praying he was done, he spoke to her. In all the other times, after he had spilled his seed into her like a beast, he had left her for his own cot. Or to carry on drinking with his men.

'Your belly does not show, but you are with child, slave, is it not so?' He had whispered into her ear. It had taken all her will not to flinch, which would have brought on another beating. He stroked the palm of his calloused hand across her abdomen. 'You are with child?' He repeated. 'I hear all that goes on in my lands.' She had heard the usual maliciousness in his voice turn to something else. What was it? Excitement?

'Yes.' Was all she had uttered, fearing to say more.

'It is mine?' His voice became fierce. 'Don't lie to me bitch. I will know.'

'Yes, it is yours,' she said. 'Your men fear you too much to come near me.'

'Why have you kept it from me? You hoped to rid yourself of it, perhaps?'

She shook her head. 'I wasn't sure,' she lied.

Since then, he had left her alone, not coming to her as he had done before. Nor did he speak to her, other than to give her orders. Though she often caught him staring at her, with a thoughtful expression.

A few nights later, there had been much excitement in the settlement. A hunting party had returned with news of a warband landed on the eastern side of the island. Blue Dog had quickly gathered his men to meet them. They had returned the following night in triumph, but not a word passed the lips of his warriors on who this mysterious band had been.

Two days later they had set sail for the north. He had told her she would be coming with them. All Alyn had been able to glean from the other men's women was they were to journey to their holy place. For a king making.

The destination held no interest for her. As she rested against the smooth wood of the mast, Alyn gently smoothed her hand across her belly. She had her own small hope in all her despair. Perhaps, she thought, the timing worked.

They had been following the river's course for much of the day. The hills had begun to close in, the fields disappeared and dense woods of red pine pressed near to the bank. Their escort continued to shadow the small flotilla, though they had to work hard to keep up.

As the sun descended behind the trees on the west bank, the winding river presented the five boats with another bend to negotiate. As they made the turn, Alyn gasped at what she saw. What could only be described as a lake lay before them. But this lake's surface was hidden by a solid covering of tall reeds that rippled in the evening breeze.

The course ahead, however, was clear. As the river ended, an arrow straight channel cut through the tall grasses.

Blue Dog left his usual place at the aft of the boat, coming to stand in the bows, placing his hand on Alyn's shoulder as he passed. Not to give comfort she knew, only for balance as he made his way forwards.

'There,' he said, pointing through the channel and the sea of reeds. He turned to Alyn, his watery gaze upon her. She shuddered involuntarily at the mixture of excitement and madness she saw there.

'There, I will be made king,' he said to her. She noticed two of his men surreptitiously glance at one another. In this instant of unguardedness, she saw the fear in their eyes. What frightens them? But the question vanished from her mind upon seeing what Blue Dog had meant.

Rising above the continuously swaying grasses of the lake, as if it floated on the very air, was a fortress on a hill. It was not like the Novantae's sacred hill, near her home. This one was smaller and appeared to grow from the grey rock upon which it sat. Hearth-smoke rose from the peaked roof of a large stone-built hall. It spoke of age and grandeur. And even though they were still at some distance, she could hear the screams.

31

A shout. No, a command was barked from amongst the circling horsemen. Though Cai didn't understand the words their meaning was clear.

'They want us to lay down our weapons,' Barra said, his voice strained.

'Fuck that,' Hrindenus said. Keefe spat onto the shingle, in agreement with the Tungrian's sentiment.

The group stood in their circle. Five swords pointing outwards with Castellanos and his ever present box along with the hunched and shivering prisoner at the centre. Their feet crunched continually in the shingle of the beach.

A spear landed between Barra's feet. The shaft fell to the pebbly ground, the point unable to penetrate. The threat was explicit. Cai was sure the next spear cast would not be a warning.

He was barged aside. The Damnonii prisoner burst from the frail protection of the circle of swordsmen. He ran across the pebbled beach, in the direction of the boat. The mist swallowed him.

'Come back you fool,' Barra shouted. An instant later a piercing scream emanated from the murk. Instantly cut off. There was a brief silence, before the commanding voice shouted once again.

'We have no choice,' Lucius said. 'It's either die here on this godsforsaken beach or release our swords and hope for mercy. Perhaps escape later.'

'Fool,' Keefe growled. 'The Epidii don't suffer uninvited guests in their lands.'

'The Tribunus is right, my friend,' Barra said. 'Whilst we live there is always hope.' He turned to the Hibernian and nodded, tossing his sword onto the ground before him. With a sigh Keefe followed the example of his lord.

'Bollocks,' Hrindenus said, dropping his blade. Cai and Lucius next. All waited with arms helplessly by their sides. All except Castellanos. The medicus still clutched onto his box. For a short time, the only sounds to be heard were their own heavy breathing and the shushing of the unseen waves on the shoreline.

Moments later dark shapes crunched out of the mist on foot. Spears levelled. The largest of the warriors looked at Cai, hatred in his eyes. He bellowed another unrecognisable command, jabbing his spearpoint at the ground.

'I believe he wants us to kneel,' Barra said.

'We really are fucked,' Hrindenus responded.

Cai knelt, his knees pressing painfully against the pebbles. The others followed his lead. Castellanos continued to stand. The Greek cast around wildly as if for some way to escape. The big warrior screamed his order once again, the greased points of his hair shaking erratically with his movement. The medicus remained standing, as if his feet were transfixed.

'Kneel, brother,' Cai hissed. 'Before they—'

The warrior swung his spear shaft in an arc. Its butt-end struck the side of Castellanos's head. The Athenian dropped like a stone, his box, released by his powerless fingers, tumbled onto the beach.

Hrindenus began to rise. 'You bastards,' he shouted, swiftly silenced as the point of another's spear appeared before his eyes. The Tungrian lowered himself once more to his knees.

Warriors stepped amongst them, binding their hands with strips of hide. They were manhandled to their feet. The big warrior, clearly the leader of this band, jabbed his spear in a direction that would take them away from the shoreline. He snarled another order. There was no need for Barra to attempt a translation as the five stumbled from the beach.

Cai watched as two warriors bundled Castellanos's unconscious body across the neck of a pony. His precious box was taken by another. He hoped the medicus was not badly hurt.

The captives soon passed through the tortured woodland in which they had hidden and into a green landscape filled with waist-deep swathes of fern and bracken. The undergrowth was wet from recent rainfall and within moments Cai's troos were sodden. The material chafed his thighs, soon making each step uncomfortable.

The ground rose steadily. The mist cleared, revealing a dark green and purple coloured sweep of mountains. The party snaked up a narrow pass, with Barra at its head and Cai bringing up the rear. The horsemen, fifteen at Cai's count, flanked their prisoners.

They walked for what felt like an eternity. At one point, reaching the saddle between two summits, Cai realised he could discern the Hibernian sea before him and to his rear. He remembered Keefe's description of the Epidii land jutting into the sea like an arm. As the day's light was fading, the group crested a final rise to reveal a wide valley below them.

At its heart was a heather covered hill, its heights encircled by a stout palisade and single ditch. Sheep and cattle grazed on the surrounding heights and valley floor.

Within the bounds of the palisade were a number of roundhouses, with many more cradling the foot of the hill from which a pathway made its way up to a narrow gateway in the defences. Cai could see people moving about the lower settlement.

Some of the riders kicked their mounts into a trot, rushing ahead of the others.

'Going to announce the arrival of honoured guests I assume,' Lucius said over his shoulder.

'I'm sure we'll be afforded a warm welcome,' Cai returned, his levity forced.

As the riders reached the settlement, sounds of excitement arose, quickly spreading. Soon Cai could see groups of women and children rushing eagerly up the hill towards them.

'Oh great. A welcoming committee,' Hrindenus said. 'If my hands were free, I would be holding onto my balls.'

A small band of wiry, swarthy-skinned children were the first to reach them. They screeched with excitement. The nearest, a slight, dark haired boy, approached Barra with no sign of fear. Without hesitation, he kicked hard at the chieftain's shin. The Novantae spat a curse. The mounted warriors laughed at his discomfort.

'Little shit. I'll have your balls,' Barra growled at the child. Who, encouraged by the laughter of the warriors and the wild calls of the other children came in for a second go. This time, Barra sidestepped the attempt and the boy slipped onto his arse with a heavy thump. The other children howled with laughter and the boy's filthy face flushed a dark crimson.

Moments later the first group of women arrived. Some ran to the horsemen, greeting them warmly. Most turned to the five bound prisoners, spitting their hate into men's faces. One crone loosed the bindings of her dress, baring her wrinkled and flaccid breasts at Keefe. She shook them with enthusiasm at the Hibernian, cackling all the while, her lips wide in a toothless grin.

'I think she's taken with you,' Hrindenus said. 'You should—' The Tungrians' words were cut off as the hag grabbed between his legs. Cai saw her raise a smile that, on a younger woman, would have been alluring. But, on her warted lips was more akin to an old she-wolf sizing up a cornered prey.

The baiting of the bedraggled group continued until they reached the settlement at the base of the hillfort. The riders warned off the women and children as they approached the winding pathway leading to the palisade above.

Cai felt exhausted. His troos had dried during the forced march and had become salt encrusted, increasing his discomfort. His thighs burned as they ascended the steep hillside. He could tell his companions were in a bad way too. Underfoot the ground had become loose. Lucius slipped and with his hands bound behind him was unable to prevent his fall. He turned his head at the last instant, landing with his cheek in the dirt.

A rider appeared from the rear and shouted another command in their unintelligible tongue. Lucius struggled to his knees and onto his feet.

'Are you all right, brother?' Cai asked

'Fine,' Lucius said, his voice terse.

Eventually they reached the entrance to the fortress. Its doorway was only wide enough to allow only two horsemen to enter side by side. They passed through the portal and into an open area, crowded with the fort's inhabitants, all with the tribe's dark complexion. Unlike the people in the settlement below, they stared back in silence. Their eyes seemed hooded and doleful as if from long grief.

151

The five were halted by the crush of humanity. One of the warriors shouted what, to Cai, sounded like a warning and the crowd moved slowly aside with a hush of whispered conversations.

'Cheery bunch,' Hrindenus said.

'Something is amiss here,' Keefe said, his voice low.

They were ushered between multiple roundhouses, the smell of cooking from hearth fires torture for the hungry men. There was a larger hut at the heart of the settlement and, at first, Cai thought they were being driven towards it. But, as they neared, one of the riders growled, pointing his spear towards a small stock pen. It appeared to have only recently been vacated by its previous occupants. The ground was mud-splattered and caked in drying animal shit.

The warrior dismounted and unlatched its small gate. The five walked through, their wrist bindings cut one at a time. There was no dry area to sit without their troos being heavily soiled. They congregated at its heart.

'Where's Castellanos?' Lucius asked. Cai had forgotten about the medicus, lost in his own travails. There was no sign of him amongst the horsemen. Barra stepped forward and, haltingly, managed to converse with their leader. The discussion with the big warrior was short and terse, but fruitful.

'He lives,' Barra said. 'I think he is being cared for in one of the other huts. It appears he has not yet regained consciousness.'

'What next?' Lucius asked.

Barra shrugged. 'We wait.'

An instant later a child's scream pierced the air. The tortured sound came from the largest roundhouse.

'I hope that's not what's next,' Hrindenus said

HUNT

32

The animal skin covering the doorway was flung open and a young woman ran out. The anguish on her face was plain to see. She dashed between the other buildings, disappearing from sight.

'A child's pain. Not torture, it would seem,' Lucius said.

Moments later the woman reappeared. Moving urgently, she held a green-leafed plant. The instant before pulling the door-skin back once more, she glanced towards the pen where the captives stood. Lucius saw her eyes narrow for an instant, before she ducked inside.

'A real beauty,' Hrindenus said, his voice filled with awe.

'Beyond a wretch like you,' Keefe said, his voice terse.

'I don't know,' Hrindenus replied. 'Your sister, now there's a beaut—' Keefe's hand clamped around the big man's throat.

'Don't speak of my sister, Roman,' Keefe roared into the face of the Tungrian. 'You're not fit to utter her name. Do not even think of her.'

'Enough,' Barra growled. Keefe did not relent, Hrindenus's face turning bright red. He grasped the big warrior's wrist in both hands in an attempt to break the other's grip. But the Hibernian did not yield. Lucius had seen this red mist of transitory hatred in men's eyes before. He moved to intervene. As he took his first step the Hibernian collapsed to his knees, releasing his hold. His fall was accompanied with an almost woman-like yelp.

Hrindenus gasped for breath, all the while rubbing at his neck, as red welts appeared on the skin's surface.

153

'Bastard,' he wheezed. 'I hope your balls turn black.' Keefe remained on his knees, his head tucked into his broad chest, his red hair hiding his bearded face. After a few moments he slowly raised his head.

'I'll make you pay Roman.'

The Vexillarius straightened, holding the other's stare. 'Well, I suppose I'll just have to take Niamh as my wife without your consent.' A sound more akin to a beast than of a man filled the air. Keefe launched himself at Hrindenus. But the Hibernian made little progress as Barra's boot connected with his jaw. The big warrior collapsed onto his face in the mud and shit. The guards, standing nearby, laughed uproariously.

'You fool,' Barra spoke quietly into the ear of his stunned friend. 'Save your strength for the real fight to come.' Keefe groaned, slowly raising himself from the mire once more. Standing on unsteady feet, he turned to Hrindenus with a look of loathing, holding it for a lingering moment before shuffling to the far side of the animal pen.

'Get over there,' Cai ordered Hrindenus, nodding towards the opposite side of the pen. 'I don't want to hear another word uttered from that idiotic mouth of yours.'

Another scream came from the largest hut, the sound more pitiable than the first. The young woman did not reappear. Darkness began to descend and the group slumped into silence.

Torches were lit outside of each roundhouse and along the palisade. As the sky turned to blackness, they heard the sound of hammering from deeper within the fortress. It lasted some time before all was silent once more. Lucius began to feel uneasy.

The roofs of the roundhouses were silhouetted by the glow from a large fire, hidden from the five at the other

side of the settlement. A slow chanting began, arising
from the throats of many men. The sound undulated. At
its heart was a single word, repeated over and over.

'What is it?' Cai asked.

'They are calling upon one of their gods,' Barra said. 'It
is not one I have heard before.'

'It is Arawn,' Keefe said, his voice low. Respectful. 'My
people know this god too. He is the dark one. He who
escorts the dead to the otherworld.'

The chanting continued unabated. The animal skin to
the entrance of the largest hut was pulled back, for the first
time since the young woman had re-entered. A grey-
haired head emerged first, followed by the frail body of
an old man. He seemed ancient. He was clothed in the
same skins as the doorway and swaddled like a babe in
arms. He held a stout pole in one hand on which he leant
for support. He turned back to the doorway, offering his
free hand. The young woman appeared, gently clasping
the palm of the elder. Neither glanced towards the pen and
the captives there. They processed side by side, chins held
high, the woman supporting the old man as they
disappeared from view.

'I have a bad feeling about this,' Hrindenus said, from
the deeper darkness at the back of the pen. No one replied.
They all felt the same.

The chanting ceased. It was replaced by the sound of a
reedy voice, raised to speak to an audience and yet weak.
Was it the old man? The chieftain? I'll have answers soon,
Cai thought, as a group of warriors appeared from the
direction of the fire. Joined by their two guards the men
entered the animal pen and began to bind their hands.

'We should never have given up our swords,' Hrindenus
said, his voice sullen. The warriors jostled the group out
of the small stockade, pushing them towards the light of

the unseen fire. They reached the open area before the small gateway. It was filled, once again, with what must have been the entire population of the village. Men, women and even a number of children. The chant was taken up again. This time, with a greater note of urgency.

At the heart of the crowd was a solid, wooden pole, much like the mast of their fishing boat. The timber was freshly cut and had been thrust into the ground to the fore of the barred gate. Cai's heart sank as he saw the branches of dressed kindling surrounding its base. A small fire, much like a hearthfire, had been set next to it. Except there was no pot set to boil hanging above its flames.

Close by the fire sat the old man. He perched in a high-backed chair, the parody of a throne of a great king. To Cai, he had a birdlike appearance. A crow staring at carrion. The beautiful young woman stood by his side, her hand resting on the bird's shoulder.

Cai heard a bustling in the crowd. Two warriors pushed their way through on the opposite side from where the captives waited. Between them they chivvied along a white-faced Castellanos. His head was bound in a rough material. He was led to the others and shoved unceremoniously amongst them.

'Glad to have you back with us,' Lucius said.

'I only hope it isn't for the final time,' he replied, his voice quiet.

The old chieftain arose on stiff legs from his chair, aided by the woman, who held him gently by his arm. Only when he was steady did she release her hold.

The ancient one raised his hands into the air. Instantly the chanting ceased. He began to speak, in the same reedy voice they had heard from the pen.

'Do you know what he's saying?' Cai asked Barra.

156

'It's difficult,' he said. 'I think the woman is his daughter. He said something about a grandson.'

'They are asking Arawn to exchange the grandson's place in the otherworld. They offer us instead.' Keefe said, his voice emotionless. 'One life for six.'

33

At a rasping command from the old chieftain, two warriors stepped forward. Cai feared they were coming for him. Instead they grabbed Lucius. Each held him roughly under an arm, hauling him towards the post.

'Lucius,' Cai stepped forward. A spearpoint was thrust at his face, halting him in his tracks. With his hands bound, there was nothing he could do. He spat at the guard impotently. The warrior simply grinned back, revealing dark, tainted teeth.

Lucius struggled as they attempted to tie him to the post. His knees buckled as a wild punch connected with his jaw. His head lolled onto his chest.

'Bastards!' Cai screamed. But his attempt to get to Lucius was met with the thrust of a spearbutt into his ribs. An Epidii warrior snarled and threatened him with the spear's point this time. Cai remained still, teeth bared in fury and frustration. He could do nothing.

In short order Lucius's arms were bound to the post. His head too was strapped to the wood with a thin tongue of leather. His eyelids fluttered open, a dazed sheen to his eyes. Suddenly, realising where he was, he began to struggle. To no avail; his bindings held him tightly.

Cai could not tear his sight from his friend. He had expected the kindling at Lucius's feet to be set alight immediately; instead at a nod from the old chieftain a bare-chested warrior tore Lucius's tunic, neck to navel, baring his upper body. Next, he stepped to the small fire, retrieving something from its hot heart. Cai couldn't see what it was until the man turned. It glowed red. A long iron blade. Not quite a sword, more than a dagger.

The warrior moved to Lucius, who struggled frantically. The crowd began its chant once more. 'Arawn.'

The silhouette of the warrior blocked their view of Lucius, like a malignant shadow. A scream, part shriek, part howl mingled with the low tone of the chanting. The tortured sound continued for what felt an eternity. He saw his friend's legs thrash. The smell of burning flesh hit Cai like a blow. Bile filled his mouth. He would have vomited but his stomach was long empty.

Eventually, after Lucius let out a final piercing scream, the chanting ceased and a chilling silence descended. The warrior stepped away from his grizzly work. Cai wretched at the sight. Lucius's head appeared to rest on his left shoulder. He had lost consciousness. But it was his friend's chest that drew his attention. The blade had left puckered red and black welts raised on the skin. The air smelled of roasting meat, and opaque juices slid across Lucius's muscled stomach. He had soiled himself.

This was no random torture before an execution. On Lucius's chest the Epidii warrior had carved a face. Its round head contained two large, blistered eyes. A long nose ran between the orbs to meet a slit for a mouth. Not a man's face. For, surmounted on top of its skull were two stubby horns.

'Arawn,' Keefe said in awe. 'The horned god.'

Lucius's trial was not over. With another rasping word from the chieftain the warrior stepped to the fire once more. This time he retrieved a burning firebrand. Cai could not take his eyes from his friend, whose head now lolled over his chest. Perhaps he would not wake as the fire took hold. Perhaps he would not feel the agony.

'Barra. Speak for me,' Castellanos said, as he pushed past Cai, nudging him aside. The medicus stepped to the fore of the captives. A guard thrust a spear towards him, the medicus ignored the threat. Instead, he stopped, holding his head high.

'I am Castellanos the Greek,' he shouted. 'I am a healer. I can save your grandson.'

Barra, initially caught by surprise, now translated the Athenian's words and added some of his own.

'I am Barra, chieftain of the Novantae people, my words speak true. This man healed my own nephew.' He had spoken some Epidii words but mostly in the language of the People. The effect was instantaneous. The young woman stared at Castellanos. Cai had never seen such a look of hope.

'She understands your language,' Cai said to Barra. He watched as she spoke urgently to the chieftain who, for the first time, became animated. He raised his hand, halting the warrior who held the burning brand over the kindling.

The chief spoke in the language of the Epidii, waving both Castellanos and Barra forwards. They were nudged by the spear shafts of two of their guards.

'You are truly a healer?' The young woman asked, failing to hide the note of hope from her words. She spoke confidently in the language of the People.

'Yes,' Castellanos said, in his professional voice. 'If you return my box to me, I can tend to the one who suffers. But you must first release my attendants and let me care for my man there.' He nodded towards Lucius, who still hung unmoving from the post.

She raised herself up, truly a chieftain's daughter, Cai thought. 'Very well,' she said. 'But, if you fail, I will make sure you all suffer much before you meet Arawn.

34

Lucius's chest was on fire. He saw the snarling warrior's face in the darkness, whose laughter accompanied each of his screams.

'The honey will help.' Why could he hear Castellanos in the night? Where was that damned Greek?

'One of the cuts has exposed bone.' Cai was there too. Lucius tried to call out to his friend, but his tongue seemed caught.

'I cannot sew the wounds, they're too tender. I will simply have to bind them and let the honey do the work.'

His eyes opened. The searing pain tore a shriek from his throat, forcing his eyes tight shut once more. In that instant he had seen a low roof, part hidden by hazy hearth smoke.

'Drink this, Tribunus,' Castellanos said. Lucius felt his head being lifted. He opened his eyes once more to see the concerned face of Cai staring back at him. The medicus appeared. He felt the coolness of a small clay pot touch his lips and bitter liquid slide across his tongue.

'No, don't spit it out,' Castellanos said, and Lucius felt his jaw held shut by a warm hand.

'You will sleep for a time,' the Greek said. As consciousness began to slip from him once more, Lucius heard his friend speak as if from a great distance.

'Will he live?'

'It will depend on whether the burns become infected. The next day should tell.'

Blackness embraced him.

Moments later, the burning returned, though less intense. There was a tightness restricting his breathing. He attempted to draw a deep breath, hissing through his clenched teeth as pain lanced sharply across his chest.

'Are you back with us, brother?' Cai said. Lucius tried to open his eyes, they seemed gummed together. He felt a cool, damp cloth pass over his brow. His eyes fluttered open.

Cai's face materialised through his fogged vision. His friend's chin was showing the fair stubble of an early growth of a beard. *How long have I slept?*

'Where—' Lucius croaked.

'Wait a moment,' Cai said, disappearing from his view. When he reappeared to hover over Lucius once more it was to raise his head, putting a beaker of cool water to his dry, cracked lips.

'Where are the others?' Lucius asked, breathlessly, after he had taken a final, glorious gulp.

'They're being held in another of the huts. I've not seen them since we were brought to this dwelling. Castellanos and I have been allowed to stay by your side whilst he also tends to the boy. Look.' He nodded over his shoulder. Lucius turned his head and could see two silhouetted figures huddled over a cot by the hearthfire. One was clearly the medicus, the other must be the young woman. Their heads were close together as they talked in murmurs.

Lucius was confused. 'How long?'

Cai smiled. 'You have slept for two days and a night. The sun is setting on the second day since they did that to you.' Lucius saw a flash of anger in Cai's eyes as he stared at the bindings.

'I can still feel the blade.' Lucius winced, his voice barely above a whisper. 'Did the bastard carve a pretty picture?' Cai nodded, almost imperceptibly, not able to bring himself to speak of it. 'What has happened as I slept?'

'You should rest, brother. I can tell you later.'

'I've slept enough.'

Cai sighed. 'Very well,' he said. 'Keefe was right. The grandson of the old chieftain was dying. He had a canker the size of a fist on his neck. When I caught a glimpse of it, I thought we were doomed. The boy was all bones and no flesh. His skin as white as the winter snows.

'Was dying?' Lucius croaked the question.

'Well. After he had seen to your wounds, Castellanos examined the boy. He poked and prodded at the canker. The boy moaned a bit but didn't move. He spoke to the chief's daughter and told her the lump had to be removed. When he showed her his implements, in that box of his, she blanched a bit. When he explained there was no choice, if he was to save the lad's life, she accepted his word without question. I thought she might threaten us with a painful death again. Instead, she simply stayed by Castellanos's side to assist as best she could. The Greek certainly has a way with him.

'He asked me to help. We prepared battle dressings and sharpened the blades of the small knives he calls scalpels. We soaked them in a golden drink that looks like piss and sets a fire in the belly when drunk. I tried some.' Cai pulled a face. 'When it came to the real bloody work of cutting out the lump the woman took over from me.

'I've never seen the likes before. Castellanos cut around the canker like he was dislodging a rotting fruit. The gods only know how he managed to avoid the arteries. But he did. He put some evil smelling compress against the open wound and swaddled it in a dressing. He's changed it a couple of times since. The boy hasn't moved, though colour has returned to his cheeks.' Cai shook his head in wonder.

At the sound of further murmuring, Lucius turned his head and saw Castellanos place a gentle hand on the young woman's shoulder. Leaving her side, he came to join them.

'Well, you're back with us, Tribunus?' Castellanos said, with a slight smile.

'Thanks to you,' Lucius said, wincing as he attempted to raise himself onto an elbow.

'Lie still. Those burns will take time to heal and will open easily with too much movement. There's still a great risk of infection.' Lucius blew a long slow breath through his pursed lips as the pain abated.

'What of the boy?'

'Only time will tell. I carved a grievous wound into his neck. I did not expect him to survive. As time has passed the signs of recovery are growing stronger. Perhaps he'll live.' Lucius noted the doubt in his friend's voice.

'You have not carried out such a procedure before?' Cai asked. Castellanos shook his head and Lucius could see the deep fatigue in his features.

'When I was learning my trade in Athens, I assisted my master as he carried out a similar procedure on a client, a member of the city council. The patient was in his late twenties and an athlete.' Castellanos closed his eyes briefly at the memory. 'It was a work of great skill. My master did a magnificent job. The operation, at first, appeared to have been a success. Unfortunately, three days later a fierce infection took hold. He died two nights later. The canker on the boy was twice the size. I have tried to give Reagann hope. I have prayed to the gods that it is not a false hope.'

'Reagann?' Lucius asked.

'The chieftain's daughter,' Cai said, grinning at the medicus. 'They have barely left each other's side. Not that I blame you, brother. She's a real beauty.'

Castellanos frowned. 'Let's see if you still think the same as your feet are roasting over the fire, should her son not live.'

ALISTAIR TOSH

35

Cai kept a close watch over his friend. Despite his protestations, Lucius slept much over the following three days and nights, aided by weak doses of juice of the poppy.

At Castellanos's request, Reagann had spoken to the old chieftain who had given permission for Cai to support Lucius in short periods of exercise. This mainly consisted of a slow shuffling walk around the interior of the fortress settlement. An armed warrior their continual shadow.

'The boy grows stronger,' Lucius said. This was a refrain both had used regularly to one another. More in hope than certainty.

'Aye,' Cai returned. 'I'd be happier still, if the little shit would wake from his long sleep.' Despite Castellanos's assurances that it was not unexpected, as the lad's body worked on its recovery, the friends remained concerned.

They had reached the small pen where they had been held on the first day of captivity. Lucius leant against the wooden gatepost of its gate. Cai noticed he was less flushed than the previous day and had walked unaided for a time. A good sign.

With Lucius's tunic in bloody shreds, he had been provided with a smooth, black skinned jerkin. It was sleek and gleamed darkly in the late autumn sun. Seal skin, they now knew, following a question to Reagann. The young, dark haired woman had become more amiable towards the pair, if not quite friendly. Friendship she reserved for Castellanos.

She and the medicus could be seen at most times of the day in deep conversation. Either heads together over her

166

son's cot, or across the hearth, where they talked of many things. Cai had seen how enthralled she was by his tales of the city of Athens and Greece, his homeland. He in turn listened intently as Reagann told of her previous life. She had been taken by the Damnonii in a raid when still a child. Living as a slave amongst her captors for years, learning their language and ways. Before, one day, she had the opportunity to escape in a winter blizzard, spending days crossing the mountains, back to her own people. She was wed to the chieftain's son and bore him a boy. But her man had been lost in heavy seas, whilst out fishing with the other men of the settlement. Many had been lost that day, she had said.

Castellanos had become quite adept at speaking the language of the People. He was not yet entirely fluent and Reagann's girlish laughter could be heard frequently throughout the hut following one of his errors.

'Well at least he isn't dead,' Lucius said, 'And the longer that remains so the better.' Cai could sense his friend slipping into one of his darker moods. They had come upon him regularly since regaining consciousness. It was understandable after his ordeal, Cai thought. But they came more often with each passing day. He saw Lucius lightly touch his chest.

'What is troubling you, brother?' Cai asked. 'I know you do not fear death. So what is it?'

Lucius's fingers caressed the seal skin jerkin that hid his dressings. He appeared momentarily overcome, turning his head away from his brother-in-arms and greatest friend. Cai heard Lucius draw in a stuttering breath, gathering himself.

'I don't know if I can go on, Cai,' Lucius said, his voice strained.

'Your wounds will heal soon enough, Lucius. If the old goat of a chieftain ever lets us go, we can wait until—'

'I am marked,' Lucius said. 'Marked by their god of death. The dreams keep coming. I try not to sleep but my exhaustion eventually takes me. And there he is, awaiting me, with his blood red eyes. At first it was the face of the warrior who wielded the blade. But it has changed. Now I see him.' Lucius placed the palm of his hand against his chest. He circled it slowly, marking the area of the dark one's image. Cai was quiet for a time, taking in his friend's anguish, considering his next words. Platitudes would not do.

'After the battle under the Novantae's hill,' Cai began. 'I was lost.' He paused for a moment, seeing through his mind's eye. 'The wounds to my body healed. Those to my mind were not so easily mended. Not only did I lose many of my comrades that day, some I had known since joining the Eagles, I had lost my brother too. My boyhood friend, my anchor, the only real family I had. It took some time to get back to myself and, if I'm honest, it was not until I found a new purpose that my true recovery began. Keeping my promise to Adal. Watching over his family.' Cai paused once more.

'There is one thing I know with certainty, Lucius. You must face the world. You must not hide from it, no matter the fear or pain it may cause you. You have a permanent reminder of the agony inflicted upon you. Embrace it. Make it a part of you. I watched you do this once already. After we almost lost the cohort, below the Novantae's hill. This may be tougher still. But you will do it, my friend. And you will not be alone.'

Cai looked at his friend. Lucius's eyes glistened. After a long moment, he placed his hand and Cai's shoulder.

168

'Come. Let's go see if the patient still breathes and if we can keep our skins for another hour or two.'

Lucius entered the chieftain's roundhouse first. The old man had said little over recent days. Once in a while he quietly enquired as to his grandson's wellbeing, before returning to his own shielded area at the rear of the hut where he slept. His gentle snores could be heard at most times of the day. Women of the settlement came and went at intervals, seeing to his needs.

'What's this?' Lucius asked.

He was immediately drawn to an excited bustling around the boy's cot. There were several women and Lucius was surprised to see the old chieftain.

'Is he dead?' Cai said under his breath, his voice tight.

'No, the lad lives, it seems,' Lucius had moved closer and between gaps in the small crowd he glimpsed the young woman's son. He was sitting up and swaddled in furs. His mother was helping him to drink, whilst Castellanos examined the dressing. The boy still appeared white and weak as a newborn lamb, but he smiled wanly as his grandfather spoke to him.

Castellanos noticed the pair and a broad grin crossed his lips as he nodded his head in affirmation of the unspoken question in their eyes. The boy would live.

Sometime later the medicus came to find them and the quiet Greek could not hide his happiness. 'The wound is healing well and the boy's strength is returning by the minute, it appears.' He sat with them as they ate their evening meal of dried seal meat. They had to dip the tough slivers into beakers of water before they could chew it. 'It seems all of my prayers to Apollo have been heard.'

'I think it has more to do with your skill, brother,' Cai said, 'than any divine intervention.'

169

Castellanos smiled again. Over the years, Lucius had become used to his slightly morose presence and it was puzzling to see this new side to him.

'Perhaps, as the chieftain and his daughter are now in your debt you should ask them to release us?' Lucius said. He spoke in Latin so as not to be overheard. 'We haven't seen Hrindenus and the others for days either.'

The smile disappeared from the medicus's olive-skinned face becoming pensive. 'Yes,' he said. 'You speak true. I'll find the right time this evening to bring it up.' He turned his eyes to Lucius's seal skin tunic. 'How is your wound?' he asked.

'It still stings with movement and the itching is maddening, but it's healing, I think.' Castellanos put the back of his hand to Lucius's forehead.

'Well, you're still free of fever. I'll give you a little juice of the poppy to help with the pain.'

'No,' Lucius said, his words abrupt. 'I'll live with the pain. The concoction is dulling my senses. I must manage without it.' Castellanos turned to Cai as if he might intervene. He simply smiled and shrugged his shoulders.

'Very well,' Castellanos said. 'But let me change your dressing.'

Later, as Cai and he relaxed by the hearth, Lucius motioned with his head, towards where Castellanos and the Epidii woman sat close together. 'I think our medicus is enamoured by the beautiful Epidii princess.'

Cai nodded. 'And it's plain to see his feelings are returned.'

A short while later, the young woman departed the roundhouse. As she raised the door skin she nodded to Lucius and Cai, the faintest of smiles playing across her lips. Then she walked into the night.

170

Castellanos remained sitting apart from them for a time. He opened his box and made an appearance of reordering his implements and potions. The medicus seemed to be buying time for himself. Putting something off, Lucius thought.

Eventually, he set the dark wooden container aside.

'I think our Greek friend may have something of import to speak of,' Cai said.

Castellanos approached, seating himself between the two men. He stared into the low flames.

'You're not coming with us, are you brother?' Lucius said. Castellanos shook his head and looked at the men who had become his friends.

'You and the others are to be released tomorrow. You'll be given horses and guided to where the Epidii lands border the Damnonii's.' He gazed again into the fire, the dying embers glowing red. Neither Lucius nor Cai interrupted. They sensed there was more.

'The price for your freedom is that I stay behind and care for the boy until he is fully recovered. He's greatly treasured by the Epidii. He will one day lead all the people of the tribe. If his grandfather dies before he comes of age, his mother will rule as some kind of regent until he is ready.' Castellanos fell silent, puffing out, what seemed to Lucius, a breath of relief.

Cai reached over, resting his hand on the medicus's shoulder. 'I get the feeling, brother, this duty will not be too onerous a chore for you.' A smile crept onto the Greeks lips. He turned to Cai and Lucius once more.

'I've spent much of my life in duty to the empire. I have lived through the horrors of the wars in Palestine and Britannia, trying to fix the broken bodies of men. Or, more often, in the boredom of barracks, lancing the boils or strapping the training injuries of recruits. For a time I soothed myself with drink. I cursed Fortuna at being left behind in what I thought of as the arse end of the world, never believing my life could be something else. But here, on this strip of land beyond the empire, I believe it finally could be.'

Cai laughed. It was a great burst of joy. 'And it has nothing to do with the dark haired beauty, does it my friend?' Castellanos returned the mirth with a wide, toothy grin, his cheeks burning a bright crimson.

'Are you sure about this, brother?' Lucius asked. 'You're a long way from civilisation if things turn sour.' He understood the Greek's desire to stay, it was still a great risk.

'I am,' Castellanos said, his expression serious and his words calm. 'These people need me. For once I will be able to put my skills to use outside of the realm of war. And perhaps...perhaps I will have a family of my own.'

Lucius nodded, a slow gentle smile lighting his face. 'Now, that is something worthy of the risk.'

36

'Fuck me, I'll be glad to be out of this shit hole,' Hrindenus said. 'Being cooped up for days with that lump of a Hibernian has not been my idea of a fun night out at the taberna.' The Tungrian talked as he strapped the sword to his hip.

'Now, Barra, there's a man who can tell a good tale. He got up to all sorts when he was fighting with the Damnonii.'

'And you managed to avoid exchanging blows with Keefe?' Cai asked.

'Well, every time I tried to raise the oak branch, so to speak, and engage him in a civilised conversation, he just gave me a filthy look and turned away. Eventually I took the hint and left him alone.'

'Good. Now get mounted up. I'll go and see what's keeping the others.' Cai pushed past two Epidii warriors who each held a brace of the stocky ponies, awaiting their riders. Since word had spread of the boy's recovery the atmosphere in the palisaded settlement had changed. It seemed to Cai less oppressive somehow. He even received a smile from one of the younger women.

As he approached the chieftain's roundhouse, the door flap was thrown aside and Barra stepped through, closely followed by Keefe. The red-headed Novantae nodded in greeting.

'Since we have been treated as honoured guests the old goat has deigned to speak with me.' Barra said. To Cai, he seemed more amused than angry. 'The site of our sacred place is close to the border with Epidii lands. He says, for several moons, parties of Damnonii have been

173

seen heading towards it. It would appear our unfortunate captive spoke true. There must be a new kingmaking for the Damnonii,' He looked meaningfully at Cai. 'Let us hope Blue Dog does not gain the other warchief's support. It would not be good for their people. Nor you Romans, I think.'

The door skin was pulled aside once more and Lucius, Castellanos and the young woman stepped through. The medicus had been attending to Lucius's wounds one final time. The Greek handed Cai a small leather sack.

'It contains the last of my dressings and a pot of honey,' Castellanos said. 'There's only a little of the yellow pus seeping through in parts. The burns are drying nicely. But you must help Lucius with the bindings each evening for a few days more.'

'Thank you, brother. I will.'

'He's not really fit to ride. I suggested he remain here with me for a time, but...' Castellanos shrugged. 'He was insistent that he make the journey with you.'

'I'm not deaf you know,' Lucius said. 'Nor am I a child. Let's get going, shall we?'

Moments later the party of five was mounted. In spite of Lucius's protestations, Cai helped him onto horseback.

'Well, my friend,' Cai said. 'I wish you well in your new life.' He held out his arm and Castellanos grasped it.

'And you, Cai. I hope you find Alyn and can leave this life of war behind.' Cai nodded, turning his mount.

Lucius nudged his pony forward and he too extended his arm. 'Good luck, brother,' he said. 'Although, from what I can see, divine Fortuna has already presented you with all of the luck you will need.'

Castellanos smiled, almost bashfully, and he turned to look at the beautiful Epidii woman. Her dark, almost black hair lay across her shoulders, shining like Lucius's seal-skin jerkin. She beamed back at him. 'Please take care of that wound, Lucius. I don't want all my good work undone.'

Lucius laughed. 'Fare well, my friend.'

Three Epidii warriors led them through the settlement's small gateway. Descending the hill, Cai saw the inhabitants of the lower village awaited them. He anticipated another reception like the one on their day of arrival, but the population simply looked on in respectful silence as they passed.

"It appears news of Castellanos's good works has spread,' Hrindenus said. 'Mind you, these scrawny bastards need the medicus more than we do.'

They rode on for the remainder of the day, along valley floors cut through by fast flowing, rock-strewn streams and over steep, brush-covered, mountain sides. The little ponies were in their element. No obstacle seemed too difficult to overcome. At times it appeared that the animals barely drew breath. Cai thought of Adela then. Though he knew they would be no match for his great warhorse in a battle, he doubted she could keep up with these stout creatures on this terrain.

There was a sharp chill amongst the hills and heavy grey clouds had lowered to cut off all view of either coastline. The first snows might soon be upon them. Cai prayed they would hold off until they reached their destination.

As night began to fall, the Epidii warriors left them. They had reached the peak of a mist shrouded hill. Their leader simply pointed north. 'Damnonii,' he said. The three turned and rode away, swiftly swallowed up by the mist.

'Do we push on?' Cai said to Barra.

'No. It's rarely a good idea to approach another tribe's land in darkness and expect a warm welcome. No matter

175

who you are. We should drop down into the valley below and make camp.'

They kept a cold camp, not yet wishing to alert the Damnonii to their presence. They stayed warm as best they could, wrapped in a mixture of the deerskin cloaks they had scavenged from Blue Dog's island and the sealskin garments provided by the Epidii. To Cai, they looked a dishevelled bunch, hardly a king's warband.

The horses had been hobbled close to a nearby stream. Keefe kept the first watch out in the deeper darkness. Cai shivered. There was no wind to speak of only a near constant mizzle he was sure would keep him from sleep.

'There are things you will need to know,' Barra said. 'If you are to have a chance of getting through the next few days with your skins intact.' Cai had anticipated Hrindenus would interject with one of his usual quips but the dark outline of the big Tungrian was unmoved.

'The holy place sits in the lands of the Damnonii. But it is neutral ground. It is a fortress defended by warriors who are adherents of the holy ones. They are raised from childhood by the priests and owe loyalty only to them. They are fanatics who will brook no breaking of the laws that govern them.'

'What if you do break one of their rules?' Hrindenus asked from the darkness, his voice humourless.

'The punishment is almost always death. And it is seldom swift. So, once we enter their domain, you must follow my lead in all things. Barra became quiet for a time, gathering his thoughts. 'We know now that mine will not be the only king-making. Our task has become more complicated. The death of our prisoner means it will not be possible to confront Blue Dog directly.'

'Why?' Lucius asked, letting his frustration get the better of him. 'Does the word of the ruler of the Novantae tribe carry no weight here?' Cai saw Barra bridle.

'I am not of their people, even though I have friends here. Blue Dog is mistrusted. But he has the tongue of a snake and may already have turned some of the tribe's leaders to his side. The only chance to convince the Damnonii of Blue Dog's murder of their king is to speak, in private, to those I trust. They may listen, though nothing is certain.

'But you must know this. Above all else, I have made this journey to have my own rule sanctified and return to my people, who are in desperate need. The Damnonii throne is of little concern when it comes to my own tribe.'

Cai could feel his anger and frustration growing within him. 'If you cannot help us, why are we here? Are you walking us to our deaths?'

'Peace, Nervii,' Barra said. 'Surely you have come to know me as an honourable man?' Cai grumbled, it was neither an acceptance nor an outright denial. Barra continued. 'I have been thinking on this as we have travelled. I am resolved we have only one true course to win back your woman.' Barra pulled his cloak tighter around his shoulders.

'And what is that?' Lucius asked, not hiding his irritation. Cai realised the burns must be chafing again.

'The holy one's value courage above all else. Courage in battle and the bravery of a warrior in facing his fears.' Barra ran his fingers through his long, damp hair. 'We must enter the fortress gates together as equals, you and I. You must not disguise yourselves any longer. Rather you should announce your intentions to the priests. Let me say my piece first, then I will introduce you and why I have aided you.'

'You must tell your life's tale. Hide nothing. Tell them of your friend the Centurion. Tell them of the battle at our sacred hill. And make sure they know it was you and your friend here who led your men to victory at that damned fortress.'

'Then what?' Cai wasn't sure he wanted to know the answer.

'Then, Nervii, you must challenge Blue Dog for the right to take back your woman. Blade against blade, in a fight to the death.'

37

Lucius was cold, stiff and sore.

He had slept only in a few, short snatches. The bitter, sodden ground and thoughts of the day to come prevented a deeper slumber. His chest throbbed, though the honey continued to do its good work. Cai had changed the strapping one final time.

He had taken the last watch and woken the others at the first hint of light. The incessant drizzle had ceased at some point during the night and the low cloud had withdrawn back up the mountainside, leaving an iron grey sky clear of the tops. He chewed at the last of his cured seal meat, working it slowly until it was soft enough to swallow. He found the sensation surprisingly pleasant and at least it stopped the growling of his belly.

The five rode in silence for around an hour. A dark mood hung over them. Cai in particular seemed shrouded in his own world. They descended a tree covered hillside, making towards a slow-moving river in the valley floor. Abruptly, the trees ended and they found themselves on the river's bank.

'We follow its course northwards,' Barra said. 'We'll reach the fortress by late morning.'

'This country is empty,' Lucius said. 'Where are its people?'

'Never fear, Roman,' Keefe said from behind. 'We'll not be alone for much longer.'

Minutes later the Hibernian's words appeared prophetic. As the small band rounded a long bend of the

179

river a party of mounted warriors emerged from amongst the reeds and scrub trees lining the riverbank. There were at least twenty by Lucius's count. Armed with shield and spear, their iron points, held aloft, gleaming dully in the morning light. All had the familiar shaven scalps and dark tattoos. Lucius wondered if he had fought any of these men on the walls of the Sack. His beard had grown longer. He hoped it was a good enough disguise to fool them. At least until they reached their destination.

A rider nudged his mount to the fore of the band, halting within hailing distance. 'Who is it that comes to the lands of the Damnonii uninvited?' The warrior's voice was strong and sounded unconcerned.

'I know this man,' Barra said. He kicked his own mount forward raising his hand, palm open. 'Hail, Tomag. It has been a long time, brother.'

'Barra?' The Damnonii's puzzlement quickly turned to delight. The warrior kicked his mount into a gallop, Barra doing likewise. The pair met, leaping from horseback to embrace. They spoke in a flurry.

'I presume this is fortuitous?' Lucius asked Keefe, who had halted his mount at his side.

'Tomag is the son of one of the Damnonii chieftains,' Keefe said. 'He and Barra saved each other's lives more than once, fighting you Romans. They were inseparable for a time.'

Lucius sensed something in the Hibernian's manner.

'There's more?' Keefe snorted.

'They parted on difficult terms. Tomag backed his father's decision not to take his own people to fight in the lands of the Novantae. He and Barra exchanged sharp words when last they were together.'

'What does it mean for us?'

Keefe shrugged. 'It means we will at least reach the holy place alive.'

For a time, Barra rode at the front of the column with Tomag, deep in conversation, heads close as they rode. After around an hour of following the river, moving at a steady trot, the Novantae chieftain rejoined them. Lucius noticed his grave look.

'Bad news?' Lucius asked.

There was a gap of a few paces between them and the rearmost Damnonii riders, still Barra spoke quietly. 'Blue Dog has been chosen as king of the Damnonii.'

'What?' Cai gasped. 'How can this be?'

'It gets worse,' Barra said. His next words were uttered with a quiet vehemence. 'It seems my cousin arrived yesterday along with a boat-load of his hearth-warriors. He is to make a claim for the Novantae lands tomorrow.'

38

Cai's mind roiled.

He had accepted long since it would come down to this. A fight to the death with an enemy he hated, but had never met. And yet, he also felt a strange kind of fear. Not fear of battle. Nor fear of death. Rather, of seeing Alyn once more.

She would be changed, he knew. Would she be so different that her feelings for him would have changed too? Would she be lost to him? He had failed to protect her, after all.

'You must know she couldn't fight him anymore.' The conversation with the woman Moira came to his mind like salt to an open wound. Swiftly followed by her first words to him. 'I am Moira, Cai of the Nervii. Alyn said you would come.' Did she still hold onto her love for him? Or would contempt grip her heart? He was certain now how he felt for her. But what of the unborn child? He shook his head. He must clear his mind for the day ahead.

Lucius nudged his mount alongside Cai's. He knew his friend worried for him and had tried to speak of it over the last day. Cai had not felt able to. Now he welcomed his presence, if only to distract from his own destructive thoughts.

'How's your chest?'

'Itches like Hades, brother. I long to run naked into the waters of this river to cool it off.' Lucius spoke with humour, relieved his friend had, at last, broken out of his self-imposed seclusion.

'It'd make your balls shrivel to little acorns. The water must be close to freezing.'

Lucius coughed a laugh. 'Aye, it'd be worth it though, to be rid of this torment for a few moments.' Lucius became quiet and Cai knew his friend was working up to saying something. And he suspected he would not like it. In the end, Lucius blew out a gust of breath. Cai spoke first.

'I'm sorry, Lucius.'

'For what?'

'For getting you into this mess. I aim to kill this Blue Dog, and I fear for what will happen to you and Hrindenus should I fail. If he should prevail, he will not be able to touch you in this holy place, it seems. But if Barra's accounts of this madman are accurate, I doubt he will let you leave Damnonii lands, his lands, alive.'

'Don't fear for me, brother. I came willingly and would do so again. As you would for me, had the tables been turned.'

'What of your family lands? Recovering them has been your heart's desire for so long.' Lucius nodded once in recognition of the point.

'Perhaps I have desired it too much,' Lucius said. 'Yes, I wish to see my father's lands restored. I seek vengeance on the murderers who took him from us. I have every confidence you will kill Blue Dog. If Fortuna is not with us, I'll gladly pay the ferryman, knowing I have died with my friend. The only family I have known these past years.'

Cai coughed, feeling his throat constrict. All he could do was nod his thanks.

'Besides, Adal would never let you live it down if you lost to that savage. So, if you don't want an eternity of sitting around the campfire whilst my old First Spear relentlessly takes the piss out of you. I suggest you kill the fucker.' This time Cai coughed harshly, choking down his own laughter.

As he recovered himself the pair crested a small rise. They pulled up.

'Well, that's a sight to be sure,' Hrindenus said from the rear.

For a considerable distance they could see what could only be described as a sea of winter-brown reeds. A sea rippling in the light breeze. However, it was something else that drew their full attention. What appeared to be an island emerged from the tall grasses.

After a few moments of scrutiny Cai could tell this was no ordinary island. Ashen coloured smoke drifted above the settlement, emanating from the peaked, reed-thatched roof of a large and solidly built stone hall. The island itself appeared to have been rough-hewn from dull, grey rock. It was clear to Cai that this was no ordinary chieftain's homestead. It was a fortress.

On its own, the large hall was enough to speak of great power. Its lower slopes were surrounded by thick ramparts of quarried stone, perhaps ten feet in height and topped by a wooden palisade. Even though still at a significant distance, Cai could discern men patrolling its parapet. This was not all. There was an outer palisade wall too. The sharp points of its wooden struts peered menacingly above the gently waving reeds. If there was a gateway, it wasn't in sight.

This wetland was plainly the source of the river they had been following. From the waterway's ending, a channel had been cut through the reeds. It was arrow-straight and led directly to the fort. So, it could be approached by boat, Cai thought. Was there another way?

Soon afterwards, the Damnonii turned west. They took a route passing along the edge of the reed lake, the fortress always out of reach. They continued for a time along a well-worn pathway. Eventually Cai saw the smoke of campfires in the middle distance rising above the treeline.

Barra returned from the head of the column. 'Do not be alarmed with what you see. Following Blue Dog's anointing, several chieftains have remained and are in the holy place.' Upon seeing Cai's confusion, he clarified. 'The fortress,' he said, nodding in its direction. 'Their warbands are not allowed to accompany them, so are encamped at the water's edge awaiting their lord's return. We'll not linger. We must leave our horses with them and continue on foot.'

'How do we cross these waters on foot?' Cai asked, perplexed.

'There is a route through the marshland. You will see.'

Moments later they emerged into a wide sandy area by the shoreline, upon which a village nestled. There were several roundhouses as well as lean-tos. It was immediately obvious this was no permanent settlement. There were no women. No children ran to and fro. There were only men. Warriors.

Barra turned to Cai. 'Blue Dog's men will be here too. You must not engage with them. They must not know where we have come from.' Cai simply nodded.

As the horsemen entered the settlement, Cai perceived all was not well. Warriors looked on in sullen silence as Tomag and his band dismounted. They congregated in groups, each remaining apart from the others. He felt an undercurrent, as if fighting could suddenly erupt at the least provocation.

As Cai and the others were noticed, a hubbub of low conversations broke out within the groups of Damnonii. None though, approached or called out. Until they recognised Barra.

'Barra, you Novantae dog,' a great bear of a man shouted from amongst a dishevelled pack of warriors. His head was shaved like most of the others but a broad brush of a beard ran across the warrior's chest and much of his broad belly too. 'Have you returned to us?'

'Horas. I see you've become even fatter since we parted.' Barra dismounted and both men embraced warmly.

'Will you stay and drink my beer, or is it still too strong for your Novantae tastes?'

'You cannot linger,' Tomag interrupted. Barra's erstwhile friend wanted them away from the encampment as soon as possible, it seemed.

'Well, Horas,' Barra said. 'It would appear we must put off our reunion until I return from the holy one's isle. Keep that ale cool for me, my friend.' The bear Horas simply smiled, until his sight landed on Keefe.

'Well, well. You still haven't found your way home yet, Robogdii?' Keefe twitched a smile. 'You owe me a fight?'

'You mean a return fight, don't you?' Keefe said. 'How is that forearm of yours? Have the bones knitted back into place yet?' The big man unconsciously touched his left wrist with his right hand. The warrior Horas roared with laughter.

'A return fight it is,' he said.

'We'll be back soon enough,' Barra said. 'There will be time for fighting and drinking then.'

Tomag led the way on foot, following another pathway along the shoreline. The dense wall of reeds continued, unbroken, as the marshland curved northwards. Barra walked, unspeaking, at the Damnonii's side, Lucius and Cai behind them. Hrindenus and Keefe brought up the rear. At any moment Cai expected to see a boat pulled up on the water's edge. Caught by surprise, he jerked to a halt to avoid walking into the back of Tomag as the Damnonii came to a sudden stop.

'I must leave you here, my friend,' Tomag said to Barra. 'You know the way.'

'I do.'

'I wish you well,' Tomag said, placing his hand on Barra's shoulder and flashed a wide grin. 'Kill the runt and make him squeal.' Barra simply nodded. The Damnonii turned without another word and strode back along the track.

'This way,' Barra said, continuing along the lakeshore, the reeds obscuring any sight of the fortress. Moments later the Novantae abruptly changed direction as if to walk amongst the tall grasses. The reason soon became clear. A little into the murky waters were two tall wooden posts. Markers, Cai realised. Beyond the posts was a walkway, supported on wooden stilts keeping the footbridge an arms-length above the water. A handrail on its left side enabled travellers to steady themselves as they progressed along the narrow planking.

Without halting, Barra waded in calf-deep and passed between the posts. 'This way. Follow my lead. We must cross in a single column.' The Novantae reached the walkway, stepping up the short ladder and onto the slender platform. Cai followed, feeling the chill of the water around his knees. Lucius came next.

Upon stepping onto the walkway, the fortress came into view once more. Still Cai couldn't discern an entrance in the palisade. Barra had not waited for the others, Cai hurried to catch up. The timber creaked continually with their passing. He noted the wood was new. The route was well maintained.

The marshland was strangely silent. There were no bird calls or screeches of startled waterfowl. The only sound was the hissing and shushing of the reeds as the wind passed through the tall grasses.

Unlike the arrow-straight waterway, the wooden passage meandered as if following the course of some unseen river.

As if reading Cai's own thoughts, Barra spoke over his shoulder. 'It prevents an enemy from seeing what lies ahead of them.'

'We know what lies ahead,' Cai said. 'The ramparts are plain for the eye to see.'

'The fortress is not what is being hidden,' Barra said, suddenly raising his hand to halt the small band. 'We must descend into the waters for a time.' Cai was confused. He examined the walkway ahead of them. As far as he could tell the route progressed unabated. Why should they not continue? Barra descended a short wooden ladder. This time the water came up to his waist. He grinned up at Cai.

'Trust me, Nervii. You do not want to step onto that next plank. Not unless you wish to have a second arsehole cut for you.' Cai followed the Novantae's lead, descending into the chill water. His feet touched the soft, muddy lakebed, the movement disturbing the sludge, turning the water around him a filthy rust colour.

Cai saw what Barra had meant. The footing was held aloft by a single spar. Neither end of the wood was fixed, so stepping onto it would plunge an unsuspecting enemy into the waters below. Though before they reached the lake's surface their bodies would be impaled on the wicked sharp stakes.

'I'm glad we have a guide,' Cai said.

'The spar in front of each trap is marked with three deep knife cuts. Only those familiar with the route know this.'

Barra became serious. 'There are more, so ensure you keep a watch out for my signal.' The warchief waded to a ladder at the other side of the trap and ascended once more. The others followed his lead. Cai heard Hrindenus grumbling to himself.

'You have been here before?' Cai asked, following Barra closely.

'Once. With my uncle. I acted as his shield-man at his anointing.'

'You were close to him?'

'Cymbel was as a father to me. After my own was killed on the end of the boar's tusks he'd been hunting.'

'As you are a father to Herne.' Barra grunted.

'One day he will be king too. And walk this very path.' Cai heard the pride in the Novantae's voice.

'He and Beren have become firm friends,' Cai said.

'Perhaps he will be Herne's shield-man one day?' It was said in jest, Cai knew.

'That boy has his heart set on following in his father's footsteps.'

'Your footsteps, I think,' Barra said. 'He wishes to join your horsemen, does he not?'

'He does.' It was Cai's turn to speak with pride.

The process of descending into the reed-filled water was repeated on three further occasions. Each time their troos were drenched to their waistbands.

After the final time, Cai was perplexed. 'Surely any enemy would not be fooled by these traps once beyond the first. A force would still reach the island intact.'

'That is true, Nervii,' Barra said. 'Think on it. They would be wet, tired and miserable and would then have to face the defenders behind the walls of the sacred place. Not a welcome prospect. You'll soon see.'

189

For around thirty minutes they had followed the narrow walkway, with the fortress growing ever larger. Until, at last, feeling cold and thoroughly miserable, as Barra had foretold, the party reached the island.

Cai surveyed the defences with a professional eye. There was a short stretch of moss-and-heather-strewn rocky ground before the stout outer palisade appeared to grow out of the grey stone. There was not the usual outer ditch. It would have been impossible to dig one out of this terrain.

Atop the wooden ramparts he got a sight of its defenders for the first time. Two whitewashed faces stared down at the small band. Their chins were clean shaven, hair pulled into long, blade-like spikes and coloured white by the same concoction.

39

There was still no sign of a gate. Only a path continuing to the left, which Barra led them along. More of the painted warriors watched them silently as they progressed around the base of the palisade.

Not long after, Cai saw boats pulled up on the island's shore. A dozen or more.

'It would appear the Damnonii chieftains take the waterway to attend the king-choosing,' he said.

Opposite the craft was a gateway. Its solid oak doors closed to them. It was no great portal like the Sack's porta praetoria, only wide enough for two men to pass side by side.

A warrior appeared on the battlements above. He leaned on the parapet and observed them quietly. A chainmail shirt sat lightly on his broad shoulders. Roman-made chainmail. His face too was plastered with whitewash. This warrior, however, did not watch them impassively; rather a strange kind of leer creased his lips.

'It would appear we are to be blessed with the presence of another of the high and mighty of the Novantae people,' he said. 'We are already entertaining one who has declared himself king of your little tribe. We cannot admit another.'

'You know who I am, Neacal. I am the rightful king of my people. I seek the anointing. I will deal with my cousin if it is the Holy One's price for it.'

The warrior Neacal snorted. 'Only chiefs and their shield-bearers may enter, you know this. I can see that big lump of a Hibernian,' the white-painted warrior nodded towards Keefe, who stared back impassively. 'Who are these others? They are not of the People?'

'No. They are under my protection. This man seeks an audience with the Holy One.' Barra indicated Cai, who came to stand by his shoulder.

'What could an outlander wish to say to the Holy One? Why should he even allow this thing into his presence? It is unheard of.'

'That is for his ears only. I, Barra, king of the Novantae people, have given my word to aid him in this. I stand as surety on pain of death he will do the Holy One no harm.'

The whitewashed warrior scrutinised them in silence for a time. Finally, coming to a decision, he waved his hand at someone unseen within the fortress. Moments later the narrow gate creaked slowly open.

'With me,' Barra said, keeping his voice low. 'Side by side as equals.' Together Cai and Barra strode across the short stretch of ground, entering under the gateway together. The others, Cai hoped, would be following closely behind.

They emerged into a narrow space, no more than two spear-lengths in width. It was a sheer-sided passage cut through the very rock itself, as high as the palisade that hid its presence.

Whoever had opened the gate was nowhere to be seen. But at the end of the passage was a wall of shields and spears. White-faced warriors stared passively from behind the barrier. Atop the passageway too, more warriors were positioned. These held bows, with arrows fitted and strings pulled back to chins. The warrior Neacal stood amongst them. A grin creased his face, causing some of the whitewash to crack and splinter from his cheeks.

'You will leave your weapons here,' he said. 'Including your eating knives.'

Barra nodded, to Cai and the others. The five men lifted scabbarded swords from their belts and placed them on the rocky ground before them. Barra stepped forward and the shield wall moved apart, making a narrow passage. Cai's shoulders brushed against the shields' deerhide coverings as he passed between them.

The white-faced warriors escorted the party through a small settlement of squat, reed-thatched huts. A small number of pigs and cattle rooted and chewed in pens set against the outer palisade. There were no indications women and children resided in this place. Cai recognised a barracks when he saw one, even if they were unlike the ordered lines of huts seen within any fort of the Eagles. He scrutinised the interior, searching. There was no sign of Alyn. He was unsure if he felt relieved or disappointed.

The six and their escort traversed a steep rise and approached the inner palisade Cai had first seen from the shoreline. There was a second entranceway set into yet another narrow rock defile. Again, a narrow door awaited. This one was open.

The grinning warrior appeared before them. He held a short-shafted axe in his right hand. From the nicks and scratches, it was clear it had seen battle. Cai noted the blade of its broad iron head was clean and wetted. One swing would take an arm off. The warrior's stance told Cai the warrior was an expert in its use.

'Only you three may enter,' the warrior Neacal said. He pointed purposefully at Barra, Cai and Keefe.

'But—' Cai began, only to be cut off by Neacal.

'Don't worry, outlander,' he said, his leer returning to his lips. 'My men will treat our new honoured guests well.' Cai turned to Lucius, who simply shrugged.

'This gets better and better,' Hrindenus said.

The three passed through the gateway and into the narrow defile greeted by another doorway at the far end of the passage. At a barked order from Neacal, the door of this final entryway swung open. In the dull light, Cai could see more warriors awaiting them.

They emerged onto a flat open area, perhaps fifty strides across. At its heart were four sandstone pillars. Each was the height of two men and marked out the corners of a broad square. The brown pillars stood incongruously against the grey of the fortress's natural rock. Each was carved with swirling designs that writhed around the stout stone.

Cai scrutinised the patterns for a moment, unable to discern what they signified. At their centre were the blackened remains of a large fire. He pushed away his thoughts of what it might have been used for. Perhaps it was simply to roast a carcass in celebration of Blue Dog's anointing.

At the hill's summit was the great hall, similar in shape to the large round houses of other chieftains he had seen. Only this one was larger still, and constructed of layer upon layer of well-dressed stone, cut from the same grey rock. Its roof was thick layers of reed thatch, through which grey-white smoke permeated before drifting lazily to the east in the light breeze.

More warriors stood sentry duty atop the stone platform on which the hall rested. Their eyes were alert, faces expressionless. This was a well-run garrison, Cai thought.

'You are expected,' Neacal said to Barra.

'I am?' Barra replied.

'The Holy One has eyes everywhere, Novantae.' The warrior grinned once more and made a great show of a mock bow, indicating the way with an outstretched arm.

194

Ignoring the warrior's insolence Barra headed towards the stone steps leading to the hall. Cai followed, heart hammering.

40

Upon taking the last of the steps, Barra halted, turning to face Cai.

'Are you ready?' he asked. Cai took a deep breath and nodded. One of the warrior sentries pulled open the heavy pinewood door. He and Barra stepped through in unison.

Cai had anticipated the usual badly lit, smoke filled hall. Instead, many torches were ensconced in the walls of the wide open space. Each cast bright, yellow-gold haloes, enabling him to see the whole interior.

The floor was laid with great slabs of the familiar grey stone. The walls of the room were covered with many skins of game. Cai recognised; deer, seal, wolf and otter. There were others, stranger, he did not. Dominating the room was a large hearth, perhaps four long strides across. Two hogs were slowly roasting on spits, turned by a pair of boy slaves.

Cai had taken all this in with his first glance. It was the faces staring back at them that now drew his full attention. There were twenty or more men sitting, with legs crossed, in a wide circle about the fire. A matching number of warriors stood at their backs. Chiefs and their shield-bearers. Many faces were impassive. A few, no doubt former comrades, smiled in welcome to Barra. Some, however, held undisguised hatred.

One such Cai recognised instantly. Frang, Barra's cousin. His face was consumed with loathing, teeth bared in a feral snarl. A gruff growl emanated from behind Cai. Keefe had seen him too.

Chiefs and shield warriors alike wore fine animal-skin cloaks, a symbol of their status. All were bare chested. It was the sight of the tattoo on the chest of one man that shook Cai. He felt like a rope had been tightened around his own chest. Keefe's description suddenly came to mind.

'He calls himself the Blue Wolf. He has a tattoo of what he supposed was that fierce beast, etched across his chest. Though the work was poorly done and is more akin to a mangy dog.' It took all Cai's strength not to throw himself at the new Damnonii king. Blue Dog.

The bearded face of the Damnonii met Cai's fierce stare. Puzzlement entered his eyes at the glare Cai directed at him. Cai forced calm upon himself. It would be pointless to lose his life now. Not when Alyn was so close. Instead, with a physical effort, he switched his gaze to the warrior at Blue Dog's back.

A mountain of a man. A head taller than the other warriors. His shoulders were broad, his arms and chest bulging with solid muscle. His skull was shaded with the dark blue tattoos of the Damnonii. His sunken eyes gave him a daemonic countenance. The warrior met Cai's stare and dismissed him with a contemptuous snort.

From amongst the seated gathering, one now moved. Aided not by a shield warrior, rather by what must be a priest, draped as he was in a plain green garment of wool covering the entirety of his body to his ankles. His long dark hair was tied by a thin cord of leather, revealing startling blue eyes. This young man assisted one much older to stand. He too was garbed in a similar fashion. Instead of green his garment was all white, closely matching the colour of his long straggly hair and beard. Two white painted lines ran in parallel from his forehead across his eyelids and down onto his chin, where they met.

'The Holy One,' Barra whispered. The old priest was ancient. Cai couldn't begin to guess his age. His face held the broadest of smiles.

'Barra of the Novantae,' he said, his strong voice belying the frailness of his body. 'You are most welcome here. Come forward. All of you.' He waved his hand, his arm moving like a thin branch in a light breeze. The movement revealed blue tattoos covering his hands and forearms.

'Before you speak,' he said. 'You must drink. The Damnonii ale is actually quite good this year.' He smiled again, taking in the gathering. Perhaps he had intended his mirth to be returned, but the obvious tension within the gathering prevented it. As the three stepped into the ring of chieftains, Cai had a feeling of what it must be like to place his head into the maw of a great bear, its teeth waiting to snap his neck.

A slave boy appeared with three cups of the dark frothing beer the northern tribes so favoured. Cai found it bitter. Barra took his and poured a little onto the stone floor. 'To those who have gone before us,' he said. He downed the beer in great gulps. Cai followed his lead, whispering his own prayer to Jupiter.

Barra let out a huge belch, before handing the cup back to the slave. The old man nodded and smiled before returning to his seated position, again aided by the young priest. The Novantae chief stepped forward.

'Holy One,' he began, addressing the wizened old man. 'You know who I am. I stood at Cynbel's back, in this very room, as his shield-bearer and heir to the Novantae kingdom. Our king is dead, killed honourably in battle with the Roman invaders. He feasts now with our forebears.' Cai observed the gathering as Barra spoke. Most nodded at his words, including the old priest. Others did not. Amongst those was Blue Dog, whose eyes remained fixed upon the Novantae.

'I have led my people in war against our enemies. I have fought with many who are gathered here today.' This was met with a hooming sound from many of the chieftains. Barra continued. 'I now take my uncle's place as the *rightful* king of the Novantae and come to you Holy One for the anointing, as is required by our laws.'

'You lie!' The words were screeched by Frang, who sprang to his feet, fists clenched at his sides. There was a sharp intake of breath from the gathered men. Angry looks flashed across the faces of some. 'I am the rightful king. My uncle gave me his blessing before he died. I was with him on the battlefield. And here is a usurper before us, come with his Roman spies to unseat me.' Shouts of consternation and surprise erupted around the room. Barra ignored them all.

'That battle raged for days on end.' He shouted to be heard. 'If you were ever in the heat of the fighting, I did not see you. It is you who lies. You are a mongrel dog and you will die, by my own hand.' Cai had expected Frang to leap at Barra for the insult, instead he spat impotently, his lips twisted into a snarl. He fears Barra, Cai thought. The very air crackled with the anticipation of a fight.

'Enough!' Cai was startled by the shout, and more surprised it had come from the old man. 'Our laws forbid fighting in this place of the gods.'

'Holy One, may I speak?' It was Blue Dog. His words grated in a way that reminded Cai of Nepos, the old Tungrian Decurion. Though there was none of the veteran warrior's humour in it.

The ancient one smiled and nodded slowly. 'If the Blue Wolf wishes to speak, it is his right. Go ahead, brother.'

199

'Frang speaks true, Holy One. I was with him and his uncle as he took his last breath. Cymbel gave him his blessing as the new king of the Novantae.'

'You lie, Blue Dog,' Keefe spat the insult. Cai continued to watch the Damnonii king, whose face flushed. His lips pulled back to reveal dark and twisted teeth. 'You were not to be seen on the battlefield. And believe me I searched for you. How then would you know what our king's final words were?'

'You dare call the king of the Damnonii a coward?' Blue Dog screamed back. 'I will have your liver for this.' Cai saw Blue Dog's shield-bearer reach for the sword at his hip and curse silently as he realised it was not there.

The hearth fire blazed into sudden life. Green flames thrust briefly towards the ceiling before, almost instantaneously, returning to their former state an instant later. There was a hissing and crackling sound as fat dripped from the roasting hogs. The slave boys fell to their knees in fright. Even a few steps away, Cai had felt the surge of heat. The gathering was shocked into silence by the display.

'There will be no killing here on pain of your own lives. You know our laws.' The shout, this time, came not from the elderly priest. Instead from the young acolyte who had been standing quietly, behind his master. His voice sounded more like the battlecry of a warrior than a servant of the gods. 'Keefe of the Robogdii people,' he glared at the Hibernian. 'You will absent your place at your chieftain's side.' Keefe took a step as if to argue, but Barra grasped the shield-bearer's arm and shook his head.

'Wait for me outside,' Barra said. Keefe seemed stunned for a moment before giving the briefest of nods and departing. The heavy door slammed hard behind him.

The ancient one arose once again. To Cai he appeared wearier than he had only moments before. 'My thanks, Seoras,' he said to the young priest. He walked slowly around the circle of chieftains, hands clasped firmly in front of him. Cai watched his progress closely. In the absolute silence, his white robes made a shushing sound as he moved. The only other sound was the occasional snap of a log in the fire, and whimper of the slave boys who had stayed on their knees, foreheads pressed against the stone floor.

None of the gathering, chiefs or shield-bearers, met the priest's fierce glare.

'I knew Cynbel from a young age. He was a fierce warrior and a just king. Above all else he was an honourable man. Always true to his word. And is why I encouraged you all to support his call for aid against Rome.' Cai saw many of the chieftains nodding. 'Cynbel spoke to me on two occasions, where he told me, if he had not fathered a son of his own, then Barra would be the next ruler of the Novantae people.

'However, I do not doubt the word of the king of the Damnonii,' the old one turned to Blue Dog, whose hooded eyes, it seemed to Cai, glimmered with barely contained hatred. Or was it the madness that Barra said filled this man? 'However, I must question if Cynbel was still in his right mind when he spoke these final words to Frang.' Barra's cousin opened his mouth to speak, Blue Dog's sudden grip of the Novantae's arm stilled him. 'I must reflect on this matter.' He was silent for a time as he continued his slow circuit. 'I will commune with the gods tonight. They may deign to give me a sign for the path to a resolution.'

He turned, slowly, taking in each chieftain at the gathering. 'None of us wishes to see conflict within a land of the People when the Legions are so close at hand.' He pulled his long spindly fingers through his scraggly white beard. 'Let us now go to our rest places and make ready for the night's feasting. I will give you my ruling in the morning.'

A murmuring of voices struck up at these final words and some of the chieftains began to rise. Barra stepped forwards once more.

'Holy One, there is another matter. An oath I must fulfil concerning this man standing at my side.'

'Indeed,' said the old priest. 'Is this your Roman spy as Frang accuses?'

'He fights for Rome, it is true. But he is no spy. He comes to you of his own free will.'

'Why have you given an oath to this man?' The ancient one seemed perplexed, and not a little angry.

'He saved the life of my nephew, Herne, who will be king of the Novantae after I am gone.' Barra paused as if considering his next words. 'Following the battle for the Roman fortress, I was under his sword. He spared my life.'

The room erupted. Chieftains rose swiftly to their feet. Raised voiced filled the air, none of it intelligible. All faces, now flushed with anger, turned towards Cai.

41

'Silence!' the young priest roared. Some chieftains stilled their cries of indignation; many did not. 'You will be silent or you will face sanction.' This time the shouting died down, though low murmurs continued.

'I will speak, Holy One,' Blue Dog said, his voice rasping and offended.

'Make it quick,' the old priest snapped. 'I tire of the Damnonii behaving like children in this place of the gods. Even kings will show respect.'

For an instant Cai saw Blue Dog's madness. In that one moment his face was unable to hold its disguise. His teeth bared, a line of spittle joining his top and bottom lips. However, it was his eyes that gave away his true essence.

'I beg your forgiveness, Holy One,' he began. 'It is the nature of this affront to the gods that has made me speak so.' The old priest nodded, mollified for the moment. 'How can it be a man of the People, one who comes to this place with his demand for the anointing, also brings an enemy into this holiest of places?' Blue Dog smirked at Barra. 'Perhaps the favour of the Novantae has been bought with Roman gold.'

Cai knew hot anger must be pulsing through Barra's heart. Somehow, he kept it in check. His next words were icy calm.

'Your insult cannot go unchallenged, Blue Dog.' Barra put heavy emphasis on the second word. It had the desired effect as the Damnonii king bristled. 'We will meet king to king, swords in hand, at a place of the Holy One's choosing. I will put an end to the madness that resides within you.'

An incoherent sound erupted from Blue Dog's shield-bearer. The giant flew past his master and leapt towards Barra. Cai was taken aback by the speed of the man as he closed on the Novantae. The young priest was faster, however. One moment the shield-bearer was in full flight; the next, he lay face down on the stone slabs of the hall, his head coming to rest at Barra's feet. Unconscious. Or dead. Cai couldn't tell.

The acolyte halted in the circle of chieftains. He gripped a long staff of oak as if it were a mere walking stick. Its knotted end stood a foot taller than the young man. Cai had not noticed it earlier, nor barely seen the movement of the Holy One's man, so quick was his movement. Even now he appeared calm, simply taking in the gathering with icy disdain. When he spoke, his voice matched the coldness of his stare, which he turned on Blue Dog.

'If I had not stopped your hound from reaching lord Barra,' he said coolly, 'he would have been dragged from this place and joined tonight's other sacrifices to the gods.'

Cai scrutinised the priest, who was perhaps no more than twenty summers, hold Blue Dog's returned glare. The taut muscles of his forearm rippled as he gripped his staff harder. This man was no mere holy man, he thought. He had the bearing of a warrior. Seoras turned to the ancient one and dipped his head. The older man returned the acknowledgement with his own nod, before addressing Barra. He spoke, ignoring the body of the unconscious shield-bearer, whose slow rise and fall of his cloaked back revealed he still lived.

'There will be no fights between kings, this day. It must be settled at another time.' He was still for a time allowing his words to resonate. 'Continue, lord Barra. You said this Roman spared your life?'

'My thanks, Holy One,' Barra said. 'Yes, this man spared my life and saved that of my nephew. When he came to our lands seeking my help, I was honour-bound to give it. Though I did not agree unwillingly. He is an honourable man and courageous. And I count him a friend.'

Cai turned to the Novantae chieftain, surprised by this last. Barra did not take his eyes from the old priest.

'Very well. Let us hear what this Roman has travelled so far to seek from us.' He turned his intense stare upon Cai. 'Step forward and tell your tale, Roman.' The final word seemed to hold a threat.

Cai advanced a single step. He stood at ease, arms behind his back, as if he simply waited on a parade ground for the orders of the day. At first, he met the old man's fierce, though watery, eyes. Until, with a conscious effort he took in the faces of the chieftains before him. He felt a trembling in his legs, though when he spoke, was relieved his voice did not waver.

'My name is Caius Martis of the Nervii people,' he began. There was a snort of derision from someone unseen to his right. He did not react. 'I am the Praefectus Ala of the First Nervana and lead its mounted warriors.' He paused for a moment, taking a slow deep breath.

'I have served with the Eagles since I left my village as a boy. I have fought my emperor's enemies in many places and have done so for more than ten summers on the Isle of the Mighty. My cohort locked antlers with the Novantae people beneath the ramparts of their sacred hill. Their fierce warriors all but destroyed us, so great were our losses. Amongst those gravely wounded was my greatest friend and brother. Before he joined our ancestors around the hunting fire, I gave my oath to him that I would watch over his wife and son and see no harm come to them. I have done so these past years.

'This woman moved with her boy to the village outside of my fort. As time passed she became my woman and the boy as a son to me.' Cai could not hide the warmth from his voice. 'But, once more, war came to the lands of the Novantae. You know of the great battle at our fort. For many days we held the combined might of the Novantae, Damnonii and Selvogae. At last, the point came where we could hold on no longer, and our defences were overwhelmed. If not for the arrival of the Twentieth legion none would have survived.' There was complete silence in the room. Cai had expected to be cursed for the enemy he was and for the death he and his men had brought to the tribes. Instead, most appeared to be lost in their own memories.

'As the tribes withdrew, my woman was taken. I learned from Barra she had been captured and made a slave by the Blue Wolf.' A lascivious grin crossed the Damnonii's lips. Cai felt the red mist of his anger begin to rise. A firm hand took hold of his shoulder. Barra. He held tightly. Calm settled upon Cai once more

He turned back to the Holy One. 'I have come before you to ask she be freed so she may return to her son. I will pay whatever price you ask of me.'

Blue Dog began to rise, as if to speak, but was waved down by the old priest. 'You are courageous indeed to walk into the heart of the lands of your enemies, Roman. An oath holds great power to honourable men.' His voice took on a note of bewilderment. 'Yet surely your dead friend would see you have already fulfilled your vow to him. This is a mere woman. I do not understand why you have risked your life and the lives of your companions to rescue a wife. One who could so easily be replaced? Why?'

And it came to him, a way out of this. Cai turned to face Blue Dog. 'Because she carries my child.'

42

'How much longer until they have us skewered on a spit?' Hrindenus asked, his voice morose. 'I don't fear the pain. I fear the boredom of their chatter as I wait for the fires to cook me.'

Lucius knew he did not really need an answer for the Tungrian's question. Every man had his own way of dealing with their impending death.

They had been brought to this low hut. Its sides were well made of wattle and daub. The roof was reed thatch. There were six wooden cots lined against the walls, with a cold hearth at its centre. Lucius lay on his back with his hands behind his head, eyes closed, though accepting sleep was impossible. Especially as Hrindenus paced continually around the room.

'Sit down man,' Lucius said. 'You're making me dizzy.' Hrindenus harumphed, dropping heavily onto the cot opposite causing alarming creaking and cracking sounds from the straw-covered bunk. 'It's pointless imagining whatever this Holy One has in store for us. We'll just have to wait and see if Cai and Barra are successful.' Hrindenus snorted though did not pursue the point, for which Lucius was grateful.

After a few minutes of silence, Lucius heard a rustling at the doorway as the flap was pulled aside. He caught a glimpse of one the sentry's hide-covered troos. It was not a warrior who entered, but a woman.

She was bent over a small reed-thatched tray that held bread and cheese. Hrindenus leapt to his feet, ready to make a grab for the food. They had not eaten since early morning. The big man stopped in his tracks as the woman stood to her full height. Lucius's breath caught.

She wore a leaf-green coloured dress. Her dark hair was tied back in a single plait. Normally her dress would have been cinched at the waist with a tongue of leather. Instead, the bulge in her belly prevented it. The woman looked up suddenly, her grey eyes startled as she heard the catch of Lucius's breath.

'Alyn,' he said. She squinted in the gloom of the hut's interior, trying to discern his face. Instantly her expression changed.

'Lucius,' she said, wonder in her voice. She took a step, reaching out a hand, instantly withdrawing it. The momentary delight quickly turned to something else. She lowered her head.

'Alyn,' Lucius said again. 'We've found you.' He reached for her hand and he felt her stiffen as he took it. She did not pull away, nor did she seem to welcome his touch.

'You should not have come,' she said, after a moment, her eyes remained averted.

'Cai has come for you, Alyn,' Lucius said. 'He is, even now, speaking with this Holy One.' Her eyes instantly rose to meet his. Lucius saw fear.

'They will kill you all, Lucius,' she said, turning to Hrindenus as if seeing him for the first time. 'They do terrible things here to their enemies.' She began to weep. Fat tears raced across her cheeks, one dripping onto her swollen belly. 'My son is dead. I did not wish to lose the man I loved too. Even if it meant never seeing him again.'

'Alyn,' Lucius said gently. 'Beren's not dead. He was very much alive when last we saw him.' Her hand went to her mouth as if preventing a scream. Lucius saw the wildness in her eyes turn to suspicion.

'I saw him cut down,' she said, her voice challenging, and yet unable to hide the hope in it.

'He received a blow to the head, but soon recovered with Castellanos's help.'

'Aye, and he led us on a merry dance too,' Hrindenus chimed in.

Alyn scrutinised the face of the Tungrian, as if searching for the lie. 'Beren lives?'

'Aye,' was all Hrindenus could manage as a smile creased his face.

She sat heavily onto the nearest cot, the basket of bread and cheese resting on her lap, forgotten. After long moments she turned to Lucius once more, shaking her head slowly, her grey eyes desolate.

'You should not have come.'

43

There was an instant of complete stillness in the large hall as if the building itself held its breath. The fire crackled and spat as fat from the roasting hogs spat furiously into its flames. All heads turned from Cai to Blue Dog whose eyes roved the room. Thinking furiously, it seemed to Cai.

'The child is mine,' Blue Dog said, breaking the silence, his words snarled. 'I fucked her day and night on the retreat to Rerigon. I pleasured her more when I returned to my village. She begged for it when we awoke in the morning and when night fell. We rutted like deer in the mating season. We couldn't get enough of each other. And why not? Why would she want a Roman slave when she could have a king?' He smirked, and some of the Damnonii laughed.

Cai felt Barra's firm grip on his shoulder once more. 'Not here, brother,' he whispered. Cai felt the fury coursing through his body. Every fibre of his being demanded that he charge headlong at the Damnonii. Instead, he turned to the old priest.

'The child is mine, and Blue Dog is a liar,' Cai said, his voice icily calm. 'I will place my life before the gods and let them decide.' He turned to the Damnonii king who met his gaze. 'Let us, you and I, meet sword in hand, warrior to warrior in combat.' Cai noticed the calculating look in Blue Dog's eyes return, weighing up his odds of success, no doubt. A further jab was required. 'Unless the king of the Damnonii truly is a coward?'

The room erupted. Shouts of indignation came from many of the chieftains. Some jumped to their feet, faces red, as they screamed their fury, fwords almost unintelligible. Again, Cai noted, not all were so moved. Some merely watched Cai, faces inscrutable.

Blue Dog remained seated, his face outwardly calm, though his eyes were ever on the move.

'That should do it,' Barra whispered. 'But remember, he's cunning.'

'You will be silent.' The priest, Seoras, stepped forward into the ring of men once more. He swung his stout staff wide, forcing many of the Damnonii to step back, less they be struck by its knotted end.

'This cannot stand.'

Cai was surprised to hear the voice of Frang. Barra's diminutive cousin had remained standing as the other chiefs began to withdraw to their seats once more. 'Are the Damnonii going to allow their king to be insulted by an enemy?' Voices became raised once more, another a wide, arching swing of Seoras's staff instantly stilled them.

'You do not speak for us, Novantae.' This voice came from behind Cai and Barra, and, although quietly spoken, its words carried a force. Cai turned to see another of the Damnonii warchiefs was standing. Unlike most, his head was not shaven. Long locks of dark hair streaked with grey hung down his back. His long beard was neatly divided into three long plaits. He ignored Cai, instead staring at Blue Dog. 'I wish to hear what our king has to say about this challenge.' A few heads nodded in agreement.

There was a groan from the still prone body of Blue Dog's shield-bearer. The Damnonii king studied his man for a time, before turning his mad eyes upon Cai, a sneer twisting his lips. 'So be it,' he said. 'If this Roman whelp wishes to die for this woman, I won't stand in the way of his folly. The gods are with me and will decide in my favour. I am a king and will not sully my hands on this invader.' He looked again at his shield-bearer who had risen, slowly and unsteadily to his feet. 'Taog will deal with this fool.'

As if awaking from a dream, the huge warrior shook his head before turning to Cai. A smile grew slowly on his lips. One that did not reach his bloodshot eyes.

Taog spoke in a low rumble. 'Death awaits you, little Roman.' His smile broadened and this time his eyes creased with joy.

The old priest called an end to the gathering of chieftains. Cai noticed they did not leave in unison. Instead, most gathered into small groups. Knots of three or four of the Damnonii leaders spoke in lowered voices. The low hum gradually dissipated as they exited the hall. Blue Dog and Taog were amongst the last to leave, with Frang on their tail like an obedient hound.

'You have unsettled them.'

Cai turned sharply. He had not heard the young priest's approach. Seoras looked at both Cai and Barra in turn. Barra's face split into a wide smile and both he and the priest embraced warmly.

'It is good to see you again, Seoras.' Barra said. 'I didn't have the chance to thank you for your support when I was last in these lands.' They pulled apart and Seoras smiled sadly.

'My help came to nought in the end, it seems.'

'Perhaps. I thank you nonetheless.' There was a momentary pause before Seoras nodded towards the main door through which the chieftains had exited.

'They do not welcome this claim of Frang's. Most, it is clear to me, do not trust him and have no wish to see strife within the lands of an ally. More importantly l some of the fools fear they have chosen poorly in selecting the Blue Wolf as their king. The decision was close run, and now we find he may have lied about his woman.' Cai bristled at his words. 'Peace friend, I meant nothing by it.' He continued as Cai relaxed somewhat. 'Many too, did not like their king's refusal to face you. It is a craven act.'

Cai's attention was drawn by a rush of activity behind Seoras. More priests, similarly, dressed, appeared from a doorway at the rear of the great hall. Perhaps ten in total. At first, he thought they were going to clear away the detritus of drink and food left by the chieftains. Instead, they progressed past the three, each carrying something. A few held clay pots filled with strangely smelling concoctions. Others held sharpened knives, like those Cai had seen in use by the butcher in the Sack's village. Another carried rope coiled across his shoulders. When Seoras noticed the question in his eyes he shook his head.

'Do not ask,' he said. 'You will not like the answer.'

'Now what?' Barra asked.

'The Holy One has invited you all to the feast tonight. Sacrifices to the gods will be made and much drinking will be done. In the morning he will rule on the Novantae leadership. He is caught. He cannot call the king of the Damnonii a liar. We cannot, however, have a weak king of the Novantae in these difficult times. We need strong rulers. Which Frang will never be.' He flashed a smile at Barra. 'You may have to put the whetstone to your sword, my friend.' He turned to Cai. 'I will tell you tonight how Taog can be beaten.' Without another word, he bowed his head slightly and retreated through the internal doorway from which the other priests had appeared moments before.

214

44

Lucius heard the murmur of voices from outside of the hut. He couldn't discern what was being said, and moments later they moved away.

He tentatively moved the door flap at the entrance aside a handspan. The guards were gone. He pulled it fully open. The white-painted warriors were nowhere to be seen. There were a number standing on the palisade walkway and others moved through the fortress going about their duties. They showed no interest in Lucius.

'Well, either the sentries have abandoned their post, which seems unlikely given their fierce commander. Or, they have decided we are no longer a threat.'

'Perhaps they aren't going to skewer us after all?' Hrindenus said

'I don't think we can be confident of that yet. It may be they simply don't care if we attempt to escape. They know we won't get far.'

'You really are a cheerful soul aren't you, sir?'

Lucius scratched absentmindedly at his healing chest as he contemplated the fort's interior. There were numerous grain pits, as well as a stone-lined well. It really was a formidable edifice. He watched as two men, slaves from their gaunt faces, strained against a taut rope as they hauled up a large wooden pail from the well's depths. Water sloshed from its sides as they heaved it onto the stone-walled lip. This fortress could outlast a long siege. He would not want to be the officer tasked with attempting to storm it.

What an uncanny set of events had led him and his companions to this mysterious place beyond the edge of the world. He momentarily wondered what his life would have been like had his father not been murdered. More mundane, certainly.

The encounter with Alyn had shaken him. He had felt her flinch at his touch. The Carvetii woman was strong. He knew she had suffered. She was not the same Alyn Cai had come to know, even if they were able to free her from the clutches of Blue Dog. The memory of her as she moved energetically about the Sack tending to the wounded came to him. At the very least, it would take her some time to return to a semblance of the woman who had once appeared so full of life.

How would Cai react when they met? If they met. What about when the child was born? Could he treat the infant as his own, even if it became obvious it was not? Lucius already knew the answer. They were *his* family now. Alyn, Beren and yes, the unborn child. His friend would do what he must.

The crunch of approaching footsteps snapped Lucius from his reverie. Cai and Barra strode through the gate of the inner palisade. They were unescorted. Perhaps the audience had gone well? The looks on their faces told a different tale. Cai raised his hand in greeting.

He had intended to be more measured when he first spoke to his friend. Instead, he blurted it out. 'We saw her, brother. We saw Alyn.'

Cai stopped short, momentarily stunned. He grabbed both of Lucius's forearms. 'Where is she?' Excitement lit his features. He cast around, seeking.

'She's gone. I'm not sure where. The sentries came to collect her not long since. But we spoke to her, Cai.'

Cai continued to cast around the fortress's interior. He started to move; Barra grabbed him by the arm. He turned to face the Novantae, fury creasing his features.

'You must not seek her out,' Barra said. 'It will give Blue Dog an excuse to have you killed. Without the need for a meeting of swords to decide the fate of your woman.' Cai attempted again to pull away, Barra held firm. 'The chieftains will have returned to the village on the shoreline. They are not permitted to stay in this sacred place. They will return in the evening for the feast. You may have the opportunity to speak to her there. Though he will surely keep her close now.' Cai still seemed unmoved by the Novantae's words. Lucius intervened.

'Brother, what has happened? Was your plea listened to?' Cai kept his gaze on Barra, though his features softened, accepting. He shook his arm from Barra's grasp.

'Damn it all,' Cai snapped. 'So close. It's unbearable.'

'It will be decided soon,' Barra said.

'What will?' Hrindenus asked, as he appeared through the hut's doorway.

'I'll leave you to explain,' Barra said to Cai. 'I must go and find that damned Robogdii fool. Before he causes any more trouble with the priest-kind.' The Novantae strode away in the direction of the main gateway.

'Well, brother,' Lucius said. 'What happened in there?'

Cai sighed. He still felt an almost overwhelming desire to leave the fort in search of Alyn. Barra was right. It would achieve nothing. Only his own death. 'Let's go inside, away from prying eyes,' he said. 'And I will tell you all.'

'So,' Lucius said, as Cai finished his tale. 'You are to get the chance to fight for Alyn. That is more than we could have hoped for when we began this quest. You are a skilled fighter. I would give you decent odds.' Lucius heard the fake bravado in his own voice. Cai was well aware of the uncertainties of a one-on-one fight.

'He's a bull of a man,' Cai said, and Lucius heard the doubt creep into his friend's voice.

'You know as well as I,' Lucius said. 'Size can be a disadvantage. You will be quicker and he will tire.'

'Besides,' Hrindenus chimed in. 'Few men have been in the number of scraps you have. He will not have your guile and you must use this to your advantage.' Cai said nothing.

'When is the fight to take place?' Lucius asked. Cai shrugged.

'That's for the old priest to decide. As everything seems to be in this place.'

'Well let's remain alert. All of us,' Lucius said. 'I wouldn't put it past this madman to try to even up the odds tonight at this feast. We must watch our backs in this nest of snakes.'

45

Tiny snowflakes settled on the giant's shoulders. The low, heavy cloud-cover added to the otherworldliness of the land around her. Alyn sat in the bows; her eyes fixed on Taog's back as he hauled on the oars. The wooden paddles made rhythmic splashing sounds as they dipped in and out of the still waters of the channel.

Blue Dog was in the stern, keeping his own counsel. He had said nothing to her when he and the shield-bearer had arrived at the shoreline below the fortress ramparts where she had been instructed to wait. He had simply grabbed her arm, manhandling her into the wooden craft.

His moods were often unpredictable. On his island, Alyn had come to accept his casual violence. The cuffs across her cheek with the back of his hand had been most commonplace. Usually, she didn't get to know the reasons why. He simply revelled in the power he had over her. But when he had discovered that she was with child, his brutality had ceased. Blue Dog had even begun to talk to her occasionally. Not that she was expected to speak. She was merely his audience. He especially had not been able to contain himself in regard to his ambitions. He would be king, he had said, and she would be his queen.

She had recoiled internally at the thought of it. Though such status, she rationalised, would at least give her child a chance of survival. However, Alyn sensed something had changed. The old gut-twisting feeling returned. She dreaded what would happen once they reached Blue Dog's roundhouse in the settlement of the men.

She had seen Lucius. In his presence, Alyn had felt shame. But also joy. Beren lived. With the warmth of that knowledge, she could withstand any punishment.

Cai had found her. She had known, even in her darkest moments, he would seek for her. The hope had sustained her, even though she feared for his life. Had he seen Blue Dog? How would he free her from this beast? She feared the answer and tried to push it from her thoughts.

She shivered despite the woollen cloak. The sea-green garment had been a gift from Blue Dog. It had appeared on her cot shortly after he had become aware she carried his child. It had reeked of fish. Alyn had washed it over and over before she could bear to wear it. She was glad of it now.

The boat juddered to a halt as it crunched across the pebbles of the lake's narrow beach. Alyn stepped quickly over its wooden side and into the shallow, icy waters. She walked briskly onto the shore to escape its chill.

In the first days following their arrival at this desolate place, Alyn had often been greeted by coarse remarks from the bored Damnonii warriors. Always when not in the hearing of Blue Dog, whom most seemed to fear. However, on one occasion, as she had passed through the settlement on her way to cut wood for the hearth fire, Taog had overheard a comment made by a young warrior. He was barely more than a boy; the big man had struck him so hard it had taken him much of the remaining day to come back to consciousness. When he did awaken, the sight in one eye was blurred. It had remained so. After that, no one dared say anything to her. Not even in kindness.

Alyn crossed the hard ground, worn bare by many boots. She averted her eyes from the inevitable stares of the small bands of warriors. Bawdy laughter erupted to her right, though no comments were directed her way.

The snow was becoming thicker. It was late in the day and the freezing air had turned her fingertips a reddish-blue colour. Even so, she did not welcome the warmth of the hearth fire that would have been built up by Orla, Taog's woman. There would be no escaping Blue Dog once she entered the roundhouse's gloomy interior.

As Alyn approached the doorway the flap was flung back and Orla's head poked through. Her red hair, always seeming to stand upright in a parody of perpetual fright, now hung damply across her rounded shoulders.

'Oh, it's you,' Orla said, her words filled with disdain. For reasons Alyn had not been able to fathom, the Damnonii woman had taken a dislike to her from their first meeting on the island. Once it had become known she was with child, dislike had turned to hatred.

Orla had given no children to Taog. He did not appear to bear her any ill will because of it. Indeed, the pair were clearly very fond of each other, often behaving like lovers in the first flush of their coupling. Under different circumstances Alyn might have found it endearing.

'I'm away for more firewood. The broth is in the pot. Don't let it burn.'

Orla breezed past her without another word, waving at her man in greeting as she did. Taog was pulling the boat up onto the firmer ground. Blue Dog was animatedly conversing with one of his band. The Frog. The warrior's stout belly and long skinny legs gave him a comic countenance. He was regularly a target of fun for the other warriors. She could not feel sorry for him. On the island he had been her shadow. Though it was not her protection that he sought.

Blue Dog kept his voice low so as not to be overheard. Whatever it was appeared urgent.

She stared across the tall reeds of the lake to the stone fortress beyond. It was a dark smudge in the increasingly heavy snowfall. She hated that place. But somewhere inside its grey ramparts was Cai. An instant feeling of hope filled her. The sensation was quashed as she saw Blue Dog striding towards her.

She waited for him outside by the doorway. If she stayed within sight of the other bands of warriors, he might be less savage. It was a forlorn hope, she knew.

'Inside.' The order was brusquely given. His face was outwardly calm. Fear gripped her.

Alyn entered into the gloom of the hut's interior. It always smelled damp in comparison with the huts of the fort across the water. In the near silence she jumped at the snap of a burning log in the hearthfire.

She waited as Blue Dog followed on her heels. He stared at her; she did not dare meet his eyes.

He slowly raised his hand to the hilt of the dagger at his belt. He withdrew it from the leather scabbard. Alyn felt the fingers of his other hand interlacing amongst her hair, softly, at first, like a lover. Suddenly he gripped it tightly, yanking hard so she was impelled to meet his eyes. Those mad eyes.

She felt the cold of the iron blade as it caressed her neck. She could smell his breath. It was sweet from whatever it was he had been drinking in the Holy One's hall. Blue Dog played the keen blade lightly up and down her soft, pale skin.

'Is the child mine?' He breathed the words into her ear.

'You know it is,' she said. 'I have been with no other man.'

'That's not what the Roman says,' he whispered. 'Is the child his?'

'I swear I have lain with no one else. Only you. The child is yours.' There was near complete silence for a time. The only sound coming from his breath and the thrum of her heart as it beat against her chest.

'If the babe is born with fair hair, I will rip it from your arms and dash its head on a rock.' He licked her earlobe. It took a great effort not to flinch. 'Then, I will take this blade and slice you open from cunny to tit.' He played the flat of the blade between her legs, slowly drawing it to the top of her dress.

He turned suddenly from her and strode towards the hearth. Alyn released the breath she had been holding. She looked at his retreating back. The terror drained from her body to be instantly replaced by the white heat of fury.

You will not get the opportunity, she thought. I will slit your throat long before the child is born.

46

Would he be able to see Alyn before the fight? The thought had plagued Cai since Lucius had told him of his encounter with her.

The fire at the heart of the gathering burned fiercely. The flames licked like a myriad of great serpent's tongues towards the night sky.

The heavy cloud cover had cleared as night fell leaving a dark, star-filled cloak in its stead. Snow blanketed the rooftops of the fortress buildings. Underfoot it had been cleared by the passing of many boots across the stony fortress interior, leaving only a wet and filthy slush.

Wrapped tightly in his cloak, Cai silently observed these men of power as they interacted with one another. The chieftains had returned and were seated on long, low pine benches in a wide circle around the four stone pillars, the great fire at their heart. Even at this distance Cai felt its heat. He watched as the dancing light of the flames played across the surfaces of the sandstone, making the spiralled carvings appear to twist and writhe in life.

The old priest was seated on the opposite side of the ring from Cai, with Blue Dog on his left. The chieftain who had questioned his king at the gathering in the great hall was on his right. Perhaps the old man was trying to smooth ruffled feathers?

Taog no longer stood at his king's back, instead relaxed at his side. The weasel Frang had positioned himself next to the giant. Cai stared at the shield-bearer, trying to pick out some physical weakness. He could not.

'Big bastard, isn't he?' Hrindenus drawled. Since the feasting began, his Vexillarius had been consuming the dark ale as if he had an unquenchable thirst. Pork fat stained the fair hair of the scruffy growth of his beard.The Tungrian's lips split into a wide, idiotic grin.

'No need to look so damned happy about it, Hrindenus.'

The big man laughed. 'Don't worry, sir,' he said. 'I have every confidence you will prevail.' He slapped Cai on the back before taking another great swallow from the cattle horn, wiping a cascade of the liquid from his chin with his forearm. 'You just need to keep moving. He'll never catch you.'

Cai snorted a laugh despite himself. 'And when is it you decided to start calling me sir again, anyway?' Hrindenus laughed again.

Lucius was in a deep conversation with Barra, their heads close together like conspirators. Keefe had positioned himself next to his chieftain. His king. The big Hibernian appeared to be brooding as he stared silently into the flames, a horn of ale held loosely and forgotten in his sword hand.

'Your friend is wrong.'

Cai jumped with surprise. The priest, Seoras, had appeared, unheard on his left side.

'How in the name of the gods do you do that?' Cai said, not hiding his annoyance. The younger man continued as if Cai had not spoken.

'Taog is not slow. I've seen him fight many times. He will move quickly, using his reach and strength to overpower you.'

'I really am surrounded by helpful fuckers tonight,' Cai said. The priest smiled wanly. 'You said you would tell me how to beat him.' Seoras nodded slowly and turned to stare into the fiercely burning fire.

'Before I was taken from my family as a child, for training within the brotherhood, I lived in the same village as Taog. We weren't exactly friends though we ran in the same pack of boys amongst the forests and mountains near to our home. Even in those days he was much larger than his peers. Over the years he has developed into a hard and unforgiving man. In those days he was, in many ways, soft hearted.'

'On hot summer days, all us boys would swim in a deep spring that was surrounded by tall walls of rock. The bravest, or most stupid, amongst us would climb one of the more accessible cliff faces and, once the summit had been reached, jump into the pool below.

'It was not an easy climb and the surface of the rock was always slick and moss covered. Taog's great size made him less nimble than most, and he was wary of the climb, though never a coward. He made the ascent as many times as his peers.' Seoras took a quick swig of beer from his horn cup, warming to his tale. 'However, this one day, perhaps he was reckless. Or the rock wall was more treacherous than usual. Taog fell. Fortunately for him he was only a part of the way up, or it may have been worse for him. He struck the jagged rocks at the edge of the pool. His right leg was shattered above the knee.

'He lay in his father's home for months, his leg in a splint. He took a fever and perhaps a less brawny lad would have succumbed to it. With the help of one of the brotherhood, he survived. However, his leg thereafter has pained him. See how he holds it even now.' Cai glanced across the circle to the big Damnonii warrior. His right leg was stretched out and although he gave no outward sign of pain, Taog continually adjusted his sitting position.

The young priest continued. 'This is why he tries to finish any confrontation swiftly. After a time the pain becomes a burden. And this is how you can defeat him.

You must keep him moving. Fend him off until he begins to struggle. Then strike.'

'How often has he been beaten in this way?' Cai asked, his eyes wide with anticipation.

'Oh, Taog has never been beaten. There is always a first time for everything, is there not?'

Hrindenus who had been listening, enraptured by the priest's story, roared with laughter. Seoras looked at the Tungrian, perplexed by his mirth.

'One final thing. Since his fall, Taog is quick to anger. Goad him. Make him lose his reason.' The priest took on a thoughtful countenance for an instant. 'His woman. He has an inexplicable soft spot for the harpy. She has also failed to bear him children. Perhaps you could pick at that scab.' Cai nodded glancing across at the shield-bearer and jumped inwardly to see the big man staring back at him. Did he sense he was the subject of their conversation? Cai turned back to the priest.

'Why are you helping me?' he asked.

'Because choosing the Blue Wolf as their king was a mistake by the Damnonii chieftains. He will unleash chaos in these lands. Defeating his man and taking back your woman will be another humiliation. One, I am not sure, he will recover from. Our people value strength in their kings above all other qualities. And besides…' Seoras lapsed into silence, shrugging his shoulders.

'What?' Cai said.

'You have shown great courage coming here. Barra admires you too, for more than your bravery. Perhaps…perhaps one day you will be of use to our people.'

Cai did not question what use the young man meant. Another thought had come to him. He must see Alyn before the fight. He had been considering attempting to steal out of the fortress when the festivities reached a peak. Perhaps his absence would not be noticed. He had seen the white-painted warriors on the main gate and the walkways of the palisade. They were ever vigilant. It was a virtue hammered early into any new recruits to the cohort. He had cursed to see it in his enemies.

'You would like to be with your woman,' Seoras said. Cai looked back at the priest, unable to keep the surprise from his face. It was not a question, simply a statement of the truth. He continued to watch Cai, his face unflinching, as if searching for something.

'Would you help me to meet with her tonight? I'll not run.'

Seoras held Cai's earnest gaze. Considering. 'I can get you beyond our walls. After that it will be up to you. If you're caught, it will mean your death.'

'So be it,' Cai said. 'When?'

'Not until after the sacrifices. If you leave before, it will be noticed. One offering in particular could have been designed to provoke you into a rash reaction. You must not intervene, no matter what you see. Or hear.'

'Let me guess,' Cai said, his tone sardonic. 'If I do, it will mean my death.'

'Not only yours. Those of your company too.'

47

Two muscular priests pulled hard at the rope. It was attached to an iron ring that pierced the bull's snout. The animal resisted, perhaps sensing its imminent demise. It was encouraged to continue its ponderous progress towards the fire by the two slave boys. Each whipped at its flanks with thin branches of birchwood.

The beast was huge. The long, tan coloured hair of its tangled coat hung low, hiding its belly, making it appear even larger as its silhouette was framed against the flames. Seven more priests walked in procession a few steps to the rear of the boys. All were dressed in the familiar light coloured robes. Now, however, their faces were painted in the same whitewash as the men who garrisoned this place. Instead of their hair being fashioned into stiff, blade-like points it was slicked back against their scalps by a concoction that shimmered in the firelight.

Two priests to the fore of this group each held a pair of wickedly sharp, long-bladed knives. A third carried a small wooden pail. As far as Lucius could tell from the way it swung in the priest's hand, it was empty. The remaining four were split into pairs, each supporting a large wicker basket between them.

The sight, in a strange way, was a familiar one to Lucius. In his childhood, his father had taken him and his brother each year to the feast of Saturnalia in the local town of Acinipo. There they would watch the usual troop of actors perform at the theatre atop the cliffs. The highlight of the day, though, was the sacrifice of a bull by the priests at the temple of Saturn. Afterwards the meat was distributed to the poor of the town. Or so it was said. It seemed priests, the world over, were expert butchers.

From the far side of the circle, the Holy One arose. His movement, like the bull's, was slow and ponderous. With no supporting hand from Seoras, he instead used a stout wooden staff. The young priest had vanished from Cai's side some moments ago. Lucius had wanted to question Cai on his conversation with the strange young man. But the appearance of the bull had taken everyone's attention.

The old man raised his staff two-handed above his head. He began to sing. More of a chant, his voice strong and surprisingly melodious. The words were in a language Lucius did not understand, even so its sing-song rhythm was inviting to the ear. After a period of several minutes the ancient priest's performance came to a slow ending. The melody petered out. An instant after the last note left the Holy One's lips, he lowered his staff.

A strangled bellow erupted from the bull, quickly cut off. The animal collapsed onto its haunches as one of the priests sliced through the big arteries of its neck. Another of his brethren, garments spattered with the animal's blood, held a pail under the stricken beast's throat, collecting the gushing red liquid. In moments the bull breathed out a last great gust of air as it slumped onto its side.

The priests set to work. The pair who had held the long knives removed the bull's head and began skinning the animal. At an impressive pace the hide was removed in one piece. It soon resembled a blood-spattered rug, which the two slave boys immediately began to scrape with wide-bladed knives of their own.

Next the animal was butchered. Huge cuts of meat were flung into the large baskets. In no time, almost nothing remained save a darkly glistening patch of ground and the broad skin that the slave boys continued to work at with a zeal.

The activity did not stop there. Once the meat had been carried from the circle of chieftains, the priests reappeared, this time bearing prepared timber of and struts. Lucius continued to watch, curious as to what was being constructed. It soon became apparent it was to be a great spit, for cooking. His stomach bulged from the mound of pork he had already consumed. He couldn't bear the thought of eating a pile of beef too.

He turned to the Novantae warchief. 'Surely they are not about to begin cooking a second course,' he said. 'I'm full to bursting already.' Barra didn't look at him. His face remained impassive, though his eyes held a pained expression.

'It's not the kind of meat you are going to want to eat. Another sacrifice is being prepared. It will cause you great pain to witness. You and the others must bear it, no matter the cost to you. You cannot intervene. The consequences for you and your men would be severe. I tried to intercede but Blue Dog insisted it should go ahead. I am sorry, Nervii.'

'What is it?' Lucius asked, a sick feeling settling in his stomach. The Novantae simply shook his head, saying nothing more.

'What are those lads up to?' Hrindenus said. The Tungrian had slid closer to Lucius as Cai also looked on. The two slaves were using long bone needles to thread animal gut through the bull's thick hide. The wiry, muscled youths worked swiftly and in tandem. One held two sides together whilst the other sewed making a seam. Soon what resembled a huge egg sat before the fire. The dense hair of the animal was on the inside. One seam had been left open. Waiting.

231

Lucius's attention was caught by movement from across the circle. The old priest was rising once more. Again, he raised the staff above his head, though this time he did not sing. Instead, he simply slowly lowered it until it was level with his hips. There he held it, clasped by his bony fingers.

It was then, Lucius noticed Blue Dog. The Damnonii king was watching him. His piercing eyes took on a red hue in the light of the flames. His lips were twisted in a sneer. He knew what was coming and his enemy would not like it.

Barra leaned across Lucius so that Hrindenus would also hear his words. 'Remember, whatever happens you must not react. If you wish to keep your lives, you must watch and do nothing.'

A commotion flared up out in the darkness. A voice was raised in anguish, getting louder as it neared the fire. It was a man's voice, though high pitched. It babbled hysterically, in a language Lucius did not understand. It was not of the People, nor was it Latin, though its sound was strangely familiar.

A group of four priests emerged from out of the night, still wearing blood-spattered robes. Between them they held a struggling, writhing captive. His skin was darker than all those present. He was stripped to the waist. Deep welts covered his chest, oozing with infection. It was his troos, however, that confirmed it for Lucius. They were a deep red in colour and ballooned loosely along his legs, cinched at his ankles.

'Oh gods,' Hrindenus groaned. 'He's a Hamian.' The archers from the empire's distant east were well known and perhaps the most easily recognisable of all the troops in the north. With a rising feeling of rising horror, Lucius recognised what was about to happen. He tasted acrid bile.

'You must stop this,' Lucius said to Barra.

'I cannot.'

Lucius began to rise. Instantly he felt a firm hand take hold of each of his shoulders.

'You must not, Roman.' It was Keefe. Barra's shield-bearer held him fast. 'There is nothing to be done.'

Lucius felt impotent. He turned towards Cai. Anguish twisted his friend's features. And yet he sat rock-still, as if Keefe's hand held him too.

The archer continued to struggle, kicking out in increased desperation. His hands were bound at his back. The priests trussed his ankles, before feeding him feet first into the open seam of the huge egg. The prisoner writhed. The hide bulged as he kicked at its side. It was to no avail.

With the help of the priests the slave boys sewed up the last remaining seam. They had left a small gap open in its top. Lucius's stomach lurched as the Hamian's head popped through the hole in a parody of birth.

The chieftains' howled with laughter. Most of them. Lucius noted Frang appeared to be enjoying the archer's terror most. Even whilst seated, the Novantae's legs danced a jig in his excitement.

'If you don't kill that shit. I will. I swear it.' Lucius, though addressing Barra, could not bring himself to look at him. The Novantae king was silent.

The priests began to haul the egg-shaped hide, with its frantically babbling human inhabitant, towards the wooden frame. A horse-hair rope was passed through slits in the animal skin, its other end looped around the frame. Four of the priest-kind strained at the rope. It rose, inch by inch, until it almost touched the frame's topmost wooden spar.

The sweating priests moved the frame over the fire. The flames had been allowed to die down over the course of

233

the evening, so they merely licked the bottom of the egg's skin. At first there was a hissing sound as the moisture left in the hide dried out. It smoked and steamed, temporarily obscuring the container.

The Hamian's pleas for mercy became more desperate, his words screamed unintelligibly across the circle of watchers, who continued to laugh uproariously at the entertainment.

The slave boys rushed forward carrying a wooden bucket between them. Water sloshed over the sides as the heavy bucket knocked against their scrawny legs with the movement. In turn, each tossed the liquid contents against the bottom of the egg to prevent the hide from scorching. They did not want the Hamian to be charred, Lucius realised. They wanted him cooked.

The Hamian's terrified cries ceased. Instead, a long, lingering scream pierced the air. The egg moved wildly as the prisoner thrashed in his desperation to escape his agony.

'You damned animals,' Lucius said, the snarled words drowned out by the tormented screams and the accompanying laughter.

48

The poor wretch had taken an age to die. His inhuman shrieks had pervaded the fortress. There was no escaping them. At one point the archer had passed out, only to be forced awake again by showers of cold water cast by the slave boys. An aroma akin to cooking pork had filled the air and Cai knew he would not be able to eat of that meat again.

Abruptly, the screams had ceased. Cai had prayed, he knew not who to, for the Hamian's heart to give out. It seemed his prayers had been granted. The death had been greeted with a wild cheer from most of those gathered and the feasting arose to new heights of revelry. Although the old priest was no longer amongst them.

Where was Seoras? He had said he would come.

'That was no way to die,' Lucius said. Cai turned to his friend, seeing disgust and pity warring on his features.

'No,' Cai said, his voice barely a whisper. Lucius sat on the bench next to him.

'What were you and the priest talking about? You appear to have formed quite the friendship.'

'He said he would help me.'

'With what?'

Cai turned to Lucius. 'To get out of this fort tonight.'

'You are going to seek out Alyn.'

'If I can. She's being held in that shit hole of a village we passed through.'

'It's one thing to get out. How do you plan to get back in? You've seen how vigilant these damned white-faces are.'

Cai shrugged. 'Seoras said he knew how.'

235

Lucius looked like he was about to object. In the end he said nothing, instead his friend's hand rested gently on Cai's shoulder.

'May the divine Fortuna be with you, brother. Hrindenus and I will do our best to cover for you.'

'Thank you, Lucius. For everything.'

Lucius returned to the others. Cai saw him speak in low tones to Hrindenus and Barra. Keefe was there too, the Hibernian's gaze remained on to the chieftains across the low burning flames of the fire. Who was he watching? Frang? It was hard to tell.

His own thoughts drifted. If he reached her, what would he say? How would she react to him? He feared she would reject him.

He yelped at a piercing sting against his shoulder. He turned sharply, searching for the rock thrower. In the darkness he saw an indistinct shadow. It must be the priest. Cai glanced back at the chieftains. None were taking any notice of the Romans. He slipped away from the bench and into the night.

'Are you sure about this, wise one?' Neacal said. The lead warrior waited by the main gate, his face no longer covered in the chalk paint. Blobs of it still clung to the corners of his eyes. His hair too had been washed clean.

'Yes. Do this for me, Neacal. I have my reasons or I would not ask such a thing.' The warrior stared at the young priest, light from the flames of the torches above the gateway flickering in their eyes as they met. Cai saw the resemblance between the two was unmistakable.

With a snort of frustration, Neacal raised the locking spar, pulling the heavy door open. Cai had expected it to creak, instead its movement was soundless. Seoras nodded his thanks to the warrior and passed through the opening. Cai followed swiftly.

'He's your brother,' Cai said as the pair reached the shoreline. In the near-complete darkness the only sound was the soft rustling of the reeds in the chill breeze.

'Is it so obvious? Yes, he is my elder brother, by more than three years. He followed me when I was chosen. Not to become a priest. To protect me. Not that he would ever admit to it. Our father was furious,' the young man laughed softly. 'We were both happy to leave the cruel bastard behind.' Abruptly he strode off into the night. 'Follow me.'

They crunched along the shoreline until they reached an area, lit dully by two tall torches, where the chieftain's boats had been pulled up onto a patch of land below the fortress's ramparts, further away from the main gate this time. 'This one,' Seoras said. Without waiting he pulled the smallest of the boats towards the entrance to the channel. At the water's edge he lifted a paddle from the bed of the craft, handing it to Cai.

'You have perhaps an hour. Two at most. Don't linger. Blue Dog is no fool. After the events of this afternoon, he will have put a watcher on your woman. You will have to deal with them first. His roundhouse is the largest and is nearest to the channel. Now go.'

Cai did as he was bidden. He pushed the boat away from the shoreline, feeling the near-freezing water soak into his boots. He stepped carefully into the craft and began to paddle towards the far shore.

Once he entered the channel it wasn't long before he was able to pick out the first of the flickering lights from the village. He couldn't hear any revelry though men must be about. He must find a way into the settlement not requiring him to cross the open ground from the water's edge.

His memory of their arrival told him the village was nestled on a narrow strip of land between the lake and woodland. He formed a plan. It meant leaving the small craft amongst the reeds, hoping he could discover it once again on his return. If he returned.

Cai removed his cloak and slipped over the side, the cold of the water taking his breath away. It wasn't deep, reaching his chest. He pushed the boat amongst the reeds, far enough it would not be seen by the casual eye. Then he began to swim for the entrance to the river. The route, he prayed, would keep him out of sight of any in the village.

Cai felt his limbs begin to stiffen, his hands becoming numb. He slowly passed the village. There were two fires, around which a number of warriors warmed themselves, talking in quiet tones. He heard laughter.

He entered the mouth of the river. The slow-moving current took him past the last roundhouse and out of sight. He kicked for the river's bank, pulling himself onto the shore. In moments he was amongst a dense tangle of trees. Water dripped from his hair and he began to shiver uncontrollably.

Without light he would have to move with great care, picking his way towards Blue Dog's hut. He heard laughter once again, this time muffled by the buildings and the dense woodland. At least he could be sure he was headed in the right direction.

It took much longer than he had hoped. A number of times he had to stop to untangle his tunic from the thorn bushes. Finally, he reached the rear of what he thought must be the roundhouse. Where Alyn was held.

He crouched, listening. Other than the distant sounds of men conversing by the fires all seemed at peace. Most would be sleeping. He hoped any guards would be too. Cai braced to rise once more.

Someone coughed and spat. Cai froze. A man's cough, no more than twenty or so paces to his left. He heard a giggle, a woman's laugh, followed by the deeper chuckle of a male voice. The woman laughed again, coarsely this time.

'Come on my little Froggie. I need you to fuck me hard one more time with that big prick of yours. Before Taog returns from the feast. You don't want him to catch you not guarding the bitch, do you?'

'It's freezing, Orla, my dear. You need to warm me up a bit first.' Another coarse female laugh.

'How about this, Froggie?'

Cai couldn't make out the smothered response. He took his chance. Alyn was unguarded. He left the treeline, soon reaching the rear of the roundhouse. He moved swiftly around its edge. Snowmelt ran from its eves onto his head and under his tunic. The first of the fires came into view. It was a good spear's throw distance, still its light cast the warriors' long shadows against the hut's wattle.

It was now or never. He dashed the last few steps, reaching the entrance to the hut. Without pause he pulled back the door flap and entered. He halted inside the doorway, his heart thudding against his ribcage, but ready to deal with an attack from within. Other than the crack of wood burning in the hearth fire, there was only silence.

The flames gave out the only light. It took a moment for Cai's sight to adjust. A sitting figure was hunched by the fire, wrapped tightly inside a thick cloak. A hand reached out from within its folds for a piece of firewood and added it to the flames. She seemed unaware, or uncaring, that someone had entered the hut.

'Alyn,' he breathed her name. She didn't move. 'Alyn,' he said, hearing the crack in his voice.

The woman turned, tentatively, as if not quite believing her own senses. Her eyes squinted into the gloom beyond the fire's halo. Her face was pale and her hair covered by the hood of the cloak; still, there was no mistaking who this was. Alyn. Cai stepped into the light.

Her eyes widened, and her hand went to her mouth. She shook her head as if this might be a deceitful vision.

'Is it really you?'

Cai rushed to her. Kneeling, he took hold of her hand in his. 'Yes, my love. It's me. I'm a little late, I know'

She touched his cheek gently with her fingertips. 'Your beard?'

Cai laughed gently. 'A ruse to fool any we met. It's growing back though. I will soon return to my handsome best.' Alyn smiled, a fleeting flicker of her lips. She looked to the doorway, fear filling her grey eyes.

'You must go. I'm being watched. If they catch you...'

'Don't worry, we have a little time. Taog's wife is keeping the wretch occupied in the woods.' He gently squeezed her hand.

'You can't free me. We will not get far.' Alyn's hand drifted to her stomach hidden by the heavy folds of the cloak. She lowered her head. 'You don't know it all.' Her voice was barely a whisper. Cai heard the anguish in it.

Cai squeezed her hand gently again, raising her chin with his other. 'The woman Fiona told me.' He rested the palm of his hand on her belly, feeling its firmness.

She met his eyes. Hers glistened in the firelight. 'It may be his? I cannot be sure.' Her words fearful. She gripped his hands tightly. 'I tried to fight him at first...'

'The babe will be mine, no matter the colour of its hair,' he said. Tears flowed in rivulets across her cheeks. Cai pulled her into an embrace. 'Do not worry, Alyn. We'll soon leave this place.'

Alyn pulled away from him to gaze into his eyes once again. 'What price must you pay for my freedom? He will never let me go. All the Damnonii believe the child is his.'

Cai met her eyes again. 'In front of this Holy One and all the Damnonii chiefs, I laid claim to the bairn. I challenged him. But the coward wheedled out of it. I am to fight his champion instead.'

'No,' Alyn gasped. 'You cannot fight Taog. He's a beast. Please don't do this. I can survive here. I could not bear it if I knew you were dead.'

Cai took both of her hands in his. They trembled. He raised them to his lips, kissing both in turn. 'It will not be easy. The gods have shown me favour over the many years in this land. They will not abandon me now.' He turned to look towards the doorway. 'Besides, after tonight I know how I will defeat him.'

Cai pulled the boat up onto the dry ground under the palisade of the fortress. He couldn't remember the last time he had been this cold. It had taken him an age in the water to find the boat amongst the reeds. Now, even with his cloak wrapped around him once more, he felt frozen to his very bones.

'This way. Hurry.' The whispered words urged in the darkness. It was Seoras. The young priest appeared on the edge of the torchlight, beckoning. Cai moved swiftly, seeing he was in earnest.

'What is it?' Cai asked.

'Your luck has held. Blue Dog and the chieftains are only now leaving.' As if to confirm it, he heard laughter along the shoreline. 'We'll conceal ourselves here and wait for them to leave.' Seoras lead Cai through a dense patch of tall scrub. As he crouched, he was still able to see the flickering light of the torches. The laughter and raucous calls were getting closer.

'You saw her?' Seoras whispered.

'Yes.'

'And you weren't seen?'

'The guard was occupied elsewhere.'

The Damnonii had reached the boats. One chieftain was singing a bawdy song, his voice slurred. Much of it was unintelligible, though Cai discerned the words Roman and arse. Some of the chieftains joined in the chorus.

There was a splash, followed by an eruption of laughter from the others. 'Ach, I'm soaked. Who pushed me?' More laughter.

'A race to the other side,' someone shouted. Cai heard the sound of many feet splashing into the water. Chaos reigned as the Damnonii chieftains and shield-bearers began a drunken race. In minutes they had gone, their shouts and laughter resounding back along the channel.

Cai began to rise, only to be pulled back by Seoras. 'Wait,' he whispered. 'More are coming.' Moments later he heard them.

'Have they gone?' Cai recognised the voice of Blue Dog.

'Yes lord.' This, from Taog. It was quiet for a time as the crunching footsteps continued towards the boats.

'The Holy One will surely decide the shield fights will take place before the sun reaches its highest mark. Are you ready, Taog?'

'Yes lord. I will not take long to deal with the Roman.'

'Don't be overconfident my friend. He's no coward.'

'I will crush him.'

'And you, Frang,' Blue Dog said, his voice menacing. 'Are your preparations complete?'

242

'Yes,' Frang said. 'Barra will not see out this night.' There was silence for a moment. Cai slowly released the breath he'd been holding. The Novantae king must be warned.

'Are your men ready to make the return to Novantae lands tonight? The white warriors will hunt you down if you are not.'

'Yes, we will be gone as soon as I return to the village.'

'You understand the Holy One will not consecrate your reign. But…you will have my support and the support of its warbands to aid you in holding your lands.'

'And what price must I pay for this service?' Frang said, not masking his suspicion.

'You will swear fealty to me. You will pay tribute after each harvest season. You will be my man. Do we have an agreement?'

'You forget I have the support of the dark Roman.' Frang's voice had become shrill. 'He has rewarded me richly for my information over the years. More will come for the word I sent on the threat of war from the Novantae. He will come to my aid if I have the need and with another bag of his silver.

Blue Dog laughed. 'Well little Frang, do you think you are Urbicus's only spy amongst the People? Why do you think I brought my band to Caden? I was to kill the old bastard if the opportunity presented itself. In the end the fool came to me. Urbicus has built his wall and has left the Isle of the Mighty. Rome is on the other side of the world. You are alone, my friend.' Again, the silence returned, with only the sound of the wind rustling through the reeds once more.

'Well? Do we have an understanding?'

'Yes, lord,' Frang said, his voice almost inaudible.

243

49

Lucius and Hrindenus returned to their hut. The Tungrian had staggered most of the way from the feast at the standing stones. He had become subdued following the torture of the Hamian. It had not slowed his drinking. If anything, he drank with complete abandon. Lucius had helped him into his cot and his snores reverberated around the room.

There was no sign of Cai. Nor the young priest. The Damnonii appeared not to have noticed his absence. Or, at least, none had challenged it, so consumed were they by their revelry. The bull-hide ball had eventually been hauled away by the priests, the body of the archer still inside. Lucius had been grateful for that. It would be some time before the man's agonised pleading left the forefront of his mind.

Barra had remained by the fire, talking quietly to Keefe. The Novantae had told Lucius he expected the old priest would decide both fights must take place on the following day. Lucius feared for his friend. Cai was one of the most courageous of men but, the Damnonii might be the ending of him.

'Where are you, brother?' he whispered.

The answer was not long in coming. Lucius heard running footsteps approaching. The skin to the doorway was flung back. Cai's head poked through.

'Lucius. Thank the gods. Where is Barra?'

Lucius jumped to his feet. 'He's still by the fire with Keefe. Why? What is it?'

'He's in danger. Come.' Cai disappeared, the sound of his running feet heading in the direction of the earlier gathering. Lucius followed, leaving Hrindenus snoring. The Tungrian would be of little use.

'Lord.' The shouted warning was unmistakable. Keefe. A sound part roar, part scream erupted an instant later.

'Keefe. Traitors. I'll—' Barra yelled. The Novantae king's voice was cut off.

'Brothers! Raise yourselves! We are attacked.' Lucius recognised the voice of Seoras from deeper in the fortress.

As he approached the circle of benches Lucius saw Cai crouched over a prone body. It was Barra. Keefe was standing at the farthest side of the circle screaming his defiance into the night. Lucius could see no enemy in the darkness.

'Stay still, Barra.' Cai spoke firmly. 'Let me see the arrow.'

'This is your chance to finish me off, Nervii,' Barra's attempt at humour was partly hissed through gritted teeth. As he reached the scene, Lucius could see the agony writ across the Novantae's features. Lucius moved to the other side of Cai for a better view. His heart sank. An arrow was buried a handspan deep into his side.

'Lord?' Keefe had returned and knelt by Barra, the despair in his eyes making him seem almost child-like. The Hibernian's face was white and it was only then Lucius noticed the arrow protruding from the big man's shoulder.

'From the shape of the entrance wound I don't think the arrowhead is barbed,' Cai said. 'I can pull it?'

'Do what you must,' Barra said.

'Hold your hand,' Seoras said, his voice commanding. 'Let's get him into the hall. My brothers will see to his wound.' He turned to Keefe. 'You too.'

The Hibernian shook his head.

'No,' he said. 'That snake Frang has done this. I will find him and rip out his innards.'

'You're right. It was likely Frang. I've already sent Neacal in pursuit. And you will be of no use to your lord if you bleed to death. Come.'

A small group of priests emerged from the darkness and into the light of the dying fire. Lucius saw one of them still wore blood-soiled robes. 'Carry lord Barra into the great hall.' Seoras said. 'And be careful of the arrow.'

In moments, Barra had been laid on a pile of animal furs, near to the hearth. More priests appeared from the doorway at the building's rear carrying an assortment of implements. Some appeared familiar to Lucius, much like ones he had seen in Castellanos's box.

The priests ushered Lucius and Cai away from the Novantae's side.

'Sit, Keefe,' Seoras said from behind the pair. 'You are too big for me to see the wound properly if you stand.' The Hibernian slumped heavily onto a low stool, not taking his eyes from his lord as the priests fussed around him.

'Just get it out, priest,' Keefe said. Seoras turned to Lucius and Cai, waving them over to his side.

'When I remove the arrow, you must hold this compress firmly against the wound.' The young priest held a strange-smelling pad of material to Lucius. 'You,' he said to Cai, 'must quickly bind the compress to the shoulder.' Cai nodded his understanding, taking the proffered dressing.

Seoras gripped a pair of iron tongs. 'Are you ready, Keefe?' The Hibernian grunted. Seoras nodded to Lucius and Cai. The priest clasped the arrow shaft with the tongs and took a deep breath. 'Prepare yourself.' Keefe tensed. He yelped like a foxcub an instant later as Seoras yanked hard. The shaft came most of the way, though not cleanly. The young priest had to gently lever the wood from the meat of the big man's shoulder, the shaft cracking as he did so. With a sucking sound and a growl of pain from Keefe, the arrowhead was freed. Blood flowed freely from the wound, Lucius swiftly covered the gash with the compress and soon Cai had the bindings done.

'Here, drink this.' Seoras handed Keefe a small clay bottle. 'Drink it all.' Keefe took it, gulping it down as he went to his lord's side.

Seoras stretched his back as he observed the activity by the hearth. 'We must pray to the gods that the arrow did not pierce his lung,' he said, as he went to attend his brethren.

'Did you see her, brother?' Lucius asked, turning to Cai. 'Did you see Alyn?'

'Yes,' he said, his voice terse. 'I saw her. And the sooner I kill Blue Dog's man the better. I want to be gone from this place.' He turned then to his friend, unable to meet his eyes. 'She has suffered enough at the hands of these animals.'

Lucius's attention was caught by the appearance of the old priest from the doorway at the hall's rear. His white hair hung in long straggles across his shoulder. He wore a simple white tunic and walked gingerly with the aid of his wooden staff. Seoras had seen him too and went to his side. They spoke together in low tones. Seoras, at one point, glanced in Cai's direction.

'Do you know what is going on?' Lucius asked.

'Frang has attempted to murder Barra, instead of having the courage to face him. He's in league with Blue Dog. The runt and his band will be making a run for it. Seoras's brother is hunting them.'

'Seoras's brother?'

'The leader of the white faces is the priest's brother. His name is Neacal. There's more. Frang is Urbicus's—'

The main doors burst open, banging hard against the internal walls, the sound resonated around the chamber. In strode Neacal, his face still clear of the white paint. He halted for a moment, searching from face to face, until he saw Seoras and the old priest. Lucius and Cai followed as the warrior walked briskly towards them.

'Holy One,' Neacal said, dipping his head, his voice firm but respectful. 'Frang and his band have fled. They've taken their boats from the village.'

'It is a desperate thing to attempt to navigate the river at night,' Seoras said. 'He aims to usurp the Novantae lands. As I said, Holy One. He spurns the consecration.'

'His people will not accept him,' the old man croaked.

'The Damnonii king has offered him his protection in exchange for fealty,' Seoras said.

'More than that, Holy One, both Frang and the Blue Wolf have taken Rome's silver. The other chieftains must be told.'

The old priest shook his head before turning to look upon the place where Barra lay, surrounded by the priest-healers. 'We must ensure king Barra lives. He must bring the usurper before us. This insult to the gods cannot go unpunished.'

'What of the Blue Wolf?' Seoras asked, addressing Neacal.

'He acts as if nothing is amiss. He is drinking with his hearth warriors. He claims he did not know Frang was leaving. Nor, he said, did he care. The Novantae lands are lost. Those were his words to me.' The warrior turned to the old priest. 'Should I bring him before you, Holy One?'

'No. He is king of the Damnonii. We must tread with care. It will be your word and the Romans' against his.'

The old man looked beyond Neacal, taking in Lucius and then Cai. 'Are you ready to fight his champion?' Cai nodded. 'Good. I will pray to the gods that you slay him.'

50

There was barely a breath of wind as the snow began to fall. Although the sun had risen long since, the low-lying cloud cover made it feel like dusk.

Cai waited on the rise where the Damnonii boats had been pulled onto the shore. His back was to the fortress's stout outer palisade, where many of the white-faced warriors stood on its parapet. A silent audience.

Lucius was at his side. His friend had been full of good advice. None of it was new, said more in comfort and for want of something else to say. His commander was silent as he held Cai's shield.

Before he left the fortress, Seoras had come to him in the hut he shared with Lucius and Hrindenus. 'Take this,' he had said. 'It will be of greater use than the blade you brought with you.' Cai had untied the bindings of a deer skin, to reveal a magnificent sword.

The steel glistened in the light of the hut's small hearth fire. Its grip was bound in new leather strappings. The end of the hilt was decorated with a snarling bear's head of silver. A Roman officer's spatha. Cai gave the priest a questioning look. Seoras smiled briefly. 'He fought bravely before I killed him,' was all he had said.

Cai had made a number of practice strokes. The balance was superb. Lighter than the sword he had left on the farm with Mascellus, and its blade was keen. It rested in its scabbard at his hip. He gripped its hilt for comfort.

'Here he comes,' Lucius said. Cai watched the channel, so different in appearance in the daylight. There were three men in the boat. One pulled at the oars. Blue Dog sat in its bows, his back towards the island. It was the

Damnonii king's shield-bearer, however, that his sight fixed upon. Taog was seated in the aft of the small craft, his bulk forcing the sides of the boat low to the waterline. Across his knee rested a huge, scabbarded sword.

The Damnonii spotted Cai on the rise. The big man's eyes narrowed at first, before a wide grin broke across his lips. Cai met his leer with a calmness he did not feel. He did not release his own stare until the boat crunched against the shoreline. Cai had thought Blue Dog might bring Alyn. She was not in the boat and he felt an unexpected feeling of relief.

Taog was first to come ashore, wading across the ankle-deep water. He was greeted with a chorus of cheers from some of the waiting Damnonii chiefs. A few kept their silence. Blue Dog followed next. His face held a wide smile. It didn't reach his eyes. Cai sensed his discomfort.

The giant and his king paraded through the gathering and made towards the rise where the old priest awaited them, a few short paces from Cai, and supported by the ever-present Seoras.

'Drink, sir?' Hrindenus held up a leather skin to Cai. He shook his head.

'I would kill for a piss right now,' Cai said. 'But I don't want the big lump to think I fear him.'

'Just skewer the fucker, sir.'

The snow began to fall more heavily as Blue Dog and Taog reached the top of the rise. The Damnonii king bowed his head to the old priest.

'Greetings, Holy One.' The old priest returned the greeting with the slightest of nods but said nothing to the king. Instead, he walked, supported by the young priest, to the centre of the rise where Cai waited with Lucius. Blue Dog and Taog followed in his wake.

251

In a sudden and unexpected motion, Seoras swung his own staff out in a wide circle, forcing the advancing Damnonii to halt where they were, creating space between the two adversaries. Blue Dog frowned, his mad eyes glinting at the affront, but held his tongue.

The old priest surveyed the Damnonii chieftains, who waited at the base of the rise. 'This will be a fight to the death,' he began, his voice reedy though firm. 'The king's shield-bearer stands as his champion.' Cai noticed frowns on the faces of some of the warchiefs. 'The fight will be with sword and shield. No one will interfere.' The old priest was silent for a moment, letting his words take hold.

'If the Roman wins, he has the right to take the woman and return in peace with his companions whence they came. They will be unmolested.' Again, he waited a few moments before continuing. 'If the Roman should lose, his head will be hung from the gates of this holy place until the flesh falls from its bones. His companions will see out the remainder their days as slaves to my brothers on this sacred isle.'

'They'd better not come anywhere near my arse,' Hrindenus grumbled under his breath.

The old priest stepped back to be replaced by Seoras. 'When I lower my staff, the fight will begin. Do you understand?' he said, taking in Cai and Taog by turn. Cai nodded, Taog simply aimed another grin at Cai.

'May divine Mars and Fortuna be with you, brother,' Lucius said, holding the shield for Cai to slip his arms through.

'If not, I'll see you around the hunting fire, Lucius.'

For a short time, Cai was on his own. He felt the heft of the leather-bound shield and adjusted his grip. Next, he drew the sword from its scabbard. It felt good. For an instant he heard the mocking laugh of his old friend.

'Be with me, Adal,' he whispered into the increasingly heavy flurries of snow. 'Or be ready with a cup of ale, you old miser.'

He heard a laugh, this time not from the otherworld. 'Praying to your gods, are you Roman? Even they can't help you now.' Cai said nothing, simply holding his enemy's stare until he saw Seoras step forward. The young priest gripped his staff in both hands, holding it horizontally over his head. Cai tensed. Ready. The staff lowered.

51

Taog roared. He covered the open ground between them in an instant, quicker than Cai would have believed. Had he not been forewarned of Taog's usual tactic he would have been felled swiftly. As it was, he barely had time to sidestep the charge. Nonetheless, his shield took a heavy back cut from the warrior's sword as his momentum took him past, the impact jarring Cai's arm.

Taog turned, bellowing his frustration at Cai's escape. The Damnonii came again, giving Cai no respite. He had little choice other than to retreat before the onslaught, all the while accompanied by the jeers of the Damnonii chieftains. Cai was forced to fend off blow after blow with shield and sword, giving him no opportunity to counter.

His shield arm was beginning to numb. At least the giant had been unable to get beyond his guard. Still, all Cai could do was withdraw in the face of the unrelenting onslaught. Taog halted suddenly. He stared across his shield at Cai, his breath coming in great heaving gusts.

'Is this how you cowardly Romans fight? Run, little mouse, your time is nearly up.' The big man moved again. This time instead of a rush he made a jab at Cai's exposed right knee. Cai drove his shield rim downwards to parry the blade. It had been a feint. Taog changed the blade's direction, slicing upwards at Cai's sword hand. Cai withdrew his blade instinctively and the crash of steel rang across the battleground. The impact, so close to his hand, had come near to driving the sword from his grip and sent a shock of pain along his arm.

Cai stepped back. It gave him an instant of space. Taog's face was twisted in hatred. This was not the way he had expected the fight to go, Cai thought. However, despite his heaving breaths, there was no sign the Damnonii was done. Cai knew he must try to stem the tide of the shield-bearer's storm of attacks, or he would soon be done for.

Cai aimed a wild thrust at Taog's face. The big man had no time to raise his shield and was forced to quickly retreat a step. Now it was Cai's turn to feint. He reversed his blade, whipping it downwards towards his enemy's knee, who withdrew it swiftly. The sword's point ripped through the wool of the Damnonii's troos but did not bite into flesh.

The momentum, however, was with Cai, as Taog withdrew to fend off his enemy's fast moving blade. Cai kept changing direction of attack, aiming blows at the warrior's face, body and often at the knee. Each time the big man parried with his sword or blocked with his shield.

Both were tiring. Cai couldn't maintain his attacks and Taog gasped for breath. They pulled apart.

Cai was dimly aware of the shouts and jeering voices surrounding him. His mind unconsciously pushed them away. The two enemies locked eyes across the small space that had grown between them. The snowfall was settling on the bare ground, creating a thin carpet of white. Taog's stern face broke into a grin.

'So Roman, my boyhood friend Seoras told you about my old injury, did he? You have taken rather a fancy to my knee, I noticed. Never fear, it will outlast you. When this is over, I will escort my king back to the village, where he can set about planting more of his seed into *his* woman.'

Cai allowed a slow, deliberate smile to cross his lips. 'As you are so interested in other men's seed, Damnonii, perhaps it is your woman you should be more concerned with.'

A look of confusion furrowed the big man's brow. 'Don't talk of my woman, whelp.'

'Be done with him, Taog.' The shout was from Blue Dog.

'I left the feast last night and crossed the lake to visit my woman,' Cai said. 'It was easy to get into your hut because the guard was preoccupied, you see.' The frown deepened. 'Now, what was it your woman said? Orla, isn't it? Oh yes, I remember,' Cai's face became sombre, before the grin returned. 'Come on my little Froggie. I need you to fuck me hard one more time, with that big prick of yours. Before Taog returns from the feast.'

A sound erupted from the Damnonii at odds with his huge stature. It was almost effeminate, and all pain. Pain he now released at Cai. Taog tossed his shield aside and came at him, sword raised two-handed. His blade sliced downwards at Cai's head, with all his might behind it.

He had overreached. Cai sidestepped the blow. The blade met only air. Off balance, the impetus took Taog past Cai. He slipped on the snow-slick ground, tumbling full stretch onto the wet earth of the rise.

For the first time Cai let rage fill his mind. With swift, lithe steps he leapt onto the prone warrior's body as he rose to his knees. With all his fury, Cai slammed the rim of his shield into the base of Taog's neck. The snap resonated around the gathering. Taog was dead before his body slumped back to the earth. Still the battle mist consumed Cai.

He cast his shield aside. And, with wild two-handed strokes, Cai hacked down onto the neck of the Damnonii's lifeless body. Again the blade swung. And again. Blood pooled into the dirt, staining the thin coating of snow red.

256

Cai bent down and embedded his fingers in Taog's nostrils. He lifted the severed head away from its shoulders, holding it high for all to see. Blood cascaded from its stump, flowing along Cai's sword arm and staining his leather armour. He found the face of his enemy. The Damnonii king looked on in horror. Cai bellowed at the man who had taken Alyn from him.

When he was finished there was complete silence from those on the rise. The only sound was the shush of the tall reeds as the wind blew through them.

52

'The woman is mine. This Roman filth can't have her. I will not let him take my child.'

'No lord. Your champion is dead.'

Lucius searched for the speaker. The indignant voice had come from amongst the Damnonii chieftains.

'Snake.'

Lucius turned at the sound of his friend's curse. Cai's face was twisted with hatred as he tossed the head towards Blue Dog.

'Here, coward,' he said. 'Your shield-bearer is returned to you.'

The Damnonii king took a step backwards as the head bounced towards him. Taog's head came to rest between Blue Dog's feet, his dead face looked up at its master as if in appeal. For a moment he held the stare, before turning back to Cai.

The madness was no longer concealed, it was there for all to see. 'You may have her back,' he said, with a smirk. 'But the babe is mine. I will cut it from her belly before I return her to you.'

The battle-mist enveloped Cai's mind once more. He gripped Seoras's sword, his knuckles white. He saw again, the leer on the madman's face. He would have the Damnonii king's head too.

'No, sir. Not today,' Hrindenus said. Cai felt huge arms wrap around him, pinning his own. Cai roared, struggling to free himself. Another pair of hands gripped his sword arm.

'No, brother. Calm yourself,' Lucius said. Cai continued to struggle, though the battle-mist slowly slipped from him. Eventually, he eased his shoulders and released this grip on the sword. Lucius took it.

'Let me go, Tungrian.' Hrindenus tentatively removed his hold on Cai as if he expected his commander to fly at the Damnonii king at any moment. 'You will be long dead before you reach her,' Cai said. 'You are a mad dog and must be dealt with as such.'

'There will be no need for further killing,' Seoras said, stepping between the Damnonii and Cai. 'The woman has already been removed by my brother priests and is being sheltered within the sacred isle.'

Blue Dog turned towards the wooden palisade as if he might see Alyn through the stout barrier. He was met by the grinning face of Neacal, standing tall upon the parapet. The warrior, whose face was once more covered with the familiar whitewash, waved back at the king.

Blue Dog's face flushed. His lips twisting as he turned towards the old priest, who had not moved from this position below the fortress's ramparts. 'This was your plan all along, wasn't it, old man?'

'Peace, brother,' the old priest said, raising his palms outward. 'There is no ill intent here. We only wished to ensure the woman's safety from unwanted attention should your champion lose.'

Blue Dog bared his teeth. 'She is mine. Let's see how far these Romans get if they attempt to pass through Damnonii lands. They can't hide behind these walls forever.' The Damnonii king strode towards the boats, shoving his way through the waiting chieftains. Most of them followed their king. Some did not. A small group watched the others go, speaking in low tones to one another.

'All is not well amongst the great men of the Damnonii people,' Lucius said.

'That may well be,' Hrindenus said. 'But there's more than enough of them to finish us as soon as we step off this island.'

53

'I must return to my lands,' Barra said. 'I cannot allow Frang to consolidate his power. He must be dealt with before he turns my people upon one another.'

'Agreed,' Lucius said. 'But how? We're trapped here. Blue Dog is watching the route to the river. I doubt he is fool enough to let us slip away in the dark as Frang did.'

Lucius, Barra, Hrindenus and Keefe were seated by the hearth fire of the great hall. Cai was with Alyn. He had not seen the pair for some time.

Barra's face was ashen, though his wound had not been as grievous as first feared. The arrow point had not penetrated the lung and as yet an infection had not taken hold. Even so, Lucius wasn't sure the Novantae king would have the strength for a long journey. Keefe, on the other hand, appeared unaffected by the rent in his shoulder. Whether the Hibernian could swing a sword as well as would be needed had yet to be tested.

'Could we cross the lake to the west and cut back towards the lands of the Epidii?' Hrindenus said, his voice hopeful.

Keefe snorted. 'Do we really want to push our luck again, Roman? Even if they don't skewer us on sight, I doubt they will have boats big enough to carry us back to Novantae lands.' Hrindenus grinned back at the Hibernian. The Tungrian's usual good mood had returned since Cai's defeat of Taog.

'Then there's no choice,' Lucius said. 'We must take the longer land route and make for the Wall.'

'We'll be run down long before we reach your cursed new wall,' Barra said. 'The distance is too great.'

'We must become tricksters.' All heads turned to see Seoras approaching, his brother Neacal at his side.

It had taken two days to make the preparations. Seoras and his brother, along with four of his warriors, had taken a pair of boats northwards through the lake. Once they had dealt with the watchers, ensuring at least one was left alive, they would be met by another of the young priest's contacts, who would have the horses ready for them.

'I thought the priest looked the part, all made up in women's clothing,' Hrindenus said in mock seriousness.

'Let's hope he fooled Blue Dog's watchers, Roman.' Keefe replied. 'Otherwise, our clever scheme will come to nothing.'

Seoras had set out in the darkness of the early morning. Now the sun had set and the long wait inside the fortress had preyed on all their nerves. It was time to move. Lucius for one was glad of it.

Despite Keefe's reservations the Damnonii appeared to have taken the bait. One of the sentries on the ramparts had reported seeing a large group of horsemen leaving the village in haste, heading northwards around the lakeside. The trickiest part of the plan was yet to come. The small band had no boat big enough to carry them all. They must take one of Blue Dog's craft from the village.

They gathered by the main gates of the fortress. It had stopped snowing, leaving a thick white covering. Even in darkness and the low cloud cover, Lucius feared their silhouettes would stand out in the stark whiteness. Knowing there was little choice. It was a risk they must take.

HUNT

He observed his friend. Cai stood next to Alyn. She had said little over the last two days, other than to Cai. However, Lucius sensed the fierceness that had always been a part of her was still there. One day it might return in full measure. She was wrapped in a thick cloak, a new deerskin cloak tightly about her shoulders. Cai had told him that she had tossed the old one into the hearth and watched it burn.

Cai fidgeted with the pommel of his sword. Seoras's sword. Gifted to him by the young priest before he departed. At last, there was Barra and his shield-bearer. The Novantae king was pale and worn. He tried to disguise it with a brusque manner when speaking to others. Lucius had seen the ruse too often over the years to be fooled. Barra was in considerable pain. Keefe knew it too and had barely left his lord's side.

Earlier in the day Barra and Keefe had been summoned by the old priest. An hour or so later the shield-bearer had reappeared on his own. When Hrindenus in his usual manner had asked what it was all about, Lucius had expected the Hibernian to turn on him. Instead, he said simply. 'My lord is now the true king of the Novantae.'

Lucius shook his head at the strangeness of these people. Only a matter of days ago he had been forced to watch as the Hamian was tortured to death. He would never forget the cruelty. And yet here they now were, those same priests aiding them in their escape from the Damnonii.

Lucius turned at a clicking sound. The old priest was approaching, his long staff of dark age-worn wood in hand. He was assisted by another of his brethren to prevent the old man slipping in the slushy ground of the fort's interior.

'So, it is time for you to leave, king Barra,' he said.

'It is, Holy One. My thanks for all you have done for me and my companions. And for the Novantae people.' The old man smiled.

'Your People have a new, strong king to lead them. And this land will have need of strong kings in the years ahead. Do not forget your vow, and when the time is right, your boy will stand on this island.' Barra gave the slightest of bows. The old priest turned to Cai.

'Your gods are with you, warrior of the Nervii. May they stay with you on your journey home.'

'Thank you, Holy One,' Cai said simply. The old man smiled once more. With the farewells done he held out his hand to the assisting priest and progressed gingerly back to the hall. The click-clacking sound accompanying his journey.

'Time to go.' Barra nodded to the warrior by the gateway, who pulled one of the heavy oak gates open, the locking spar already removed. The party left the fort, making their way silently to the west along the base of its palisade. Lucius glanced at the parapet surprised to see no white faces staring back. They were on their own.

The lake-boats were moored under the ramparts. Reaching them, Cai and Lucius immediately hauled one into the freezing water. They carefully placed their shields and small supply of food into its bottom, then steadied it for Alyn to step into. She's holding up well, Lucius thought. They took up the paddles. Barra, Keefe and Hrindenus were in another of the small craft and were already paddling slowly towards the channel.

In moments the boats were sliding past the tall reeds as they made towards the village. There was no hint of light from any fires. The dull glare from the heavy snowfall showed them their destination. Barra's boat came to a halt mid-channel and Keefe indicated the others should come alongside them.

Barra silently pointed towards the shore of the settlement. At first Lucius did not understand. He could see the first of the roundhouses and was relieved none of the inhabitants appeared to be abroad. Perhaps they had all left in pursuit of Seoras and his men?

Then he picked out what appeared to be several, snow-covered burial chambers, close to the narrow beach. The boats. Turned over to protect them from the elements. They set off again, making slow, careful strokes.

In moments the hulls crunched onto the bank. No one made a move to step into the water. They surveyed the settlement, watching and listening. All was still.

Keefe was first out, closely followed by Hrindenus and Barra.

'Wait here,' Cai whispered to Alyn as he too stepped ashore, Lucius following. Keefe swept snow from the keel of the nearest boat. He growled in frustration and moved to the next, repeating the action. He pointed vigorously at the upturned hull. He had found what he was searching for.

The big Hibernian made a lifting motion with his hands, his intent clear. The five men gathered at one side and heaved. The heavy boat moved. What they had not bargained for was the noise it made as it righted itself. The mast, lowered and tied loosely in place, clattered against the rowing benches. The sound was sharp in the still night air.

Hands instinctively reaching for sword pommels. They waited, frozen in place. The village inhabitants must surely rouse, so great was the din. Lucius could hear little above the hammering of his own heart. Moments passed.

No warriors appeared from the roundhouses to challenge them. Only silence greeted them.

Barra nodded to Keefe. They pushed the boat towards the lake. It crunched across the ground, Lucius grateful for the snowfall which muffled the noise somewhat. Soon the boat floated in the lake. With the support of Hrindenus, Cai helped Alyn over its side. Lucius followed with their equipment and food, leaving Barra and Keefe last of all.

'I knew it was a trick.' A voice croaked from out of the darkness. Barra and Keefe spun, swords freed, in a single motion. The speaker came into view, hands raised. 'I knew Barra of the Novantae must know he would be run down if he dared take the land route.'

'It's one of the Damnonii chieftains,' whispered Cai. 'I recognise him from the hall. He's the one who challenged Blue Dog.'

'Have you come to stop me, Harailt?' Barra said, his voice calm, sword remaining raised. The chieftain smiled.

'How can I stop what I do not see?' The Damnonii approached Barra. 'He will come for you, Barra, even if you make it back to your lands. Some of the warchiefs of our tribe fear him and will follow where he goes.'

'Not you?' Barra asked.

'No, not I. Nor a number of the others. We are strong enough in number to defend our lands against our new king, should the need arise. Yet he will still have a considerable force at his back. Kill your cousin and you have a chance.'

'Never fear. I will deal with Frang.'

The chieftain held out his arm. Barra clasped it. 'Fare well, brother. I enjoyed those years when we fought the invaders. Perhaps we will get the chance again.' The chieftain turned on his heels and disappeared back into the night.

54

The boat slipped into the river.

Cai felt the tug of its flow as soon as they left the lake of reeds. He was seated on the rowing bench, making slow, steady strokes in time with the others, keeping a continual eye on both banks, which the snowfall had given a ghostly visibility. Trees crowded close to each side of the river, making it feel like they passed through an endless tunnel. His mind played tricks on him, imagining arrows streaking out from the shadowed depths of the woods. He found himself continually fighting the urge to flinch.

Barra was at the steering arm. The Novantae was still too weak for the strain of long periods of exertion. Alyn sat against the mast, which Keefe had raised as soon as he boarded. Her eyes, dark pools in the wan light, watched him. He was her beacon, he knew. If he was gone, she would be lost. And yet, on the times he had touched her to bring simple comfort, he had felt her stiffen. Was the old Alyn truly gone? Or would the passage of time heal her?

His thoughts turned to the child she carried. How would she be once it was born? Would she take to the infant? Would he? These were questions for another time. First, they must survive, and the journey would be hard on her.

'Slow your strokes,' Barra ordered. 'I can no longer see the way ahead.'

'We can't stop now,' Cai said. 'It won't be long before Blue Dog uncovers our ruse.'

'If we wreck the keel by blindly moving ahead, Blue Dog *will* overhaul us before we even reach the sea.'

'We can use the oars to fend off if we need to,' Lucius offered.

'Very well,' Barra said, after a moment. 'Slowly.'

The four oarsmen set a sedate pace. Barra peered, wide-eyed, into the blackness ahead. For a few short minutes they progressed into the black of night. Cai occasionally made out fleeting shapes on the left bank, but all else was shrouded in a deep darkness.

There was a sharp crunching sound from the bows. In the same instant Cai was thrown backwards from his bench. The boat juddered from bows to stern. Cai cried out as his back cracked against one of the ribs of the boat, the pain jarring along his spine.

'Get up, Roman,' Keefe said to Hrindenus, who also lay sprawled on the rough . 'We must push the boat away from the bank.' The Hibernian clambered towards the bows.

'Gods, my head,' Hrindenus groaned.

'Get up here. Quickly. Bring your oar.'

Hrindenus scrambled to his feet. 'I think the damned thing has fallen over the side,' he said.

'What! Find it,' Keefe said, his voice terse.

'I'm not a damned owl. I can't see in the dark. We need torchlight.'

'There is none,' Barra said. 'I checked as we boarded. You'll have to go over the side and feel for it.'

'You steered us into the bank,' Hrindenus said. 'Why don't you go for it.'

'You dare speak to our king, like you are his equal. 'I'll—'

'Enough,' Lucius said. 'I'll do it.'

'No, sir,' Hrindenus replied. 'I'll do it. It's my oar after all.'

The Tungrian stripped to his waist and lowered himself over the side. 'Gods.' he exclaimed as he entered the water. Splashing sounds followed his progress as he searched around the keel.

'Anything?' Barra asked, as the Tungrian reached the stern of the boat.

'I'm not having a bit of fun splashing around in the river. It's damned freezing,' Cai could hear the quaver in Hrindenus's voice as he began to shiver. 'Wait. I've found it. Here.' He raised the oar, Barra grasped hold of it.

'Help me get him out,' Cai said. But the big Hibernian was already leaning over the side.

'Take my hand,' Keefe said, banging his palm against the boat's side.

Keefe hauled him up and Hrindenus flopped onto a rowing bench. Water cascaded from his body and he shivered uncontrollably.

Alyn moved next to him. 'Here, wear this,' She said, laying her cloak across his shoulders.

'M-m-my thanks,' Hrindenus said, pulling the furs tightly around him.

She returned to her seat at the mast. Cai smiled to himself despite the situation they were in.

'We must wait until first light,' Barra said.

'Every moment we delay will bring Blue Dog the chance to recover ground on us,' Cai argued.

'I know,' Barra replied. 'I didn't see the bend in the river, and there are many more before it runs into the sea. We can't risk it.' Cai knew the Novantae king was right.

'We should move the boat to the river's centre,' Keefe said. 'We can drop the anchor stone there.'

They manoeuvred the craft away from the bank. Hrindenus heaved the heavy stone over the side at the boat's stern.

'We may as well try to rest as best we can,' Barra said.

'I'll keep first watch,' Lucius said.

Cai moved to sit next to Alyn at the mast. She was shivering slightly without her cloak and Cai placed his arm gently around her shoulders. He was pleased to feel she did not stiffen this time in his embrace. She rested her head against his shoulder. For a time they sat in silence, sharing the warmth of their bodies. As he was beginning to drift off, Cai felt Alyn's head turn against his shoulder.

'Cai,' she whispered into his ear.

'Are you well?' he asked.

'You won't let him take me, will you?' Her voice sounded small. Distant.

'He isn't going to catch us, my love.'

'I know. But if he does. You will do what must be done?' Cai hesitated only a moment, knowing he must give her only one answer. He placed his forehead against hers.

'If the time comes, I will ensure he cannot take you.'

'You promise.'

'I promise.'

55

Lucius jerked awake. Keefe, who had replaced him in the night, roughly shook his shoulder.

'The light is returning,' he said.

'Ach,' Hrindenus exclaimed. 'My feet are wet.'

'What?' Keefe said, alarmed. He scrambled over the benches to reach the Tungrian. 'Damn the gods. We're taking on water.'

'And here,' Cai said, from the mast, where he still sat by Alyn.

'How bad is it?' Barra asked.

'About a handspan deep at its worst,' Keefe said. 'We'll need to bail her out.'

'Can we do it as we row?' Lucius asked, feeling the anxious knot in the pit of his stomach tighten.

'It will mean fewer at the oars,' Keefe said.

'I'll do it,' Alyn said. Cai frowned, letting his concern show. 'Don't fuss,' she said.

'Here, take this,' Keefe said, handing her a small bucket. 'Start from the mast and work forwards.'

'Do you think the boat was damaged as it struck the bank?' Barra asked.

'Hard to say. Let's hope it doesn't worsen or the sea might finish her off. And us.'

'Neptunus! He's the Roman god of the sea is he not?' Barra asked.

'He is,' Lucius responded.

'Well, I suggest you start praying.'

Lucius could discern the outlines of the trees on the bank to his left as he took to the rowing bench.

'I can see well enough ahead to steer by,' Barra said. 'Let's see if we can make up for lost time. Put your backs into it.' The Novantae king grinned. 'I have a cousin to kill.'

They rowed hard and relentlessly for another hour. Lucius's tunic clung to his back and sweat dripped from his forehead. He could see his breath before him as the snow began to fall again. They exited the tunnel of trees and a blustery wind drove the freezing snowflakes into their faces and numbed their hands, until Lucius could no longer feel his.

Alyn worked continuously with the small pail. She threw never-ending buckets of water over the side. No sooner had she cleared one spot than another filled. At one point she sat back, red-faced, resting her right hand on her extended belly.

'You must rest,' Cai said. She simply shook her head. Instead, reached for a water skin and passed it amongst the small crew. Once they had all gratefully drunk their fill, she returned to the bailing process again. This was the Alyn Lucius remembered.

The rowers had set a steady rhythm. Even so his arms screamed and his lungs ached. And for the first time he felt the chill of the water seep into his boots. The river was entering the boat faster than Alyn could bail.

'The river is widening, we are approaching its estuary,' Barra shouted. 'We will soon be able to raise the sail.'

'Thank the gods,' Hrindenus gasped.

A matter of minutes later they passed low, muddy banks and screeching seabirds wading amongst the silt of the shoreline. The boat lurched and rolled as the river met the incoming tide.

'Ship oars,' Barra shouted. 'And hang on.' Keefe unfurled the sail. In moments a dark, salt-stained sheet flapped wildly in the growing wind. The Hibernian worked at its guide ropes, and, in moments, it filled.

Alyn held a steadying hand to the mast and gripped firmly to the pail with the other. Cai took the bucket from her.

'Rest now,' he said, brooking no further argument. At first the boat rocked alarmingly, but soon they passed into the sea proper and it steadied.

'We'll take turns,' Lucius said to Cai. 'I'll—'

'Lord!' Keefe shouted in alarm. Barra was slumped over the steering oar as if in sleep, his head lolling against his arm.

Lucius scrambled to his side. He patted his hand against the Novantae king's bearded cheek. 'Barra. Barra,' he said. The Novantae moaned but his eyes remained shut.

'He's bleeding,' Alyn said from behind. 'Look at his tunic.'

'His wound has reopened,' Lucius said. 'Keefe, take his place. Hrindenus, help me lift him.' With the Tungrian's aid they moved Barra to the centre of the boat and laid him on a bench.

'No,' Alyn said. 'Sit him up. I need to see the wound.' She tried to tear at his tunic, it was made of tough hide and wouldn't rip. 'I need a blade.'

'Here,' Hrindenus handed her his eating knife. She worked its sharp edge along the seam of the blood-stained tunic to reveal the bindings of his wound. Blood oozed through the dressing.

'Is it the lung?' Lucius asked.

'I don't think so. The priests were right in this I believe. There's no bubbling of the blood. A good sign at least. The stitching must have torn. Where's my pack?'

'With the food,' he said, retrieving a small sack from the storage box below the mast.

274

'I can close the wound and rebind it,' Alyn said. 'But he must have time to rest and recover or his blood loss may kill him.'

'Perhaps we could take him to Castellanos,' Hrindenus said. 'I haven't seen a wound the Greek scab-lifter can't fix.'

Lucius shook his head. 'No. The distance is too great. And we would have to carry him across land. It would kill him.'

'We could make for the western garrison on Urbicus's new wall?' Cai said. Lucius hesitated. It was still a long journey around the many isles.

'Perhaps,' he said. 'It would at least give us somewhere safe to lie-up for a few days. We'll have to come up with a good story though. It seems our best option.' Lucius turned to Keefe. 'We'll make for the port at the western end of the wall. I don't know how we get through this myriad of islands though.'

'I know where it is, Roman,' he said. 'We attacked it enough times as it was being built. Why would they help the king of the Novantae? They would kill him and hang his head from their gate.'

'We won't reveal who he is—'

'No,' Barra croaked. They all turned to the Novantae king, his eyes remained closed and lines of pain furrowed his forehead. 'There's no time.' His eyes flickered open. He hissed through clenched teeth.

'You must let me see to your wound,' Alyn said. 'Then you must rest.'

Barra continued, as if she hadn't spoken, not taking his eyes from Keefe. 'We cannot turn from our path. Frang's hope will be either I am already dead or Blue Dog will kill me if I attempt to leave the fortress. What do you think he will do next?'

275

Keefe frowned at the question. Quickly turning with a look of concern. 'Herne.'

Barra nodded feebly. 'Yes. He will move to end my line.'

'Beren,' Alyn gasped.

56

As the day wore on the low cloud lifted. They could clearly see the fells on either side of the long sea lake. At times they discerned smoke drifting skywards from the rooftops of settlements on the shore.

Cai watched Barra. The Novantae seemed somewhat stronger since Alyn had restitched his wound. He sat next to Keefe at the tiller. The two spoke together in low tones. The king and his shield-bearer.

Neptunus was with them. Despite the sharp wind that froze their faces and hands, the sea had remained calm enough they could continue the journey without the need to seek shelter. Cai sat at a rowing bench. His back ached from the continual need to bail. The influx of water had not yet worsened, though the effort was relentless. He, Hrindenus and Lucius were working in short shifts. Alyn had wanted to take her turn; he had insisted she must rest. Despite giving him a piercing stare that would have wilted a veteran centurion, she had acquiesced.

They anchored off Blue Dog's isle as night fell. Keefe had chosen a long bay on its eastern coastline. Alyn had become quiet once again in the shadow of its large peak. She had rested her head against the mast, keeping her eyes shut for the most part, until night had fully descended. Cai, watching her, thought of the woman Moira. He hoped she fared well.

Deep into the afternoon of the second day, they were approaching the strange, loaf shaped, rock of Ailsa's Isle. Its dome held a white cap of snow. So much had come to pass since the night they had first anchored off its rocky shoreline, he reflected.

'To think I used to complain about long days on horseback,' Hrindenus said, as he tossed another bucketfull of water over the side. 'What I wouldn't give for a day's patrol out in the hills rather than being tossed around in this leaking bucket.'

'You won't be transferring to the Classus upon our return then?' Cai asked. 'Although, the navy needs their sailors big and dumb and good at the oars.'

Hrindenus guffawed, a deep throaty sound. He stood to his full height, stretching and arching his back, legs splayed to steady himself with the boat's motion. 'No, I'll leave that to—' The Tungrian squinted into the distance beyond the stern.

'What?'

'I thought I saw…' Hrindenus moved to the mast and stepped onto the small box store. 'A sail,' he said. 'No wait. Two. Three sails.' Keefe crossed to the mast as Barra took the tiller. The Hibernian scrutinised the distant horizon.

'What do you think, Keefe?' Barra shouted into the wind.

'It can only be Blue Dog,' he said. 'Who else would be out in this weather?' He continued to scrutinise the three sails as the wind whipped his long red hair across his eyes. 'They've seen us.'

'Can we outrun them?' Lucius asked. Keefe ignored the question, instead going to the mast and ascending nimbly.

'He has his men at the oars and the benches are full,' Keefe hailed from above. 'They'll catch us before nightfall.' Keefe turned to the way ahead, shielding his eyes from the strengthening wind. 'That might aid us.'

Cai spotted what the big warrior had seen. A great bank of cloud, like an impenetrable dark wall, risen from the sea itself. He turned to Alyn. Her eyes were locked in terror on the approaching storm.

'We must take to the oars too,' Keefe said.

'We're still shipping water,' Cai said.

'Your woman must bail,' Keefe replied tersely.

'No. She—' Cai began.

'Yes. I must,' Alyn's voice was firm. The terror transformed to determination. 'We must reach Beren.' Without waiting for a response from Cai, she took the wooden pail from Hrindenus. The Tungrian raised his eyebrows at Cai, who shrugged.

For the next hour the four men strained at their oars, Barra at the tiller. Each could see the three sails growing larger by the minute and the storm was fast approaching.

For a time, it appeared to have changed direction, slanting towards the coastline. Now it came on in full force. The three chasing ships were swallowed by the dense mist. Ailsa's Isle was a dim shadow to the east, the great rock's fading presence allowed them to maintain an accurate course.

It began to snow heavily once more. The driven, icy flakes stung their faces. Barra, at the tiller, squinted into the whiteness.

Cai was glad to be at the oar-bench. His body was warmed with the nonstop effort, though he had lost the feeling in his hands long since. More worrying was his feet. They were covered by bitterly cold seawater as it continued to rise, despite Alyn's efforts.

'They won't be able to track us if we change direction,' Cai shouted to Barra. 'We could head for land and try to pick up horses. Go overland.'

'No,' Barra returned. 'There are few Novantae lords left on this part of the coast. Most have taken refuge in the great forest. Only they would have enough mounts to bear us all.'

'We can't keep this pace up for much longer,' Lucius said, through gasps of breath.

'We don't need to. Darkness is already beginning to fall.' Barra was right. The light had been so poor for much of the day he had not noticed it had begun to fade. 'We can turn towards the coastline and drop anchor. Blue Dog will pass us by in this murk. We can wait them out in the darkness until morning.'

Barra steered a course towards the distant shore, Keefe kept a close watch out for rocks. When the Hibernian deemed they had gone far enough they dropped the anchor stone. Soon night embraced them.

The wind began to lose some of its earlier strength as if it too was tiring. However, the snow did not relent and they each huddled into their cloaks, shrouded in misery and exhaustion for a time.

Lucius shared out what was left of the food, mainly strips of cured beef and hard bread. They settled down for a miserable, wet night, each again taking turns to bail.

Cai and Alyn sat close together by the mast once more, where he slowly drifted into a fitful sleep.

'Roman, cease your snoring.' Keefe shook Cai roughly. 'Wha—'

'Quiet,' he said. 'Listen.'

All in the boat had become alert.

At first, all Cai could hear was the lapping of the waves against the boat's hull and Alyn's quick breaths. She had tensed against him at Keefe's words. Then he heard it. Alyn did too. She gripped his arm. A splash of oars. It had continued to snow heavily, obscuring the light of the approaching torches. A faint glow was emerging through the whiteness.

'Get down,' Keefe said in an urgent whisper. Cai heard Barra groan. They lay, unmoving. Alyn had not released Cai's forearm. Chill water soaked through his troos and cloak.

The sound of the regular stroke of oars was almost upon them. There could be no escape.

57

'Have a care. You're too close.' The shout of alarm came out of the darkness.

'Quiet, you fool!' The voice of Blue Dog.

Lucius raised his head. The nearest torch shone clear. Yet there was no excited shout of discovery. The torch passed on. The regular slopping sound of multiple oars dipping in and out of the water faded, along with the light. Until the lapping of the waves against the hull was all that could be heard.

'How in the name of the gods were we not discovered?' Lucius asked. 'I could see their torchlight as clear as a harvest moon.'

'Fortuna watches over us,' Hrindenus murmured from the bows.

'It was the snowfall,' Keefe said. 'It would have reflected their own light back at them. They probably couldn't see more than a few spear-lengths in front of them.'

'They're ahead of us now,' Lucius said. 'If Blue Dog comes to realise it, they can wait off until first light and ensnare us. Or turn back and continue the hunt.'

'Perhaps,' Keefe said. 'Only the foolish or desperate blunder around in the dark in these waters.'

'Or mad,' Alyn said, her voice barely quiet. Keefe grunted his agreement.

'We'll have to see what the morning's light reveals,' Barra said.

'Pass me the bucket,' Hrindenus said. 'Perhaps the effort will warm me up. My balls have shrivelled into my stomach.'

Lucius managed snatches of sleep. Though exhaustion repeatedly pulled him under, the need to continually rotate the bailing duties, combined with the cold, prevented any real rest. After an interminable time had passed, the first light of morning revealed the sunken eyes of a fatigued crew.

Keefe huddled against his lord in the aft of the boat. Barra's head rested on the shoulder of the Hibernian. Cai and Alyn were wrapped together in their cloaks. Both were awake and stared, with dull eyes, to the east. Hrindenus was again toiling away with the bucket. His rate of work had slowed dramatically. The water was deeper still. If they did not make land soon, they must surely sink.

'Raise the sail,' Barra said. 'Let us see what this morning holds for us.'

Their supply of food was gone, so Alyn passed around the remaining waterskin. As yet there was little to see, only the outline of the distant coast, a shadow against a darker background. The snow had ceased, the only mercy. Slowly the weak winter light strengthened, though there would be no sunrise to see, the sky again a heavy iron grey. No sea mist obscured what lay ahead.

Keefe climbed the mast. He searched to the south and east. Then to the west and north.

'Nothing,' he shouted. 'I can see the mouth of Rerigon's sea lake. They may have headed there to join with Frang. But they would have needed great luck. Or someone who knows these waters well enough to navigate it in darkness. Blue Dog has neither.'

'Perhaps he sailed directly for your own village?' Cai said. Lucius heard the anxiety in his friend's voice.

'I doubt it,' Barra said. 'He doesn't know its location. Perhaps the gods are with us after all. We should reach my home as the last light is falling.'

'If this wreck can stay afloat long enough,' Keefe grumbled.

They continued along the coastline for the remainder of the day. Keefe steered a course far enough out they would be concealed from any watchers along the shore. The snowfall continued unabated. But, as Barra had predicted, they approached their destination as dusk approached.

The keel crunched onto the sand and pebble beach. Lucius was the first of the exhausted crew to step into water. It swelled above his knees and he stifled a gasp. The waves beat in from behind and he was forced to grasp the side of the boat again to prevent a stumble.

He felt near to exhaustion as he helped drag the boat up onto the shingle before following Barra into the sand dunes. Icy snow matted his hair as the small band stood in a tight circle amongst spikey tufts of marram grass. They had landed in a bay near to Barra's village, out of sight.

'Keefe will go ahead,' Barra said. 'We must know what we are up against.'

'I'll go with him,' Lucius said. 'It won't hurt to have an extra sword.' To his surprise Keefe nodded his assent without argument.

'I'll come too,' Hrindenus chipped in enthusiastically. 'I'd rather not sit here freezing my arse off.'

'Just don't get in my way, Roman,' Keefe growled and strode from the dunes.

Days at sea had weakened Lucius. He struggled to keep up with the big Hibernian, who moved with a grace and swiftness belying his size. Hrindenus too seemed unaffected by their long journey. Lucius could guess at the Tungrian's desire to come along. Keefe's sister. He couldn't recall her name.

He didn't truly understand Hrindenus's desire to see her. Lucius had never been taken with a woman enough to settle down. There was rarely the time or opportunity. Occasionally he had entertained dignitaries in the fort's praetorium. Some had tried to foist their daughters upon him. None had ever been that appealing. At home on the family estate his father had begun to suggest he should find a wife for his eldest son. Nothing had ever come of it, and now never would.

They were making their way through the low, tangled undergrowth of a sparse woodland, whose wind-gnarled trunks were silhouetted against the last of the sky's dying light. The sound of the crashing sea came loudly from the right. The choking calls of gulls filled the air around them. Suddenly they met the treeline.

'There,' Keefe said. The palisade of Barra's settlement nestled on its clifftop perch. Torches blazed on the parapet from which men stared out into the near darkness. The makeshift settlement around its ditches was alive with movement. The flames cast by many hearth fires flickered as shadows walked between them.

'Either the village has grown since last we were here, or a new force has arrived,' Hrindenus said.

'There are too many men on the walls to be of our warband,' Keefe said. 'We must get closer.'

They left the woodland moving silently until they were close to the first of the meagre huts. 'Wait here,' Keefe whispered. 'I'm going to find someone I trust. Come running if you hear my shout.'

'A mysterious type, isn't he?' Hrindenus said, after Keefe had slipped into the darkness of the settlement.

'You mean your future brother-in-law?'

Hrindenus snorted a laugh. 'If he lets me live long enough. Though Niamh is worth the risk.' Lucius smiled at the wistfulness of the Tungrian's words, which were so incongruous with this fierce warrior.

'Does she feel the same?'

Hrindenus was quiet for a short while. 'At the time I was sure of it. After so many weeks have passed since we last set eyes upon each other, I am beginning to doubt my memory.'

'Well, when you see her again, I'm sure your worries will be settled. Just remember to take a sword and shield when you ask Keefe for his sister's hand.' For once the Tungrian had nothing to say.

From their hiding place, Lucius observed the activity in the village. In many ways, other than the poor quality of the huts, it appeared normal life carried on. But, he sensed an undercurrent of threat. Perhaps it was imagined. After all, they had been running for their lives for the last few days.

Keefe had been gone some time and Lucius began to worry. He was on the point of going to investigate when he saw movement in the darkness. A hunched figure moving stealthily. In moments Keefe reached their hiding place.

'Let's go,' he said, moving off in the direction they had come.

'What did you find?' Lucius asked.

'We must go,' Keefe said. 'I'll tell all once we return to the beach. He has Herne and your friend's boy.'

'Who does?' Lucius asked.

'Frang. Frang has taken the settlement.'

'He brought a warband to the village two nights since,' Keefe said, moments after their return to the dunes. 'I managed to reach old Colm. No one ever seems to notice his hut by the shore. It would appear Frang has convinced some of the men of Rerigon he has been anointed king and you are dead. Killed by his own hand. Our men did not believe a runt like him could have brought you down, though they were too few to resist. They are being held in one of the houses inside the palisade.'

'And you're sure the boys are alive?' Cai asked.

'Aye. Old Colm saw them at noon when he brought his day's catch to trade. Though they are being closely watched.'

'Frang would not dare kill them if he had the least doubt I had met the demise he hoped for,' Barra said. 'He will bide his time and wait for word from Blue Dog.'

'We must attack. This very night,' Cai said.

'It would be good to know the fate of the madman,' Lucius said. 'Before we make our move.'

'How many warriors did he bring?' Barra asked.

'Colm counted thirty. He said half have been billeted outside of the walls.'

'Even so, not good odds,' Lucius said.

'No. We do have two things on our side. He won't know yet of our escape from the holy isle. I also know my home like my own sword hand. Which includes the best places to gain entrance and not be seen.'

58

'You can't leave me here,' Alyn said, her voice becoming panicked. 'I'll be alone in the dark. Not again.'

Cai was stung by her words. He felt guilt at having to leave her, but she couldn't possibly make the climb. Neither could anyone be spared to watch over her; all would be needed for the fight to come.

'You'll be safe here,' Cai said. 'Out of sight. I'll come for you as soon as we have rescued the boys.'

'What if you do not return? What will become of me? I won't return to that life.'

He reached for her, holding her close. She was trembling. Her terrors had taken hold of her once more. He had hoped she was beginning to heal. The fear of what lay ahead was overwhelming her.

'Take this,' he said, pulling away from their embrace. He handed Alyn his knife. It wasn't his old pugio, though the blade was lethal enough. It was as long as his forearm and the steel keen. 'You'll not need to use it.'

Alyn shook her head, refusing to take it. Cai took hold of her hand, surprised by how warm it was. He placed the dagger's hilt into her palm and gently closed her fingers around it.

'I'll return soon,' he said. In the darkness he could not tell if Alyn looked at him. She remained silent. He squeezed her hand once more and left. He did not know which was worse, her anguished words or her silence.

He joined the others by the old fisherman's hut. 'Colm has confirmed the way to the western cliff face is clear,' Keefe said, keeping his voice to barely above a whisper. Cai saw the old man, a bent silhouette near to the open doorway of his hut, where a dim light glowed from its interior.

'I'll lead,' Barra said, his voice sounding stronger than it had for days. 'Remember, the pathway is narrow and the drop is sheer to the rocks below. Tread with care. It will take time to locate the hidden entrance in the palisade, we must not make a sound. And pray our enemy is complacent and not watching this side of the defences too closely.'

They set off into the darkness. Cai brought up the rear of the five, holding on to the hilt of his scabbarded sword to prevent it catching on any of the coarse underbrush. A chill wind blew in off the Hibernian sea and he wished he had not had to leave his cloak behind. Waves crashed against the rocky shoreline to his right. He hoped it would be enough to hide the sound of their approach.

Soon they came upon the bracken and dense fern Barra had described. Once through, they would reach the narrow pathway leading up the cliff face to the ramparts of the Novantae king's village. The dense bush shushed as the party pushed through it. Cai winced at the sound, sure they must be heard by sentries on the palisade walkway. He anticipated hearing a shout of alarm at any given moment. The only other sounds were the wind and the rhythmic assault of the sea.

Lucius was ahead of him. Cai was glad of his friend's presence. He sent a silent prayer to Fortuna they would both survive this night. The scratching and shushing sounds of their passage through the bush came to a sudden end. As they left the cover of the bracken, the wind freshened.

The boom of the surf now came from directly below them. Cai sensed though could not see the drop.

Unconsciously he put out his left hand to grasp hold of the dry winter grasses lining the cliff face.

Lucius tapped him on the shoulder. 'It's here,' he whispered. 'Follow me.'

Cai heard a slight crunching sound as Lucius began to move along the narrow pathway. Cai tentatively took a first step, relieved to feel firm ground. He had found the path. Looking upwards into the darkness he sought out the wooden palisade. A faint light from within the settlement revealed it as a shadow against the night sky. There was no sign of movement on the parapet.

Taking slow, deliberate steps, Cai made steady progress as the pathway climbed steeply. His thighs burned and his breathing became ragged. He could still hear the faint sound of Lucius's passage further ahead. It seemed his friend was getting away from him.

From out of the darkness ahead, Cai heard a hiss of breath, followed instantly by the clattering sound of falling stone, becoming louder as the scree tumbled down the cliff face reverberating into the night. He froze. Hearing a gasp of effort. Lucius.

Cai moved quickly, despite the unseen chasm. A rapid scrabbling sound accompanied by panicked breathing came from immediately ahead. More small stones were freed to cascade down the rockface. How could the sentries above not hear it?

The sounds led Cai to Lucius. He couldn't see his friend. It was clear, however, he was desperately clinging to the precipice. Getting onto his knees, Cai reached out blindly, groping for any contact. He felt the skin of Lucius's forearm, grasping it tightly. The path was too narrow. All he could do was hold onto his friend. He would not be able to lift Lucius without help.

'Shit,' Lucius said, barely above a breath of sound. Cai felt the dead weight. Lucius's other hand had lost its grip on the cliff edge. Only Cai now prevented his friend's certain death. He grasped frantically to Lucius's forearm. His arm was slick with sweat and Cai felt hopelessness begin to overwhelm him as it began to slip from his fingers. His shoulders screamed. He couldn't hold on for much longer. Cai dug his fingers in deep, a last desperate attempt to prevent the fall. His desperation grew. Lucius was going to die on the rocks below.

59

Panic overwhelmed Lucius's mind. He still fought the scream demanding release. It would mean death for his companions.

His hand had lost its grip on the dry brush. He flailed, trying to find it once more. Cai held on fiercely. He was losing the fight. Another hiss escaped Lucius's lips as he slipped through Cai's grasp. But instead of falling, Lucius rose, pulled upward. Someone held the neck of his tunic in a talon-like grip. An instant later he stood on the pathway once more, heaving quick breaths. He pressed his head against the scrub grass of the cliff face, suppressing the desire to shout his relief.

A great hand patted him on the shoulder. Hrindenus's hand. The Tungrian disappeared, back along the pathway. Lucius felt Cai grip his arm in reassurance. He took a deep, calming breath and followed Hrindenus, his heart still pounding. He was alive. The laughing face of his father flashed, unaccountably, into his mind. Instantly gone.

He moved off again, pressing hard against the long grass that grew from the cliff face. In moments he came up short as a hand was placed on his shoulder. Again, it was the Tungrian. They were immediately below the wooden palisade. The faint light from within the settlement was sufficient to see the silhouettes of Keefe and Barra disappear over the lip of the clifftop.

Lucius could hear the heavy breaths of Cai at his shoulder. The three men waited in their exposed position. His calves burned at standing so long on the narrow ledge.

Had Barra been able to locate the hidden entrance? A way only he and Keefe knew of? The question was answered shortly after as the dark bulk of Keefe reappeared.

He waved them forward. Hrindenus was up and over the cliff top with surprising stealth. In moments he, Cai, Hrindenus and the big Hibernian were gathered under the palisade. Keefe leaned against the stout timber staring at the ground. There was no sign of Barra.

Lucius heard a scraping sound. Shortly after, the dark shape of a head appeared next to Keefe's feet. 'It's clear. Come.' It was the Novantae, his head disappearing again. Keefe got onto his knees and slid into the dark gap. Hrindenus followed. Then it was Lucius's turn. He slid onto his front and felt for the hidden entrance, a gap between two of the palisade's wooden posts. A short piece of the timber had been removed. Lucius slithered through, to slide through lying on his side and using the wooden post as leverage. He felt hands drag him the last part of the way.

The smell of rotten vegetation and animal waste was strong, the ground soft and churned over. He heard shuffling snorts and low squeals. They were in a pigsty, he realised, set between the west facing defences of the village and one of the roundhouses. He recognised the hut he and the others had been held in on their last trip here. Barra was nowhere to be seen.

Cai slopped onto the ground at Lucius's feet. He helped his friend up. Keefe slid his sword from its scabbard. Lucius and the others followed his lead. Ambient light filtered through the wattle of the roundhouses, enabling them to discern the dark outlines of the buildings. A howl of laughter came from further into the settlement, perhaps from Barra's hall. Shortly after, the drunken refrain of a song of the People floated through the settlement. The warbling tune was taken up by others. A warrior's song, the words thick and slurred.

Barra reappeared, his shadow sliding between the slats of the pigsty's fence. He gathered them close.

'Most of Frang's men are in my hall. The boys are with them. From what I could see they are unharmed. They are being held at the rear. I couldn't see my cousin amongst them, but we won't wait for his return. We must be swift. Herne and Beren are quick-witted; they will find a way out if we keep the others occupied.'

He became pensive. 'My hearth warriors are no longer in the village. They may be held in the settlement outside of the gates. We must deal with the sentries without their help.

'There are two at the gates. Two others are on the walls watching east and west.'

The singing momentarily grew louder. Someone had left the hall. The five listened intently. Lucius heard footsteps coming towards their position. A deep voice still croaking the words of the song in accompaniment with the drunken gathering. Lucius assumed he would be making his way to some latrine bucket. Instead, his trudging footsteps grew louder.

Keefe ushered them into the darkness under the roundhouse's thatched roof. The Hibernian slid his sword back into its scabbard, instead drawing a long bladed dagger. The footsteps were nearly upon them, the words of his song replaced by an off-tune hum.

Lucius heard a rustling of clothing and saw a vague outline near to the sty's fence. There was a splash of liquid and a sigh. A shadow flashed past Lucius.

'What—' the word was instantly replaced by a gurgling noise and the sound of thrashing feet. Then silence. Keefe reappeared.

'One less,' he said. 'Three of us can take the sentries at the gate. The parapet is too narrow for more than one at a time.'

'I'll take the watcher on the east side,' Lucius said.

'I'll take the west,' Cai said.

'Good,' Barra said. 'We'll meet by the gate once we are done. Let's move.'

60

Alyn shivered. The biting wind cut through her tightly held cloak.

Her eyes had adjusted to the darkness and she could discern the shapes of the wind-bent trees around her. Despite her terror at being left behind she had spurned the offer of taking refuge in the old fisherman's hut. She couldn't bear the thought of being trapped, alone, with an unknown man. She held firmly to her courage. She would not panic. Cai would return for her soon.

Cai. Even after several days in his presence, it was hard to believe her prayers had been answered. He had found her. She had always known he would try. But, when Blue Dog had sailed from his island, taking her with him deep into the lands of the north, she had lost hope. Cai hadn't. She fought to control another wave of panic. What if he was killed? Beren would surely die with him. She fingered the hilt of the dagger and was surprised at the comfort it provided.

She had been crouching amongst the tangle of branches, discomfort forced her to stand and move position. What was that? A voice on the wind? She froze. Was it a trick of her mind? It came again. Closer. Another voice responded, though she could not discern the words.

Alyn lowered herself slowly back amongst the twisted branches. Her cloak caught. There was a snapping sound as it came free. The voices stilled. Only the wind could be heard once more. Without thought she pulled Cai's blade from her belt.

The voices did not come again. Perhaps they had passed? She prayed.

A hand grabbed the neck of her cloak. 'Hello again, slave.'

Alyn lashed out, instinctively. She blindly sliced the dagger at the shapeless figure. He shrieked, releasing his grip. She ran into the night, swallowed by the darkness, her cloak billowing behind her, all the while accompanied by the agonised howl of Blue Dog.

'Kill the bitch!'

61

Cai slipped through the village, accompanied by the refrain of the warriors' drunken song.

He moved between pens and storage huts. At one point, in the darkness, he kicked over an unseen bucket, its contents slopping across his foot, its smell acrid. He pushed away the thought of what it might be. A dog barked from somewhere in the settlement outside the ditches. No one within the palisade stirred.

He remembered where the ladder was placed from his previous visit. He tested the first rung. It held steady. He ascended with care, edging upwards, rung by rung. As his head crested the walkway he looked left and right along its length. There was only darkness, no sound of the sentry. The crash of waves and the gusting wind enough to smother the sound of any movement. He had no time to wait. He must choose a direction. He chose to head in the direction of the gate.

Climbing the rest of the way he stepped from the final rung onto the parapet. He was immediately assailed by the strengthening wind whipping his fair hair across his face. He drew his blade. Moving on light feet, he progressed as quickly as he dared. He had picked well, for in moments a man's dark shape began to emerge.

'Is that you, Da?' A boy's voice. Shit. He ran, sword raised to strike.

'Da!' It was a frightened cry for help. Cai struck. The boy collapsed onto the walkway. He didn't stop, instead running on towards the main gate. As he reached the corner of the palisade, he saw a flurry of movement by the gateway. There was no resounding clash of weapons.

Though the urgency of the activity left him in no doubt as to its cause.

Cai descended a ladder nearest the gates. The tip of a blade pressed against the back of his neck. 'Is it you, Roman?' Keefe said, his voice a low, menacing growl.

'Yes,' Cai felt the pressure of the blade released, to be left with a sensation of warm liquid sliding across his skin. He put his fingers to his neck. Blood. Not his.

'You dealt with your man?' Keefe asked.

'He's down. All done here?' The big Hibernian grunted in acknowledgment.

'We await your warleader.' Cai followed the Hibernian to the gateway.

'A damned deserter,' Hrindenus was saying to Barra, who was crouched next to the Tungrian. 'One of my own people.'

'We have seen them before, Roman,' Barra said. 'Some have come to us over the years. Few are allowed to live long enough to become one with the people.'

'A Tungrian,' Hrindenus spat the words, when he saw Cai approach. 'Can you believe it, sir?'

'How can you tell?' Cai said, scrutinising the body. 'His hair is fair to be sure, so are many of our Germanic troops.' Hrindenus bent once more, pulling back the sleeve of the dead warrior's tunic.

'Look at the ink,' he said. Cai scrutinised the arm in the poor light. In the dark blue colour used by the tribes of the Isle of the Mighty was scrawled the word *I Tungrii.*

'The First Tungrians,' Cai said. 'When I inform his Tribunus, I'm sure he will be glad he's accounted for. It will save him the effort of a crucifixion.'

'It's a damned disgrace, that's what it is,' Hrindenus began.

299

'What's a disgrace?' Lucius asked, appearing out of the night, his face blood spattered.

'Hrindenus here is shamed by one of his countrymen. There's no time to explain. We must finish the task at hand.'

'You're right, Roman,' Barra said, with a leering smile. 'It's time to be rid of my beloved cousin.'

They moved silently through the village, soon reaching Barra's hall. There was a small hole in one of the slats of its doorway, left by a knot in the wood. The Novantae peered carefully through.

'Still no sign of Frang,' he said.

'Let's get it done,' Cai said. 'Where are the rest of his men?' The singing had ceased moments earlier; still, laughter and drunken insults could be heard within.

'Seven are seated at the hearth-fire. I can see four others sprawled in their cloaks. There must be more in the shadows.' The Novantae king drew his blade. 'Are you ready?'

Without waiting for affirmation Barra burst through the door, Cai on his shoulder. The stink of ale and vomit was strong.

They rushed the warriors who sat at the hearth. All stared, open mouthed and unmoving. Barra ran the first of them through. His blade carved deep into the neck of the nearest warrior, whose dying heart sprayed blood across the others.

One bare-chested warrior turned in a panic, searching frantically for his own sword. Cai felled him with a scything blow cutting deep into his unprotected ribcage, tearing through his lung. He died where he lay, blood bubbling from the gash in his side, like a pot on the boil. He looked for another assailant, only to see Hrindenus and Keefe finish the last of them. One had babbled for mercy;

the big Hibernian swiftly cut off his pleas, driving his blade through the unfortunate's eye. Deep into his skull. He yanked the sword clear, its exit accompanied by a squelch.

The five turned to the remaining warriors in the hall. The blood lust filled Cai. All he wanted was to kill his enemies. But those who were not on their knees begging for mercy were still unconscious in a stupor from their night of revelry. Still Cai wanted them dead. He moved to the nearest, sword dripping red globules onto the rushes of the hall's floor.

'Cai!' Beren's shriek jolted him. He searched the gloom at the back of the roundhouse. His blood cooled. A grey haired warrior gripped Beren's long fair hair in his fist. He held a short blade to the boy's throat. It was only an eating knife. Sufficient to end Beren's life. Vomit was drying against the warrior's bare chest and crusted his red-grey beard.

Herne stood in front of them, sword in hand. It was too heavy for the Novantae boy, and he struggled to wield it. Still, he held his ground.

'Let me go free,' the old warrior slurred. 'Or I'll gut him.' Cai took a step forward. The warrior yanked Beren's hair, baring the boy's thin, white neck. Beren stared at Cai, his eyes wide with terror.

'Release the lad,' Barra said, his voice calm. 'You have my word, none of my men will harm you.'

'You?' The old warrior said, his voice dripping with derision. 'How could I trust what you say?'

Barra took two steps towards the warrior before halting. 'Because,' he said. 'I am not my shit-of-a-cousin. I am Barra, anointed king of the Novantae people. Let the boy go and I swear by all the gods neither I, nor my men, will harm you or stop you leaving.'

The old warrior stared at Barra, doubt warring with hope on his face. In an instant, he made his decision. 'Very well,' he said. He released his grip on Beren's hair, shoving him towards Herne. The Novantae boy grasped his friend's hand, leading him towards the hearth.

'Go,' Barra said, his words commanding. The old warrior began to walk-stagger towards the doorway. The Novantae king turned to Cai, nodding once. Cai drove his blade deep into the vomit-splattered belly of the old warrior, twisting the hilt in swift movements to prevent the steel becoming stuck. As the dying man collapsed to the floor he looked accusingly at Barra.

The king of the Novantae grinned at the dying warrior.

'He's not my man.'

62

'Frang has escaped.'

Lucius turned sharply. By the entrance to the hall, whose doors now hung precariously from the frame, stood a woman. Her long, dark hair was dishevelled and the neck of her green dress torn.

'Niamh!' Hrindenus and Keefe exclaimed simultaneously.

Lucius noticed Keefe's sister flashed the briefest of smiles at Hrindenus.

'What has happened sister, are you hurt?' Niamh waved her hand dismissively.

'The rat and one of his men tried to have their way with some of the women, I gave him more than he anticipated. He said you were dead. I knew he lied.'

It was then Lucius noticed the knife in her other hand. Niamh raised it for all to see.

'His face is even less pretty now,' she said defiantly. 'He heard your attack on the hall and made a run for it. I saw him scramble over the wall.' Her voice became respectful as she took in the sight of Barra. 'Lord,' she said. 'Frang has been boasting he is king and a mighty army is coming to deal with his enemies amongst the Novantae people. Led by Blue Dog.'

'We know, sister. He overtook us in the night. If not for the poor weather we might have found ourselves on the end of their spear points.' The big Hibernian turned to his king. 'We must free our men. Before your cousin and Blue Dog can come for us.'

Barra took in the sight of the remainder of Frang's men, now trussed hands and feet, their expressions a mixture of

303

confusion and fear. One had still not woken from his stupor even as Lucius bound him.

'Lord,' one of the men raised his voice. 'May I speak?' Lucius thought he was in his middle years and did not appear to be one of the warrior-kind. A fisherman perhaps? He bowed his head, falling silent. Disgust creased Barra's lips.

'Why should I listen to a slug who could not stay loyal to his king?' Barra said, disdain dripping from each word.

'Frang told us he had killed you, Lord, and he was the rightful king of these lands. He said we must come here to suppress a rebellion against his reign. We did not know, lord. I swear.'

Lucius saw many of the other prisoners nodding vigorously in agreement. He turned to Barra. 'We could use more men if Blue Dog reaches this place.'

'If his boats haven't been dashed on the rocks,' Keefe said. 'We saw no sign of him when morning broke. We can't trust them, Lord.'

Barra had continued to stare silently at the men, few of whom could meet their king's eyes. 'Let us first free my hearth warriors from captivity. Then I will decide what must be done.'

'Lord,' it was the same man. Barra turned to him once more.

'My boy,' he said. 'He was keeping watch on the wall. Does he still live?'

'He may live,' Cai said, 'I felled a sentry with the side of my blade. He was a young lad, I think. I hit him hard.'

'I will look for him,' Niamh said, the gentleness in her voice at odds with what had taken place in the hall.

'There's no time for this,' Keefe said. 'We must go. Now.'

Moments later, Lucius and the other four men were outside of the village ditch. Keefe had extinguished the torches over the gateway, plunging them into complete darkness. All was quiet, apart from the sound of deep snoring coming from one of the ramshackle huts nearby.

'How could they not have been disturbed by our attack?' Lucius whispered.

'They must have assumed it was a part of their drunken revelry,' Cai replied.

'There is only one building large enough to hold our men,' Barra said. 'This way.'

'What—' Keefe began. A man's scream carried to them on the wind. There was no mistaking the agony in it. Lucius froze as did the others.

'Kill the bitch!'

'Blue Dog,' Barra said

'Alyn,' Cai said, instantly drawing his blade and ran in the direction of the scream.

'Go with him,' Barra said to Lucius and Hrindenus. 'Keefe and I can manage alone.'

Lucius raced in the direction he had seen Cai disappear. Hrindenus was at his side. The sound of Cai's passing as he crashed through the undergrowth enabled Lucius to follow.

'Shit.' Hrindenus had stumbled, falling hard, crunching amongst the scrub grass. Lucius didn't slow; the Tungrian would have to catch up. He ran on. Bracken, still wet from the recent snowmelt, soaked his troos. The wicked points of blackberry bushes tore at the skin of his forearms. For a few short moments all he heard was the wind as it blew hard off the Hibernian sea.

From close by, Cai roared his warcry.

'Nervana!'

ALISTAIR TOSH

The clash of steel on steel sent a shock through the air.
Lucius ran on into the night. Towards the sound of battle.

63

He shouldn't have left her. The thought played like a continuous refrain as he ran. The sound of his gusting breath competed to be heard with the beat of his heart. He shouldn't have left her.

Cai ran recklessly, descending the slope towards the beach. He instinctively followed the natural lay of the land, crashing through dense undergrowth, not caring the sound of his passing might alert his enemies.

Abruptly the brush came to an end and Cai was out in the open. He halted. Dark shapes ran towards him. There seemed many, panting heavily as they ascended the steep slope. One silhouette led the pack. It stumbled and fell. A woman's shriek cut through the driving wind. Alyn.

Cai raised his sword two-handed. He charged towards the writhing, dark mass of men.

'Nervana.' The warcry burst from his chest, called up by his rage. Cai's only thought was to protect Alyn. He reached her prone figure, struggling to rise once more. He didn't stop. His momentum took him headlong into the warband. The leading figures had halted, shocked by this unexpected, ferocious assault out of the darkness.

Cai's blade sunk deep into the skull of the leading warrior. He barrelled into the already dead body, driving it to the ground. Ripping his sword free with a crunch of bone and slop of brain he struck out blindly. The nearest warrior had recovered from his temporary stupor and desperately parried Cai's wild swing. It wasn't enough to save him. Using his impetus, Cai slid his sword along the other's blade, sinking its point into the warrior's throat. Warm liquid coursed along the cool metal.

'Nervana!' The cohort's warcry came from behind him. Lucius. An instant later his friend was by his side striking out with ferocious strokes, forcing the leading warriors back. They wouldn't be able to hold them for long.

A bestial roar erupted from their rear. The big Tungrian had come. Hrindenus had no thought of defence. His huge shadow flashed past Cai and Lucius and rammed like a charging stag, driving deep into the confused ranks of Blue Dog's warband. Cai and Lucius followed in his wake, in their battle madness. They drove the enemy back.

Hrindenus was formidable and terrifying to his enemies in the darkness. Two bodies lay at his feet and he continued to scream his defiance. The three friends fought side by side, forcing Blue Dog's men to withdraw further down the slope. In an instant, they broke. One moment the three seemed to be fighting against a solid wall of warriors. The next, they had melted back into the night. Black outlines of men running towards the shore. Hrindenus made to follow, but Cai grabbed him by the arm. The Tungrian tried to dislodge him, shrouded still in the killing lust. Cai held firm.

'No, brother,' he said. 'It's first blood to us, but we shouldn't test the gods. They have been good to us this night.' Hrindenus relented, but his eyes retained their wild countenance.

'We must return to Barra,' Lucius said. 'Blue Dog has found us after all.'

'Alyn,' Cai said, turning sharply, desperately peering into the darkness towards where he had last seen her.

'I'm here,' she said. 'I'm well.'

Cai ran to her, taking Alyn in his arms. She wrapped hers around his neck squeezing it tightly. He felt cold metal brush against his ear. He reached for her hand, feeling the dagger.

'Shall I take care of this?' he asked.

'No,' she said. 'I need it to finish what I started.'

64

A grey early morning light filtered across the fields. Occasional patches of white, the last remnants of the previous day's snowfall, punctuated the dullness of the landscape. A heavy rain had battered the buildings of the village during the night, driven by the ever-present wind. It passed quickly. As Lucius watched from the parapet over the gateway, an oppressive gloom of low cloud had settled about the land, matching his mood.

Would he ever again see Baetica and the warm lands of his birth? He shook the thoughts from his mind. They were fruitless. Who knew what the gods had in store for him? Would they have brought him all this way just to dash his hopes? Probably.

He turned at a metallic scraping sound. Barra's warriors were readying their weapons.

Sharpening swords with the whetting stone, affixing bright feathers to spear shafts and testing the flights of arrows. They had two bowmen. Four if you counted Beren and Herne. Lucius smiled at the memory of his old First Spear's son, demanding to be allowed to take his place on the ramparts. His smile faded, knowing the boys would have their own dangerous part to play in the battle to come.

Barra had sent the people of the village and its ramshackle settlement into hiding, led into the great forest by one of his warriors. All who remained were the men capable of fighting and a handful of their women who had refused to go. Including Niamh. She would not leave Hrindenus's side, much to the annoyance of Keefe.

The Hibernian warrior appeared to sense he had lost the fight with his strong willed sister. Or perhaps it was set aside until this greater battle was done. Instead, he studiously ignored the pair as they huddled together gazing out over the sea from the palisade. Lucius shook his head. How could a man lose himself to a woman so quickly?

The night battle with Blue Dog's men had been short and fierce, the three soldiers matched against a warband, and they had prevailed. The coming day was unlikely to bring such easy success. The most surprising outcome of the fight had been Alyn. She had become less fearful. Less in need of Cai's continual presence. Perhaps the thought of her vengeance on t her tormentor had helped? He was glad of it, nonetheless.

Where was their enemy? This was the worst part of battle. Waiting for it to begin. The memory of his cohort standing resolutely under the Novantae's sacred hill flickered into his thoughts. His first engagement as an inexperienced commander. Waiting as the storm lashed the faces of his men. Hearing another kind of storm on the hill's obscured ramparts as the legions battered their way through the hilltop's defences. It had been unnerving, anticipating the tribe's warriors would break at any moment. And break they did, against the steady ranks of the Nervana.

'Still no sign of my cousin?' Barra asked. Lucius had not heard the Novantae's approach. He was dressed in his full finery. The scales of his Roman-made armour shone even in the dull light, framed by the blue curling tattoos on his arms. His red hair was set in new plaits and his beard combed. He appeared every bit the warrior king.

Lucius shook his head. 'Perhaps we scared them away for good last night,' he said, with as much humour as he could muster.

Barra snorted. 'My cousin will feel emboldened with an army at his back. He will come. He's impatient to have me out of the way and to begin his rule.' Barra became sombre. 'But he's a fool. Even if he prevails over me, it will have been achieved with the backing of the Damnonii king. Blue Dog will be the true master of these lands and Frang his vassal. If he lets him live.'

'We'll have to make sure he doesn't, won't we?' Lucius said.

Barra snorted a laugh.

'What's so funny?' Lucius asked, puzzled.

'You said 'we', my friend. The Novantae and Rome fighting side by side. Who said the gods don't have a sense of humour?'

Lucius joined in the mirth, barking a short laugh.

'Perhaps this could be the beginning of something,' Lucius said. 'Perhaps the Empire and the Novantae people can coexist in relative harmony.'

'It's possible,' Barra said, becoming thoughtful. 'For my part, I will try to make it so, for as long as I am king. It takes two sides to create a lasting peace and Rome always wants to extract its own price for it. It will depend on how high that price is.'

'Lord!' A hail came from further along the parapet. 'To the north.'

Two horsemen were emerging from amongst the bracken and gorse bush. At first the low cloud gave them a dark countenance, making it difficult to see the riders clearly. Soon there was no doubting who approached Barra's village. Blue Dog and Frang.

'Look at the little shit,' Barra said. 'He's like a child riding his first horse.'

'What could they want?' Lucius said.

'He has come to offer terms. None of which will be acceptable to me. His real aim will be to assess our strength.' Keefe appeared at the top of the ladder next to the gateway. 'Keep the men out of sight.' The Hibernian nodded his understanding, disappearing once more.

'Now I see why Alyn is more her old self this morning,' Lucius said. 'It seems her dagger found its mark.' The Damnonii king wore a bronze helmet, with broad cheek pieces that could not hide the bindings covering his left eye.

Barra grumbled a laugh. 'It seems my cousin, too, has suffered from the wrath of a woman.' Lucius saw he was right. A gash sliced Frang's right cheek. The flesh of the wound was puckered and coloured a deathly white.

The two horsemen reached the outskirts of the shambling buildings of the temporary village. Blue Dog held high a leafless branch of oak. Barra raised his arm, acknowledging the symbol. The riders nudged their mounts forwards. The pair carefully picked their way along the pathway through the settlement, until they reached the outer edge of the ditch. They halted where it met the causeway to the main gate. Barra's face was a mask of calm.

'Greetings, Barra,' Blue Dog said, his voice raised in a tone that spoke of friendship.

Barra nodded in return, maintaining his silence.

'Good morning, cousin,' Frang began. Barra cut him off, snarling back.

'When you speak to your king, you say lord. But your father was a fool too, who didn't know his place.'

Frang's face burned red. 'Why you—'

313

'You must forgive your cousin, Lord Frang,' Blue Dog interrupted. 'He has had a long arduous journey and must be tired.'

'What is it you want, Blue Dog?' Barra said, still watching Frang. 'Do you seek a healer for your face?' Lucius saw the Damnonii bridle at the use of his hated moniker. Hatred flashed in his eyes, quickly disguised. Instead, he made a great show of looking along the length of the palisade.

'You have so few men. You know a battle is pointless. It will only lead to your destruction, and I would prefer to avoid any unnecessary deaths amongst my own people. So, I have come to offer you an arrangement.'

'What arrangement could I trust from a man who murdered his own king?'

Blue Dog was stunned into silence. Lucius saw the truth of Barra's words written on the face of the Damnonii king, the madness returning to his eyes.

'How could you so easily be taken in by lies?' he said, feigning hurt. 'Who would say such a thing?'

'We came across your shithole of a village. Only to discover you had sailed north to stake your claim to be king. Which puzzled me. After all, I'd seen Caden only days before. It took only a little persuasion for one of your faithless hounds to tell us the full story.

'You ambushed Caden and his men on the shore, where their boat had foundered. Instead of offering your king aid, you slit his throat.'

Blue Dog's eyes had narrowed. 'You would believe the word of this dog?'

A slow smile emerged on Barra's lips. It seemed one of genuine mirth. 'My father taught me to trust a dog's instinct. If he growls at a man, do not trust the man.' Barra's smile broadened further. 'This man still lives,' he lied. 'Perhaps I will bring him before the Holy One and your warchiefs and let him tell his tale.'

Blue Dog stared up at Barra, his face a red mask of fury. After a moment Frang leant over and whispered something to the Damnonii. Blue Dog turned in his saddle, making a show of appearing to be in search of something to the north. Then in mock frustration he turned back to the palisade.

A smile returned to his face. 'My army lies to the north, hidden yet by the mist. At best you have a handful of warriors and you cannot hide behind your little walls for long. I offer you this. Hand over the woman and I and king Frang will allow you and your people to leave unmolested. You can run and hide in Roman lands with your Roman friends.' With a glance at Lucius, Blue Dog spat a fat globule of phlegm onto the sodden ground below.

Barra's face took on a stern countenance. 'I do not need your filthy little deal. A wise man doesn't put his trust in a rabid beast. You are a coward and your men will run when they see you run. As for you, cousin, I would never abandon my people to your tyranny. Nor will I cower behind these walls. We will meet you shield to shield on the fields over yonder. If you have the balls?

Blue Dog leered back at the Novantae king. 'Very well. You will die on the ends of our swords and when we are done with you, I will take back my woman. When my son is born, I will give her over to my men to do with what they will.' The Damnonii cast the oak branch aside, turning his mount and kicking her into a gallop, followed by a surprised Frang. In moments the pair were swallowed by the low cloud once more.

65

'They have seventy men, lord,' Keefe said, breathlessly. 'I counted sixty shaved Damnonii heads. The rest must be what's left of Frang's hearth warriors.'

Keefe had returned moments before, through the hidden entrance in the sea-facing palisade. He had been gone no more than an hour, leaving during the run-in between Barra and Blue Dog.

'Not much of an army,' Cai said, as he stood by his hall's hearthfire with Barra, Lucius and Hrindenus.

'No,' Barra said. 'Though, still twice our number.' The Novantae was thoughtful for a time. 'We must meet him in battle. I'll not shrink behind these walls like my craven cousin would. Nor can we prevail if we simply meet them head on. They will eventually overwhelm us.'

'Perhaps you have forgotten what the Novantae did to my men?' Cai said, smiling at Barra's puzzlement. 'At the battle under the ramparts of your sacred hill?' Cai's smile broadened. 'On the day you tried to kill me.'

Cai saw understanding dawn in Barra's eyes. He returned the mirth. 'As I recall, the plan didn't succeed,' he said.

'No, thank the gods. But it almost did. And this time there will be no reinforcements coming to the rescue.' Cai outlined his plan. 'I will also take the archers, including Beren and Herne.'

'No, brother,' Lucius said. Cai turned to his friend, taken aback. 'Blue Dog will sense a trap if he doesn't see you amongst the men facing him. He hates you. More even than lord Barra, I think.'

'He's right, Roman,' Barra said.

'I'll go,' Lucius said. 'He's less likely to miss me.'

'Then take the big lump here,' Cai said, indicating Hrindenus with his thumb. The Tungrian simply smiled back.

Lucius shook his head. 'You'll need him in the shield wall. They will fear the sight of Keefe and Hrindenus standing behind our wall of shields.' Cai saw a briefest of glances pass between the two big men. As close to an acknowledgement of mutual respect he had seen. Cai felt a rush of comfort at having these fiercest of warriors at his side.

'Let's prepare,' Barra said.

'Do everything Lucius asks of you,' Cai said. 'And if he orders you to run, you run. Understood?'

'Yes, Cai,' Beren said solemnly.

'Good. When I eventually meet your father again around the campfire, I don't want to face his wrath for getting his son killed.'

'No, Cai.'

'Good lad,' Cai smiled down at the boy. 'You look more like him each day. He'll be bursting with pride as he watches you grow towards manhood.'

'Do you think so?' Beren said, his eyes lighting up.

'I know it. Now off you go with Herne. Get yourselves ready.' He watched the boy, his boy, run towards his waiting friend. He held a hunting bow in one hand and used the other to stop the quiver of arrows from bouncing against his back.

'I'm trying, brother,' Cai whispered into the sea breeze.

'Saying a prayer to Fortuna, sir?' Hrindenus said, as he appeared beside him.

'Well, she hasn't let me down in all the years I've served with the Eagles. Let's hope she doesn't choose to break the habit of a lifetime on this day.'

'You Nervii really are cheery fuckers, aren't you? Now, us Tungrian's we're of a more genial disposition. I put it down to our mothers' milk.'

'Just make sure you and your cheery disposition don't leave my damned side when the hard fighting starts.'

Hrindenus smiled. 'Have I ever not been there to pull your arse out of trouble, sir?'

'No, but—'

'Cai.'

He turned to see Alyn, waiting for him by the door to Barra's hall.

'I'll see you in a moment, sir,' Hrindenus said, not hiding his amusement.

Cai moved to her side. Alyn took his hand in hers and her grey eyes glistened as they met his. He sensed she wanted to say something of import and was unable to give voice to it.

'I have no intention of dying this day,' he said, guessing her intent. He squeezed her hand. 'I plan on living a long life with you and the boy. Perhaps we can be farmers like Mascellus? Or horse traders?' Alyn laughed at his enthusiasm, wrapping her arms around his waist and resting her head against his chest. He felt her hard belly press against him and was surprised at how protective he felt of the unborn child.

'If the worst should happen, you know where the fisherman's boat is. You and Niamh must get to it. The boys will meet you there.' She shook her head against his chest. 'You must Alyn. You must do it for Beren and our child you now carry.'

She stared into his eyes with a mixture of sadness and wonder at his words. 'I will,' she said. 'We'll wait by the shore until you come to us.' And with that, they parted.

66

Lucius scratched roughly at his chest. The itch of the healing wounds at times was unrelenting. He was first through the narrow gap in the palisade. The waves crashed against the rocky shore below him. He scrambled onto the narrow path and waited for the others to emerge.

Beren was next, followed by Herne. Both boy's eyes were alight with excitement. Lucius's small force consisted of seven warriors, two of whom carried hunting bows. With the boys and himself, there were ten. Not his biggest command. He hoped it would be enough to make the difference.

They inched along the precarious route, made more difficult by the need to carry shield and spear. How had they managed this in the dark, he thought? All the while they were buffeted by a strong wind.

Fortunately, it wasn't long before they left the path and were amongst the scrub. The bracken and dense blackberry bushes would hide their presence for a time. He hoped. At least until they reached the dunes.

A hum of voices in the wind. He halted. He signalled those following. All crouched as he had done. They waited. The voices came again. At least two. Nearby, their conversation was relaxed. Not expecting trouble?

Blue Dog is not a complete fool, he thought. They are watching their rear. Lucius signalled the others should stay. He edged forward. He approached the end of the undergrowth's protection. The voices were close. Peeling back a branch of winter dried bracken, he got his first glimpse of his enemy.

There were two. Less than a spear's throw from his concealment. Both sat on a grass-covered sand dune, staring out to sea, spears and shields abandoned on the sand close by. Both wore their long, dark hair in plaits. Not Damnonii then. Lucius set his shield aside and gripped tightly to the ash shaft of his spear.

'Frang will see us right, no worries.'

'But lord Barra lives. He said he had killed him. We can't trust Frang no more.'

'Who cares? Barra will soon be dead and Frang will be lord of these lands. Then, it will be the easy life for us, my friend. Think of all the women of Rerigon who will be wanting to suck on the cocks of the king's hearth warriors.'

'Aye. You might be right. Not that you've got much to suck on.'

Lucius burst from the bracken and onto the shingle, moving swiftly on light feet.

'You fucker I'll—' The watchers turned in unison.

Lucius cast his spear, low and direct. Surprise and agony warred on the nearest warrior's face as the spearpoint cut deep between his ribs. For an instant his mouth opened in the silent parody of a scream. Lucius slid his sword from its scabbard with long-practised ease.

The second warrior scrambled on his hands and knees, in a desperate panic to reach his own spear. All the while emitting a strange pig-like squeal. He was already too late. As Frang's man clasped his spear shaft Lucius swung his blade in a wide arc, cutting through vein and windpipe. With hands held to his neck, the warrior made a futile fight for life, as blood pumped freely through his clutching fingers, draining onto the windswept sands.

Lucius didn't stay to watch his final death throes, instead returning to his waiting men. He led them from

321

their hiding place out onto the dunes. Beren and Herne did not so much as flinch as they passed the bodies of the two watchers.

He skirted the old fisherman's hut, following a route Keefe had described. Eventually his small warband reached the stunted and wind-bent trees, the point at which the Hibernian said they should turn eastwards.

They stole forward in a skirmish line. The archers, including both boys, nocked arrows to bow strings. The ground underfoot was soft, for which Lucius was grateful. It would help mask their approach. At times they were forced to bend under low branches; at one point they crawled on hands and knees to get through the increasingly dense woodland.

At the sound of coarse laughter his men froze. Lucius signalled they should lie flat, whilst he moved forwards once more. He crawled over the sodden ground, his hands chilled as they sank into saturated moss and leaf-covered earth.

Someone coughed, the harsh sound followed by a hawk and spit. Lucius pressed himself into the soft ground of the woodland. The dense trees blocked his view. A sound of splashing hit the earth nearby.

'Where are you, Aodhan?'

'I'm taking a piss.'

'Well hurry it up. We're on the move. The fools have opened the gates.'

The splashing ceased. 'Ha. The fun is about to begin then?'

Lucius heard the squelching of running feet, moving away. He quickly got to his feet. He must risk it. He dashed forwards, advancing from tree to tree. Ahead there was more laughter and the sound of many feet slopping over the saturated ground. He came upon a clearing time to see the last of the enemy moving towards the settlement before it was swallowed by heavy snowfall. It must have commenced, unnoticed, whilst they moved through the woods. A blessing from the gods, perhaps.

He followed the rear ranks of the enemy, keeping out of sight from any casual eye that happened to glance back the way they had come. A sudden gust of wind cleared the way ahead and, for the first time, he had a view of what lay before him. The battlefield.

Blue Dog and Frang had committed their full force, anticipating an easy victory. The pair rode at the fore, the only ones mounted. Their warriors moved forward in two ragged lines; spear points raised skyward. The tattoo-covered scalps of the Damnonii gave the impression they wore helmets. Though, only the two lords had any kind of metal armour.

The enemy too had abandoned their cloaks for the fight to come and wore a mixture of coloured tunics. Some with leather vests, most not. They walked, heads bent, into the face of the wind-driven snow. Beyond the enemy was Barra's palisaded holding. The gates were indeed open.

Momentarily his heart sank as he saw the full strength of the warband that faced Blue Dog's. They seemed so few, straddling the roadway at the point it met the first of the buildings of the ramshackle, temporary village. They too were in two ranks, much shorter lines than the enemies. At the heart of the front rank were his companions. Four big men, standing side by side, like rocks on the shoreline waiting for the incoming tide to break against them. The snowfall drove in once more, like the drop of a curtain, obscuring the field.

Lucius ran. It was time to bring his men to the fight. It was time to shed blood.

67

'I hate those bald-headed bastards,' Hrindenus said. 'Why can't they grow their hair long like real warriors?'

'They say it is because the creatures their tattoos depict enable them to communicate better with the gods,' Keefe said, his voice a grumble. 'But I think it is because they are riddled with fleas.'

Laughter broke from the Novantae warband. They had watched the slow approach of the Damnonii, and Frang's allied Novantae, from the edge of the makeshift village. Cai knew the laughter would be a welcome release of tension for all. They were positioned on a slight rise, straddling the pathway leading to the open gates of Barra's home.

To each side of them were the disordered huts of its inhabitants, meant to be temporary, now taking on the appearance of a more permanent settlement. Thatch of bracken dressed the low rooftops that dripped continually as the thick snow tried to settle, unsuccessfully for now. He prayed it would catch when the time came. Or this would be a very short-lived battle.

'It's a shit day for a fight too,' Hrindenus said, warming to his subject. 'Who decides to start trouble in the midst of winter's grip when it's pissing with snow? Fools and those who have never known the warmth of a woman. That's who.'

'We'll have to kill them quickly then, won't we, Roman?' Keefe said. 'So we can return to the hearth and our ale.' For the first time since he had known him, Cai heard a smile in the Hibernian's voice.

'Aye,' Hrindenus replied. 'We will.'

Blue Dog and Frang could be clearly seen astride their short, dappled mounts. Their bronze helmeted heads lowered into the face of the driving, near-horizontal snow. The two broad lines of warriors following could so easily envelop them once they engaged shield to shield. As the enemy came within the range of a long arrow shot, Cai turned to Barra.

'It's time, I think.'

'This village needs to be rebuilt in any case,' Barra said, turning to Alyn and Niamh who waited, shivering, nearby. Both protected smouldering brands and unlit torches beneath their cloaks. He nodded once to the women. Alyn ran to one side, Niamh to the other, both disappearing amongst the tangle of buildings.

Cai hoped Alyn would obey him and make for the boat as soon as she was done.

All twenty of their warriors held a shield. Each man in the front rank held a spear, along with a sword. Those in the rear rank held a mixture of spears and farming tools to use as best they could when the lines closed. Most of Barra's hearth warriors were in the leading line, the cream of the Novantae, with a smattering in the rear to bolster the less experienced men.

These were mainly the fishermen who had come with Frang and Barra had let live. Cai had been pleased to see the young lad he had struck on the parapet. His face was a livid purple and black colour, his right eye swollen. But he lived, and stood at his father's side.

As the enemy ranks came within a spear's throw of the village, the Damnonii king raised his arm aloft, halting his men. For a time, the two bands stared silently at one another. Each side seeming reluctant to cast the first spear.

Cai scrutinised the buildings of the village. There was no sign the women had been successful. He spoke quietly to Barra.

'Is it just too damned wet?' he asked.

'It'll catch,' Barra said. 'But let's buy the women some time. And have some fun, shall we?'

Barra stepped from the line and strode towards the waiting Damnonii. He halted midway.

'Ballsy,' Hrindenus said.

'A pain in my arse, is what he is,' Keefe said, unable to hide his pride.

'Blue Wolf, lord of the Damnonii people. I, Barra, king of the Novantae people, challenge you to single combat. Let's not spill our men's blood unnecessarily. Meet me, king to king, to decide this day.'

'Ha. Why should I fight someone who is not my equal? The true king of the Novantae people rides beside me, as my friend. We'll soon deal with your pathetic little band. It's your blood that will be spilt on this day.'

'As I thought, Blue Dog,' Barra said, putting heavy emphasis on the slur. 'You're a coward. You hid behind Taog, afraid to meet the Roman who had come for his woman. Now it is me you fear to meet. Very well, let me see if my cousin has the heart. So, Frang, what of it? Blue Dog claims you are the rightful king, even though it was I anointed by the Holy One. Let us end it here. The gods can decide who has the right.'

'Why would I waste my time on you, Barra?' Frang shouted, his voice shrill. 'Your blood will soak this ground soon enough.'

Barra nodded slowly and deliberately so all before him could see. 'As I thought, you too are a craven stoat of a man. Why should I be surprised? Both of you were bested by women. Each of you carries the wound to prove it. Is this what the warriors of the Damnonii want to fight for? Two cowards who will run when the battle turns against them. Which it will. They will abandon you to your deaths to save their own skins.'

Cai smiled as he saw many of the dark-headed warriors turn to one another. A deep-throated rumble of a laugh came from Keefe.

'He always had a way with words.'

'Look,' Frang shouted.

Cai glanced left along the line, in the direction Barra's cousin pointed. Smoke was billowing through the thick bracken rooftops of the nearest buildings. Turning to the right he saw a similar scene. The strong wind was blowing dense white clouds towards the enemy, partly obscuring their ranks.

Barra reappeared out of the smoke like a god from the otherworld, his bronze scale armour reflecting white. His face held a broad smile.

'That was fun,' he said, taking his place next to Cai.

'Kill them all!' Blue Dog screamed. A roar of massed voices filled the air.

'Here they come!' Cai shouted. 'Ready your spears! Remember. Hard and low.' The smoke from the burning village had mingled with the low cloud cover, obscuring the battlefield. Only fleeting glimpses of the Damnonii could be seen. Their warcries rose in volume as they closed with the Barra's small force.

'Now!' Cai bellowed. He cast his own spear into the smoke and snow, along with the others of the front rank. He didn't see the impact. The agonised screams that rent the air an instant later told its own tale. He slid his sword from its scabbard, seeing Barra in his periphery doing likewise. He braced his legs and gripped tight to his shield as he waited for the impact. An instant later the first warriors of the dark-headed Damnonii flashed into view, emerging from the murk, faces contorted, screaming their hatred. Now, once again, would come the time for blood and death.

68

Smoke billowed across the battlefield.

Lucius could hear the screams of the living and the dying. But he could see little more than flitting dark smudges of men moving within the gloom. His eyes watered. He stifled a cough.

'We have to get nearer. We'll hit them close in. Remember what I said. When I say run, you run. No questions.' Both boys nodded vigorously, their earlier excitement replaced by trepidation.

He turned to the other two archers. 'Once your arrows are spent, join the fight.'

'Yes, lord,' the two Novantae warriors answered in unison. Lucius found their words jarring. The strangeness of the respect directed towards him by his former enemies. He addressed the remaining five warriors, in their own tongue.

'The smoke is a gift from the gods. We'll take them up the arse as soon as the first volley flies. Let's move.'

The ten ran towards the tumultuous sound of battle. As they closed to the rear of the enemy line, Lucius halted them. 'Seek out your targets. Have a care for our own men.'

The two archers along with Beren and Herne drew back their bowstrings. Lucius had an instant to appreciate how expert the two boys had become as he saw them pick out a target.

'I've got the one with the red jerkin,' Herne said. 'You take the one to his right.'

'I see him,' Beren replied.

Shield held close to his shoulder. Fingers, numb from the cold, gripped the hilt of his sword, he released a long slow breath. Lucius prepared to charge. The four released a ragged volley of arrows.

Cai sliced into the groin of the Damnonii. He twisted his blade and Damnonii's scream of fury turned to agony, his features contorted. Cai shoved hard with his shield, forcing the dying man into the tribesmen behind. He quickly looked around him.

The fire was achieving its intended purpose. Protecting their flanks. Where was Blue Dog? Cai had caught glimpses of the Damnonii king through the billowing white smoke. He had remained on horseback. Perhaps he had dismounted?

He had no time to wonder further as another assailant struck the iron rim of his shield. They pressed shield to shield for a time, neither able to bring their weapons to bear. This warrior, young and red-headed, must have been one of Frang's men. He was inept. He simply tried to out shove Cai as if he might push him over. Their faces were so close Cai felt the spittle on his face as the other screamed his rage. Cai smiled back, feeling calm, wrapped as he was in the battle-heat. He slammed his forehead into the bridge of the other's nose. The young warrior's blood burst across Cai's face. The Novantae collapsed, falling from sight.

Although Blue Dog may have been cowardly, his men were not. They were being pressed relentlessly by the Damnonii. Gradually, step by step, they were being pushed back along the pathway, slick with mud.

The fire had taken hold. The ramshackle buildings of the village were perfect kindling as the flames spread rapidly from hut to hut. The heat was intense and the white

330

clouds of smoke continued to cast the battlefield in a fog-bound otherworld. All the while thick snow continued to fall.

Cai tried to see over the ranks of the enemy to the fields beyond, this time not seeking Blue Dog, but his friend. All was a thick cloak of whiteness.

A spearpoint flashed out. He moved his head instinctively. Its iron point missed, though the smooth wood of its shaft kissed his cheek. What he wouldn't give to have his old helmet right now. He ducked into his shield to avoid the next attempt, flicking his sword point out, meeting only air. No fool this one, he thought.

A yell came from his left. It was not in the language of the people. Keefe, Cai realised.

'Up you come.'

Cai saw Hrindenus reach down. The Hibernian had slipped and was on his arse. The Tungrian had raised his shield to cover himself and Keefe. He was still badly exposed. A Damnonii saw his chance. A big warrior, clad in a dark seal fur tunic, snarling, revealing dark and twisted teeth, struck hard. He swung his long blade downwards in a fierce arc.

Cai reacted, flicking his own blade out to parry what would be a death blow for Hrindenus. In doing so he knew he had left himself open to his own assailant. The spearman would not miss a second time.

The clash of steel resounded loud in his ears. His arm jarred; pain lanced along it as his sword took the full impact of the other's strike. He braced, anticipating the burning agony of sharp iron driven between his exposed ribs. It didn't come. He regained his position. He had given Hrindenus time to pull the Hibernian back to his feet. Cai risked a glance beyond his shield, the Damnonii spearman was nowhere to be seen.

He glanced to his left to see Barra, effort creasing his face as he pulled his sword from an unseen body at his feet. The spearman? There was no time to question further as both he and the Novantae king were assailed once more. They were driven back another step. Where are you, brother?

The arrows struck home. A difficult shot to miss at such close range, even for unpractised bowmen. Each point punched deep in the back of an enemy. Lucius saw one warrior drop his sword and shield and attempt to reach for the shaft. He turned in Lucius's direction, dumbstruck confusion etched on his face. He opened his mouth to yell a warning, an instant later the light fled from his eyes.

Lucius ran into the smoke and snow, towards the writhing mass of the enemy obscuring Barra's small band. So deep was their desire to kill the men before them, none of the enemy host had noticed the fall of their own comrades at the rear.

Crossing the short distance quickly, mouth open wide in a silent warcry, he did the first thing that came to mind. Gripping his shield aside, Lucius raised his sword. Two steps from the rear rank he swung. With a splintering crack of bone, his blade bit deep into a Damnonii's shoulder.

Lucius could not stop. He smashed into the back of the stricken warrior, driving the body before him, like a second shield, into the heart of Blue Dog's men.

He was dimly aware of more screams as the rest of his own small command struck. Lucius tried desperately to free his blade but it held fast. What was worse, the deadweight of the body dragged downwards taking him with it. He crashed onto the boggy morass of the blood tainted snow. He was face down. What a fool he had been. He was a dead man. He waiting for the end.

A hand grasped the rim of his leather tunic. He was yanked to his feet.

'Hello brother,' Cai said, a grimace creasing his lips. 'Nice of you to join the fight. There's no time for rest. We have an enemy to kill.' And his friend was gone. Lucius looked wildly around. The battle had turned into a tumult of disorder. No longer were there two lines of enemy facing each other. The abrupt intervention of Lucius and his men had shattered all order. It had become a brutal fight between individuals and small groups.

'Kill them all!' Barra screamed from nearby. 'Kill them all!' The Novantae king appeared possessed, a manic gleam shone in his eyes. Shieldless, he swung his sword left and right, killing and maiming with each stroke. The Damnonii fled before him, disappearing into the smoke filled gloom.

Lucius recovered his sword and searched for an enemy to kill. Fleetingly he thought of the two boys, he hoped they had gotten to safety. Where was the mad king? Where was Frang? As if in answer he heard the rumble of horses moving at a gallop. The outlines of two mounted men appeared out of the murk.

'Lord!' Lucius heard Keefe's warning from his right. He had seen the danger. The two riders must have been drawn to Barra's wild battlecries. They burst into view. Blue Dog, and Frang his lap dog, riding hard, lances in hand. Barra turned at his friend's warning. They were almost upon him. The Damnonii king threw his spear, hard and direct. Barra swiped his sword wide, deflecting its flight. He had left himself open to Frang's own spear cast.

333

It struck Barra clean in the chest, throwing him onto his back.

'No!' Keefe's scream of anguish crossed the battleground.

Lucius saw Frang whoop with joy as he turned his horse to ride from the field, disappearing amongst the smoke, following the fleeing Damnonii.

But Blue Dog reigned in his dappled mount, turning it in a wide arc, to face his enemies. His warband had fled the field, running for the cover of the nearby woods. He was alone.

The Damnonii king giggled like a child, the laugh transforming into hysteria. He looked to where Barra lay, hidden by the broad back of Keefe who knelt by his lord. Finally, with an effort, he was able to control himself.

'You should have taken my offer to run, *king* Barra,' he laughed again, instantly becoming a choking cough. 'Your lands will be ruled by Frang under my guidance. And your nephew will be hunted down.'

A spear flashed out of fog. 'Bastard,' Keefe's shout was part grunt from the effort of his throw. The Damnonii saw it at the last instant, but it had not been aimed at him. The spear's point punctured deep into his mount's rump. The animal shrieked, collapsing onto its flank. Blue Dog fought desperately to stay on its back. The king of the Damnonii was thrown backwards from his saddle, not by the movement of his dying horse but by the two arrows that had punched through his mail shirt, deep into is side.

Lucius ran towards Blue Dog, who was struggling to rise. Cai was quicker. He rushed in as his enemy had risen to knees, coughing up blood over his chin. He fumbled for the sword at his hip, until Cai's boot connected hard with the Damnonii's back.

A hiss was the only sound from Blue Dog as air was driven from his body. He rolled onto his back, snapping the arrow shafts. His face contorted as he gulped for air. Cai wasn't finished with his enemy. Lucius had halted a few steps from the scene, staying clear of the thrashing legs of the horse. He watched as his friend stamped one booted foot firmly onto Blue Dog's chest. Without a word, he drew a dagger from his belt. Blue Dog was still unable to speak, but his single eye pleaded.

'I'll not waste another thought on you. But know this. The child is mine and he will never know your name.' Cai bent, and with a quick, single movement sliced the short blade across the Damnonii king's windpipe. He stepped quickly back as Blue Dog's life blood pumped relentlessly onto the snow covered battleground.

69

'He is asking for you,' Alyn said.

Cai turned from where he was sitting by the hearth of Barra's hall.

'How is he?' Cai asked, already knowing the answer.

'It won't be long now.'

Cai looked at the wicker screen at the rear of the hall, marking Barra's sleeping place. He turned back to Lucius and Hrindenus who sat across from him, knowing his own face mirrored the grief he saw in theirs.

He stood, Alyn placed her hand onto his shoulder, squeezing it gently. He walked towards the screen, his legs feeling like they were filled with lead.

Niamh waited by the entrance to the small space as if on guard duty. She watched his approach, her eyes glistening as tears cascaded across her cheeks. She didn't speak, simply standing aside to allow Cai to enter.

The small space was dimly lit. There were three people inside. The huge crouching figure of Keefe seemed to fill most of the far end. The boy Herne sat on his haunches, nodding as the third person spoke quietly to him. Barra, his uncle.

The king of the Novantae was propped up in his cot. His face was pale and moisture dappled. His long red hair was sweat-soaked. His chest had been strapped by Alyn; the white dressing blood-stained. An old memory flashed into Cai's mind, quickly quashed.

Barra's eyes lit on Cai and he smiled weakly. He addressed Keefe and Herne in words Cai couldn't make out. Both arose and left his side. Neither met Cai's eyes as they passed him.

'Sit with me, Roman,' Barra said, his voice seeming stronger.

Cai smiled. 'We have never called each other by our given names. Why is that, do you think?'

'It is hard for men who were once enemies to fully embrace friendship, I think. Let us start now. Please sit with me, Cai.'

'Thank you, Barra.'

The Novantae silently looked at Cai for a time, as if wrestling with a decision. 'I have a great favour to ask of you. It is a burden and I will understand if you were to refuse it. But you are one of only two men I would trust with it.' Barra had looked in earnest as he spoke, and the effort of speaking took its toll.

'Ask it, Barra. I'll not refuse, whatever it is,' Cai said.

A smile twitched on Barra's lips, and he gave an almost imperceptible nod. 'Frang will claim lordship over the Novantae lands and its people. He will say he killed me in battle, rather than as the assassin he is. There are none who could refute it. He will aim to quickly bolster his position. Now Blue Dog is dead, he cannot rely on the Damnonii for support so he must persuade people by cunning and strength of arms of his right to be king.' Barra rolled his tongue across his dry lips. Cai retrieved a waterskin hanging by the cot, filling a cup. He gently raised Barra's head to help him drink. The Novantae nodded his thanks.

Barra took some time to regather himself. Marshalling his remaining strength.

'My cousin can never be secure in these lands whilst my nephew lives.' Cai nodded his understanding. 'Herne will be king of the Novantae lands one day, if he lives long enough to fight for them. Frang will do all in his power to ensure he does not.' Barra had become agitated, his chest rising and falling rapidly. 'Keefe would take him to his people, but that holds its own perils.' Now the Novantae reached for Cai's arm, holding it firmly. 'I would ask that you take Herne to Roman lands. Teach him your ways. If he is to be lord here one day, he should be immersed in the worlds of both of our peoples. He must not return to these lands until he is ready.'

Barra released Cai's arm, raising his hand to forestall Cai's response. 'Before you answer you must know that if Frang hears of his whereabouts he will send men to kill him. It will put your own family at risk.'

Cai answered without equivocation. 'I will protect him as I would my own,' he said. 'I will teach him what I know so he will be ready when the time comes. Besides, I'm not sure those boys could bear to be parted from one another, so close have they become. Like brothers, almost.'

'A friendship that may one day help both of our peoples,' Barra said. The Novantae closed his eyes, either from exhaustion or fighting a fresh wave of pain, Cai couldn't tell. After a moment his eyes met Cai's once more.

'When he is ready. When you judge him to be a man. I ask that you give him this,' Barra placed his hand on a sheepskin bundle by his cot. Its shape made clear what items it held.

'I will,' Cai said simply.

After a moment Barra held out his arm. 'Now, before my nephew returns, wish me fair travels.' Cai clasped the Novantae's arm, surprised by the strength of the grip. He looked upon the warrior king's face and returned its smile.

'Farewell, brother,' he said. 'It has been my honour to know you.' Cai held his former enemy's arm for a few moments longer. With a final nod he took up the sheepskin and left the small sleeping area without looking back.

Outside of the wicker screen he came across Herne, with the big warrior Keefe his shadow. The boy looked up at Cai's approach and then at the bundle he carried. A question formed on his lips. Instead he asked, 'My uncle still lives?'

'Yes,' Cai said. 'He needs you now.'

The boy slipped past Cai, the face of the young warrior from the day before now gone, replaced by the lad of ten summers he was. Keefe followed in his wake, a lost soul.

70

'You will take care of her?' Keefe said.

Lucius wasn't sure if it was a question or an instruction to the Tungrian. Hrindenus chose to treat it as the former.

'You have my word. Niamh will want for nothing.'

'Listen to them talk about me as if I'm one of their horses,' Niamh said, as she appeared at Lucius's side. He snorted a laugh.

'I'm just glad they aren't punching chunks out of each other.'

It was the day after Barra's death. That morning they had set the Novantae king upon a pyre of dressed oak branches. Keefe, and what remained of Barra's hearth warriors, had carried out the task, going into the woods before sun-up. They had completed construction of their king's last resting place before a weak winter sun struggled above the eastern horizon. Smoke still drifted skywards from its blackened remnants. But now they must be on the move.

A scouting party dispatched by the Hibernian had returned during the night, reporting no sign of the Damnonii. Perhaps they had already taken to their boats and left these lands. Of more concern was Frang. He had not returned to the Novantae capital and Lucius feared they might be trapped here and overwhelmed if Frang was successful in gathering a new warband.

Keefe embraced Niamh. 'You know where I will be, sister, should you ever have need of me.'

'I do. And just because I may not have a need of your assistance, it does not mean you cannot visit us. I will miss your gruff company.' A broad smile split the face of the big Hibernian warrior and he embraced his sister once more.

'Where will you go?' Lucius asked.

'My king left me instructions. Whilst you protect the boy, I will keep his memory alive. Our people will know who their true king is. Barra was descended from the eastern folk of the Novantae lands. There he is known and loved. They will return to those lands from the great forest once Rome has lost its anger. I will ensure we are ready to move when the time is right.'

'Will there be war between the Novantae?' Lucius asked.

Keefe scratched his bearded chin that had been freshly set in three long warrior's braids by Niamh. 'I will work to avoid it, though it may be inevitable.'

'I'll send word about the boy when I can,' Cai said. He had appeared at Keefe's side. pulling the Hibernian's mount by its bridle.

'My thanks,' Keefe said. Taking hold of the horse he leapt onto its back. He looked upon his sister once more, whose eyes glistened. His chequered cloak rippled in the wind. He smiled weakly. 'It is time, brothers,' he yelled, kicking his mount towards the main gate. Barra's four remaining hearth warriors followed, the thunder of hooves filling the interior of the village. The noise quickly dampened as they reached the snow covered ground. The group watched them go until, at last, they disappeared from sight as they entered the nearby woodland.

'Well, Lucius,' Cai said. 'At long last you can continue your own journey. Urbicus must be wondering what's taking you so long.' Lucius grimaced, placing his hand against his chest. A habit that Cai noticed his friend had developed in recent days. That night still preyed on his mind, it was clear.

341

'Indeed. But now that we have done what we set out to do I find myself filled with misgivings. We've seen the nature of the men that he has used as his agents. I wonder at his ruthlessness. Can he be trusted? Even with the Numidian's help, will it be enough to overcome the forces set against me?'

'Us, brother,' Cai said, placing his hand on Lucius's shoulder. 'You'll not be alone.' Cai looked back into the village at those awaiting them on horseback. Beren and Herne, heads close together, chatted away, or at least Beren spoke to his friend, attempting to raise his spirits. Alyn smiled back at him from her white pony, her hand resting on the bulge of her dress.

'For more than one reason,' Cai said, 'it will be good for us all to leave these lands for a time.'

Lucius had known his friend would offer his support, and he was glad of it, but there would be great risks. 'The journey in winter will be difficult, brother,' he said. 'Alyn is surely only a few weeks from her time.'

'We have talked,' Cai said. 'I did try to dissuade her, but she would not hear of it. We're coming, Lucius.'

Lucius smiled broadly. 'Well then, shall we get going?'

HUNT

71

AD 149 Tiddis, Numidia

It had been a long journey from the coast, though a familiar one. How often would she have to return here, she wondered?

The voyage from Baetica, too, had been uneventful. The Mauritanian trader, and owner of the ship, had at least been entertaining company. The tales of his journeys to the cities dotting the Mare Nostrum had been enthralling, if embellished. But all the best stories contain exaggerations, if not outright lies. Their love-making had been most enlightening too.

She had been ordered, via a one line message, written on papyrus in his hand, to make haste to his home. That fact alone had told her this was a matter of some import to him. And perhaps some risk too.

She sat on a stone bench under a small grouping of palm trees. A cooling breeze blew in from the surrounding hills as the last of the sun's rays lit up the ordered grounds. The Garden, they had called it as children. The low hedges and flower beds ran almost from the villa itself, descending the long slope of the hill and on down to the slow-moving river. Nearly dried out in summer, it carried deep and cooling waters at this time of the year.

She looked up at the sound of quick footsteps crunching along the gravel path. A woman of around her own age approached. She was dressed in a long white tunic, with fair hair bound and braided. Even though she walked quickly the woman held an aura of serenity. As she reached the bench, she bowed her head slightly.

'Good evening, mistress,' she said.

'Good evening, Livia. How nice to see you again.'

'Thank you, mistress. Dominus asks you to attend him in his rooms.' The slave bowed once more and returned the way she had come, her light footsteps crunching along the path once more.

She felt an instant of sadness as she observed Livia's retreating back. As children they had been close, they and their mothers, household slaves. Their paths seemed set to follow the familiar pattern. When Dominus had taken a special interest in her, eventually granting her freedom, friendship had turned to resentment, on Livia's part at least.

She stood and adjusted her stola, attempting to brush the creases from the light blue material. She softly touched the loosely held bun at the back of her head and tucked a stray strand of her dark hair behind her ear. Once ready, she followed the slave who was some distance ahead. But she already knew the way.

She passed through the inner courtyard. Moving sedately, between the low walls that contained the water of three ponds, their surfaces covered with lily pads and bright pink and yellow blossoms. At its heart, each held a slow flowing fountain in the form of an animal. One, a lion, reared on its hind legs and pawed at the sky. Another, an elephant, its trunk held high, spraying water into its pond with a gentle tinkling sound. The final, and most impressive, was a large snaking crocodile, whose wide jaws gushed water, constantly rippling the pond's surface. She had so loved them as a child.

She progressed through columned outer passageways, and on into the inner rooms of the villa she had once considered home. Most, these days, were unused. Once they had regularly been filled with the sound of laughter and conversation, accompanied by the sound of light music of lyre and lute. Now their master reserved his entertaining for Rome and the great figures of power.

As she reached his rooms, Livia was standing by the door her head lowered in obeisance and a respect she knew the slave did not feel.

'The Dominus is in his study, mistress.'

'Thank you, Livia.'

She entered through the arched doorway, its frame and solid door made of the oak he had brought with him upon his return from Britannia. After adding more of that island's savage northern lands to the empire. Once inside, the study was more intimate. Three walls were covered floor to whitewashed ceiling with shelves. Each was stacked high with books of parchment and rolls of papyrus, hiding the colour of the walls entirely.

And there he was, sitting at his long, dark-stained desk, reading one such book. Quintus Lollius Urbicus.

He looked up, a warm smile slowly spreading across his lips. She was surprised to see how much grey now peppered the dark of his well-groomed beard.

'Ah, you are here at last,' he said.

'Greetings, father.' She returned his smile

She noticed his brow furrow and the smile faded slightly.

'Don't worry father. Livia has gone.'

'Come then daughter, let me see you properly.' She approached his desk. Urbicus stood and embraced her. He smelled of the eastern perfume he so favoured. Not unpleasant, but a little too strong.

'How was your journey?'

'Tiring. Though the weather at sea was fair given the time of year. And the company was pleasant. I came as

345

soon as I could make the arrangements. Given the nature of your communication.'

She had been gifted with his dark hair and complexion. She was tall too, even so he still towered over her.

'Sit,' he said, indicating the chair opposite. He poured two cups of wine, the red liquid emptying into the delicate glasses of different hues of blue and green.

'How is your work progressing?' he asked, handing her the wine.

She took a sip, collecting her thoughts before responding. 'I have established that the Castriciae are acting on their own. None of the other powerful families are involved. But their web of activity extends across all Hispania, not simply Baetica. They have made huge land-grabs across the peninsula. Not only agricultural properties. They control mines of iron, copper and gold. I have proof of extortion, fraud, and now, with the Faenii we have a murder to complete the list. Once we have our hands on the assassin, we can move on them.'

Urbicus ran his fingers through his beard, not taking his eyes from her.

'I have been recalled by the emperor to Rome,' he said.

'Yes. Praefectus Urbi. Congratulations father.' His eyes widened and she suppressed a smile.

'Nothing gets past you it seems. Your network must indeed be extensive.' His eyes became piercing as he held hers. She was used to this habit of his and did not flinch or look away as she once would have. 'Yes, I am to be bestowed with that great honour upon my return. But there are other matters that will affect my performance in the position once I take it up. For which I might need additional support. Financial support.'

Now it was her eyes that widened. 'You mean to squeeze the Castriciae for it.' It was not a question.

Urbicus smiled, cocking his head to the side in acknowledgment. 'How does this affect the operation? Ah I see. If you go to the emperor and get the odious family's business dealings closed down, all the proceeds of the sale of their lands and properties will go to the imperial coffers. You would get nothing. But, if you approach the Castriciae elder with what you have on him, he will be only too glad to donate hefty sums to whatever projects you need finance for.'

Urbicus spread his arms wide, his smile broadening once more. 'You are as perceptive as ever, daughter. However, I won't be approaching him directly. You will.'

'But what of your Tribunus in Britannia? Does your promise to aid him no longer hold?'

'Oh, help him if you can. Unless it looks like he might get in the way of my enterprise. Then you will have to deal with him.'

'You mean kill him.'

'Isn't that one of the skills you have honed so sharply, daughter? Those skills I have invested so much time and money in giving to you.'

ALISTAIR TOSH

Acknowledgements

As ever, by far the most important thanks to be proffered by an author must go to my closest family, Jenny, Mike, Robbie, Tess and Abbie. Not only for unfailing encouragement but also for their, always excellent, insights and feedback.

Once again my good friend in writing, Marian Thorpe, has been a terrific help in smoothing out the rough edges in the manuscript and for spotting the odd embarrassing anachronism. Marian is an excellent storyteller and you can see her novels at marianlthorpe.com

Thanks too, must go to my good chum Max Bigham for guiding me around the stunning and mystical sites of Argyll during the research phase. And for introducing me to Dunadd fort, what a find that was. Jane, his wife, was the best of welcoming hostesses and an excellent cook. I still have those extra few pounds, gained on my stay, to shift.

Also to you dear readers. My thanks for buying this book and also because it means you likely bought book one, for which I am eternally grateful.

Finally to my wife, Jenny. We moved house twice during the months that I was writing Hunt and you were no less supportive despite the topsy turvy-ness of our lives. Thank you my love.

Author's Note

Edge of Empire: Hunt is a work of fiction. There are both deliberate and inadvertent historical inaccuracies throughout. In part to fit the story narrative but also because of sparse detail and dates in the written record. Two characters however, did exist during the period that the tale is set. Lucius was the Tribune of the I Nervana Germanorum, an auxiliary cohort originally raised in the lands of the Nervii tribe in modern day central Belgium. Also Quintus Lollius Urbicus, who we first meet in 'Siege', makes a brief appearance in Hunt and was governor of Britannia for a time. He was indeed awarded the honour of Praefectus Urbi in Rome by emperor Antoninus Pius

In Hunt I have used existing locations that are contemporary with the story;

For Barra's settlement I used Barsalloch Fort close to the Isle of Whithorn on the coast of Galloway. It has been identified as a fortified farmstead and associated with the Novantae tribe.

The Novantae capital of Rerigon was an abbreviation of Rerigonium, the city recorded by Ptolemy. It is believed the site has been located on the shores of Loch Ryan near Stranraer. Unfortunately there is no visible evidence remaining above ground. Today the site is home to a very different tribe. Caravan Holiday makers.

ALISTAIR TOSH

The Holy Isle is based upon Dunadd fort in Argyll and situated in Kilmartin Glen. Although more well known for its association as the royal power centre of Gaelic kings in the 500s to 800s AD, it has been a significant site since the Iron Age. This lovely, ancient place is well worth a visit.

Lucius Faenius Felix and Cai Martis will return.

Alistair Tosh

Printed in Great Britain
by Amazon

18445288R00205